A KISS IN THE DARK

COPYRIGHT

NYLA Publishing
121 W 27th St., Suite 1201, New York, NY 10001
http://www.nyliterary.com

A KISS IN THE DARK

SUZANNE ENOCH

1

Samantha Jellicoe kept her head down, edging forward with her hands and her toes. Another ten feet should do it, and then she meant to take at least four showers. For crying out loud, just because most people didn't spend time in air ducts didn't mean they shouldn't be kept reasonably clean. This was the crap people below would be breathing, after all.

Ten feet. "Okay," she panted into her walkie-talkie, "I'm at the far northwest corner, about four feet from the outer wall."

"No, you're not," a male voice returned crisply. "Midway along the south wall, twelve feet above the floor, arms out in front of you, ankles crossed."

She grinned. "Awesome. That makes this place as bulletproof as I can get it. I'm coming out. And stop looking at my boobs on the thermal, Kymo."

"They're just hot blobs," James Kymo commented. "Not enough to get my motor running."

"I'll have you know these are very fine hot blobs. Somebody meet me with a towel before I mutate into the Toxic Avenger."

"Right, boss," another male voice chimed in, South Florida thick in his voice. "I'm in the utility room now."

That would be Luke Bodrie, her most recent hire. If he was in there by himself, somebody was going to get their ass kicked. Probies didn't go anywhere alone. Not under her watch. Thieves were experts at breaking into places and snatching things. That made them handy for security system installation, but it also meant they had to resist temptation. Sometimes, a lot of temptation. And some of these guys, whether they put "former" thief on their resumes or not, weren't that great at resisting.

Blowing out her breath, Samantha resumed inching her way through the ductwork. It was definitely doable as a way into the building's inner offices, but only for people who ticked the petite box. Bruce Willis would never have survived the attack on Nakatomi Plaza if these had been the ducts he had to navigate. Still, it could happen. And if it did, security would now be able to see whoever it was scurrying through the air conditioning system, hot blobs and all. Yippy Kai Yay.

By the time she emerged through the section of panel they'd taken down, she felt like a sweaty dust ball. Blech. Bodrie offered her a hand, and she squirmed out the last two feet and stood upright again. He stepped back again as Bobbi Camden moved up to hand her a bottle of water. Good. She'd chosen Camden to keep an eye on the newbie. In fact, Bobbi was proving to be somebody Samantha could see promoting to job supervisor. Go, girl power. "Thanks," she said aloud, drinking sloppily, letting the cool wet run down her front.

"You sure you're Martin Jellicoe's kid?" Bodrie asked, eyeing her as he tossed her a towel.

"That's the rumor," she replied, wiping off as many layers of grime as the towel could handle. "We can't all be glamorous cat burglars, I guess."

"True enough," Bobbi said. "I may be getting dirtier than I

did in my old gig, but I also don't have to worry about getting shot or thrown in the slam after a day's work."

"Exactly. Listen to Bobbi, Luke. She knows what she's talking about." Someone whose former career had mostly involved acting like a bimbo and getting men to spend cash on her, Bobbi Camden had managed to turn that into a skill for getting a bunch of macho guys to do what she told them to on site.

Setting aside the water, Samantha stripped out of the formerly white painter's garb she'd donned for her trip into the ductwork. Underneath it her jeans and T-shirt were damp with sweat, and she still felt like the grime had made its way beneath her skin.

When she'd started this company eight months ago, word had spread fast that the daughter of Martin Jellicoe was hiring thieves looking for a chance to go legit. Retired safecrackers, a couple of thugs, a few con artists, and even a cat burglar or two had appeared, and with one exception she'd agreed to give them a chance. So far, they hadn't disappointed her, but she wasn't a charity. Jellicoe Security had been gaining lots of new business lately, but it would only take one guy lifting a Rolex or a sensitive file to put her out of work and derail her entire go-legit plan.

Yep, new business was good, and the last three jobs had been recommended by previous clients, which was awesome. She knew as well as anybody that the first couple of security-installation jobs had been mostly courtesy of her boyfriend—and now fiancée—Rick Addison, recommending her to his fellow mill- and billionaire buds.

The fact that her British gentleman had put his reputation on the line for her made it even more important that none of her employees screw up. So, ironically enough, to protect the guy trying to keep *her* on the straight and narrow, she was relying pretty heavily on Martin Jellicoe's extremely crooked reputation to keep everyone else in line. She had to; she couldn't use her own reputation for shit.

She was one hundred percent legit now, and running out the clock on all of the statutes of limitation still hanging over her. Yeah, she'd done some exceptionally hairy things, and yeah, she'd been more successful at high-class thievery than even her legendary dad, but the reason she'd had the option to retire was that nobody knew who'd pulled any of the jobs she had under her belt. The rumor that it *might* have been her didn't hurt, though—not with these guys, anyway.

"So, what's worth more in here?" Bodrie asked, leading the way back to the security room where they'd set up their base. "The technical stuff, or the artwork?"

By "technical stuff," she assumed he meant the business the people on the computers were doing, and not the computers themselves. The equipment was top-of-the-line, too, though, so she couldn't be certain what he was thinking. "It doesn't matter," she said aloud. "Firewalls and passwords and shit are somebody else's problem. We're setting up a system to keep this place physically secure. As soon as we clean up our equipment, I'm calling that done."

"Yeah, but this is a fucking accounting firm, right? How do they afford a Picasso for the coffee room?" he blurted out, his Florida twang deepening.

"First, it's a Jasper Johns, not a Picasso. Second, this is an accounting firm that has some of the wealthiest guys and companies in the world for clients. Third, they hired us to protect their stuff, so that's what we're doing. Are we clear?"

Luke shuffled his feet. "Yeah. It's just that their stuff is...right there." He gestured with his hands like a teenager grabbing his first pair of boobs.

Samantha squared up on him. This was the thing she wasn't used to—lecturing thieves about morality. Hell, she'd had her hands on a Jasper Johns painting or two in her time, even if her clients tended to favor the older, more classical works. "Luke. You get it, don't you? That this is your one chance? Your last and only chance to do something you're good at and still be able to work days, sleep nights, and not wake up every morning wondering if your shit has caught up to you?"

The newbie grimaced, looking down at the floor before he nodded his head. "My dad keeps telling me the same thing. I screw up again, and he's tossing me out. So I get it. No jobs while I'm on the job."

"No jobs at all while you're in my employ," she amended. "None. Not even shoplifting gum. And if you do some shit, I'll know about it, because you leave a sloppy trail a mile wide. I know, because I looked. Can you do legal? And be honest, for fuck's sake, and spare me the trouble of putting you on the payroll full time if you can't keep your hands to yourself."

"O—"

"I'm willing to give you guys a chance," she said, deliberately interrupting. She knew the macho, self-confident attitude that went into being any kind of lawbreaker, that sense of superiority at being able to take other people's stuff on a whim. Every one of these guys had at one time or another thought him or herself the smartest, most talented person in the room. "I figure maybe if my dad had had one good chance, he might not have died in prison. If I find out you lifted something during a job or if you break back into a place after you do an installation, I'll do more than fire you. I will hunt you down and drag you into the nearest police station by your lovely golden locks. Do you believe me?"

He looked at her for a minute, his pride clearly warring with what he knew and what he'd heard about her. "Yeah. I believe you. And I get it. The straight and narrow it is."

"Good. Bobbi, get the company credit card and take everybody out for a burger."

5

"You got it, boss. And you can tell Aubrey that I've learned my lesson and I *will* get a receipt."

Samantha grinned. "He's a stickler, that Aubrey."

"He's one of those guys you can't con, because he's way too concerned over the numbers to go with his heart." Bobbi shook her head, managing to make her dark brown ponytail look sexy. "And it would take way too much effort to look prettier than he does, anyway."

Snorting, Samantha gestured for them to precede her. She didn't know if Bobbi had tried to put the moves on Aubrey Pendleton or not, but she was pretty sure that Aubrey didn't swing that way. Aside from that, he had to be in his mid-sixties, a good thirty years older than Bobbi Camden and forty years older than herself, but he did know how to put himself together. "I will never criticize anyone for knowing how to choose an outfit."

"Ha. You comin' with us for lunch?"

"I am going to go take a shower and then make sure that my next hire is somebody smaller than I am, so I don't have to go duct crawling anymore."

The curvy woman with way bigger hot blobs than she had laughed. "You should have thought of that before."

"Yes, I should have. Pack up the truck first."

With mock salutes Bobbi and Luke went off to collect the rest of the gang from the security room. Samantha finished off her bottle of water and sent a text to the head of security that they were wrapping up here and that James Kymo would be on site for the rest of the week to teach and demonstrate the security system. If she hadn't been covered with yuck, she would have told him in person, but according to her office manager, grimy people didn't make a good impression. And in addition to being a snappy dresser, Aubrey Pendleton was the Superman of knowing how to impress people.

Official stuff done, she headed out to the parking garage, put the towel on the seat of Rick's night-blue Porsche 718 Boxster, and hopped behind the wheel. Yeah, she generally chose to drive something that didn't stand out, but here in rich-people central West Palm Beach, Florida, the Boxster fit in pretty well. Aside from that, it was damn nifty.

Once she had the top down, she zipped out onto the street, heading for Worth Avenue and her office and wondering if she was leaving a stream of dust and dirt, Indiana Jones style, behind her. Before she could even turn the corner, her phone rang to the tune of "Heigh Ho" sung by the Seven Dwarfs. Off to work, she went. "Hey, Aubrey," she said, hitting the answer button on the steering wheel. "We just finished up. I'm heading in to take a shower. And then another shower."

"I've got a call for you," her office manager and sometime professional escort for mature West Palm Beach single ladies said in his soft, Colonel Sanders drawl. "Anne Hughes, with Sotheby's New York."

"Ooh. Put her through."

Sotheby's was one of the key words, along with *castle*, *auction*, *priceless*, *museum*, and *treasure*. When somebody uttered one of those, Aubrey knew to find her and put the call through. "Here she is."

"Sam Jellicoe speaking," Samantha said, adopting her most professional persona and straightening in her seat a little.

"Hello, Ms. Jellicoe. This is Anne Hughes, with Sotheby's New York. I'm told you are the woman to go to when valuables need to be protected."

Samantha pumped her free fist in the air as she stopped at a light. "That's me," she answered coolly. "What can I help you with?"

"I am preparing a collection for exhibition and auction here in New York, and I would like to hire your firm to handle security."

Yes! As soon as the light went green, Samantha changed lanes and pulled over in front of the Mark Borghi Fine Art shop. Tiffany's was next door, and petty or not, she always wanted to give the blue-box store the finger—Rick had gotten her engagement ring from Harry Winston, and it had immediately become her favorite piece of jewelry, ever. Even better than the Hope Diamond. "I'm happy to hear that," she said aloud, putting up the Porsche's roof to cut down on the street noise. "Out of curiosity, how did you hear about us? Jellicoe Security is based in Florida."

"I spoke with Joseph Viscanti at the Met, and he said you've done some work for them. You specialize in both protection and recovery, yes?"

"Yes, I do. We do."

"Joseph spoke very highly of you. But I want to make it clear, Ms. Jellicoe—I wish to hire *you*. *Your* expertise. *Your* presence on site."

"Understood. What's your time frame?"

"The exhibition opens in ten days. The auction is in two weeks."

Samantha blinked. "That's not much of a heads-up. I can't advise you on security if you already have your displays set up."

Silence. "I don't," Ms. Hughes finally said. "I have a venue and I've tried to begin setting it up, but I've…I have had issues with burglary before, and I have a great deal on the line with this project. I…could use your assistance, Ms. Jellicoe. Sotheby's could use your expertise, and they have already agreed to fund the extra security."

Swiftly Samantha ran the name Anne Hughes through her memory. It sounded vaguely familiar, but then if Hughes worked for Sotheby's, that made sense. She'd hit them a couple of times. Mentally crossing her fingers that she wasn't the one who'd caused that tremble in Ms. Hughes's voice and that karma wouldn't therefore be throwing a bowling ball at her head, she took a quick breath. "I can be there first thing in the morning. Where do you want to meet?"

"Oh, thank you. Um, I'll email you the details. Does that work?"

"Yep. And call me Sam."

"Sam. And I'm Anne, of course. Thank you. Thank you so much."

"You're welcome. See you in the morning."

Hanging up, she checked over her shoulder and pulled back into traffic. "Hey, Siri, dial work."

Siri responded, and a second later Aubrey picked up. "Well? Do we have a job?"

"We do. Will you book me a flight to New York for sometime this afternoon? I'm meeting her in the morning. She's emailing the details to us—forward them to me, please."

"You have a private jet, you know."

"Rick has a private jet. I'll fly commercial."

She could almost hear his eyebrows furrow. "Samantha, y—"

"This job probably wouldn't pay for the fuel for the jet, Aubrey. Business class. Me. Today. I'm being fiscally responsible."

"I can't argue with that. Give me ten minutes."

"Will do. I'm heading home to pack and take all my showers, not necessarily in that order. The crew is having lunch and should have the truck and the credit card back this afternoon."

"Ten-four. I'm still doing the 'how to talk nicely to people' seminar in the morning, if that's okay."

"Sure. Send out a text this afternoon to remind everybody. The sooner they can get it through their thick heads that not everybody is a mark, the better."

The fact that Aubrey had volunteered to teach some etiquette to her Jellicoe Security squad had initially surprised her, but then he kind of made his living by knowing the right thing to say at the right moment to the right person. Aside from

9

that, Mr. Pendleton had been supremely helpful since he'd decided to start showing up at her office. He might not be so slick at figuring out how to store things in—on?—the Cloud, but the man knew how to talk to people. And like Bobbi had said, he was good at crunching numbers.

Whatever the reason he'd decided to employ himself at Jellicoe Security (and she still really didn't like that name), he'd figured out some things that probably never would have occurred to her. After all, while she'd had a legit job or two in her life, employee withholding taxes, insurance—that was just Mars alien language, and she was glad enough he'd shouldered that shit that she'd been relieved to put him on the payroll. She supposed being a social escort left him a lot of time on his hands; the social season in West Palm Beach was like three or four months long, at most. So, win-win.

Like now, when she could drive home for a shower and have somebody else make her plane reservations, and she wouldn't owe him a favor for doing it, because it was part of his job. That was kind of cool.

AUBREY PENDLETON TAPPED the button on his earpiece to disconnect from the call with Miss Samantha. Maybe an earpiece was a bit much for a small outfit like Jellicoe Security, but it freed his hands up to do filing or printing or make some fresh iced tea in the office's small kitchen, and it looked both official and high-tech, which was a good image for the company.

Lately business had been ticking up, anyway, to the point that the earpiece was actually useful rather than just lending him an air of authority. And the authority angle was helpful, too, considering some of the questionable characters Miss Samantha had been bringing into the business. Mostly they stayed on the straight and narrow, but he knew enough to realize that these men—and a few women—had some credentials. The bad kind of credentials. But they'd already done their time, or were trying to go straight, and he couldn't fault that.

Spinning his chair around clockwise, he sent the computer looking for nonstop flights from Palm Beach to New York. With this short notice tickets would be ridiculously expensive, but Miss Samantha seemed mostly to operate on short notice. *Sotheby's*. That was big, the kind of job that would keep Jellicoe Security elevated far above the rest of the three-letter-acronym security installation companies.

Of course, it also sent her to New York, where he wouldn't be of much use except to give more of his how-to-deal-with-humans talks in the office. As he'd discovered when she and Addison had jetted off to Scotland a couple of weeks ago, he didn't like being that far out of the loop. Hell, she'd sent for Walter Barstone, but good ole Aubrey had been stuck in West Palm Beach answering phones.

On the tail of that thought the phone rang, a number he recognized but had never put into the system. Miss Samantha answered her own phones from time to time, after all. "Jellicoe Security," he said, leaning into his southern gentleman drawl. "How can we help?"

"Aubrey Pendleton, my old friend," a familiar, much crisper voice with just the tiniest bit of Boston in its vowels said expansively. "Did I catch you at a good time?"

"I'm alone in the office," Aubrey answered, glancing toward the door anyway, "but I'm expecting a team back in about half an hour." Scrolling down the list of flights on the computer screen, he found a direct flight and checked the available seats. Samantha would probably fly in the cheap seats, but that would feel too much like he'd failed his mission. She'd said business class, and that was what he would find for her.

"You do remember you're not a secretary, right?"

Aubrey sighed. "Yes, because I'm an office manager. Why are you calling, anyway? There isn't anything scheduled, and I'm getting some information for the boss."

"'The boss'? Well, your *other* boss wants some information, too. You remember that guy?"

Pulling off the headphone, he glared at it for a second before he put it back on again. "What would be good is if you would tell me what you're after and stop trying to act like some wannabe mob enforcer, Dean. I'm doing my job. Miss Samantha's only been back from Scotland for two weeks, and she has three security installation jobs going, plus a line on a fourth. So, once again, *what do you want?*"

"What *we* want, Aubrey, is for you to get us something we can use to make an actual arrest. She's Martin Jellicoe's damn daughter, for fuck's sake. We *know* he didn't pull all those jobs by himself, and we *know* he didn't pull some of those jobs that he took credit for. You've been doing her filing for eight months now. You said she trusts you."

"I also said she's legit," Aubrey retorted. Damn bureaucrats. No interest in people or personalities or projects of self-improvement. It was all about political points and trying to outmaneuver each other for the juiciest assignments. "If she wasn't before, she is now. And I don't know anything about the before. I'm not going to lie about something."

The voice on the other end of the call went so silent he would bet it had been muted. Dean Frankle wasn't alone in his office. Which meant Ling Wu was in there, too, listening. They were supposed to be a damn team, not a bunch of hyenas looking to eat members of their own pack. Jeez, maybe he was getting old, remembering the good old days that really hadn't been all that different from what they were now.

"Okay," Dean's voice returned, "look at it this way. Samantha Jellicoe decided to announce that she exists, and you got the assignment to figure out all of her befores. Eight months in, and all you've told us is that she's legit today. No leads pointing to her or to anyone else. That's—"

"What about Gabriel Toombs?" Aubrey broke in. "She found him. He ripped off the Met, and we caught him red-handed."

"Richard Addison caught him, and then Toombs's house burned down before we could dig any deeper. Considering that obsessed as he was with Jellicoe, he probably had some dirt on her, I don't really call that a win."

"He was a sick fuck, stalking a woman just trying to go about her life, you mean," Aubrey muttered. And now he wasn't. And he was in jail, and about to go away to prison for a very long time. A definite win, in Aubrey's book.

"The fact is," a second, deeper voice took up, "she is probably the biggest fish to come our way in a decade. Maybe longer. Yes, you have seniority in this office. But eight months on a case where we've assigned a half-dozen agents, and we have exactly nothing? We have no choice but to assess whether a…younger agent might fit better in her circle and gain us more results."

"Have you looked at her circle, Wu? And considered how Addison would react to some young stud showing up and elbowing his way into a friendship? We'd never find the damn body."

"You're not getting any results there, Aubrey. And we have other concerns that could use a boost. The office in Omaha could use somebody with your experience, for example. There's some kind of medical billing scam going on at their Immanuel Village, and you're the guy most likely to not make waves snooping around. Not a demotion; just a reassignment."

He knew what that meant. "I'm not going undercover at the Nebraska version of the fucking Villages, Wu, just because you're looking for a big-enough score to move you out of an office that overlooks CVS. I've been keeping a lid on West Palm Beach for ten years. It takes someone the older ladies trust. Nobody else can do what I do here. You couldn't, no matter how much you want to get noticed so you can move to the bay office."

"This isn't about promotions, or office views, Aubrey. It's about results. You keep saying you're digging, but this isn't just some old lady stealing her neighbor's earrings or guys cooking up a pyramid scheme at a fancy society party. Maybe it's time to admit that this will take more than what you've got."

"Keep in mind that for ten years nobody's had any idea who's ratting out the old ladies or the grifters, and I'm still invited to all those society parties. I *am* digging. If there's anything to find, I will find it. And do so with some finesse, which, I believe, is why you gave me the assignment in the first place. But you have to consider that if I don't find anything, there might not be anything here in Palm Beach—other than the old ladies and the pyramid schemers—to find."

"True enough," Ling Wu returned in his smooth, professional tone. "It's also true that the FBI doesn't have unlimited funds for investigations that don't go anywhere. And you can thumb your nose at Nebraska, but we're talking millions of dollars going somewhere it shouldn't be. So this is it, Aubrey; give us enough to get an arrest warrant on Samantha Jellicoe or somebody who'll flip on her, or start packing for snow."

The line went dead before Aubrey could do the honors himself. *Shit in a bucket.* Palm Beach was *his* territory. And while he didn't particularly care if he reported to the so-called "CVS Office" rather than to the newer "Bay Office" half a mile to the east that overlooked Lake Worth, Ling Wu did. That was probably because Ling spent most of his time in his pharmacy-adjacent office, and his view was for shit. On the other hand, Aubrey had spent most of the last decade undercover, discretely putting away bored trophy wives snagging each other's jewelry or husbands, the odd stockbroker reporting an art theft to collect the insurance money, and the usual Russian oligarch money-laundering schemes.

That had been easy. It had even gotten a little boring, to the point that he'd started to consider retirement from the Bureau. The sudden appearance of Miss Samantha Jellicoe had been like Christmas, Halloween, and a dozen birthdays all rolled into one. Or it had been at first. Now it was a damn nightmare.

Until she'd stood up and said hey, all anybody, Interpol included, had had was rumors that Martin Jellicoe even had a partner-slash-kid. Just the fact that she'd so effortlessly stayed off the grid until she chose to reveal herself had had all the agencies hopping. Nobody stayed that anonymous and hidden just for fun. There had to be a reason for it. Everybody in the FBI, CIA, Interpol, and Treasury Department knew what the reason had to be, but nobody—*nobody*—had any proof of anything.

No fingerprints, no CCTV footage, nothing but a long string of high-end cat burglaries dating back nearly a decade with no evidence at all attached to them. Just a few rumors, some blame thrown by other, less-skilled cats, and her family name. Her family legacy.

Shaking himself, Aubrey finished booking the flight to New York and texted Miss Samantha the details. For the thousandth time he speculated that if she'd surfaced calling herself Samantha Jones and partnered with Richard Addison, it would only have been the entertainment news trying to figure her out, and nobody at the Bureau would have so much as blinked.

The way he looked at it, she'd wanted to be honest with Addison, and as high profile as *he* was, that had exploded everything. She'd wanted to go legit, whatever her history. And it hadn't been lip service, either. Just after she'd appeared, she'd taken down a couple of art forgers and nearly gotten herself killed in the process. But the FBI didn't like when civilians solved big cases, and they didn't trust that she hadn't been behind the entire mess in the first place. Now they wanted her taken down for everything they assumed she'd done and whatever she could possibly, potentially, be doing now, and they'd picked him to do it.

After ten years of acting as a sought-after society walker, he'd been called in to the fancy state FBI headquarters in Tampa and told to nail Samantha Jellicoe for every high-end art or jewel theft they'd never been able to solve. They'd teamed with Interpol on the international cases. And all because a reclusive young woman had stood up and said her name—and then brought down a handful of other criminals.

Hell, in just over a year she'd caught a murderer, stopped a heist at the Metropolitan Museum of Art, recovered stolen Samurai armor, and helped Addison open a museum in England showcasing the art the billionaire had spent most of his adult life collecting.

As Aubrey finished filing paid invoices, a walkie-talkie call came in from Andy Guttierez, asking if the replacement A/V cables had come in for the Hernandez job. "Not yet," he replied. "I checked again this morning, and they said Friday at the earliest. And I know you know, but do not remove the old wiring before the new stuff arrives."

"Yeah, I know. Sam's rules. We don't leave a house unprotected, even if what it's got is ten years out of date."

"Roger that." Setting down the walkie-talkie in its cradle, Aubrey returned to the filing cabinet.

Damn it. Was it his fault that sitting in this office, doing filing and giving pep talks, felt...significant? Because yeah, Samantha Jellicoe done some high-end cat burglaries. Okay, not some. A lot. He knew it, probably better than anyone in Tampa, or Langley. Proving it would be tricky, because she'd never come out and admitted to stealing anything to him, but she talked about various security systems like someone who'd dismantled them, and she'd described how cold and windy it could be hanging on the outside of a thirty-story building.

The thing was, she didn't do it any longer. He couldn't name another crook who'd given up that life without being caught and forced into bar-surrounded honesty. But she *had*. And she'd started a company that specialized in keeping other thieves at bay, plus recovering things if anyone did manage to steal them. She had to know she was taking a risk, because until the statute of limitations ran out on every job she'd ever pulled, *everything* was a risk.

Maybe if she'd been some rough, boozy, arrogant old man, digging around enough to stop her would have been easier—on his conscience, if not in fact. The thing of it all was, though, he liked her. He even admired her. He liked Addison, too, and the risks the billionaire was clearly willing to take to keep her in his life.

Did he like her more than he liked this comfortable assignment in Palm Beach, though? Did he like her more than he detested the idea of being sent to Nebraska—which his boss had mentioned not because he had the most experience in insurance fraud, but because he was the damn oldest agent he knew?

He slammed his fist against the top of the file cabinet, making a dent that rebounded with a loud metallic thud. Yeah, he could turn Miss Samantha in. Now. Today. Except that he wasn't ready to do that. Not quite yet.

2

———

Tuesday, 12:47 p.m.

Checking the time on the car's dash, Samantha headed out toward Solano Dorado, Rick's massive estate that backed up to the bay known as Lake Worth. With an early lunch meeting scheduled at business attorney Tom Donner's office, she doubted Rick would be home yet—especially since she hadn't thought to be finished until twoish, herself.

It wasn't that she needed to report to him or ask his permission before she went anywhere. Cripes, she'd practically been on her own since she turned fifteen; being independent wasn't a thing she had any trouble with. No, this was more about her knowing how much he worried about her, both in her current occupation and because she could still be arrested for her previous one.

"Hey, Siri, call Rick's mobile."

The call didn't ring through, but rather went straight to his voicemail. "Hey," she said after the beep, "I'm flying to New York in a bit. A quick consult job for Sotheby's. I shouldn't be more than a day or two. If I don't see you before I go, I'll call you when I get settled tonight. Love you."

That last bit still felt a little awkward on her tongue, even though she'd known Rick Addison for over a year now, and had been in love with him practically since the first minute. Bombs had literally gone off, then, fire and explosions. Like fairy-tale fireworks, only deadlier. It was the L word, itself. It made her feel…squishy. Vulnerable.

And of course now that she'd said it on the phone, he'd probably never delete the message. Yep, gorgeous British billionaire, bonafide English aristocrat, and sentimental as hell—where she was concerned, anyway.

Rick had proven to be a way better partner in semi-nefarious activities than she'd expected, too. For some reason he put up with her shit, to the point that in a couple of months, if she ever settled on a date, she would be Samantha, Lady Rawley. Not bad for a girl who'd met her guy while trying to steal a premium piece of antiquity from his house.

Her phone rang, to the tune of James Bond. Grinning, she hit the car's answer button. "Hey. You got my message?"

"I did," Rick's suave British accent returned, the sound of his voice alone sending warmth tingling beneath her skin. "Morgan's having the jet fueled as we speak. I'll meet you at the hangar."

"I'm grateful and all, but I doubt providing some security recommendations for a Sotheby's exhibit would pay for a trip on the jet. And it's just a consult. One day, probably."

Silence. "Is this one of those times where I clench my jaw and wave goodbye as you fly commercial?"

Half of her had kind of been hoping he *would* insist on joining her in New York. Realizing that shook her up a little bit. It wasn't that she needed his help, because damn, nobody knew more about how to break into places than she did, but that she liked having him around. She liked it a lot. "If it takes more than a day or two, I may change my mind about sleeping alone."

"See that you do. I already don't like it."

She glanced into her rearview mirror, even though the massive glass building across from her office hadn't been in sight this afternoon to begin with. "Are you still at Donner's office?"

"I am."

"Invite him over for steaks or something so you don't get lonely. Or adopt a dog. Less trouble than the boy scout."

"You're an ass, Jellicoe," came over the car's stereo, the voice deep and Texas southern.

"Don't ask Rick to put me on speaker if you don't want to hear me insulting you, Donner." Grinning, she flipped on the turn signal. By now the distrust between her and the boy scout lawyer Tom Donner had pretty much faded to territorial grunting, but she wasn't about to pass up a chance to get in a jab. "Almost home. Gotta shower and get some clothes, and then I'm heading to the airport. I love you."

"I love you, Samantha. Be safe."

"I don't love you, Jellicoe."

"I hear the words, Donner, but I also sense your inner turmoil. Be strong. And maybe see a therapist."

As she tapped the call off, the ten-foot stone walls surrounding Solano Dorado came into view. Pulling up to the call box, she waved at the camera set above it. Man, her life had changed. A year ago she'd climbed up the wall, cut through a glass window, and snuck into the house. Now she tooled up the long, palm tree-lined drive in the owner's convertible, top down and her face out there for all the cameras to see and record. *Christ.*

Reinaldo met her at the front door, pulling it open and standing aside as she strolled in. "You're back early, Miss Sam," he said.

"Unexpected business trip," she explained, trotting up the stairs. "Just grabbing a couple of things."

"Shall I pull out any of Mr. Rick's suitcases?"

Samantha paused on the landing. "I could use his blue carry-on, if you don't mind. My backpack kind of leaves things wrinkly."

"I'll bring it up."

"Thanks, Reinaldo."

In the old days she'd kept a backpack beneath her bed. In there had been everything she would need for a quick, don't-look-back escape. Now she kept a backpack in the closet, but it had stuff for a weekend getaway—to the Keys, or the Poconos, or NYC. Fun places. Places from which she expected to return, because now she had a place to return to. And a guy with whom she traveled.

Shaking herself, she hopped into the big shower and scrubbed until her skin was pink. She didn't mind getting dirty —she never had, but getting clean definitely felt good. Once she had put herself back together again, she pulled her spare toothbrush and deodorant out of the holiday backpack, depositing them in the carry-on Reinaldo brought upstairs for her. A pair of slacks and a nice blouse would do for her meeting, but she threw in a dress in case she changed her mind. Meeting somebody was nothing new, but meeting somebody for business, and with her posing as the most competent version of herself instead of a bimbo or lawyer or photographer—or whichever of those was most likely to help her get information about her gig —still felt a little awkward.

She also tossed in a pair of blue coveralls and sturdy shoes, because her new line of work still entailed crawling into airducts from time to time. In a way it was a relief that thievery and preventing thievery had so many elements in common. If the latter had entailed learning…embroidery or something, making the shift would have been much trickier.

That put her in mind of something, and she pulled out her phone again. One ring later a low-toned voice picked up with a noncommittal, "Go."

"Hey," she said in response. "Is that how you greet everybody these days?"

"Just because the phone says it's you, doesn't mean I have to believe it. Mobiles are handy, but every time I turn it on, I feel like I've been tracked to within two feet of where I'm standing."

Samantha sighed, sitting on the edge of the bed. "I'm discovering that I know a lot of paranoid people, Stoney. And you're the king of Paranoid Land."

"The only people you can still talk to *are* paranoid," Walter "Stoney" Barstone, her former fence and current surrogate dad-ish type, countered. Big and solid, he'd always reminded her of a black Hulk Hogan with better hair and tailoring, and a bottom-less knowledge of where the most vulnerable and valuable works of art and jewelry could be found. "That's why we're still around to take your call." He cleared his throat. "So, hi, Honey. You bored already today? I told you, the straight life and a born cat burglar are not simpatico."

"Thanks, Stoney," she returned, smiling at his refusal to give up on her returning to the more lucrative criminal life. "I appreciate the way you keep trying to drag me back into danger."

"Nah. It's not that," the high-end fence argued. "You have a very rare talent. Wasting that is a crime against nature."

"Putting me in jail for a hundred years would be more of a waste, as far as I'm concerned."

"There is that. What's up, then?"

"Have you heard anything about a grab going on in New York, maybe involving a Sotheby's exhibition coming up in the next couple of weeks?"

"A Sotheby's exhibition," he repeated in a soft, slow voice, the way a pie addict talked about a fresh lemon meringue.

"Stop drooling. I'm not in that line of work anymore."

"Maybe not. But we're not in an exclusive relationship, you know."

That made her frown. Her second worst nightmare would be Stoney lining up a job for one of his other "guys," as he called them, where she ended up taking the assignment to recover the item, or stop the theft in the first place. So far Stoney had been reluctantly…supportive, if there was such a thing. He knew she could have made them both a ton more money if she'd stayed in the business, but he also knew that her life expectancy had dramatically increased since she'd hung up her cat burglar suit. Of course, he'd also pointed out that her freedom expectancy would be better off if she hadn't started co-habitating with a famous rich guy, but some things were just worth the risk.

"Mm-hmm. Stay away from anything with the name Anne Hughes attached to it. And if you do hear anything, I—"

"Yeah, I'll let you know."

"Thanks, Yoda."

"Just remember, Han Solo couldn't go straight, either, even after he married Princess Leia."

She snorted. "I'll let *you* tell Rick that he's Leia." Not that she had any objection to being Han Solo. "Talk soon."

"Be smart."

"So, I'm Princess Leia in your little scenario?" a cultured British drawl came from the bedroom doorway. "I always thought I was more of a Lando Calrissian."

Heat swept along her skin. At the same time, she should probably have realized he'd show up. Rick Addison had a tendency to appear when he thought she might be getting into something sticky, especially when it involved them sleeping in different bedrooms. In different states. "You definitely have the suave," she said, tossing in the Jimmy Chu's that would go with both the dress and the slacks. Comfortable and stylish all at the same time. "Did you abandon Donner at the office? You'll make him cry."

"We got enough done to keep the contract people busy for the rest of the day." He pushed upright from the doorframe. "Aside from that, I'm the boss. I called it a day." Rick strolled into the room, sexy as hell in a dark blue suit with a dark blue tie. The effect deepened the color in his Caribbean-blue eyes to the deepest azure, and the amused quirk of his mouth made her want to kiss him—and do a few other things that would make her miss her flight.

"And then you practically flew back here at light speed. You aren't checking up on me, are you, Lando?" Samantha asked, only half teasing. "Because I'm a big girl. I even remembered to pack a toothbrush."

"A toothbrush? You're staying at the hotel, then? Not at the apartment?"

"I don't cook. If I stay at the apartment, I have to mobilize the cooking and cleaning staff. I'll be there for a day. Two at most. I'll get a burger from room service and Wilder and Andre won't have to cancel their weekly poker game."

"My butler and my chef hold a weekly poker game?"

"It's a small one. Upper crust house staff only."

"I have no idea whether you're joking or not."

Samantha grinned. "Good."

Shoving the suitcase out of his way, he sat beside her on the bed. "The hotel it is, then. This 'gig' or whatever you call it came up quickly, though. I didn't hear any secret code words for 'run, the coppers are onto me,' but I still don't know all the code words." Rick took her hand in his. "We did have dinner plans this evening, and as you don't generally miss them, well, I had a thought. A vaguely worried one. And so here I am."

Shit. Burgers with the Donners. Generally, she looked forward to the monthly barbecue, to seeing what normal family life looked like and to playing video games or tossing a ball with the two youngest Donner kids. Stiff-assed as Tom Donner was, he had a good family, and his wife Katie was probably the closest she'd come to having a female friend. Hell, Katie Donner even knew her secret identity.

"I'll call Katie and see if maybe we can reschedule for Thursday or Friday. I should be back way before then."

"I'll take care of it," he said, twining his fingers with hers. Even after a year together, he seemed to take every opportunity to touch her. She didn't have a single complaint about it, either. "You certain you don't want some company?"

"Only if I get to walk into your negotiations whenever I want."

His pretty eyes narrowed a little. "Point taken, if not appreciated. When's your flight?"

"Don't know yet." She checked her phone, to find both the meeting details from Anne Hughes and her flight information courtesy of Aubrey. "Three-twelve this afternoon. I should get going."

"If you took my jet, we'd have hours and hours here yet."

"No fair tempting me with sexy times." Grabbing a spare phone charger, she tossed it on top of her clothes, added the newest Karen Hawkins Dove Pond book, and zipped the suitcase up.

"Every so often," Rick said, taking the carry-on out of her hand and hefting it himself as they headed downstairs, "I remember just how...mobile your life used to be, and how much it isn't that way, now. An entire suitcase for a two-day trip, when you used to carry everything you needed to last you a year in one backpack."

"I did have stuff stashed around in a couple of places," she conceded. "Clothes and shit. But yeah, I used to travel lighter." She knocked the carry-on with her fist. "That is a *small* suitcase, though. Give me a little credit."

"I give you all the credit, Samantha. Am I stepping on your toes if I drive you to the airport?"

"Nah. That's some understated support, that is. Very manly and progressive all at the same time."

He grinned, the expression making her insides gooey. "I'm British. It comes naturally."

She'd been happy with the Porsche, but for Rick that was too ordinary. His brand-new deep-red Aston Martin DBS Superleggera Volante had a name almost as long as his, but damn if it wasn't an actual James Bond car. And he'd let his cousin Reggie sell it to him, which was both nice and a good sign that he'd finally begun making a serious attempt to include his extended family back in his life.

Rick put the carry-on in the trunk while she climbed in on the passenger side. Since they'd met, they'd been apart a couple of times, mostly when Rick had an unexpected business meeting somewhere and she had a local security consultation to finish, but this was the first time she was the one leaving.

Probably because word had gotten out that Rick was at home, a pair of photographers stood outside the main gates of Solano Dorado now, and as the Aston Martin left the property, one of them actually chased the car for about twenty feet, camera raised. She knew, because she watched him in the side view mirror until the road curved.

"Two is better than twenty," Rick said into the silence.

"I know. I still think maybe we should have stayed in Scotland. The only people hounding us there were your relatives." She chuckled, mostly to let him know that she was okay with two members of the paparazzi tagging them. "And some angry villagers and a ghost or two, and the weather."

He smiled back at her. "For a city girl you did surprisingly well in the country."

"The *snowy* country," she pointed out. "I get even more credit because of snow."

"I *am* missing the snow—and the Highlands—right about

now." Rick glanced down at the dash display. "The middle of October, and it's ninety-two."

"And ten thousand percent humidity. Don't forget that."

"Hm. New York is beginning to sound more attractive by the moment." A brief scowl touched his mouth. "I mentioned to Tom that we were considering a move there."

Samantha twisted in the black leather seat to face him, curling one leg beneath her. "You don't have to do that."

"I don't have to be a mind reader to know that you prefer doing protection and recovery for valuables over installing security," he commented. "Or that the jobs you've most enjoyed have been in New York."

"But the Donners are here. Solano Dorado is here." She knew that before her, Rick had lived a pretty mobile life, too. He had homes or apartments in New York, London, Scotland, Paris, Hong Kong, Florida, and San Francisco. As far as she'd been able to figure out, his main reason for purchasing Solano Dorado had been because Palm Beach was where Tom and Katie Donner had settled with their three kids. A guy needed his damn friends. Rick needed the connection to a genuine good guy and his awesome kids to remind him that the world wasn't all business, and that he shouldn't be all about work. Hopefully she played a part in helping him realize that, too, but the Donners had been there first.

She had her own attachments to Palm Beach, too. Stoney lived there, in his unassuming little house with his sliding eyes cat clock in the kitchen. He was the reason she'd set her perimeter around Pompano Beach and Palm Beach, with safe houses and bolt holes scattered across the county in a rough circle. Now, when everybody who watched entertainment news knew where she lived, the idea of safe houses seemed even more vital—even if she hadn't set foot in any of them for a year.

"That's why I mentioned it to Tom," he said, yanking her out of her thoughts. "To see if he might be amenable to relocating."

He sent her a glance as he turned them up the highway toward the airport. "I'm beginning to think you and I aren't quite on the same page about it ourselves, though."

"I thought we were just talking about it." She unrolled the window. Heat blasted against her face, and with a grimace she rolled it up again. "Don't start trying to crane the Donners out of here until we've figured it out, for cripe's sake."

"I'm not moving anyone yet. Tom and Katie need time to consider the idea, just like we do. No one's packing boxes."

By "we" he apparently meant "her," and that was weird. "I'm the most mobile person I know," she said aloud. "I can't even tell you how many places I've lived."

"You, with the near photographic memory?" he drawled, obviously teasing.

She shrugged. "Okay, I remember most of them, except for the really early ones. My earliest memory that isn't fuzzy is Martin cutting a ton of my hair off and putting a baseball cap on my head so I could pass as a boy."

Rick pulled them over to the breakdown lane as a Mercedes and a Tesla honked at them. "You never told me that before," he said, putting the Aston Martin into park and shifting to face her. "That's your first memory?"

"Jeez, Rick, what are you, my therapist?" When he continued gazing at her, she frowned. "What?"

"I'm just wondering if it was your father being kicked out of your home and taking you with him that triggered that fascinating ability you have to remember everything."

"No. I was bitten by a radioactive elephant at the zoo, and that's why I remember everything. It's my superpower. Plus, I can blow water out of my nose."

His thoughtful look collapsed into a grin. "It's just a theory. Have it your way, Samantha. My first memory is having an ice cream in Hyde Park with my parents. I kept wanting to go wading in the Serpentine."

Now that was a nice, normal memory, something to warm a person up on a chilly night. Samantha didn't have many memories like that. Mostly they were filled with her learning to pick pockets and pick locks, and her dad leaving her with Stoney and then coming back flush and full of himself at having stolen and sold off some Monet or something. And the later ones of her going with him on jobs, as he called them, and then her solo excursions.

"I like your memory better," she decided. "Now get me to the airport, will you?"

At least Rick Addison had given her a new set of memories. They weren't as proficient at keeping her warm at night as the man himself, but they would do for a day or two.

3

Tuesday, 7:35 p.m.

"Uncle Rick, when is Sam coming back?" Olivia Donner asked, bouncing out the front door of Tom's house to greet him. "She said she would show me how to booby trap my room so Michael can't come in."

"No booby traps in the house," Tom countered as he traipsed by, barefoot, to toss a plastic bag into a trash can. "Has she landed yet?"

"Yes. She's on her way to the hotel." A few years ago, Richard would have swung Olivia up in his arms, but she was ten now, and so he offered her a hand. Her small fingers closed around his, and he allowed her to tow him into the house.

"I still need to know when she's coming back," Olivia insisted, her voice now a conspiratorial whisper.

Clearly the "no boobytrap" rule was going to be broken, regardless of what Tom ordered. "A day or two. If it's longer than that, I'll make sure she calls you."

"Yes, do that, please, because Michael is not respecting my space."

Michael was her fifteen-year-old brother, and while Rick doubted the lad would find much of what filled his sister's room worthy of his attention, the kids did tend to prank each other—more so since Samantha had come into their lives. "You have my word."

"Thank you. And mom said not to say anything, but just between us, do you think Sam needs any more bridesmaids?"

"I am not qualified or authorized to answer that question, Olivia." Especially when, as far as he knew, Samantha had yet to ask *anyone* to be in the wedding. He imagined Katie Donner would be her maid of honor, because Samantha had never mentioned a long-term female friend. That actually troubled him a little; she did have friends, but they were mostly male, and most of those were from her tricky, troublesome past.

"I told you not to ask," Katie said, handing him a bowl of sliced watermelon and angling her head toward the back yard. "Sam and Rick may decide not to have a ceremony at all. We don't know, and it's none of our business, is it, Livi?"

"No, it's none of our business. But I still want to know. I've been a flower girl before, when I was younger, but I've never been a bridesmaid."

"Livi. Enough."

The ten-year-old sucked in her breath. "Fine. Can we at least do s'mores later?"

"Yes."

"Only in ten-year-old world is being a bridesmaid equal in importance to a s'more," Katie commented, following Rick outside as Olivia ran off to find marshmallows.

"It might be similar in Samantha world, actually," Rick returned with a grin. "I'm not certain."

"Speaking of which, New York? Are you going to sell Solano Dorado?"

They'd set the large table on the upper deck with paper plates and plastic forks. Clearly, she'd been preparing for the dinner tonight for days, and then he and Samantha had messed it all up. Yes, he'd come, but these days Uncle Rick wasn't the big draw for the Donner family. No, that honor fell to Aunt Samantha. It was good for her, and she'd already admitted that the Donners were the nearest to normal she'd ever strayed, but both of them needed to remember that not everyone else's lives were as changeable as theirs.

"We're just considering some ideas right now," he said aloud. "Logistics and opinions and options and such."

"Well, in my opinion, the school year just started."

"Is that your only objection? Waiting until summer is rather…doable."

"That's just the first thing that came to mind. Give me time."

"That's the idea." He set the watermelon in the center of the table, beside the hamburger buns and the potato salad. "I'm sorry again that Samantha had to change her plans. She wants to make it up to you."

"She already called me. I'm considering making the two of you take Olivia and Michael to Disneyworld as compensation. For a weekend."

"Ah."

Tom patted him on the shoulder. "That'd be a good test, to see if you and Jellicoe want to reproduce."

For the first time since she'd called him at Tom's office, Rick was glad Samantha wasn't there. As skittish as she was about the wedding, he couldn't imagine how she would react to the idea of children. Babies. Hell, he wasn't sure how *he* would react. "One thing at a time," he commented, since Tom no doubt expected a response. Or for him to flee in terror.

Katie laughed. "I doubt teenagers could induce anyone to want to have children. They're barely human. I just want a weekend off."

"Done," Rick said. Even if he had to buy Disneyworld.

"And our friends!" Michael added from over by the barbecue. "Dad, should I flip 'em?"

"Let me take a look." Tom handed Rick a bottle of beer and strolled over to the smoking barbecue.

"Don't let him scare you," Katie said. "Having babies is much easier than having teenagers."

"I'm not scared." For God's sake, he negotiated deals worth millions for breakfast. "I just haven't spent a great deal of time thinking about it. The last year has been rather...eventful."

"You can say that again. And from what Tom told me about Scotland, your getaway there wasn't precisely peaceful, either."

"True, but it wasn't boring, either."

She tilted her head, her straight blond hair cut like a heart around her face. "Can I say something to you without you getting overly British about it?"

Rick smiled. "You can try."

"I've known you what, twelve years now? Through buying businesses and bachelorhood and Patricia and divorce and now Sam. Your life has been...busy, and successful, but, well, this is the happiest I've seen you. Honestly, it is."

"I feel happier," he admitted. "And I think we both know who I can thank for it. She's a whirlwind, a tornado, and my serenity, all at the same time. I've never..." Rick cleared his throat. He wasn't one for waxing poetic, and other than a quiet moment or two with Samantha, Katie was the only other human in the world with whom he would share those sentiments. "When I met and married Patricia, I was fond of her, and we had—for the moment—a mutually beneficial relationship. I discounted ever feeling head over heels about anything, and yet here I am. Giddy."

She grinned. "Giddy suits you."

He wasn't entirely certain about that. Giddy meant gale-force winds whipping him about, and he'd built his business empire based on logical, solid, reliable footing. Having his personal life be the exact opposite was terrifying, but he couldn't deny that it was also damned thrilling. Perhaps he was becoming an adrenaline junkie just like Samantha.

His phone rang in its one generic tone, and he pulled it from his pocket. Samantha had different ringtones and text tones for everyone who knew her number, but he wasn't going to have "Lady" or "I Will Always Love You" or "When a Man Loves a Woman" sounding from his pocket while he was in the middle of tearing some company into pieces and selling off the remains. Aside from potentially weakening his position, he had no idea which love song would be…hip enough for him to use, anyway.

All he needed was to see "Samantha" pop up on the screen, anyway. "Hi," he said, standing to walk to the far corner of the large yard. "Are you at the hotel?"

"I am," her voice came back. "In room 212 of the Manhattan, despite the front desk woman trying to wrangle me into the top floor suite. Something about me knowing the owner of the place."

"The suite has the nicest view," Richard grumbled.

"Mm-hmm. Then they made me wait for twenty minutes while my new digs were being cleaned, or so they said, you sly guy." She cleared her throat. "Or at least I assume you're the one who called ahead to ask them to fill the mini fridge with Diet Cokes and Hershey Bars?"

"Perhaps."

"Oh, and the fifty thousand roses covering every shelf and table. That's totes romantic, but you've already got me, Brit. You don't have to work that hard."

Rick grinned. "While I might agree that the fifty roses—not fifty thousand—might have been excessive, not even you can stop me from making the gesture."

"Was Katie upset that we had to reschedule the barbecue?"

For a half second or so Rick considered lying to her.

Samantha didn't like upsetting the "normals"—as she termed those who'd never lived a life of crime and mayhem. On the other hand, without honesty between the two of them, by the time he realized how far off-kilter they were, one of them could be in prison. "I was about to cancel," he said, lowering his voice a little, "but then Tom started talking about how long it takes to make a potato salad and how Michael had asked to be the one to grill the burgers, so…"

"OMG, you're there now, aren't you?"

"Yes."

"Keep your voice down, then. I do *not* want to be blamed for trying to prevent grilling and potato salad."

"Never fear. I made certain they knew how cranky you were at having to miss this. We've been tasked with taking Michael and Olivia and their friends to Disneyworld as compensation."

"Ooh, we could fly there in the helicopter. They would get so many fire points."

"'Fire' points?"

"Didn't you know? Good things are fire, now. But don't worry about trying to figure out how to use it. It'll probably be as uncool as 'groovy' by the time I get back home."

"Noted. And yes, your apology has been accepted by all."

The responding silence on her end abruptly had him worried, and he reviewed their conversation in his head. Rick didn't think he'd said anything to set her Spidey sense—as she called it—tingling, but her mind bore a striking resemblance to quicksilver and he frequently found himself trying to catch up to her thought process.

"Samantha?"

"I do miss it. I miss the barbecue. And the potato salad. And the Donners. Which is weird. We see them all the time. Am I domestic, now?"

Thank God. "Perhaps. My opinion depends on whether you miss me or not."

"Ask me how many days you and I haven't slept in the same bed over the past year."

Just the question had him thinking about sweaty, naked nights and the taste of her skin. He took a breath, reminding himself that he was at a family barbecue and wearing a rather snug pair of jeans. "How many?"

"Five. This makes six. So yeah, I miss you."

"Burgers are ready!" Michael yelled, clanging the metal tongs against the grill lid.

"I heard that," Samantha said. "Go eat. Tell Michael how yummy his burgers are. And compliment Katie on the potato salad."

"Will do. And I'll tell them again that you wish you were here. I love you."

"Love you back. Bye."

"Bye."

He clicked the phone off. Before and after his ex-wife Patricia, he'd played about, dating an actress here and a model there, but none of them, including Patricia, had ever grabbed hold of him the way Samantha Jellicoe had. And did, every bloody day.

"Uncle Rick, your burger's getting well done," Michael called, the boy and the barbecue surrounded by swirling, meat-scented smoke.

"Thanks," he said, scooping up a plate and bun. With his free hand he texted Jack Abernathy, letting his pilot know that he wanted to be in the air by midnight.

"Whatcha doin'?" Tom drawled, lifting an eyebrow as he passed over the mustard. "Did Jellicoe get arrested or something?"

"Why would Aunt Sam get arrested?" Olivia demanded, her eyes widening. "Did you rat her out, Dad?"

Tom scowled, obviously not liking being turned into the bad guy in this scenario. "No, I didn't rat her out. I was just joking, Livi."

"Well, I don't like it. I think that a long time ago Aunt Sam might have done some things that…" She leaned forward. "That the po-po might not like," Olivia continued in a whisper.

"'Po-po?' Where the—where did that come from?"

"From *Ant-Man and the Wasp*, Dad. That's what Peanut—her real name is Cassie—says."

"Her real name isn't Cassie," Michael cut in. "She's an actress."

"I know that, Michael. I meant her real name in the movie. But that reminds me, Uncle Rick. Do you think I should be Wonder Woman or Captain Marvel or Scarlet Witch or Black Panther for Halloween?"

Richard glanced at Olivia's parents, but one was avoiding his gaze and the other one seemed to find the whole conversation hilarious. "Which one do you like the best?" he asked, checking as his phone vibrated. Good. With any luck he should be in New York by three in the morning.

"Probably either Wonder Woman or Captain Marvel. I mean, I like Wonder Woman because she's one of the warriors of Themyscira, and they're the Amazons. But I like Captain Marvel because she's a good pilot and she helps the whole universe."

"And she knows Spider-Man, and Livi has a crush on Tom Holland."

"Michael! Shut up! You have a crush on the Hulk!"

"I do not! I like Harley Quinn."

Using every ounce of his straight-faced negotiating skills, Rick put up a hand. "Wonder Woman is a goddess, right? I think maybe the woman who wasn't born special but accidentally absorbed the power of one of the Infinity Stones might be more heroic."

"Well, look at you." Katie didn't bother hiding her grin. "Sam really has gotten to you, hasn't she?"

He shrugged. "She likes the Marvel movies. Nearly as much

as she likes Godzilla." The things she liked, he learned about. It was as simple as that.

"Are you sure she isn't arrested?" Olivia pressed. "I could help bail her out."

"You know far too much about the legal system for a ten-year-old," Tom commented with a mock frown. "Since Jellicoe isn't arrested, how's she doing in New York?"

"Fine. Her meeting's in the morning. And I'll need you to shift the meeting with Rohrbach to next week."

The lawyer thudded his fist on the picnic table. "I knew it. You're flying to New York. *Is* she in trouble?"

"No. Sotheby's is preparing an exhibition and auction. I'm an art and antique collector. If I have someone on the inside who can get me a preview of items, I'm going to make use of it." There. That explanation didn't make him sound like a lovesick puppy.

"Mm-hmm. Do you have time for dessert? Sour cream blueberry pie."

"I do. I may even have time for a round of Pictionary."

"Uncle Rick's on my team!" Olivia bellowed, holding out a fist for him to bump. "We're the Avengers. Earth's mightiest heroes. You're Iron Man, because you have lots of money and fire cars."

"Fire" was still in for the moment, then. Yes, normal was important, for both him and Samantha. Without the Donners, his most frequent human contact would be with high-powered businessmen and investors and attorneys. For Samantha it would be her fence and surrogate father Walter Barstone, the almost-magically helpful Aubrey Pendleton, and God knew how many underworld figures of infamy and renown. And so he played Pictionary and got lambasted for drawing a dinosaur with X's in its eyes to represent the word "extinct." It made a great damned deal of sense, in his opinion.

And then he went home, packed an overnight case, and had

Reinaldo drive him to the airport. Because while they'd spent nights—five of them, evidently—separately before now, and while Samantha certainly could manage on her own, he missed her. And he didn't like the feeling.

○

SAMANTHA CROUCHED, using the massive air conditioning unit on the roof to keep her in shadow. New York City could be tricky, with nearly every square inch lit up twenty-four seven and covered by somebody's camera. Roofs with lots of machinery were good, because other than the occasional piece of copper there wasn't much to be stolen, and the machinery and pipes and conduits created heat to fuck up infrared drone scanners and at the same time made for lots of hiding places.

The police helicopter crossing overhead continued on its way, and she leaned forward onto her fingertips again. The building across the street was half the size of the one on which she perched, so she had a pretty good view of the roof and the west and south sides. Lots of windows with cute mini sills breaking the flat surface of the walls, a Juliet balcony about three stories up on the back center, and a peaked, Victorian-style roof with a wrought-iron widows walk.

She'd driven by the front side already, twice, and it looked a lot like an oversize Victorian house set in the middle of some expensive apartment buildings, a museum, and a couple of fairly exclusive office buildings. Extra wide, heavy-duty doors marked the rear entrance, and the front had both steps and a wheelchair ramp. A covered front porch boasted a couple of chairs, but anyone sitting there wouldn't have had much of a view.

Nope, it wasn't anybody's house. Not any longer, anyway. Now it made for three stories of prime exhibit space, a perfect place for paintings and jewelry and small sculptures meant for a select number of viewers in a place that could encourage them to imagine the items displayed in their own home. And it happened to be only four blocks from Sotheby's, which made it pretty convenient, too.

She used to love places like this. Tons of windows, security put in well after the building itself had been built, valuables out in plain view on pedestals not meant for a domestic setting, rooms not wired for anything but motion, paintings set on hooks and not bolted to the walls—it was like a cat burglar buffet.

Her pocket vibrated. "Why aren't you asleep?" she asked, as Rick's name popped up on her phone's display. "It's late."

"Why aren't you in your hotel room?" he returned crisply.

Samantha straightened, stomping her feet to get the blood flowing back into her legs. "Why are you calling the room instead of my phone?" she countered, pulling the ski cap she wore down over her face, stepping through the roof door, and picking up the four-foot length of pipe she'd used to prop it open.

"I didn't."

"Then how do you know I'm not in the room? I know the Manhattan is your hotel, but if you have people spying on me, we're going to have to have a chat." As she descended to the fourth floor she left the stairwell, turning off the lights behind her and relocking the door.

"Don't turn this on me. Where are you?"

"I'm looking at the building where the exhibit's being set up. I have a meeting about it tomorrow." In the small corner office, she locked herself in, walked over to the open window, and ducked out onto the fire escape. Shutting the window again, Samantha removed the flattened sheet of foil she'd used to bypass the alarm and pocketed it, then hiked down the steep stairs, climbed down the escape ladder, and shoved it back up into place with the pipe before she tossed that into the alleyway dumpster.

"Alone? At night. In the middle of the city."

She pocketed the ski mask and replaced it with her black baseball cap. "I wore my big girl panties. Why are you spying on me? I thought we had this trust thing figured out."

"I'm not spying on you. I'm…here."

Samantha nearly tripped over a crack in the sidewalk, which would have gotten her double bad luck points. "What?"

"I just figured…Well, it doesn't matter now. Where are you? I'll send a car."

Accelerating into a trot, Samantha turned the corner and headed up toward Lexington. "I'm hailing a cab now," she said, lifting a hand as one turned the corner ahead of her. "I'll be back in ten. And you'd better be ready to explain what's going on, because eight hours ago we had an agreement and you were being supportive in Florida, Brit." Before he could respond to that in his low, sexy voice with his suave, sexy accent, she clicked off the call and pocketed her phone again.

Dammit, dammit, dammit. Whatever this was, it had better be good. Because leaving in the first place had been way harder than it should have been. Rick Addison tailing her to all of her meetings would not only be too distracting for everyone concerned, but it would totally knock her own legitimacy on its ass in favor of his. And she didn't want to use his.

"Where to?" the cabby asked, glancing at her in the rearview mirror.

"The Manhattan Hotel."

"Okay."

Settling her baseball cap lower over her eyes, she sat back. The news droned quietly from the seat-back TV, but she ignored it in favor of the city lights. This wasn't the first time Rick had tried to manage her, if that was what this was. His psyche tended toward macho, so he might have flown up from Palm Beach to protect her from big bad New York—and that wouldn't work, either. For fuck's sake, she knew how to be on her own, and for her that hadn't meant making her own dinner. It had meant climbing up the outside of buildings and breaking in to steal things.

She paid off the cabbie in cash, because she still disliked leaving a trail even if she did have a credit card with no spending limit. After she sent a wave to the concierge, she headed for the elevator, tapped her card at the reader and hit the second floor button.

When the doors opened, she stepped into a short hallway and headed left. Five doors down Samantha stopped, sliding the card again and pushing open the door.

She stopped just inside the room. Barry White purred through the speakers in all three rooms, while the lingering scent of the roses mixed with the softer, cookie-dough scent of vanilla candles. Abrupt amusement pushed at her, and she shoved it away as best she could. This was serious. Damn serious. "Barry White? Really?"

Rick stepped into the bedroom doorway. He'd put on one of the hotel's plush white robes, and even with it belted around his waist she was fairly certain he didn't have anything else on under it. Twiddling a rose in his fingers, he leaned sideways against the doorframe. "Hey."

God, he was gorgeous. "Hey."

"This is not a checking-up-on-Samantha visit, Samantha. This, quite simply, is a booty call."

Determined to keep her gaze from wandering down his hard, toned, terry cloth clad body, she planted her hands on her hips. "Seriously."

"I played Pictionary. On Olivia's team."

"And that made you horny enough to fly a thousand miles in the middle of the night?"

The slight smile on his face remained, though she would have been willing to bet that he wasn't amused. Rick wasn't used to being questioned, and even if he'd probably come to expect it from her, he couldn't possibly like it. "I'm wealthy," he said in his cultured British prep-school drawl. "I can work from practically anywhere in the world that has internet. And when I spoke to you on the phone, I realized I missed you. It's as simple as that."

She weighed that for a minute, along with the fact that when she'd heard him talking about being at the Donners' and eating burgers, she'd felt…what, homesick? *Her*? It didn't make much sense, but she didn't know how else to explain it. "You're not worried I'm planning some Italian Job heist or something, then."

"No, I am not. Or I wasn't, until you said that."

Trust. She was learning—slowly—to trust. And while Rick had several times neglected to tell her something, he hadn't lied to her yet. Samantha tossed her black gloves onto the chair by the window. "Whatcha got on under that robe?"

"Not a bloody thing."

"So what was the original plan?" Sitting beside the gloves on the edge of the chair, she untied her shoes and kicked them off. Planning a job, even if it was just to figure out how to prevent someone else from breaking in somewhere, generally got her adrenaline going. Tonight, she'd figured to call down for a big tub of strawberry ice cream and watch Marvel movies until she passed out. Rick sex was a much better idea. "You sneak in here, undress, and just slide into bed with me?"

Rick walked toward her, unknotting the ties of the belt as he approached. "Given that I have yet to sneak up on you, I took the room directly across from this one, changed into this, and then planned to stroll in here with a rose between my teeth."

A grin pulled at her mouth. "You are a damned magnificent bastard."

"Hm. I'll ignore the fact that you just disparaged my ancestry."

He cupped her face in his hands, leaning down to kiss her. God, she loved him. Every so often when she considered her odds of successfully avoiding arrest until after all the statutes of limitation had run out, when she thought about spending the next twenty years in prison because she'd relocated a Monet or two—or eight—back in the day, it wasn't about missing her freedom any longer. It was about not having the man standing in front of her, in her life.

Samantha slid her hands up his bare, muscular chest, shoving the robe off as she went. When she stood up, he immediately went to work unfastening her jeans, while she kissed his jaw and throat, inhaling that very expensive aftershave of his that somehow conjured images of green fields and horseback riding and nights by a cozy fire. She'd have to ask what it was called. "Virile English Lord" or something, probably.

As he lifted the front of her black T-shirt, he ran his palms up her bare skin to cup his hands over her breasts. She didn't need to look down to know that he wasn't faking wanting her, or that sex had been the most convenient excuse for him showing up to check on what she was doing.

Quickly she reached around to unfasten her cute purple bra and shrugged out of it and her shirt at the same time. "Okay, maybe I missed you," she murmured, sliding her arms around his neck, skin to skin.

"Good." Rick kissed her again, hot and open-mouthed, before he squatted down, yanked down her pants and purple underwear, and straightened again to scoop her up into his arms.

As accustomed as she was to standing on her own two feet, there was something totally arousing about this guy, who could lift her off hers. With a laugh she wrapped her hands around his shoulders, dragging him down onto the bed when he dropped her there.

Samantha wrapped her legs around his hips as he pushed into her, her throaty sigh mixing with his groan of satisfaction. He might have still been a little miffed with her for not being where he expected, but as he pumped into her again and again, she was okay with that. God, yeah, she was okay with that. The bed rocked, picking up a high-pitched, rhythmic squeak in time with their motion. The muscles across her abdomen tightened, and she leaned up to kiss him as she came in a delicious spasm.

With a grunt Rick shoved into her, lowering his head to suck on her tits as he climaxed, too. Samantha lay back again, breathing hard and tangling her fingers into his dark hair. "Now *that* is how I like to end a day," she panted.

"You and me both." Rick twisted them so that they lay side by side, facing each other. "So, you were casing the exhibit space?"

"I looked at it on Google, but I wanted to scope it out before my meeting tomorrow."

"And how secure is it?"

Samantha squinted one eye. "As it is right now? I could have gotten in with a screwdriver and made it out with as much as I could carry."

He brushed his fingers through her hair, making her shiver. "That's not good."

"Nope. Hence Anne Hughes needing me. I think I can lock it down, for a couple of weeks, anyway. If it was permanent that would be a whole different and way more expensive conversation, but it's not permanent."

"Even given your expertise, I still wish you would take someone with you when you go about climbing tall buildings in the middle of the night. You aren't bulletproof."

"Neither are you," she retorted. "And if you're insinuating that you're the one who should be going with me, you getting killed would wreck the stock market and a bunch of peoples' incomes. Plus, I'd feel bad. So, nope." She smiled a little, trying to keep from enraging his masculine sense of whatever it was that made him think he had to be the one in charge of protecting everyone else. "You have better things to do than climb rusty ladders with me, anyway."

"More useful, yes. Better, not necessarily. And you're avoiding my point. You shouldn't go alone. You aren't a solo enterprise any longer, my dear."

Well, that was true. In the old days, after she'd decided her dad was getting too reckless and taking too many risks and she'd ended their partnership, it had been just her. Stoney getting her jobs to liberate items, and her going out and doing it. She'd been so under the radar that if she fell off a building nobody but Stoney would probably even have known that the splat on the sidewalk had once been a world-class cat burglar. "I'm still not taking my boyfriend out scoping buildings with me."

"Your fiancé, Samantha. Soon-to-be husband." He eyed her. "I suppose the alternative would be that you go in the daytime and have one of your employees join you."

At least he hadn't said that the alternative was that she not go at all. That would have ticked her off. "If it didn't make you think I would use the opportunity to be training some padawan to join the Dark Side, I can work with taking one of my guys along. Mostly. I think a couple of them might actually be reformed."

"Safety can be very tempting, I imagine."

"Kymo told me this morning that thanks to Jellicoe Security, he's never going to have to explain to his daughters why daddy's in prison. I like that." She stretched. "It feels good."

Rick kissed her. "You're being very amenable tonight."

"Well, you gave me the good sex."

Putting his arms around her, he pulled her up against him. "I always give you the good sex."

Samantha laughed. "Just keep that up, then."

4

Wednesday, 7:56 a.m.

I n the past, when Samantha met with suit-types it had been in the process of scoping out a crime. She did best with her portrayal of "generic dumbass bimbo," because men loved to mansplain all their secrets to, well, generic dumbass bimbos who hung all over them and pretended to be infatuated. At the same time, she did speak a couple of languages and had also assumed the guise of a professor, a doctor, a couple of anthropologists and archaeologists, a selection of rich heiresses, and a reporter or two.

All that meant now, though, was that after a year of being on the straight and narrow she still had the tendency to run all her personas through her head while she figured out how to meet a prospective client. In those circumstances, the version of her that was matter-of-fact, cursed less, and showed some knowledge of what was being protected seemed the most practical to wear for the day.

Blowing out her breath, she tapped her clipboard against her

47

thigh and resisted pacing for another minute. Waiting sucked, no matter what the job happened to be.

"Miss Jellicoe?"

She turned from gazing up at the converted Victorian house to see a petite woman hurrying up the block toward her. Anne Hughes lacked an inch or two on her, and she considered herself pretty short—especially in comparison with a six-foot-two English lord. The Sotheby's curator had hair that had likely started out as brown but had been allowed to lighten to a honey blondish as a good portion of the strands went white.

Ms. Hughes wore it in a slightly longer version of a Helen Mirren bob, and it made her look competent and stylish at the same time. The gray slacks, practical shoes, and peach-colored blouse beneath an open blue jacket completed the ensemble, and Samantha was glad she'd decided against wearing her dress. Yay for practicality.

"Hi. You must be Ms. Hughes," she said, shifting the clipboard and proffering her right hand.

"Anne, please." Anne had a firm grip, and while that didn't necessarily mean anything, it was so much better than the soft, curled-finger howdies that overly cultured women seemed to favor.

"And Sam is fine. This place is lovely." Samantha gestured at the former house. "Way bigger than a traditional Victorian, though."

"Yes. Two homes originally sat on this lot. The rear house was demolished to make room for the extension of this one. The entire front of this house is original, with the exception of the windows and some security and accessibility additions."

Samantha sent her a sideways glance, then resumed gazing at the building. Yeah, she had it pretty much memorized, but it was a good move to look intensely interested. "Sotheby's has used this place for exhibits before, hasn't it? Why the concern now?"

"Well." Anne shifted her feet in her low-heeled peach-colored pumps. "Let's discuss that inside, shall we?" She motioned toward the front door.

"Sure. Lead the way."

They headed up the six steps to the wood and glass front door—or rather, steel and plexiglass, she amended, knocking one knuckle against it as Anne slid her ID card through the reader. Definitely not original, but if the rest of the windows had been beefed up to plexi, it would make her job a little easier.

"We did replace the front door," Anne said on the tale of that thought, pushing it open as the bolts slid open with an audible click. "And the ground floor windows. The upstairs windows are either original or replicas, since they're much more difficult to enter through."

Samantha could have disputed that, but she only nodded and made a note on her clipboard to check the alarm wiring on all the windows. Back in the day she'd almost never gone into a building via the ground floor, for exactly the reason Anne Hughes had stated.

In the foyer, which had been opened up to allow for a plexi-glass-enclosed ticket booth-looking box and an elevator, they stopped. "We have about half of the displays moved into the building," Anne said, gesturing toward the depths of the house, "but they haven't been secured or wired yet. I wanted your opinion, first."

"Not meaning to overstep or anything," Samantha commented, "but like I said, Sotheby's has used this venue on more than one occasion. Is there a particular reason you're worried about this exhibit? If you do have a specific worry, that would help me figure out where you could use some improvement."

"Yes, that." Anne took a breath. "We will be exhibiting and then auctioning a large portion of the estate of Lewis Adgerton on behalf of his family."

Samantha blinked. "Lewis Adgerton as in Adgerton Digital Media? The guy who wants his ashes flown into space and scattered in orbit?"

"Yes, that's him. He had quite a collection of art."

Boy, had he. Samantha had personally liberated a Matisse from him about five years earlier, from his summer home in the south of France, and through Stoney she'd once delivered him an original Picasso plaster of one of his weird penis-nose woman statues. Great. Her statute hadn't run out on either of those, yet. If this was karma, then karma could go fuck itself. "Wow. His family isn't keeping hold of all that stuff?"

"No. They all detest each other, apparently, and want everything liquidated and divided into nice, neat little piles of money." Anne cleared her throat. "Sorry. The sale of artwork keeps me employed, but there's something about reducing it to its monetary value that just rubs me the wrong way."

"Oh, I get it. Touching a work of art is like touching history." Sam put on a smile, trying to be disarming rather than suspicious. "If you could touch it, that is."

"Yes. Exactly. Anyway, come on, and I'll give you the tour. My team will be here at nine." Anne grimaced. "And yes, I have a specific worry. I've had dealings with a…particular person before, who's attempted to damage my reputation. I have reason to believe that he knows I am in charge of this collection and that he means to attempt to remove items."

Samantha glanced up from her clipboard, eyeing Anne Hughes from beneath her lashes. The woman looked like a competent, middle-aged, mid-level businesswoman, not getting quite as much exercise as she used to and determinedly staying in close pursuit of the better fashion trends. The idea that she had an enemy, someone trying to harm her—even if it wasn't a physical threat—seemed…weird. Unexpected. "Who is this guy?"

"I don't know if that matters, because I want to see this

collection protected from any attempts at theft by anyone." She took a breath. "However, in the interest of full disclosure, I believe he goes by various names. The one he used with me was Bradley Martin."

A metaphorical icepick drove into Samantha's brain. *Fuck, fuck, fuck.* She knew Bradley Martin. Bradley Martin, Bob Martine, Frank Bradley, and Brad Cassidy (apparently in honor of Partridge Family singer David Cassidy) were all the same guy. Martin Jellicoe. *Her dad.* There were probably even more names than that, ones he'd used both before he'd started dragging her along with him and after they'd parted ways.

"I assume from your expression that you've heard of him," Anne said, folding her hands together. "I'm impressed; I haven't heard his name mentioned in years, myself."

He hadn't *used* that moniker in years, as far as Samantha knew. "If you haven't heard mention of him, then what makes you think he could be after this stuff?"

"I found this on my desk." She opened her purse and pulled out a folded piece of copy paper.

Samantha opened it. Written on a computer and printed out, of course, probably right at Sotheby's. Handwriting would mean evidence in some file somewhere. "'Congratulations on winning the Adgerton collection gig. I might stop by and see it some time. BM.'"

"When did you find it?" Samantha asked, willing her fingers not to shake as she handed it back.

"Three days ago. I came in on Sunday to go over some logistics with the exhibit, and there it was. I went straight to my boss and offered to hand off the collection to someone else. When he said that no one had ever been able to break into the house here, I asked for additional funds to make certain it stays that way. I was pretty persuasive, I have to say. And here you are."

Well, this wasn't the way Samantha had pictured her day going. "I have heard of Bradley Martin," she admitted, nodding.

"He used to be at the top of the heap where cat burglars are concerned. And with a couple of weeks to work, yeah, I could keep him out." Frowning, she turned a slow circle to eye the late nineteenth century-inspired wallpaper in the hallway. "How long do we have again?"

She knew the answer, but this would be a good way to figure out if there was any leeway in the schedule at all. It still didn't explain why she hadn't already turned down the job and run out the door, because going up against her dad...She'd done it once, and he'd double-damn crossed her and nearly got her sent to prison. Maybe that was the lure for her, though. He'd slipped away without his prize, but neither of them could actually say they'd come out the winner in their little contest. The Metropolitan Museum of Art sure hadn't, what with having to replace fire doors and upgrade their entire electrical system.

"The timeline is firm. Six days before the exhibit opens, and it will remain open for two weeks. We've already uploaded photos of the items on the website and printed the exhibit and auction brochures. I believe we've even had some bids come in. Unofficially, of course."

That made Samantha's ears perk up. "Do you know which items have gotten the most interest?" Hell, she couldn't count on all her fingers and toes how many times one of her jobs had been to liberate something after the guy who wanted it the most had lost out on a bidding war.

"I'll inquire. It's unofficial, as I said. We use it as an indicator of our starting price, more than anything else. That said, there are some items worth more than a hundred million dollars apiece." Anne tilted her head. "Sam, I can see you hesitating. Is this something you can do? Because if it isn't, I need to find someone who can, and I have no time left in which to do that."

This was one of those times when she would have liked to be able to talk to Rick before she answered. He made for a pretty good conscience while she was still trying to find her balance in the crazy world of being law-abiding. But he was at his giant skyscraper of an office headquarters this morning, and she was standing in front of a nice lady with a very big problem. If it hadn't been her dad, she wouldn't even have hesitated. Maybe that was her answer, then.

"I can do it," she said. "I'm not cheap, though. Especially with this timeline."

"I understand. Do we have a deal?"

Samantha stuck out her hand. "We do. Let me make a few calls, and I'll get started. Sotheby's will have a contract emailed to it before noon. When your installation staff comes in this morning, make sure they know that what I say goes. Because I can pretty much guarantee they won't like some of what I'm going to say."

Anne shook her hand. Hard. "Thank you. You have no idea—thank you. Bradley Martin left a disaster in his wake the last time. I don't want to lose to him again."

Neither did Samantha.

RICHARD TYPED the address Samantha had given him into Google Maps, then clicked on street view. Ah. A renovated Victorian, just the thing to help any potential buyers imagine all the expensive pieces in their own homes. She hadn't told him what Sotheby's was going to be exhibiting or auctioning, but he imagined he could get that out of her later. With his art museum up and running in the renovated stable of his estate in Devon, he'd become even more interested in acquiring pieces than he had been before, and that was saying something.

Someone rapped at the door of the office he'd commandeered for the day, and he looked up. "Come in."

Jeniah Davis stepped into the room, a folder in one hand and a cup of tea in the other. "I have the printout of the docs you requested from Tom Donner," she said, "and a cup of Earl Grey."

"Thanks. For both. Where did Peter settle?"

She grinned. "In the breakroom. But don't feel sorry for him. We had donuts brought in this morning, and he's been looking for a reason to pop in there and eat all of them, anyway."

"Well done me, then." He picked up the folder as she set it down in front of him. "Have my car brought 'round at five-thirty, will you?"

"Sure. And I texted you the confirmation for dinner for two at the Bryant Park Grill at six-thirty." She hesitated. "Are you certain that's where—"

"It's a pretty little place, at the back of the New York Public Library," Richard interrupted. "It's interesting."

"It's gorgeous," Jeniah agreed. "It's just that I've never known you to dine there before."

Ah, the before times. Before he'd met Samantha Jellicoe. A great many things in his life had changed since then—not the least being that his first requirement for a dining establishment was no longer exclusivity. Samantha liked quirky, and historical, and interesting. He was discovering the same about himself. On top of that, he liked doing things for her. "I'm branching out."

"Good for you, Mr. A."

Evidently everyone thought adding Samantha into his life had been an improvement. He happened to agree, but at the same time he'd discovered that "old Mr. Addison" had apparently been rather cranky and demanding. And while the moniker "Mr. A" made him feel like a character in a comic book, being more approachable certainly hadn't hurt his bottom line. Just the opposite, in fact. "Thank you, Jeniah."

She left, shutting the door behind her, and Richard immediately swiveled in his chair to look out over Manhattan. He couldn't see the old Victorian house from the corner office of the Addisco headquarters on the thirtieth floor of the building he also owned, but he knew pretty much where it lay.

All day he'd resisted the urge to call Samantha, to see how her new "gig," as she called it, was proceeding, but thinking about it had put a definite damper on his ability to get any of his own work done. After he checked the time on his phone again, he went ahead and tapped her photo.

She answered after the second ring. "Hey."

"Hi. Anything interesting going on?"

"Dude, are you *bored*?" she asked, her voice dripping humor.

"I know, you told me not to come to New York. But I'm here, so how is everything going?"

"Good, with a smattering of 'holy shit,'" Samantha returned, her voice lowering. "I have about another hour here today. Wanna meet me somewhere for dinner after?"

"How about I pick you up at quarter of six?"

"As long as what I'm wearing is okay. I don't want all those women on the Rick's Chicks Facebook page trashing me again."

He grinned as he gazed out the window. "Your attire is suitable. I can't promise you won't get trashed. They do love me, you know."

"Oh, I'm well aware. They call me 'Jellicon,' which scared me until I realized they just meant that I'm conning you—not that I'm on my way to becoming a convicted felon."

"God, every time you say something like that my Fitbit alert informs me that I'm having a heart attack," he muttered, not amused any longer. "I'll see you in an hour."

He wanted to ask what it was that ranked as holy-shit-worthy on her meter, but given the way she'd lived her life so far it would have to be bad. No, it was better to wait so she could tell him in person and he could decide if he needed to throw her over his shoulder and flee with her.

At the same time, something untoward was already afoot, and he was a quarter of the way across town from her. Richard tapped his phone again. "Benny, bring the car around now, will you? I'm in the mood to go for a drive." And to circle a particular block for an hour until time to retrieve Samantha.

When they reached the building some twenty-five minutes later, nothing looked fright-inducing. A truck parked at the rear, with uniformed workers unloading what had to be display cases and stands. A van parked behind the truck bore the name of a security company with whom Samantha had worked occasionally over the past few months, and a third vehicle sat with its rear doors open to reveal boxes of cables and cameras, a Sotheby's security agent watching over all the comings and goings from beside the heavy double doors.

"There's some parking about two blocks from here," Benny said over his shoulder as he sent the SUV on up the street and around the next corner. "Do you want to wait there?"

"No keep circling."

"Okay, but the guard's already giving us the side-eye."

The downside of Samantha entering his life and making him seem more approachable to his employees was that they didn't only bring him new insight. Now they all felt free to question his choices and decisions. Admittedly overall that seemed to encourage him—and the company—to make better choices, but his ego still wasn't quite comfortable with him being...humanized. "At least once more around the block, Benny."

"You're the boss, Mr. A."

They circled again, and he took time on this go around to count the number of windows lining the front and back of the modified Victorian. If he knew anything about Samantha, which he did, she would think there were too many. The ones on the top floor even looked like they could be original to the house.

His phone rang. Samantha's name showed up in the display, and he tapped the accept button. "Hi."

"Are you by any chance driving around in a black Ford Expedition and circling my block?" she asked without preamble.

"You said you were facing 'holy shit,'" he returned, frowning. "I wanted to make certain SWAT wasn't surrounding you."

He could hear her sigh. "Okay. I'm just…I'm glad it's you. Marv wanted to pull a gun the next time you came around and start a *Heat*-type shootout."

"*Heat* being the DeNiro movie, and Marv being the Sotheby's security agent, I presume," Richard said. "We've only circled twice, so either Marv is extremely gung ho, or you have him on high alert."

"Probably half and half. Just double-park out back and come in."

"Will do." He lowered the phone. She hadn't complained that he was being pushy or stepping on her toes. To most men that likely would have signaled that she was become more accepting of having someone else in her life. To him, though, and with Samantha being the woman in question, he found it worrying. If she wanted a second opinion, or backup, she should simply have said so. "Park us behind one of the vans, Benny."

"You got it, Mr. A."

He'd been to enough Sotheby's auctions to know that armed security wasn't uncommon, but this was both an off-site venue and one that was still setting up the displays. No valuables would be inside yet. Aside from that, Samantha didn't like guns. Something had spooked her. And that, he didn't like. At all.

"Wait here for me," he instructed, as he stepped out of the SUV to approach the security officer stations at the house's open rear doors. "You must be Marv," he said, keeping his hands away from his sides just in case Samantha hadn't yet given her armed protection the all-clear.

"Mr. Addison. Sam says to meet her up on the second floor." Marv tilted his face toward the microphone extending down from his right ear. "Eagle to Nest: I have Mr. Addison on his way up, over."

"Thank you." Hiding his amusement behind years of practice, Richard walked into what Samantha would have termed the business end of the house. Stacks of metal chairs stood in one corner, while open doors on the other side gave him a glimpse of the security room, the utility closet, and a padded elevator, respectively. With a half dozen people in sight already, Samantha must have had at least three times that in the building. Hmm.

After a trio of men wheeled a four-foot-tall pedestal topped by a glass cube into the elevator, he stepped in behind them. "Which floor?" he asked, pushing the second-floor button.

"Same."

The workers exchanged glances. "You're Rick Addison, aren't you?" one of them asked in a thick Bronx accent.

He nodded. "I am."

"How does a stiff in a suit like you get a hot lady like Sam? It's the money, right?"

"Nah, she don't go for money," the second one countered. "Maybe it's that accent. You're British, right?"

"I am," Richard answered, somewhere halfway between being insulted and amused.

"Yeah, if I had a swanky accent like that, I bet I could get the ladies," the second mover went on.

"No, you couldn't," amateur comedian number three put in. "And it's definitely the money."

Thankfully the elevator opened before one of them could pull out a measuring tape and ask him to drop his trousers. With a nod, Richard exited. The walls, covered with dark, rich paneling and pin-point lights designed to illuminate particular sections, made the second floor feel like a maze. Of course, he might have asked in which direction Samantha would be up here, but he'd been too occupied with being rich and British.

Keeping his expression neutral, he headed to the right. If he could find some windows, he would at least be able to orient himself. It didn't help that there were plastic sheets hung everywhere to protect freshly re-stained wood, or that the smell was intense enough to actually make him feel light-headed.

A hand slipped around his left arm. "I figured you wouldn't be able to resist coming inside," Samantha murmured.

He leaned down to brush his mouth against her ear. "That's what she said."

Shifting, Samantha gave him a quick kiss on the jaw. "I don't know how you manage to make that sound sexy, but you do."

It likely had a great deal to do with her being an adrenaline junky looking for release, but hell, so was he. "This is…chaotic," he observed, turning his attention back to the house.

She looked up at him. "Yeah, I think I'm high on fumes right now, too. Let's find a window."

Obviously, she'd already learned the layout, because she led him around a half dozen corners, through three sheets of plastic, and into one of the corner turret rooms. All the windows stood open, and he staggered to the nearest sill and took a deep breath. "You should be wearing a mask."

"I was; you should have tried breathing in here two hours ago. I could see sound." With a grin she sank down on the sill of the next window over, unmindful of the thirty-foot drop to the ground directly behind her. "I'm glad we set up the museum at Rawley Park. It's been good practice for this."

"I'm more interested in what prompted your comment on the phone," he said, glancing at the open door beyond. As discreet as he generally was, she'd turned the damned thing into an art form.

"Nothing urgent." Straightening, she sidled toward the hallway. "If you can hang out here, I'll be about fifteen more minutes."

A silent alarm began buzzing in the back of his head. Within two minutes of him arriving, she'd ushered him into one corner and seen to it that he stayed there. She'd done a good job of it, but he knew when he was being handled. The question was, why? What, exactly, had she run into here that had bothered her? And why the hell did she want to keep it from him and keep him close by at the same time? "I'll attempt to stay out of the way," he said aloud.

That earned him a swift kiss on the cheek. The moment she slipped out of sight, he pulled out his phone and sent a text to Tom Donner, asking him to discover what he could about Anne Hughes, the building, and which auctions Sotheby's had coming up in the next month. Tom wouldn't like it, but by now he'd become accustomed to odd requests where Samantha and her business was concerned.

The response came immediately. "Christ. Gimme a damn minute."

Not bothering to respond, Richard took a deep breath out the window and then headed back into the chaos. In some ways it offended him to pretend to be bumbling or dim, and none of that would fool Samantha, but he wasn't putting on this show for her. Instead, he made for the trio of workers wiring a pedestal for light and for an alarm system.

None of them knew from where the collection for which they were preparing had come, though they seemed to think it was all from one "dead rich guy." Filling this entire building with one person's collection—that had to be someone whose acquisitions nearly rivaled his own. And that narrowed down the list of suspects considerably. Hm.

He sent another text, inquiring after rich dead guys who'd expired over the past six months. Tom's response—"What the hell are you doing, playing criminal Trivial Pursuit?"—made him grin as he strolled into the next area, this room likely a former library, or even ballroom, given the size of it.

A small woman stood in the middle of the swirl of activity,

an iPad in her hands and her neck crooked as she held a phone pinned between her ear and shoulder. This would have to be Samantha's employer—nobody else would be attempting to direct workers with Sam in the house.

She lifted her head, dropping the phone into one hand with an ease that said this wasn't anything unusual for her. He wanted to walk up and ask her for whatever information she had, but he had a pretty clear idea of how Samantha would react to her boyfriend coming to visit her on the job and then checking up on her with the boss. Nor would she be above pulling the same shit on him just to give him a taste of his own medicine.

Sidestepping, Richard posted himself just outside the door, out of the way but not quite out of earshot. There. That was fairly unobtrusive, if one could overlook the fact that he was there in the first place. And Samantha had invited him upstairs, after all.

"—Hughes, was this the cabinet for in here, or the library?" a male voice asked. "I can't read the last number on the back."

"Let me check, Terry. Is that the twenty-four inch?"

"Thirty."

"Thirty, thirty…Library," she said after a moment.

"And all this is for one guy's stuff?" the same male voice queried.

"Yes. Hard to imagine, isn't it? Even my entire Barbie collection from when I was a kid couldn't fill all this space."

"My Hot Wheels could give you a run for your money. And you should see Jamie's Star Wars stuff."

Anne Hughes laughed. "I did a Star Wars auction once. Sotheby's sold a set-used lightsaber for thirty-thousand dollars."

"Ya hear that, Jamie? Any of your stuff worth that much?"

"If it was, I wouldn't be telling you about it," a rougher voice responded. "Hey, Sam, do you collect anything? Other than British guys?"

"Ha ha," Samantha's voice came, and Rick edged back a little farther from the doorway. Spying was bad enough. Getting caught—that was worse. "I have some cool Godzillas."

She did, because he'd given her most of them. Before him, before she'd settled in one house, one place, she hadn't collected anything that he knew of. No one could flee on a whim with a collection of anything bigger or weightier than pennies or Pokémon cards. The way she marveled at the silliest of gifts told him volumes about how she'd lived her life before she'd crashed into his.

"Speaking of British guys," Samantha went on, "I hope you don't mind, Anne, but mine wanted to pick me up for dinner and showed up early. I think he's hoping to get a preview of the collection, but I didn't have the heart to tell him that nothing's been installed, yet."

A hand snaked around the doorframe, palm up. Feeling like a damned schoolboy caught smoking, Richard put his hand in hers and rounded the corner into view. "Excuse me for the intrusion, Miss Hughes," he said in his most charming tone. "I'm a collector, myself, and resisting a sneak peek at a Sotheby's auction is...difficult." He stepped forward, offering his free hand. "Richard Addison."

5

The older woman shook Richard's hand, her grip firm and confident. "Your collection is rather famous, Mr. Addison," she said with a smile. "As are you. Anne Hughes."

"Pleased to meet you," Richard returned. "Samantha won't even tell me whose collection it is that Sotheby's has acquired. I don't suppose you would take pity on me?" There. At least that sounded like he was merely curious, and not that he was controlling or felt the need to check up on Samantha.

"Hm. It's not precisely public knowledge, but it's not quite a secret, either. Lewis Adgerton. His family decided to keep approximately five percent of the collection, but they've entrusted the bulk of it to us."

No wonder Samantha had been excited. Lewis Adgerton had even outbid him on one or two occasions, though he supposed that had been mainly an old man's ego rather than a reasonable price for a Matisse and a Renoir. "Well. Some of the pieces in Adgerton's collection are legendary. Now I'm definitely interested."

"I'll get you a booklet," Samantha said. "Okay, guys, tools down. It's closing time. We'll start again at nine. And don't forget you'll need your badge, because if the house doesn't log you out, it won't let you in again tomorrow."

"You worried somebody's going to take the copper plumbing?" Somebody, Jamie from the sound of the voice, piped up.

"I've seen guys steal the glass out of windows," Samantha quipped. "Just be happy I'm keeping your tools safe."

"Yeah, fine. See ya in the morning, Miss Hughes. Sam."

Richard found himself alone with Anne, while Samantha wrangled her team. "Adgerton died nearly a year ago, didn't he?"

"Yes. It took his family some time to decide how to proceed."

"Might I interpret that as them wanting all the money but none of the upkeep for his valuables?"

She smiled again. "That would be my interpretation. Personally, I'd much rather his treasures be in the hands of someone who will enjoy and appreciate them, rather than having them languish in the custody of a family who views them as a burden."

"As would I."

"Sam mentioned that she helped you put together your museum in England. I've heard nothing but good comments about it."

"She designed most of it," Richard clarified. "And all of the security." Things he never would have thought of, because he saw through the opposite lens that she'd used for most of her life. "You're in good hands."

"She wouldn't be here if I thought otherwise. And while it's lovely that you're her cheerleader, I didn't base my choice on who her boyfriend happens to be."

Ah. Richard did throw his weight around when he found it necessary or expedient to do so, and he'd done it on Samantha's behalf on more than one occasion. Clearly Anne Hughes wasn't having any—and he found that equal parts admirable and annoying. The woman was also Samantha's employer, which considerably limited the responses he had to hand. Instead of conjuring one of them anyway, he inclined his head. "Good."

"Which is not to say that Sotheby's wouldn't be ecstatic to reserve a seat for you at the Adgerton auction."

"I imagine I'd be there regardless of who was handling the security," he returned, "though Samantha's involvement assures that whichever items strike my fancy will still be available come auction day."

A muscle in Anne's jaw jumped. "You're pretty good at this."

"It's kind of my thing," Richard conceded with a brief grin. "And whether or not I was marrying her, I would still tell you that Samantha Jellicoe is a remarkable individual."

"That, I'm beginning to believe. I thought Sotheby's was up to date on all the latest security measures. If nothing else, I thought she'd look at the plans and give a thumbs-up. Apparently, though, the higher the tech, the easier it is to get past some of it. I mean, she showed me how to keep from setting off one of our window sensors by using a gum wrapper she picked up off the street."

"We washed our hands after that, though," Samantha put in as she strolled back into the room. "Everybody's out, all their badges accounted for and scanned into the system. There's nothing much worth taking here at this point, but I still don't want anybody wandering in or out without me knowing it."

Hefting the iPad, Anne nodded. "I'm going to be staring at this thing all night, to see if any of the cameras or indicators go off."

Samantha patted her hip pocket. "You and me both. It'll give you an alert tone. And we'll both know. But don't you be driving down here if something does happen. Call the cops. The system will contact them anyway, but a live caller is good for letting them know it's not a false alarm."

"Oh, calling 911 is definitely my plan. I'm not about to be a hero. Believe me, the last thing I want to do is corner Bradley Martin." Miss Hughes shuddered. "He wouldn't come here at this point, would he?"

"I doubt it. He could try casing the building, but not all the security is in place yet. It wouldn't do him much good at this point. And there's always the chance that he was just trying to rattle you, and he's nowhere near Manhattan to begin with."

Shaking out her shoulders, the petite woman nodded. "That would be fine with me. Shall we?"

She led the way as Samantha took Richard's hand and they all headed to the elevator, flipping off lights as they went. Richard mouthed "Bradley Martin?" at her, but she shook her head and launched into a story about the Hope Diamond being delivered to the Smithsonian via the Post Office.

Once Anne Hughes climbed into her Uber and drove off, Richard frowned. "Who's Bradley Martin?"

"In the car, James Bond."

When she glanced up toward the building, he followed her gaze. A camera, mounted high enough that nobody walking by would probably even notice it, covered the entire block looking north. As far as he knew, only she and Miss Hughes currently had access to the camera, which meant she didn't want Anne overhearing their conversation. With a nod he walked over and pulled open the rear door of the SUV himself.

"Hey, Benny," she said, patting the driver on the shoulder as she slid into the car.

"Miss Sam. Glad to see you back in New York. I checked the weather in Palm Beach this morning. You could fry eggs on the sidewalk."

"Yeah, I nearly evaporated when I accidentally walked outside yesterday," she returned, taking Richard's hand again as he sat beside her. "Poof."

Richard understood what that meant. "The library, if you please, Benny," he said, cutting into the driver's laugh, and hit the button on the door handle to raise the privacy glass between the rear and the front seats.

"So impatient," Samantha observed, digging into the mini fridge for a water. "And the library? Are we going to the Bryant Park Grill?"

Frowning, he pulled out a water of his own. "You've been there?"

"No. I've wanted to go, though."

"Good. Now who's Bradley Martin?"

She blew out her breath and drank a couple of deliberate swallows of water. "One of Martin Jellicoe's aliases. Apparently, he hit one of Anne's collections a couple of years ago and rubbed her face in it. Then he sent her a note a couple of days ago congratulating her on getting the Adgerton gig and saying he might stop by to see it."

That didn't make sense. The Martin Jellicoe he knew, and the one about whom Samantha had chatted on numerous occasions, was the epitome of a cat burglar. In and out without leaving a trail of clues—unless it suited him to do so. "He rubbed her face in it? That's not very stealthy."

"Yeah. No, it isn't. In the old days Martin used to case joints sometimes by getting to know one of the marks. Somebody with access. Back when his charm and looks matched his ego. From what I can figure out without asking her something really embarrassing, he charmed her into bed, and then he robbed her collection. She called me because that note made her worry that he's back for a rematch."

"Does she know about your connection to Martin?"

"Nope. I mean, she's gotta know that I'm Martin Jellicoe's kid, but I think if she knew that Bradley Martin and Martin Jellicoe were the same guy, she'd be kicking my ass to the curb."

Richard sat back, turning his gaze out the window as the city darkened around them. The last time Martin Jellicoe decided to reunite with his daughter, Samantha had been arrested, and she'd ended up tangled into a robbery, avoiding jail, and trying to keep the Metropolitan Museum of Art from losing a good portion of its collection.

"So, what's going on in that big brain of yours?" she asked, sipping at her water.

"Two things. First, can you do this job without anyone else figuring out your connection to Bradley Martin? Because if he does hit the collection, I have a good idea that he'll make sure the blame falls on you, and that's whether he's successful or not. Second, do you *want* to go up against him?"

She coiled one leg beneath her bottom. "That's the problem. I *do* want to go up against him. I've been telling myself that he's as close to the best as there is, and if I can keep him out of the Adgerton collection, then I can be pretty sure *nobody* can get past me. That I'm the best at what I do."

"You and Wolverine," he supplied, knowing that was probably where she'd picked up the phrase.

That earned him a quick smile. "Yeah, Bub. The other part of me keeps thinking that this is personal, and that I just want to prove to myself that I'm better than he is."

"Which you are. No question."

"Stoney would agree with you," she replied, without a hint of ego, "but Martin, not so much. And that's another problem; if he's just trying to rile up Anne and doesn't actually mean to do anything, if he finds out that I've been brought in to do security, will he decide that's a challenge he can't pass up?" Blowing out her breath, she tapped the water bottle against her knee. "It would be better if I just backed off before anybody really knows I'm here."

"Better for you, yes. Better for Anne Hughes...Well, I suppose that would depend on whether Martin actually means to hit the collection or not."

"You're the business guy, Rick. Do you go after something where there's only a small benefit and a giant chance of horribleness? No, you don't. You go and find something else that's more advantageous."

Richard wasn't certain whether she was trying to convince him or herself, though he would have been willing to wager that she was trying to talk herself down before the shadow of Martin Jellicoe became the actual man himself. And he had no problem with keeping as much distance between daughter and father as possible. Martin Jellicoe was *not* good company for Samantha to be keeping.

Her frown deepened. "You're not going to help, are you?"

"I have the same concerns you do. In my opinion, we should head back to Florida now. The last thing I want is Martin trying to turn this into a way to humiliate you because you've given up cat burgling. Or worse, he could decide to inform Miss Hughes or her bosses about any one of your previous jobs where we're still running out the clock on the statute of limitations."

"Yeah." She nodded. "Yeah. You're right. We should go. Just because Martin warned Anne that he was watching doesn't mean that I'm leaving her flat-footed with a tiger prowling around. He might have been joking about planning to hit Sotheby's. He's such a kidder. Ha ha."

"We could give Interpol a call and let them know he's somewhere nearby," Richard suggested. "He's supposed to be cooperating with them, isn't he?"

"I can't do that."

He could, but she didn't want to hear that he meant to go rogue, especially when he'd invited himself along for this trip in the first place. "Then what's it to be?"

Blowing out her breath, she sent him a slow grimace. "I should bow out. Gracefully."

Thank God. "Okay. Dinner first, and then we'll work on a strategy. Find somebody else who can take over for you." Surreptitiously, he freed his phone from a pocket to text Tom and tell him the information he'd requested was no longer necessary.

"I can't think of anybody else who could fend off Martin Jellicoe," she grumbled, shifting to retrieve her own phone as it chimed with a rare generic text tone.

"You've laid a good foundation. And as you said, removing yourself before Martin finds out you're heading up the opposition will lower the chances of anything happening in the first place."

Silence. Richard looked up from his phone to see her staring down at hers. She was good at disguising her feelings, but he'd become adept at reading her despite that. His chest tightened.

"What?" he asked.

"Just a text," she said after another moment. "Possible spam. Sender unknown."

"And?"

"Hm? Oh. It says, 'You don't know everything, Sam. Since you can't keep your nose out of my business, I think it's time for a lesson. You won't forget this one.'"

Fuck. "I could mention we can't be certain that that is Martin," Richard offered, deleting the text he'd been about to send.

"Yeah, you could." She tapped on the phone's keypad. "We'd both know you're wrong."

"What are you saying?"

"'It's your fault I'm here in the first place. Leave the poor woman alone. She already regrets ever meeting you.'"

"You going to send that?"

Samantha glared at the screen, before she started hitting the backspace button. "No."

"That's probably wise."

She tapped out a much shorter set of words, then hit send.

"Samantha?" he asked after a moment.

With a sigh she lifted her phone up for him to see the screen.

She'd cut her reply down to five words, but Richard didn't think they would calm the situation, or cause Martin to reconsider his target. "'Fuck you, Martin. Bring it,'" he read aloud. "Very diplomatic."

"This is my damned job," she retorted. "And since I'm probably the only one who can keep Martin Jellicoe out of a building, then I kind of have to do that when I'm asked to, don't I?"

"No, you don't have to." He put a hand over hers when she narrowed her eyes. "But I like that your first instinct is to help someone."

"For money," she amended. "I'm helping for money, because it's my job. Because I'm legit."

"Because you're legit," he echoed. And because as little as he liked it, she *did* know Martin Jellicoe better than anyone else alive, and she *was* better equipped to hold him off than anyone else in the entire bloody world.

That still didn't make him feel any better about it, but neither could he blame her for stepping up to the challenge— even if he suspected that part of her decision had been made by her sense of competitiveness and her ego. She was an F-5 tornado, and he wouldn't be marrying her, be obsessed with her, if she was anything else.

At the same time, he was glad he'd joined her in New York. Because *he* knew better than anyone else in the world how far she would stick out her neck for someone, and how likely Martin Jellicoe would be to swing the axe if it would save his own skin. Risking Samantha and her freedom—it simply wasn't allowed. And it wasn't going to happen.

○

SAMANTHA LOVED Rick's apartment in New York. Aside from it being gorgeous and narrow and three stories tall, it overlooked

Central Park and felt like it was both at the center of the world and on the edge of it all at the same time.

The hotel had been fine for a night or two, but what she'd learned yesterday had pretty much made it a sure thing that she would be staying in the city until Anne Hughes was no longer responsible for the Adgerton collection. Three weeks, at least.

Sighing, she picked up her teacup and took a sip, lifting her pinkie because she was, after all, nearly married to an English aristocrat. Briefly she wondered if Martin knew that, but just as quickly she brushed the thought aside. Of course he knew. She had more than a hunch that he'd been keeping tabs on her all along, but for sure he'd been doing so since she'd fucked up his robbery of the Metropolitan Museum of Art a couple of weeks ago. Jeez, had it only been two months? So much had happened between then and now—it felt like years. A decade, maybe.

She'd tried to accuse Stoney of ratting her out to Martin, but that had only ticked the fence off, and she'd ended up apologizing. Yeah, Walter and Martin had known each other for longer than she'd known either of them, but Stoney had chosen sides— her side, to be more exact. Heck, he'd been more of a dad to her than Martin ever had. And while he grumbled at her going straight, he helped her out with her new gig, too.

"Are you drinking…tea?" Rick asked, pausing halfway out of the bathroom and into the apartment's ginormous master bedroom suite.

"Diet Coke. Chilled." She took another sip out of the tea cup. "It looks like tea, though. If I ever have to drink tea with the Royals, I'm going with diet Coke."

"You can't fool the Royals. They have powers."

That made her laugh. "Like a Jedi?"

"I'm not at liberty to say." Reaching into a drawer, he pulled out a plain black T-shirt and pulled it on over his head. Over his professional soccer player body and washboard abs that made her sigh.

"You're not exactly dressed for Addisco," she observed, eyeing him all over again.

"I've canceled my appointments for the week," Rick returned, digging into the closet for a pair of athletic shoes.

"Going jogging, then? In jeans?"

"I'm your apprentice," he stated matter-of-factly, as if he thought by simply saying the words, he could make it so. In most situations, and with most people, that would probably have sufficed.

"You're my boyfriend."

"Fiancé."

"Neither one gets you a security card. What are you trying to pull here?"

Rick tilted his head, his deep blue eyes going from the tea cup to her face. He was probably calculating her aim, because she could pretty well bullseye him in the forehead from where she was standing. "Martin Jellicoe threatened you, and you told him to give it a try. I'm sticking to you like glue, Samantha."

For the briefest of moments, she was glad to hear that, glad that somebody she trusted had her back, no matter who had challenged her front. But then the rest of equation didn't feel quite as pleasant. "I don't need you to hold my hand."

"I'm assisting. And being present with my wallet on the chance someone needs to bail you out of jail."

"I'm not going to jail." Crap, just saying the words gave her the shivers.

"He managed to get you thrown in the slam, as you call it, the last time you locked horns with him. And I bailed you out."

"The last time was a fluke. I thought he was dead, for crying out loud. Now I know. And I know what he's after. And honestly, you're a hell of a businessman, but Martin could steal the pants off you without you knowing anything had happened until you felt a breeze."

From the clench of his jaw Rick didn't like that, but then he didn't like the idea that anyone could best him at anything. She couldn't really blame him for feeling that way; in his line of work very few people could even come close to matching him. But where her world was concerned, he was a rank amateur. And guessing wrong, making the wrong move at the wrong time…Well, there were rarely second chances.

"I'm not leaving you without backup," he stated, dropping his shoes in front of a chair. "And I'm not negotiating."

Samantha took a quick breath. "I appreciate that. Really, I do. But Martin's a twisty, tricky guy. I might have to get a little twisty, too, and I don't want you anywhere near something shady."

"No." He shook his head, stepping over the shoes to stalk up to her. "You are not doing anything shady. I won't risk it. I won't risk you. Nothing is worth that."

"I do know what I'm doing, you know." Samantha ran her hands up his arms, locking her hands behind his neck, and went up on her toes to kiss him. At first he didn't yield, stubborn Brit, but after a moment his mouth softened against hers. Inwardly she sighed. Entanglements in her life were still something new, but God, without this one she didn't know what she would do.

"I'm still going with you," he murmured. "I may not know thiefy things, but I do know people."

Releasing him, Samantha stepped back. "I can't tie you up, so you're buying donuts for everybody on the way in."

"Fine."

Moving deliberately, she shifted the wallet she'd palmed into sight, pulled out fifty bucks, and tossed it back to him. Then she shook out her wrist, and his Rolex slid down her jacket sleeve into her other hand. "You do know people," she said, taking in his surprised and supremely annoyed expression. "So I hope you realize that protecting *you* is important to *me*. This is *my* show, and you're a guest."

When he held out his hand, she dumped the watch into it. "Don't do that again."

"Don't think you can do my job any more than I could do yours," she retorted.

Rick opened his mouth, then shut it again. Slowly he pocketed his wallet and then refastened the watch to his wrist. "Point taken. And just so you know, while I don't want Martin removing my pants, I have no objection to you doing so—as long as you don't do it in public."

Whoosh. For a minute there she thought she'd pushed him too far. "I'm good with that," she said, crossing the room to the hallway beyond. Halfway there she flipped his lucky platinum pen back at him.

"Damn it, Samantha. Am I still wearing underwear?"

At least he'd mustered some humor about it. Considering how long it had been since she'd seriously picked somebody's pockets, she was relieved both that he'd understood her motives and that she hadn't botched it. That would've screwed up the point she'd been trying to make.

She and Rick were the first to arrive at the Victorian house, and despite none of the perimeter alarms being tripped she did a sweep of the entire place just to be sure the security system hadn't been bypassed. They hadn't added all the fancy bells and whistles yet, after all. And even without this weird vendetta Martin seemed to have against Anne, the Adgerton collection was just the sort of thing that would pique her father's interest. Valuable stuff all in one place, displayed like a blingy buffet, as he'd used to call it, and left relatively alone in the evenings.

He had hit museums all the time for just those reasons. Maybe that was why she'd never gone after museums herself; it was too easy, in a sense. Plus, the stuff there was for everybody to see, and not gathering dust in some rich guy's vault for tax purposes.

"All clear?" Rick asked, as they descended the main stairs again.

"All clear. I figured it would be, but then again Martin might have decided to take an advance look or leave another stupid note or something."

"I thought one of main rules of cat burglary was not to leave a trace," he said, righting a stray dolly and rolling it against one wall.

"It is."

"So this note business isn't usual, I take it?"

Samantha frowned. "No, it isn't. Even if Martin and Anne had a fling or a bad breakup or something, it would be more like him to leave a note after he'd left, so he would already be in Amsterdam or something by the time she found it."

Rick shrugged. "New York is a very big place. Perhaps he feels like he has enough room to maneuver even if she—and you—knows he's somewhere nearby."

"Or he's just getting arrogant—more arrogant—because he thinks he's pulling one over on Interpol." Yeah, he probably was still cooperating with them *and* framing rivals for some of the jobs he continued to pull.

Her phone chimed, and she pulled it from her pocket. Anne Hughes had arrived, and Samantha watched as the older woman pulled out her badge and swiped it to deactivate the front door lock. What would it be like to have Martin Jellicoe, or Bradley Martin, or whatever name he chose to go by, after something that she'd given her word to protect? And Anne, who seemed like a smart-enough woman, for damn sure couldn't protect the Adgerton collection against one of the top five cat burglars in the world.

"Why is he picking on her?" she murmured, pocketing the phone again as Anne walked into the foyer. "Good morning. I brought my boyfriend. And donuts. Is it all right with you if they both stick around today? I couldn't find a sitter."

Rick nudged her with an elbow as he breezed past her to offer his hand to Anne. "My apologies. I decided to tag along to New York, but it turns out my company doesn't really need me here right now. I can screw in light bulbs like nobody's business."

Ms. Hughes chuckled. "If I get any flak for allowing you a preview of the collection, I will assure my bosses that you mean to be a generous bidder."

"Which I will be," Rick agreed, shaking her hand.

That was her guy, pretty much agreeing to lay out a couple hundred thousand bucks, minimum, with a smile and a handshake. All so he could hang out with her today. Yeah, he was cool. Plus, he looked very savory in jeans and a T-shirt.

Anne manned the door as the Sotheby's team and construction guys arrived, making sure they all swiped their cards and everyone was accounted for. The more comfortable she got with the tech, the better off they'd all be. In the meantime, Samantha wished it wouldn't be considered overkill if she installed a couple of pressure-sensitive plates that released stinging wasps or murder hornets or something under the smaller items.

"What are you smiling at?" Rick grunted, as he carried a pedestal into a window alcove.

"Remember when Indiana Jones takes the fertility idol and the giant boulder nearly rolls over him?"

"Yes."

"I could rig something like that in here."

"Death and dismemberment is a bit harsh, isn't it?"

"I want something that leaves a mark. Not just an alarm going off remotely and the cops showing up too late to catch anybody."

Rick looked at her for a moment. "I thought the idea was to keep him out, not to let him in and drop an anvil on his head."

"It worked for Bugs Bunny," she retorted, moving aside to

direct another one of the display cabinets. Enough distance between the furniture so the rooms didn't look overcrowded, and not enough to create blind spots for the cameras and motion sensors. It was a delicate balance between just enough and too much, and it made her think maybe she should take some interior decorating classes.

Yeah, she wanted Martin to feel it if he made it inside the Victorian House. At the same time, a visitor accidentally setting off a silent alarm shouldn't have to worry about getting electrocuted or eaten by crocodiles. Pesky visitors. This would be much easier if nobody at all was allowed inside.

"Have you considered," Rick murmured, pausing to grab a donut as he returned to her side, "that Martin might find a legitimate reason to be invited to one of the showings or to the auction?"

"If he shows his face around here, I'm calling the feds myself. I warned him to stay away."

He handed her half the donut—chocolate with sprinkles, of course. "Actually, I think you challenged him to get past you, but I'm not going to quibble if you decide to see him arrested."

"Hey, British guy," one of the installers called. "Pull this cable through here, will you?"

"Ah, work calls," Rick drawled, popping the rest of the donut into his mouth and heading into the hallway.

"I hope Mr. Addison knows he doesn't actually have to help," Anne said, notebook and iPad stacked in her arms again. "Just his presence helps ensure even more interest in the collection than we'd been hoping for."

"Don't tell him that; he likes being handy." Samantha smiled. "He doesn't get a chance to do it very often."

"I will inform the staff not to refer to him as 'British guy,' then." She sent Samantha a sly grin. "Between you and me, Sam, he does pretty up the room."

"Oh, yeah. He's the stand-in until the actual bling arrives."

"I read that you met when someone tried to burgle his home in Florida and he brought you in to consult."

That was the public story, all right. Nothing about bombs and dead security guards or the fact that she'd been the one actually breaking into Solano Dorado to rob Rick. Yep, their meet-cute wasn't for public consumption. "He did," she said aloud.

"And now you're engaged," Anne prompted.

"Yep. Wedding sometime this spring." Unless she chickened out and pushed it back.

"Ah."

Samantha frowned. "'Ah,' what?"

Anne lowered her gaze to her open notebook. "Nothing. Just that unless you're secretly a duchess, the two of you come from very different places. Other people may call it a fairy tale, but they forget that fairy tales frequently involve ogres, patricide, and decapitations."

Samantha snorted. "Oh, you have no idea."

"You'd be surprised." With another smile, Anne hefted the notebook. "You asked me to arrange the collection into twelve sections," she said. "I actually divided it into eleven and took a sample from each of the eleven to make up the twelfth. I thought the items in the foyer should be an appetizer for what lies ahead."

That was a good idea. "That works," Samantha said, tilting her head to view the first page of the list. "If it's okay with you, I'd like to have the smaller items like jewelry and coins upstairs and toward the center of the house and in the center of the rooms."

"Because they're the most portable, I would assume?"

"Exactly. The more video and human eyes on them, the better. And you're still good with having two security guards on each floor during visiting hours?"

"Definitely." Anne's mouth twitched. "I'm glad you're taking this Bradley Martin business seriously. I worried you might think I was overreacting."

Samantha shook her head, her brain spinning ways to continue this particular conversation without giving her own connection to Martin away, and without straight-up lying. "I haven't heard that name in a while, but I do know about his reputation. And I definitely take it seriously."

"How do you know about him?" Anne pursued. "In my admittedly limited experience, the idea is for no one to know the identity of a cat burglar. That's how they can keep...burgling."

For a second Samantha felt like a mammoth walking around the edge of a tar pit with the bank getting crumbly. "I built my business around the idea of protecting really valuable things for people," she said slowly. "I've done a lot of studying, learning who the best jewel thieves and cat burglars were and are. Everybody has a tell—a way they prefer to do a robbery—and if I can stop somebody at step one, I've got a good chance of either keeping them out, or making them decide to go somewhere else."

"What's Bradley Martin's tell?"

"He likes to go in through an upstairs window," Samantha answered promptly, "and he has no problem with breaking things and setting off alarms if he sees an easy way in and out."

"Then what is your step one to keep him away?" Anne asked, glancing around them at the tangles of cables running across the edges of the floor.

"Wiring the windows with pressure sensors, to start with. The second someone pushes on a plate of glass, the alarm goes off. If it gets too windy, the alarm goes off. A pigeon lands on the sill, the alarm goes off. Second, we put the most portable valuables in the interior of the house, we make the displays physically hard to bust up, and we put different-level sensors across all the walkways at odd intervals."

Taking in a breath, Anne nodded. "I like it. What if he just...I don't know, cuts the power or something?"

That was why Samantha had favored a giant boulder crashing down from the ceiling to crush any invaders. She forced a smile. "Sotheby's already has this place wired for power from a couple of different sources. Bradley Martin would have to knock out the power for about five blocks around to shut us down, and that would still leave all the sensors that have battery backup—which is going to be most of them."

"Okay. I'm feeling slightly more confident. Still, I don't suppose we could have iron bars that could shoot down from the ceiling if anybody sets off a sensor? Something to slam over the windows and doors?"

"That would be awesome," Sam returned, "but we'd have to do a total renovation of the house, which would take way more time and money than we have."

"I'm still going to talk to the director of operations after this event. Maybe we can get the house upgraded before the next show."

The idea of building an anti-thief trap literally from the ground up nearly made Samantha start drooling. And it would be here in New York, where Rick had suggested they relocate, anyway. It could be her in charge of the design, if she played her cards right. Everything she knew, everything she'd learned, she could put into thief-proofing this place. And after, if anybody wanted a look at her resume, she could point them right at the Victorian house in the middle of Manhattan.

Of course, that would also make it a beacon for anybody wanting to make their reputation. And if anybody beat it, that would be a direct reflection on her. Crap. Everything in good-guy land was such a two-edged sword. "Let's see how this version works first," she said aloud.

"That's true. If nothing happens, then I suppose we can just call it 'good enough.' And I have been consoling myself with the idea that Bradley Martin isn't as young as he used to be, and I doubt he's as good at robbery as he once was."

"Hey, Sam!" Jamie, the display assembly guy with the very cool *Star Wars* collection, at least according to the other guys, called. "You wanted to see the sun coming in the south windows, right? It's doing that."

"Be right there." She glanced over at Anne. "Excuse me. I wanted to see if the sunlight's going to reflect off the glass in the display cases. That can set off sensors, plus, you know, blind visitors."

Yep, that was her—looking out for criminals and protecting people's eyesight. And worrying a lot about where Martin Jellicoe might be right about now.

6

Wednesday, 4:39 p.m.

R ichard wiped his hand off on his chest and pulled the phone from his back pocket. According to the last three texts, Tom had some information for him about Anne Hughes, the Getty wanted him to attend a wine tasting among the masterpieces for a mere twenty-five hundred dollars per couple, and Jeniah had made the dinner reservations he'd requested at The Tyger for this evening.

Since meeting Samantha he'd spent less time at Pan Asian restaurants, though he wasn't certain if she genuinely disliked seafood or if she'd been trying to avoid coming face-to-face with a particular restaurant owner in West Palm Beach that she'd robbed. Well, they weren't in Florida, so this seemed a safe-enough test—and a challenge, and he did enjoy challenging her.

Her voice came dimly through the maze of rooms, the conversation something about sunlight and sensors and display case angles. She took pride in doing her job to the utmost, so considering the effect of sun on sensors made sense, but they both knew it wasn't the sun that would be attempting a break-in here. And he *knew*, whether she admitted to being certain about it or not, that Martin Jellicoe would at some point in the next two-and-a-half weeks make an attempt to get into this quaint old building.

Since no one was around to see, Richard took a grateful seat on the edge of a step stool and bent over to stretch his back. He was still very early into his thirties, damn it all, but running and sex and trying to keep up with Samantha did not use the same muscles as lifting heavy cabinets while attempting to avoid making unmanly sounds or scratching the newly replaced wooden flooring.

"You're very kind to spend your day doing this," Anne Hughes noted, and he shot to his feet again.

"Not really," he countered. "She doesn't need my assistance. It's more my worry that something terribly interesting will unfold while I'm sitting behind a desk drinking tea."

He could hear himself becoming more British as he spoke, but that was how he did charming. Since he'd invited himself to New York, much less to step into the middle of Samantha's gig, charming seemed the wisest course of action.

"Drinking tea while buying and selling expensive corporations," Ms. Hughes put in. "I am somewhat aware of your portfolio, Mr. Addison. And I will very likely Google you the moment I get home this evening, so our next conversation will be even less trivial."

Richard grinned. "You'll find some exciting bits, I have no doubt. I can't vouch for the truth of any of it, though."

She shrugged. "If it's exciting and doesn't put you in legal jeopardy, I say claim it." Her swift grin touched her eyes, a shade or two more gray than Samantha's springtime green ones.

"You're not the first person to tell me that." Samantha had only suggested that he invent a few adventures himself and see

84

how far the stories spread, but her grasp on truth could be somewhat slippery.

"The two of you make a good pair, if I may say so," Anne commented. "You have similar senses of humor, I've noticed. And she seems very…. grounded—or 'practical' is a better word, I suppose. As do you, actually. I've seen collectors who don't even lift their own hands to make a bid; they have 'people' for that sort of thing, don't you know." Abruptly her face reddened enough to match the sunset. "I'm going to wander off now, just in case you employ people for hand-lifting."

"I don't," he countered as she moved away. Something tickled at the back of his skull, but he kept the frown from his face. What was it? Had he actually met her somewhere before and neither of them could recall it? Whatever she'd just said felt…familiar, but that didn't make any bloody sense.

Shaking himself out of the odd déjà vu sensation, he reached for the pair of work gloves he'd set aside and returned to angling a tall, square display pedestal over the floor. Another hour of this, and he was going to have to cancel dinner in favor of a hot bath and some ibuprofen.

"Hey," Samantha drawled from the doorway, "the union guys say we have to knock off at five. You can come lift heavy stuff at the apartment while I ogle your backside, if you want."

Oh, thank God. "Are you sure?" he asked anyway. "When do the valuables start to come in?"

"Friday, if you can believe it. But we'll get the installation wrapped up tomorrow. Then I have to decide if I'm going to live in the utility closet here for the next two-and-a-half weeks until the auction."

"There isn't enough room for two in the utility closet, so that doesn't work for me."

She glanced over her shoulder and moved closer. "Sure, you joke now," she whispered, putting a hand on his arm, "but this whole thing is already giving me the wiggins. I mean, I'm already thinking that Anne and Martin had a thing. If she ever finds out I'm his kid, she will not be recommending me for other Sotheby's gigs. Or for anything else."

"She has to know you're Martin Jellicoe's daughter, so what's—"

"The buzz is that Martin Jellicoe died in prison. A dead guy can't pull a burglary. As far as I know, only a couple of guys like Stoney and me are aware that one of Martin's old aliases was Bradley Martin. And since he hasn't used that one in like, forever, it makes me think that whatever he did to Anne was back in the pre-me days, and that it was pretty nasty. The kind of thing that doesn't get Bradley Martin's offspring invited to the company picnic."

Richard twisted to catch her mouth in a swift kiss. "Anything in the pre-you days is definitely not something you should feel guilty about. I'm more concerned about coming up with a legitimate reason for me to be here again tomorrow."

"You don't need to be."

"I know that. But maybe I like being your lackey."

That made her grin, as he'd known it would. "I'd hire you as an apprentice, but I'm pretty sure you'd have to take a pay cut."

Worth it, he wanted to say, but that wouldn't make any sense. Part of the reason they worked as a couple was that they were two strong-willed, independent people. If he made a habit of tagging along with her on jobs, well, it wouldn't go well. For either of them. "I'll settle for lurking in my comfortable office close by, just in case you need my chivalrous participation."

"I'll take that," she returned. "Any day of the week."

That was the difference the two of them meeting had made; they were perfectly self-sufficient, independent people, but he, at least, had been learning that he liked the world better with her in it, and that a bit of compromise here or there was a very small price to pay.

"Good," he said aloud. "Now, I made us reservations tonight at The Tyger. You up for it?"

She sighed. "As long as you don't expect me to eat anything that could potentially turn around and eat, drown, or murder me if I swam up to it in the ocean. Karma's a real thing, you know."

"Or you could just stay out of the ocean."

"Still not risking it. Karma's tricky, and I have enough stuff at risk right now."

He couldn't argue with that. Especially with her father on the loose somewhere in Manhattan. "Something slow, small, and non human-eating it is, then."

"Cool. I'll be another twenty minutes or so, and then I really need a shower."

"We can save time and take one together," he suggested, snagging her around the waist.

Samantha grinned up at him. "That does not save time, but what the hell."

Richard kissed her, making certain to release her before she could ask him to do so. He had learned a couple of things over the past year, after all. "I'll be in here, wrestling with this pedestal."

The second she left the room he pulled out his phone and texted Tom, asking for whatever the attorney had found concerning Anne Hughes. He hadn't earned his reputation for being a cutthroat businessman by ignoring things that caught his notice, even if he couldn't put his finger on what, exactly, was bothering him.

His phone rang before he could even pocket it again. "I meant you could email the information to me," he said, keeping his voice low.

"She's one of Jellicoe's pals, isn't she? You know, one of those people of questionable reputation and ethics?" Tom returned.

Richard frowned at the phone. "What makes you say that? And hold on a moment. I'm going outside."

"Yeah, you do that, because this kind of shit makes me nervous as hell. Before you met Jellicoe, you didn't run across outright crooks more than once a year or so."

"She's...Wait a minute, dammit." Lowering the phone, he bypassed the freight elevator for the stairs, descending to the main floor and then outside, just remembering to swipe the temporary badge Samantha had given him. The boyfriend didn't get to ignore protocol, not in her book. Then, keeping in mind the cameras outside the old Victorian building, he crossed the street and jogged half a block to the east before he lifted the phone again. "Okay."

"What do you want?" Tom said, his voice still clenched. Samantha referred to him as "the boy scout," and she wasn't wrong about that. Tom Donner had an honorable streak a mile wide, which was one of the reasons they'd become friends in the first place. There were enough people around Richard willing to cut corners and use the weight of wealth and influence to bend the rules. Neither he nor Tom liked doing business that way. And even if he did want to flex some rules at times, Tom made that difficult for him—which was both good and necessary.

"What do you mean, 'what do I want'? What makes you assume Anne Hughes is a criminal?"

"Oh, maybe because she's been working for Sotheby's for fifteen years but doesn't exist before that."

Rick shifted to avoid a pair of joggers heading west toward Central Park. "Sotheby's wouldn't have hired her without a background check." Aside from that, Anne Hughes looked... normal, a woman in her mid-fifties who worked in a respectable position for a well-respected company.

"I'm not Sotheby's, so I don't know what they would or wouldn't do."

"Find more, then."

He could hear Tom's hesitation. "Who is she?"

"I don't know, apparently. Samantha's installing security for a high-profile Sotheby's exhibit and auction. Anne hired her. I was…mildly curious, but now—I need more information, Tom."

"The calling-in-favors kind of information, or the owing people favors kind of information? Because over the past year or so you've called in most of the favors you're owed."

Richard looked up the street toward the Victorian house. Was satisfying his curiosity worth owing someone a favor? Especially with a reformed cat burglar, still wanted by Interpol and half a hundred other agencies, sleeping beneath his roof? "Just see what you can get," he said finally. "Hughes could merely be her married name, after all."

"I doubt it's that simple, because Jellicoe's involved, but I'll do what I can. By the way, per your other requests, the building's been around since 1840, burned nearly to the ground in 1885 and was rebuilt, and the property's been owned by Sotheby's since 2007. Auctions in general coming up at Sotheby's are," and he paused as the sound of paper rustling came over the phone, "somebody's personal collection of *Star Trek* stuff, some banker's artwork he seems to be selling to pay legal bills, and some dead rich guy's stuff because his relatives can't decide who gets what and cash is easier to divide."

"That would be Lewis Adgerton's stuff," Richard supplied.

"No kidding. The digital media guy? Didn't he get into a bidding war with you over the Florida cable station you bought so Jellicoe could watch Godzilla movies all the time?"

"That wasn't the only reason I bought it, but yes."

"I can't really complain about that. Michael got an A on the essay he wrote about the transition of Godzilla from atomic demon to Earth protector."

"Well, I'm telling that to Samantha," Richard returned, stifling the urge to point out that he knew Tom was stalling. "Pull a few strings if you need to," he said finally, when the silence stretched his patience to the breaking point. "But don't do anything to get Anne Hughes in trouble with anyone. Like I said, it could be as simple as a misfiled name change or something."

"Okay. But when is it ever that simple?"

Never. "There's always a first time. Call me as soon as you find anything." Tapping off the call, Richard headed back down the street for the Victorian house. An older woman stopped about twenty feet in front of him to whip out her own phone and take a picture of him, but he ignored her and her companions in their matching Statue of Liberty T-shirts. Samantha would likely try to tease that they'd mistaken him for a dark-haired Chris Hemsworth, but he wasn't in the mood.

Whatever it was about Anne Hughes that had put him on alert in the first place, so far his Spidey sense—as Samantha called it—seemed to be working just fine. If it was, though, why hadn't Samantha sensed anything amiss herself? Because if this was him trying to find something wrong with every job she did so he'd have an excuse to hang about, he needed to get over it. Immediately.

"You eat your own damn charred baby octopus," Sam whispered, scowling.

"Octopus aren't man eaters. According to your mantra, you don't eat—"

"I know my own mantra. An octopus could totally pull off my dive mask or turn off my oxygen tank or something. Not risking it." She dug through her own fried rice and tofu, lifting a forkful in his direction. "Tofu isn't real, so it can't kill you."

"Shall I not point out that you eat burgers all the time, and a cow could trample you at any moment?"

"And that's why you'll never find me in a cow pasture. At

least a cow couldn't eat me. I bet a big enough octopus would make a snack of any number of handsome British lords, if given the chance."

He chuckled, and that made her grin in return. It would have been much simpler, she supposed, to admit that she just wasn't a fan of seafood, but there was also a very karmic reason that over the years, even when she'd been mingling with marks at some extravagant party or other, she'd never dined on alligator or shark or snake or on that one occasion, lion. That was all just asking for trouble, and she had enough of that every damned day.

Her phone vibrated, and she turned it face up on the table. Some guy in baggy pants and a trash bag shirt rattled the front door of the Victorian house, then staggered off. She backed up the footage and looked at it again. Odds were it had been some random drunk, but it could also have been Martin. Slowing down the replay, she paused it to peer at the half of the guy's face in view. Okay, too hollow-cheeked and too tall to be Martin Jellicoe, thank Christ.

"Is this how the next three weeks are going to go?" Rick asked, gesturing with his fork at her phone. "You were up at least twice last night viewing footage."

She shrugged. "I could say I'll feel better when all the wires are connected to my specifications, but I'd probably be lying." Grimacing, she stirred her plate again. "Most girls' dads just embarrass them in front of their dates, right?"

"That's my understanding. We'll stay in Manhattan as long as you need to, you know. I can work here as well as anywhere."

"I hit the ultimate bingo on boyfriends, didn't I?" she muttered, grabbing his fingers as he reached for his glass of wine.

His mouth curved. "Well, you did, but don't think I'm doing you a favor. You're working here. I like being around you.

Therefore, my being here is because of my own selfishness. It has nothing to do with being magnanimous."

Samantha grinned back at him. "You're so boss." Yeah, he was partly telling her the truth, she knew, but the other part, the one he denied, was that he *would* relocate to wherever she felt most comfortable because she scared him. Not "boo" scared him, but he worried that without his influence she would slip back into her old habits, start snatching shit just because it was a challenge and she was bored or something.

That idea didn't trouble *her* overmuch, but then she knew how much she valued having Rick Addison in her life. Doing something stupid just for kicks and thereby losing him? She wouldn't let that happen. It wasn't something she could just tell him, though. She'd been stealing shit since she was five, after all. Nope, she needed to prove it by being good and by letting him push harder than she liked, keep a closer eye on her than she liked, because the end result was something she liked—and wanted—very much.

"We have been discussing a permanent relocation here, anyway," he went on, going back to his wine.

"Uh-uh. This is not an ordinary job for me. I've set up systems and let them run all by themselves before, and you know it. Three weeks and other people will own the bits and pieces of Lewis Adgerton, this exhibit will close down, and I'll never think about it again."

"Y—"

"Katie already invited us to Thanksgiving. That's in what, four weeks? If you think I'm screwing that up by forcing the Donners to start packing, you're batshit crazy."

He looked at her for a long moment, Caribbean blue eyes contemplative. "Eventually you're going to run out of holidays to use for excuses and you're going to have to decide, but as I'm not batshit crazy, I concede. Three weeks and back to Florida."

"Good. Now order me something with chocolate for dessert

while I go and collect myself." Pushing away from the table, she leaned around his shoulder to kiss him. He tasted of red wine and seafood, but mixed in with him, that was okay.

Taking a deep breath, Samantha made her way around the crowd of tables to the restroom. Three women were in there gabbing about seeing both Lin-Manuel Miranda and Richard Addison at the restaurant tonight, and she slipped into a stall and shut the door.

For somebody who'd lived most of her life being mobile, ready to leave everything behind at the slightest whiff of trouble, this...need, wish, desire to keep things stable, whatever it was, drove her crazy. It wasn't like Rick would vanish in a puff of smoke if they moved to New York. There *was* the possibility that the Donners wouldn't move with them, not with both Olivia and Michael in school and Katie a member of every local animal rescue and school group ever invented. That would mean separating her from her one female friend, and Rick from the boy scout. He needed the boy scout. Donner's ethics kept him on the straight and narrow, just like Rick did for her.

She'd never really even had a female friend until a couple of months ago, and she liked it. There weren't many women in her former profession, and the ones that did cat burgle tended to pick a mark, seduce him or her, and then rob them blind. That was way too sticky for her and made continuing to mingle with the blingy class way too difficult. But Katie literally baked cookies, and they were good, and Samantha liked that. A lot.

Still, she could make other friends. She and Anne got along pretty well. Anne was twenty or so years older than she was, but they both liked art and antiques. That would make for at least a couple of conversations over a diet Coke and cupcakes.

It wasn't just about finding a new gal pal, though. Solano Dorado had become...home. A place where she could leave in the morning and return every night. A place where she'd redone the pool patio and hung up plants and dug holes for trees and made up pots of flowers. And Stoney lived four miles away, and Aubrey, who'd become part of her odd family almost immediately upon meeting him, lived just three miles away in the opposite direction. Plus, there were the Donners and the staff at Solano Dorado, and even Frank Castillo, the cop who'd almost busted her and had instead become kind of an ally and joined them for grilled burgers sometimes.

Samantha blew out her breath, reached down to flush the toilet, and left the stall. As she washed her hands, the chatty trio started speculating about Rick's sexual taste and how "nasty" he liked to get. Drying her hands, she turned around and smiled. "Oh, you have no idea," she drawled. "I've given up wearing underwear, he's torn up so many pairs."

"The...Oh. You're her."

Still smiling, she gave them a nod before she sauntered out of the restroom and back to the table. "I think I started another rumor about your sexual prowess," she said, sitting opposite him. "You're..." She trailed off as she took a good look at him.

His gaze was on his cellphone, and the utter...blankness of his expression, the gray tinge to his face, immediately set her heart pounding. Keeping her mouth shut, she watched as he pocketed the phone, finished off his wine, and then poured himself another glass. This was not good, whatever it was. God, had his uncle or aunt died? They were both in their sixties, and in pretty good health, but something had gone to crap. Something important to him, and that made it important to her.

"Rick?"

"Give me a minute."

That minute involved him downing the replacement glass of wine and him staring at his plate, his head lowered so she couldn't get much of a clue about what might be going through his head. She was good at reading people. Really good. And as well as she knew Rick, she had no idea what had happened.

Finally, he nodded to himself. "We're leaving," he said

quietly. Pulling the wallet from his pocket, he put too many bills on the table and stood.

Leading the way out, Rick put a hand behind his back which she gripped. She kept her expression cool, because the last thing he would want is somebody posting a photo of them with the caption "Annoyed Addison drags sullen fiancée out of restaurant" or something, but right now she wanted to be the one out in front, slaying dragons or anybody else who had him that unsettled.

It would have been simple to pick his pocket and check who he'd called or who'd called him, but that would have been cheating. Instead, she moved up beside him as they reached the sidewalk, keeping pace as he began a brisk walk north on Lafayette. If they were walking back to the apartment, she was going to have to take off her heels, though; it was like six miles.

She glanced over at him. Now that they were more incognito he was frowning, his jaw clenched and his gaze straight forward, not quite focused on the hordes of people around them. *Okay.* She knew that face. It was his "I'm thinking about how to tell Sam something and I'm worried" face, times six. Maybe seven. *Yikes.*

"Whatever it is, you can tell me," she commented, trying to sound soothing and settling for pitching her voice so low he probably couldn't hear her over the sounds of cars and conversation, anyway.

"We don't lie to each other," he muttered.

"No, we don't." Samantha scowled. That narrowed down the possible callers. "Did Donner say I lied to you about something? Because I didn't. He really needs to pull his nose out of your ass."

Rick looked over at her. "What?"

"Donner. Did he tell you I lied about something?"

"No. It's—I'm speculating about something. I don't know if

it's true or not. If it is, you need to know. If I'm wrong, then I should keep my bloody mouth shut."

"Well, since right now you're scaring the shit out of me, I vote that you tell me, regardless."

His hand tightened around hers. "Back at the apartment, then. I'm going to attempt some finesse."

She didn't want finesse. She wanted him to tell her what the hell had him so wound up. Obviously, he thought it would upset her, but it was something he could be wrong about. Had they arrested Martin again? Mentally Samantha shook her head. That wouldn't upset her. Her dad had more than worn out his welcome in her new life. Stoney, then? Had something happened to Stoney?

"Did something happen to Stoney?" she asked aloud.

"Walter? No. No one's hurt."

That was something, anyway. If not for the whole "what the hell is going on" thing, she would have felt a little better. "Are we walking, then? If we are, I'm taking off my shoes."

He stopped. "No. We're not walking." With that he stuck out his arm, dragging her closer to himself and the curb.

Under normal circumstances the manhandling would have pissed her off, but this was different. Whatever he was speculating about had him way off balance, and in a way that was more alarming than whatever he wanted to figure out how to tell her.

A cab pulled up, and Rick handed her in before he slid in beside her. He gave the cabby the address of the apartment and promptly turned to face the window. At the same time, his hand gripping hers didn't show any signs of letting go.

Holding her breath for twenty minutes would have been simpler than shutting her brain off and stopping all speculation by being unconscious, but Samantha settled into the fake leather seat and glared at the screen showing the cab creeping toward Rick's—their—apartment on Fifth Avenue.

When Rick pulled out his phone and started texting with his free hand, she made a point of not trying to look over his shoulder. What he'd said was true; they didn't lie to each other. Once or twice she'd omitted telling him something, but that had only been for his peace of mind, details about the last couple of jobs she'd done and how close Interpol had come to nabbing her a couple of times over the years. He knew the important stuff; that the last of the statutes of limitations on her thefts would expire in five years, nine months, and twelve days.

By the time the cab stopped in front of the white stone, steel, and glass building where Rick owned the penthouse apartment, full dark touched the sky, lightening to a barely discernable purple-gray in the west. They never went home this early when they found themselves in New York. At least this Rick stuff had kept her from obsessively checking the camera feeds at the Victorian house—though she would rather have been worrying over her dad appearing than wondering what had set off Rick.

"Okay," he said, as they stepped into the elevator and he put his card against the reader to unlock the penthouse floor. "I have to make one call, and then we'll chat."

"Don't mind me. I'll just be pacing a canyon into the living room floor."

The brown and black marble floor was, of course, too hard for her to penetrate, but she did manage to ruffle the pile of the gray and brown carpet set beneath the furniture by the time Rick walked out of his office. If he'd resolved what he meant to tell her, it hadn't improved the paleness of his cheeks, and her heart gave an unaccustomed shiver.

"If you don't tell me what's going on, we're going to have to wrestle or something," she told him, trying for a little humor. "My adrenaline is maxing out right now."

"So is mine." Rick crossed the floor to where she stood in front of the window that had the awesome view of the park. In one fluid motion he cupped his hands around her cheeks, leaned down, and kissed her.

She wasn't sure if it was passion or desperation, but damn. That kiss nearly melted her clothes right off. "If you can sex this away, then let's get to it, Rick."

Rick took a half step backward, taking hold of her left hand and pulling her toward the couch. "Let's sit."

"Jesus. Stop the buildup already. If you discovered you and Patty are still married or something, just tell me. I'll go kick her ass until she signs you over to me."

"Sit. And thank you for saying that."

"Fine, and you're welcome." She plunked herself down beside him and tried not to fidget. Stupid Brits and their patience and insistence that things be done just so.

"I asked Tom to look into some things for me once I found out Martin was tangled up in this job of yours."

Dammit. "Ah. You *pried*, you mean."

"Yes, I pried. You have your sources, and I have mine. So Tom delved into Anne Hughes, her boss Michael Sachless, and any recent reports about Martin."

"Great. So now the boy scout's checking up on me, too. I don't like that, Rick. I don't need you to babysit me, for crying out loud." Standing again, she put her hands on her hips. "Dammit."

"Anne Hughes isn't Anne's real name," he broke in.

Samantha snapped her mouth shut. "If you're going to try to convince me that Anne is some kind of criminal mastermind, I'm going to laugh at you."

Rick narrowed one eye. "Technically Hughes is her maiden name. So—"

"So it *is* her real name. Plenty of women don't like to keep an ex's last name, Sherlock. Knock it off. Either tell me what's got you all riled up, or I'm going back to the hotel."

"Her married name was Martin. Anne Martin."

All the wind sucked out of Samantha's lungs. Her legs went wobbly and her face turned cold, which she recognized as the signs that she was going to faint. She plunked herself down hard on the couch and willed herself back into control. It didn't mean anything. Martin Jellicoe had done shitty stuff all through her childhood. Pretending to marry some woman so he could get the keys to a museum or something? That was right up his alley. "It doesn't mean anything," she said aloud.

"Approximately twenty-one years ago, Anne Martin filed a missing child report, claiming her husband had absconded with the contents of a museum display she'd been curating, and with their four-year-old daughter…Sarah."

The words banged into the walls around her, whizzing past her too fast for her to catch and hold onto their meaning. They collided with what she knew—*knew*—of her past, that her mom had kicked her dad out and hadn't objected when he'd brought her along, too. That Mrs. Jellicoe had been a stick-in-the-mud who wanted fine things but turned up her nose at the only way Martin had of going about obtaining them.

Rick put an arm around her shoulders and took her far hand in his free one. He was getting good at that, she noted almost absently in the middle of the swirl of chaos, being comforting without smothering her or making her feel restrained. "I owe several people some large favors over this, Samantha," he said quietly. "Tom triple verified it before he even called me back, and I sent him to check it all again."

"It still doesn't mean anything," she said flatly. "Some lady named Anne Hughes Martin got left behind by her husband and daughter. Her daughter Sarah. I'm Samantha Jellicoe."

"Samantha."

Other things started dribbling into her thoughts—the text Martin Jellicoe had sent her about her learning a lesson she wouldn't forget if she didn't stay out of this; Martin cutting her hair and dying it a weird black until she was six or seven; the long time they'd spent in Europe when he'd turned down a couple of lucrative jobs Stoney set up for him because those had been located in the States.

In truth she remembered pretty much everything from the time he'd cut and colored her hair onward, but before that, just a hazy mush of things half-remembered and things shaped by what he'd told her. But her name? Why the hell wouldn't she remember if her name wasn't even Samantha? That wasn't something a person forgot. Especially her. It just wasn't.

"I don't buy it," she stated, shrugging out of Rick's embrace because even her clothes felt like they were smothering her now. "It's too handy. Too neatly wrapped. Like maybe he picked her for a job because of her past baggage. Because he knew it might rattle me."

"It's possible," he admitted, his tone clearly reluctant to give her any wiggle room. "I called Tom about Anne Hughes because I kept thinking I'd seen her somewhere before, even though she didn't give any indication that she had ever met me."

"Let me guess. She reminded you of me." That was just too easy. It had to be a setup. It had to be.

"I'm still not certain. But other than the twentyish years between you, there are similarities. Samantha, it...it makes a certain amount of sense."

His expression, full of compassion and worry, didn't steady her at all. Just the opposite. He believed it. He believed that Anne Hughes—Martin—whatever it was, was her... *Crap on a biscuit.* Her mind dodged way away from saying the word even to herself. She knew who that woman was. She always had. Mom was a selfish, self-centered bitch who'd been happy to be rid of Martin Jellicoe and whatever baggage came with him. Even if that was her own daughter.

"I remember everything," she pointed out. "Nearly photographically. I would remember her."

"You said your first clear memory was after it was just you

and Martin." Rick reached out a hand again, then clenched his fingers and lowered it. "I will admit, there's a very small chance I could be wrong and that I'm sitting here, upsetting you, for no reason at all. That…irks me."

Forcing her thoughts back to the present, she turned her head to look at him. Billionaire, cutthroat businessman, art collector, very accomplished lover—everything he was said he knew what he was doing, and that when he made a rare mistake, he owned up to it. He didn't make wild proclamations, especially when there was a chance they could hurt her. Above everything else, he made a point of trying to protect her.

If he hadn't made a mistake, though, that meant…stuff. Big stuff. And that made her fight or flight reflex want to kick in. Samantha stood up, abruptly unsettled in her own skin. "I need to go somewhere."

"Okay. I'll get our coats."

He hesitated there for a second, probably waiting for her to tell him that she wanted to go somewhere alone. Part of her did, but he would worry, and she wasn't just a solo act any longer. When all she did was kick off her heels and drag her Nike's from beneath the edge of the couch, he vanished into the adjoining room.

In the old days if something threw her off her game she would go for a run, or climb up the outside of some old derelict warehouse just to test her skills. The good thing about derelict warehouses was that they tended not to have security installed, so she could just climb and not worry about cops or silent alarms. Sometimes they had junkyard dogs, but they were good practice, too.

Samantha blew out her breath. Her thoughts were going everywhere, making stupid, meandering trails that went nowhere just so she could avoid following the main road. The road that said her mom had filed a missing person's report about her, and that Anne Hughes was just a regular, non-hateful human who had put her life back together just fine and did interesting stuff with art and antiques.

Rick appeared with a snazzy black trench coat for himself and a black hoodie for her, because hoodies were cool. Tying up her laces, she pulled the hoodie over her head and left the apartment. In the elevator she faced front, bounced on her toes, and crossed her fingers that nobody else would get in and hold them up with idle chitchat.

She let Rick greet the doorman, Vince, and once they made it outside to the sidewalk she jaywalked over to the Central Park side of the street, hopped the low retaining wall, and then headed into the green, dark depths.

"Stay on the pathways, at least," Rick said, catching up to her.

"That's where the muggers wait for people," she stated, continuing through the trees but staying close enough to the walkways to be able to use their lights for navigation.

"Well, I've seen this movie, and some naked guy comes running out at us with a machete in about two minutes."

"If he's naked, a machete isn't the best choice for a weapon." Yeah, she was upset, but she still couldn't let a comment like that pass.

"Samantha, if you're trying to brush me off, just tell me."

Immediately she slowed down, reaching out for the hand that grasped hers without hesitation. "I'm not trying to brush you off. I'm distracting myself, I think."

"Distract yourself at home. You need to think all this through before you see her tomorrow."

Ice spun down her arms to her fingers. "Nope. Not doing that. I'll text her tonight that I can't take the job, after all." She pulled out her phone with her free hand.

Rick took it from her. "You've already started the job. She'll never find anyone else who's a match for Martin, and you know it. That's why you took this gig in the first place."

She shot him a glare. "Don't hit me with my own slang. And

don't tell me what to do." Veering to the right, she spotted the outline of a rock outcropping and headed for it. Accelerating into a trot, she jumped for a foothold and then hitched herself up to the top, twisting to take a seat on the flat boulder.

With a muttered, "Jesus," Rick hauled himself up the craggy rock, making it halfway up before he stretched up a hand. "Give me a boost, will you?"

Bending her knees and bracing her feet, she reached forward, gripped his hand, and pulled. He outweighed her by a good seventy-five pounds at least, but he was no slouch. With a little less grace than she figured she'd shown, he heaved himself up beside her.

"I feel like a seal beaching itself," he grunted, turning to sit beside her.

"You looked much studdlier than that. A sea lion, at least."

"The hell you say."

Samantha hugged her knees. "I don't like this. I mean, I know Martin's lied to me about shit. That's one of the reasons we went our separate ways. But I should remember her. I should remember all about it."

"Not if your memory oddities happened as a result of losing your mother."

"That's stupid."

"Why? You suffered something traumatic, and your life changed overnight—or so I would imagine. Your father started trotting you all over the world and calling you by a different name. You lost all your anchors at once. Remembering things probably felt like the only way to keep hold of yourself."

"You're talking about a four- or five-year-old, you know. I thought it was an adventure."

He put an arm around her shoulders, lightly, until she leaned into his chest. Then his grip tightened. "I obviously don't know *why* things happened. And neither do you. You can spend all night twisting yourself up about things you'll probably never have an answer for, or you can figure out if you want to say anything to Anne Hughes tomorrow."

"I'm not saying anything to her. If I do, she'll know I'm Martin's daughter, and she'll think I took this gig as a double cross or something." She shuddered. "And if I give her that kind of information about me and she decides to call the cops, this is not going to end well."

"That's entirely up to you, Samantha. Tell her, or don't. But don't make up some big disaster to give yourself an excuse to keep quiet."

"What would you do, then?" she burst out. "Let's say you suddenly discover you have a brother, and that the last business you bought and tore apart just happened to be his life's work. What do you say? Or do you keep your mouth shut and maybe send him a box of cheese and crackers in a couple of months as an 'I'm sorry I ruined your life' present?"

"Sam—"

"I know, I know. Shut up for a minute." She took a breath. "Please."

"Okay. I will be silently supportive."

7

Wednesday, 10:43 p.m.

A box of cats would have been easier to manage than Samantha Jellicoe—Sarah Martin—Richard reflected. His arse was asleep, the arm he had wrapped around Samantha was halfway there, and from the dropping temperature they would have snow in Central Park at any moment. Before bloody Thanksgiving.

The weather and his blood supply, though, were the simple bits. He couldn't even imagine what was going on in Samantha's agile mind right now, just as he couldn't imagine what he would do if suddenly confronted with a parent he'd thought both long gone and uninterested. Martin Jellicoe had spun some tales in his life, but the one he'd told his daughter about his wife and the circumstances under which he had left home had to be the cruelest.

The lie had certainly made things easier on Martin, or so Richard assumed. Make up a villain, a reason to flee, and there would be no reason to look back. Not for Samantha, anyway.

And if as a side effect, her memory had become more precise, well, a thief could make good use of that, too.

He'd used her to grift, taught her to pick pockets before she could ride a bike, showed her how to follow in his footsteps without ever giving her a choice in the matter. And then, when he'd realized that she'd not only surpassed him in skill, but that she was a better human than he was, Martin had left her behind, too.

The thing that had tickled his brain about Anne Hughes, the thing that he couldn't put a finger on, had been that he *did* know her. Or at least he knew who some of her physical traits, her undercutting humor, reminded him of. The moment Tom had said it, everything had snapped into place.

Generally, when he figured something tricky out, he felt at least momentary triumph, or satisfaction. Not this time. His first thought had been that he needed to tell Samantha, and his second thought had been that he had no idea how he would go about doing so.

If he'd needed a measurement of how much his life had changed over the past year, the fact that how to give someone information bothered him more than sitting in the middle of Central Park on a moonless night made for a pretty large yardstick.

He could keep talking to Samantha, point out things she'd probably already realized, but she didn't need him for that. Other than Martin and Walter Barstone, she'd spent most of her life on her own. She dealt with—or she had dealt with—most of the traumas in her life alone. Well, she wasn't alone any longer, even if the most effective thing he could provide was his presence and a hug.

"How the fuck do I tell her something like this?" Samantha muttered, her breath fogging in the cold, damp air. "Oh, hi, Anne. I brought you some coffee, and by the way, Bradley

Martin is my dad, which makes me your daughter. I'm a crook, too. Creamer?"

God, he loved her sense of humor, the way she used it with equal effectiveness as a weapon, as a coping mechanism, and to offer support to her small, odd circle of friends and family. "You could lead her to the answer, so she figures it out herself."

Her shoulders shrugged. "Tell her my dad is Martin Jellicoe, and that he sometimes goes by other names, that he always told me my mom didn't want us, and we left home when I was four? That could work, but man, if there was a way to soften the blow…especially if she turns out to be the innocent party in all this, I'd kind of prefer that."

"*You're* the innocent party in all this," he pointed out. "Stop putting Martin's actions on your own shoulders."

"I was his partner."

"You're his daughter, you were four years old, and he didn't give you a choice."

"That's debat—"

"Hey, you dudes up on the rock," a voice called from the darkness around them. "You having a party up there?"

"Yeah. Are we invited?" another voice added.

Shit. Just what they needed. He opened his mouth as Samantha's spine stiffened beneath his hand.

"'Dudes'?" she repeated, scoffing. "That's kind of dated, isn't it? What about 'dawgs' or 'peeps,' or 'youse guys'?"

"Hey, the bitch is a comedian. Get the fuck down here."

"Come the fuck up here, so I can kick you in the face," she retorted, the touch of a Bronx accent in her speech now.

"How about I shoot you in the face?" came from below.

"'How about I shoot you in the face?'" she mimicked. "How stupid are you? We're not here for you tonight, but if you make me climb down from this rock, I will kick your ass and break your arm before I cuff you. Or you can go away, try to avoid the asshole I *am* after before he shanks you in the spine like he did the three guys in the ICU at Mercy, and try your luck somewhere else. Your choice."

"Shit," came the muttering from the shrubbery around them. "She ain't a damn cop."

Richard took a breath. "She *is* a bloody cop. *I'm* Interpol. And you don't want the shit I can send your way, either. Trust me."

"Man, they're lying," a third voice announced.

"It ain't worth finding out. Come on."

A bit of rustling and cursing faded into the distance, replaced by the steady background murmur of car horns and engines and, somewhere faintly in the distance, a mariachi band. Richard let out his breath. "Do you at least have a weapon on you?" he breathed, leaning over to kiss Samantha's auburn hair.

"I'm holding a pretty sharp rock in one hand," she murmured back, the faux Bronx accent gone from her voice again. It wasn't just foreign languages she spoke; she was hell with regional accents, as well. "You?"

"I have my Glock in my pocket. I do try not to use it, though. Christ, Samantha."

"Oh, come on. They wanted some cash, with no fuss. I gave them fuss."

"You impersonated a police officer."

"Nope. I never said 'cop.' You did. So it's your ass that would be busted, Mister Interpol."

Personally, he thought he'd added a certain gravitas and believability to her statements, but saying anything would probably only encourage her. "I was being your backup."

She straightened her legs, pointing her toes. "You did a good job. Two people telling the same lie makes it fifty times more believable." For a second, she leaned her head against his shoulder. "I'm getting cold. Let's go home."

"Yes." Standing, he offered her a hand and helped her to her feet. He'd be lucky if he didn't break his neck climbing down from the boulders, but he had no intention of admitting that. Instead, he watched her descend, then put his feet precisely where hers had been and held on with his fingertips until his shoes touched dirt again.

"I think it's going to snow tonight," Samantha observed, breathing into her cupped hands.

He tilted his head, taking her hands in his to warm them. "That's your takeaway from this evening? You just stopped three men from robbing us, you know."

Her gaze met his. "Do I lose points if I admit I was kinda hoping they'd come after us so I could punch some people? I'm glad you didn't have to shoot anybody, though."

Yes, they'd definitely grown up in different worlds. And yet there they were, together. "I love you, Samantha."

"I love you, too. My name's apparently Sarah, though." She made a face. "This is so freakin' fucked up. I need to call Stoney."

"Do you think he knows something?" Shifting, he kept one of her hands in his and started them toward the nearest line of lights.

"I'll kill him if he does and never told me. I'd bet he had a couple of puzzle pieces but no way to put them all together, but I'm going to make him tell me that. If he passes that test, I want his take on this."

Little as Richard cared for the degree of influence Walter Barstone had on Samantha's life, he did at least make for a more concerned and caring father than Martin Jellicoe or Bradley Martin or whatever the man called himself these days did.

"I can speak to Anne on your behalf, if you prefer," he offered.

"You'd probably be more delicate about it than I would be," she returned, leaning into his arm as they walked, "but no. It's my gig. I'll do it. You're going into the office tomorrow."

"That was the plan, yes. But things have changed. You don't have to—"

"I know I don't have to," Samantha interrupted, heading them more to the left. Perhaps she was using the stars to guide them, because he couldn't see any landmarks there in the dark. "It's my mess; I'll sort it out."

He left it at that, however little he agreed with her statement. All the blame for this plus some additional bullshit went to Martin Jellicoe, as far as he was concerned. How like Samantha's wayward father, to let her fall into a mess, perhaps even pull some strings to get her tangled into it in the first place, and then leave her to sort it out and face the consequences while he ran off to make snide remarks from the shadows.

For all they knew, Martin might have done some nudging to set up the meeting between Samantha and Anne to begin with. If this was his idea of being a good guy, though, Richard didn't look forward to seeing him being a bad one. A worse one than he'd already proven to be.

They reached the street just half a block south from where they'd jumped into the park, so he could mentally add "wilderness guide" to Samantha's list of accomplishments. If she'd decided to lose him in the park, he would probably still be in there, tangled in the bushes at the bottom of some ravine. But she hadn't tried to lose him. She'd wanted him there. And that in itself took some of the chill off the night.

"Do I have leaves in my hair?" she asked, as they approached the apartment and Vince pulled open the front door for them.

"No. You look as gorgeous as you always do."

She squeezed his fingers. "If I wasn't dreading tomorrow so much, I'd say you were going to get lucky tonight."

"I am lucky. I'm with you."

"Damn." Stopping just inside the lobby, she slid her arms around his shoulders, lifted up on her toes, and kissed him on the mouth.

"Though if you do want to get lucky, I'm available," he murmured against her mouth as she released him.

With a half grin she led the way to the elevator. "Vince was all googly-eyed. He probably wishes he had his phone out."

"Is there lots of money in selling photos of us kissing, then?" Richard asked, leaning back against the side wall of the elevator.

"Probably. I'm going to hit the treadmill after I call Stoney. I'm still squirming inside my skin. And yes, sex would burn off some adrenaline, but I need to think, too. I'm still not sure how I feel about all this, much less how I'm going to approach Anne. *If* I approach Anne about it."

He wanted to be close by, somewhere he could be certain she wasn't just pretending to be dealing with all this. Somewhere he could make sure she was well, physically and mentally. As he'd been learning, however, strong, independent women required space. Nodding, he tapped the pad for the penthouse. "I'll be about, probably not sleeping, either."

She walked in with him, heading straight for the great room and the wall of windows that overlooked Central Park. "I knew —know—Martin's a liar. Why would I just…accept that he told me the truth about my mother?" she muttered.

"Because you were four years old and he was not only a trusted adult, he was your only means of safety and support," Rick retorted, his tone sharper as he considered. She was formidable now; as a youngster, she'd needed people about her that she could trust. Martin Jellicoe had most certainly not been that person.

Shaking out her hands, Samantha leaned her forehead against the glass. "This could still be a mistake. Martin could be trying to wrap me up in something to distract me while he lifts the shiny stuff."

"Triple-checked. Tom Donner."

"Yeah, yeah. Okay. Is it too late for us to run away and join the circus? I could work the trapeze, and you could be the ringmaster."

"Thank you for including me. Call Walter, love. I'll be in the kitchen."

It was gratifying that she wanted him included in running away to the circus, but since he'd met her and her odd circle of friends, he frequently felt like a ringmaster already. Every bit of him that controlled companies, set agendas for hundreds of employees, wanted to hear the conversation between her and Walter. If the fence had had even an inkling that Samantha had been stolen from her mother, things were going to get brutal.

And yet, this was still all her play. He would be included as far as she would allow, and as far as he could shove himself into the proceedings. With that firmly in mind, he headed into the kitchen and made himself a strong, hot coffee. Regardless of how that conversation went, this was going to be a long evening.

SAMANTHA CALLED STONEY ON FACETIME. It was against their general policy of avoiding exposure, but she wanted to see his face, his expression, when she told him the news. He and Martin had worked together for years before she'd come along. That didn't mean he knew Martin had stolen her; her dad had fed her the "your mom kicked us out" story for as far back as she could remember, after all. But Stoney wasn't a kid, and he might have figured out some things that had flown right over her head.

"What the fuck, Sam?" he said, holding the phone so it showed just the edge of one ear and the corner of his kitchen ceiling. "Call me back off video."

"Nope. This is a face-to-face conversation," she replied, glaring at his ear. "Your face. Put it on my phone."

With an audible growl he shifted the phone so she could see both of his dark brown eyes glaring back at her. "I liked these fucking things better when they were just phones," he muttered. "What is it, then?"

"Anne Hughes," she said, her tongue tasting the words all over again. Did they sound familiar? Were they something she should have remembered?

"The Sotheby's woman? What about her?" Stoney's frown deepened, lining his forehead all the way up his bald scalp.

"Are you sure you don't know that name from somewhere?"

"Honey, it's after ten o'clock. I'm watching *Law and Order*, and I just took a melatonin because I have a dawn-hour phone call to make in the morning. What do you want?"

She took a breath. "Did Martin ever mention Anne Hughes to you? Ever?" The questioning was tough, both because she wanted him to answer in a particular way, and because she didn't want to lead him to that answer. "Think about it, really carefully."

"Martin? Why him?" he asked. "Is he tangled up in this?"

"Yes. Anne Hughes, Stoney. Focus."

"Fine. Don't tell me shit."

"Okay. Martin challenged me to a duel over the Sotheby's stuff," she snapped. "Anne Hughes."

"The…crap. Okay, okay. Anne Hughes," he repeated, his frown flattening a little as his eyes lost focus. "Anne Hughes. And she definitely has something to do with Martin?"

"Yes. Do you know the name from back in the day?"

"Back in the day Anne Hughes. That at least narrows it down a little." After a long moment he shook his head. "I know a lot of people, Sam. And Martin and I had a lot of conversations over a lot of beers. If you could give me a situation, or a place, or…" His dark face turned ashen, and the phone jumped in his hand, making his image jiggle. "Annie. I remember an Annie he had a thing with. Was— Is—" The room behind him shifted as he sat up straight. "Good God, Sam, is *that* the same Annie?"

Abrupt tears pushed at the back of her eyes. "You knew? *You knew?*"

"No! I mean, I knew your mom was named Annie, and that she got tired of Martin's lying ass and kicked you guys out. That's when you came and stayed with me for a few weeks. The first time I met you." He stared at her hard through the camera, his eyes wary, and abruptly sympathetic. "From the way you're asking questions, Anne Hughes *is* Annie. Jeez, honey. That must have been awkward. You didn't punch her, did you? I mean, Sotheby's is a nice gig for your straight-and-narrow plan."

"No, I didn't punch her."

"Smart. But how did you know—and how did she know it was you?"

"She doesn't. I only know because Martin sent her a stupid note, which is why she wanted to hire extra security, and then Rick had Donner do some digging into her past because Rick's nearly as paranoid as you are."

"Christ."

She kept her attention on him as best she could through the tiny screen, his expression, his body language, and the way all the blood had left his dark face. It looked legit, even if she factored in that she wanted it to be legit. He knew the same story she did, except that he'd had a first name—one he probably hadn't heard uttered in twenty years.

"She filed a missing person's report on me," she said. "And they were married. Did you know that?"

"No." Stoney shifted again. "Of all the…Your dad was a wild man when we were younger. From what he said, they moved in together, but he was ready to go when she booted him—you two—out." He shut his eyes for a second. "He *stole* you? If I'd known that, I would've…I mean, I work with thieves for a living, but that's too damn much, even for me."

"Which is probably why he didn't tell you. He needed you to help watch me while he went around doing cat burglar things and figured out how to get me out of the country. Until I was old enough for the 'take your daughter to work' sessions, anyway." Sam grimaced. "Apparently my name is Sarah."

His head cocked, and he sank back on his blue couch. "Oh, shit. You know, I thought you had a speech impediment at first, because you kept saying 'Samantha' more like 'Samara.' Jeez. Things make a lot more sense, all of a sudden."

"In a crazy, one-way-trip-to-the-Upside-Down kind of way, yeah."

Stoney pulled the phone closer to his face. "Do you want me to fly up there? I volunteer to kick Martin's ass if he shows his face."

"I'm never going to say no to you offering me backup," she said after a moment. "But I can kick his ass myself."

"Okay. I'm going to hang out here for a bit, then. See if I can maybe turn over some rocks and find out exactly what Martin is after."

Nodding, she ended the call and tossed her phone on the couch. On top of this evening's news, Stoney brought up a good point. What *was* Martin after? Not only was he messing with an ex, he was messing with an ex-wife and the mom of his one kid. And he'd stepped it up after said kid stepped into the story. Why?

Bare feet padded up behind her, and a shiny can of diet Coke appeared reflected in the window. "I didn't eavesdrop," Rick said, handing her the soda when she turned around. "I just glanced into the room and saw you toss the phone."

"He didn't know," she said, understanding what he was very carefully not asking. "With some prodding he remembered there was an Annie who dumped Martin and me, but that's it."

"And we're relieved, yes?"

"Yes. We don't have to kick Stoney's ass after we kick Martin's ass." She closed her eyes, leaning her right temple against Rick's chest. God, she was tired, all of a sudden. Like she wanted to sleep for a year. "Evidently I had trouble with my name change, and he thought I had a speech impediment because I kept saying 'Samantha' as 'Samara.'"

"Your father is a wanker."

In his educated, cultured English accent, the insult sounded even worse. An arm slid around her, just below her shoulders. Holding her up, as much as holding her. And that was good, because she was just about done. She wasn't finished yet, though, damn it all. "I still have to figure out how to tell Anne. No, I have to figure out how to tell Anne without her a) firing me, and b) calling the Feds on my ass."

"What say I pop some popcorn and we watch Godzilla fighting other monsters while we figure that out?" Rick suggested.

"I like it. Might even give me a few ideas. Godzilla's good in a fight, after all. Plus, atomic breath."

As much as she wanted to sleep, that was her brain just wanting all of this to go away and her body being exhausted from the multiple adrenaline punches she'd been taking all evening. She needed to think and to just...absorb everything. The movie would be good for that, because she'd seen all of them a bunch of times and could just tune most of it out. And Rick would be there, quiet unless she needed to bounce an idea off him, because he knew when to give her physical space and when to give her thinking space, and this was definitely the second one kind of night.

His phone chimed in its boring generic text tone as he sat down beside her and set the popcorn on the coffee table. "Tom," he said, looking at it. "He wants to know how you took the news. Actually, he's asking if we're both still alive."

She picked up the TV remote and called up the movie. "Tell him we ninja-fought muggers and then I started spinning really fast and burst into flames."

Rick tapped his phone keyboard, then held it so she could

see what he'd typed. "'We're managing; both still alive. Call you tomorrow,'" she read aloud. "That's good, too. Plus you spelled out 'you' instead of using the letter *U*, so he'll know I didn't murder you and answer in your place."

"That would be kind of a lame secret safety code, wouldn't it?"

"It's *so* lame that it would be brilliant. You should think about using it for real."

"Mm-hmm. Start the movie."

Sam kicked off her shoes, hit play, and curled up beside him to eat popcorn, watch a giant lizard fight a giant spider called Kumonga and a giant hedgehog named Anguirus, and figure out how to tell Anne Hughes that her daughter had been found.

STIFLING a yawn after a long night of not sleeping, Richard stood up as the door to the small, neat office he'd been sitting in opened. "On television, all of the police detectives work in one low-ceilinged room and have their desks smashed together so they can trade insults and hamburgers while they solve crimes," he observed, reaching out a hand to the tall, aggravatingly attractive man who had stopped in the doorway to stare at him.

"Well, shit," Detective Sam Gorstein said, shaking hands before he set down a cup of steaming coffee and took the seat on the business side of the spare wooden desk. "For your information, detectives credited with stopping full-blown smash-and-grabs at the Metropolitan Museum of Art get their own offices. Ms. J's not in trouble again, is she? Because I kind of used all my influence to get that window, there." He jabbed a finger at the small window beyond his right shoulder.

Samantha seemed to be in trouble a great deal, Richard reflected, but she was also more than adept at getting herself back out of most of it. This, though, was somewhat different. "I am going to remind you, once, that you wouldn't have this office or that window if Ms. J hadn't decided to give you certain bits of information a couple of months ago."

Gorstein sniffed, sitting back a little. "Oh. This is one of *those* conversations. I'm not breaking the law for anybody. And I'm not looking the other way while anybody else breaks the law."

"I'm not asking you to. In fact, I'm going to give you a few bits of information, and all I'm going to request in return is that you show some subtlety and demonstrate some patience."

Running a hand through his close-cropped dark hair, the detective eyed Richard. "We can do this dance all morning, but my coffee's getting cold and I have about thirty-six pawn shops to visit today to find some other rich guy's stolen antique firearms."

Richard nodded. "Martin Jellicoe is in town."

"Huh. He's still not dead, then? Fuck. He's Interpol's boy, though. They made that pretty damn clear."

"I don't think Interpol has the slightest idea where he is right now. Aside from that, he's planning to rob a Sotheby's exhibit before the items can be auctioned off. Lewis Adgerton's items."

"The tech guy? That's a lot of bling you're talking about. But *why* are you talking about it? He's Ms. J's dad."

Richard didn't particularly like the "Ms. J" moniker, but considering that Gorstein and Samantha were both *Sam*s, he did understand it. "She's the one installing the security systems for the exhibit."

"Wow. The Jellicoes are one fucked-up family." Gorstein blew out his breath. "She doesn't know you're here, does she?"

Almost immediately upon meeting Samantha, Richard had noticed that people with whom she had contact, she almost inevitably charmed. Along with that came a need for them to see her protected, even if generally she was the most self-sufficient human he'd ever met. "I am anonymously reporting that a known high-end cat burglar is in Manhattan, and that a high-end exhibit is about to open."

"I get it, Addison. I've received your anonymous tip." He sighed. "Which I guess means you can't tell Ms. J that I said hi. Just one Sam to another."

Richard stood. "No, I can't." Detective Gorstein had proven to be helpful in the past, but Richard wasn't insane enough to want Samantha to have law-enforcement types as friends. Not for another six years, anyway. Aside from that, Gorstein had more than a passing resemblance to Captain America, and *he* didn't want that around his woman.

Benny met him at the curb, and Richard directed him to a café a block away from Samantha's project. Yes, he was supposed to be at the Addisco offices doing studly work things, but she meant to catch Anne Hughes up on some things this morning. That meant he would be close by, just in case, even if he had to order five hundred dollars' worth of coffee and muffins while he sat and twiddled his thumbs and checked his phone obsessively.

This was the part of their relationship he didn't like. The part where they both didn't just know she was a strong-willed, capable, independent woman, but she forced him to the side-lines while she did the heavy lifting. He hated the sidelines. Until he'd met Samantha, he'd never even met the sidelines. And now he was about to spend several hours there, and possibly return to the office or the apartment without ever having been brought into the game.

As he sat down at a table, coffee, donut, three folders, and a copy of the *Washington Post* in front of him, his phone rang. He wanted it to be Samantha, but it was Tom Donner's name that popped up on the screen. "Tom," he said, keeping his voice beneath the general level of conversation and cutlery around him.

"You said you'd call me," the lawyer responded in his Texas

drawl. "It's like…Okay, it's only 8:15, but still. How'd she take it? Really?"

"Not well. She's spent most of her life relying on a nearly faultless memory. Discovering that the earliest things she remembers are untrue, and on top of that to realize that she had an entire life stolen away from her—well, she managed it better than I would have. And we did get to threaten some would-be muggers in Central Park, so that helped."

"Christ, Rick. Don't tell me stuff like that. What about Anne Hughes? Have you talked to her yet?"

"Samantha is planning on doing that this morning," Richard said, keeping his tone flat. Tom didn't need to know how very annoyed he was by that circumstance.

"*She's* doing it?" Donner returned. "Alone? Wow, you must be annoyed."

"I'm being supportive."

"So, what are you doing, lurking down the street, ready to lend her a shoulder to cry on?"

Perhaps he should have gone into Addisco, after all. "Why yes," he replied, deciding to go with sarcasm. "I'm knitting, too. Samantha's perfectly capable of dealing with this however she sees fit. I have three contracts and a lawsuit to review."

"Okay, okay. I get it. You're enlightened. But it's still weird to think of Jellicoe having a mom. I always figured she sprang fully formed from a wall safe behind a Rembrandt somewhere."

"Or perhaps you've been helping Olivia with her mythology too much," Richard said dryly, though he could imagine the very same thing. "I'll call you if and when I have any new information for you. In the meantime, I would appreciate it if you would ask Katie to give Samantha a call sometime this afternoon."

"Women bonding and all that? Will do." Tom sighed. "Between you and me, Rick, I'm glad for her sake that you were the one to tell her. Finding that out on her own would have been crappy. Or not finding out at all. Jeez."

"Thank you. I'm glad I was here, too. Talk later."

"Bye."

He *was* glad he'd flown to New York, and that he'd been nosey and cautious enough to look into Anne Hughes. Because Tom made a good point; if it had been Samantha alone here, she might never have discovered the truth. Or worse, it might have been Martin Jellicoe deciding to drop that particular atomic bomb at just the moment it would hurt her the most.

In fact, that might well have been Martin's plan. Could still be his plan. Which meant that he and Samantha were at least one step ahead of her elusive father for once. And he meant to keep it that way.

8

Thursday, 9:58 a.m.

Sam watched as Sang-Wook Rhee, alarm installation specialist for Sotheby's, attached the last bundle of wires to the pressure sensor system. That gave her protection against motion, pressure, temperature, and broken circuits—also known as opening things that were supposed to remain closed.

While she didn't like that all the mechanicals were in the basement, quiet and isolated and out of view, she did approve of the only entrance to the equipment room being inside the Victorian. If Martin wanted to disable the alarms, he would have to beat them, first. He could try cutting power to the place, of course, but they had battery backups for ninety percent of the security systems, and any power outage would trip the main alarm, anyway.

"It certainly looks impressive," Anne said.

Pushing back at the shiver the woman's voice elicited and beginning to wonder if she could just avoid having alone time with Anne Hughes at all today, Sam nodded. "You ready for a test, Rhee?"

He sat back on his little folding seat. "Yep. I've already alerted Sotheby's and the PD. What do you want to start with?"

"Let's do pressure." She lifted her walkie. "Alec? Make sure the second-floor west window is locked, then try lifting it anyway."

"Copy." Pause. "It's locked." Pause. "Lifting in three, two, one, go."

A heartbeat later the upper right panel lit up in festive red, a deafening claxon filled every room of the house including the basement, and both Anne's and her phone whooped in the ugliest, most grating tone she'd been able to find. She lifted hers. "'Pressure sensor alarm,'" she read aloud, having to yell to be heard over the alarm, "'second floor, window number 7. Police notified.' Or they would be, generally." She nodded at Rhee. "Reset it, please."

The sound abruptly cut off, leaving her ears ringing. Even if nothing else happened, that damn noise would affect *her* concentration during a robbery. That was how she'd wanted it, though—physically painful.

"It won't even wait for one of us to confirm that it's not an accident?" Anne asked, speaking a little loudly as she read the same information on her iPad.

"Nope. An alarm goes off, police are alerted."

"So even if a patron leans on a windowsill, that alarm is set to blast out people's eardrums and the police are going to show up?"

"Yep." Was it too much? Did she have the settings wound up to eleven when they should be at a one or two? Did fucking Martin have her overreacting? Damn it, she didn't even know if there such a thing where Martin Jellicoe was concerned.

"Good," Anne stated, surprising Samantha. "I'd rather have to pay the city for multiple false alarms than have it not go off when it should."

"I did tell Alec to yank on the window pretty hard," Sam admitted.

"Can we go push on something and see how much pressure it takes to set off the alarm?"

"We're clear with the PD for…"—the technician checked his phone—"another twenty-three minutes. Shove away, Anne. I'll reset when Sam gives me a thumbs-up."

Being a hundred percent without guaranteed backup on the way for thirty minutes would normally have freaked her out, but none of the valuables were coming in until tomorrow morning. They were even knocking off early today; yesterday, before Donner's text to Rick, that would have had Sam thinking of checking Rick out of work and going sightseeing or something, but now the slow day had her all jumpy and wishing something would happen to keep her from having to talk to Anne about *the thing*.

Sam blew out her breath as she followed Anne upstairs to the main floor. *Now or never.* "Hey, do you want to go get lunch somewhere after this?" she asked.

Anne sent her a glance over one shoulder. "Well, I was going to go back to the office and obsessively check my phone every four seconds, but sure. I can be obsessive while I'm eating."

All morning Sam had been doing her own obsessing, reviewing every word the older woman spoke to decide whether she and Anne did have some speech patterns or mannerisms or looks in common like Rick claimed they did. That last one did sound like it might have come from either of them, damn it all.

How did that work, when she hadn't set eyes on Anne Hughes in twenty-one years? Could a four-year-old pick up speech patterns and mannerisms when she probably couldn't even wipe her own butt? This was driving her crazy, and her fight-or-flight instincts were yelling at her to climb into an airplane and fly to Paris or Hong Kong or anywhere that didn't share a time zone with New York and Anne Hughes.

This was not the kind of adrenaline rush she enjoyed. And watching Anne nudge the window harder and harder until the alarm blasted wasn't helping her composure. Sam texted the all-clear to the basement crew but kept her finger hovering over the little photo of Rick that she would only have to tap to get him on the line and then over here as fast as Benny could drive him. He would talk to Anne for her; he'd volunteered to do it. And she could wait outside, preferably in a running car.

That, though, wouldn't be fair to Anne. Assuming, of course, that Anne really was the innocent party in all this, and that she hadn't been a rip-roaring bitch who'd driven Martin away and then filed the missing person's report on Sam—Sarah—just to spite him. Talking to Anne for two minutes, though, made that theory way doubtful, just as talking to Martin for half a second made the biggest surprise that any woman had agreed to marry his lying, self-centered ass in the first place.

All that was just more distraction, though, crap to keep her from focusing on the idea that in the next twenty minutes or so she was going to have to tell Anne Hughes that her daughter had been located, and that Bradley Martin was Martin Jellicoe. And that other thing, that ta da, Sarah Martin was Sam Jellicoe, and she was standing right there in front of her.

"If you guys are going to keep shoving and lifting and punching things, I'm going to have to call the NYPD back and tell them to ignore us for another thirty minutes," Sang-Wook Rhee said over the walkie.

"I'm convinced," Anne said with a grin. "And relieved, hopefully not prematurely. This is a nice job, Sam. Really nice."

"Thanks. I'll still be happier once everything is auctioned off and out of Sotheby's hands."

"As will I. Let's get everybody out of here and start moving the valuables in tomorrow morning."

With a nod Sam told Rhee to disarm everything until she could get the rest of the crew out. Once it was just him, her, and Anne left, he set all the alarms to active and they left the building. Yesterday she would have spent the rest of the day and night doing what Anne had suggested—obsessively checking her cellphone for anybody lurking around the Victorian. Now, though, she had a couple of other things taking up her brain space.

"Where to for lunch?" Anne asked, dumping her iPad into her bulky purse.

Oh, boy. Time's up. "How about we just head off in that direction, and see what happens?" Sam suggested, pointing east.

"Works for me. I doubt we can get half a block without running across a deli or something."

Anne made a good point, and since Sam wanted to do this out in the open where she had room to run, she took a deep breath. "I need to talk to you about a couple of things."

"Don't say you're backing out now," Anne said, glancing sideways at her. "I mean, I know the security stuff is wired in, but I want you supervising the placement of every item going into the exhibition."

"I'm not backing out. Though you may ask me to, after this."

"Ah. Is this where you tell me that your father was Martin Jellicoe, renowned cat burglar? I told you that I looked into you before I made that phone call. You have an insight that not many other people in the world possess. And you've used that insight to do good. I applaud that."

Man, any more of this, and Sam was just going to pass out. "Yeah. Thanks. The thing is, Martin Jellicoe…Well, he didn't always go by that name when he was pulling jobs. I don't know all his aliases, but sometimes he went by Bob Martine, or Frank Bradley, or Brad Cassidy…or Bradley Martin."

Anne stopped in her tracks, so fast a guy in a gray suit nearly bashed into her from behind before he flipped her off and went around. "What?" she said faintly, her face going chalky gray.

Maybe the out-in-the-open thing had been a mistake. "He might be lurking around here somewhere," Sam muttered, moving in closer but not ready to grab Anne's arm. She might get punched for one thing, or if Martin *was* watching and saw Anne flinch or something, he'd know his little game was paying some dividends. Unless he'd been counting on staying a step ahead of them, and he'd meant to spring this surprise on them at just the right time. *Hm.* That was worth thinking about—just not at this moment. "Let's keep walking, shall we?"

With a hard breath Anne nodded, setting off again at a walk that was way too fast even for New York. "I'm going in there," she stammered, pointing at a Starbuck's.

"Good. Okay."

Anne walked straight past the counter toward the bathroom at the back. When one of the baristas yelled that she had to buy something to use the restroom, Sam pulled a twenty out of her pocket and slapped it onto the counter. Then she followed Anne into the single ladies' room and locked the door behind them.

While Anne stood in the far corner and stared at the white tile walls like she could make them melt, Sam looked at her all over again. Yeah, she'd been doing that all morning, and part of her wanted to see some…difference that would mean they couldn't possibly be related, but there were still things that made sense. Brownish hair lightening as gray strands worked their way in, not her own auburn but not that far off from it, the same height within an inch or two, green eyes a little grayer than hers, the same shaped mouth…and a similar dry humor and appreciation of the absurd, even though Sam had no idea if those things could be inherited or if it was just a coincidence.

"Hey!" A male fist pounded on the door. "Get a damn room for that shit!"

"It's not like that," Sam shouted back. "She's my mom, and we're having a female issue."

"Oh. Oh. Okay. Just...don't take too long."

Anne's shoulders lifted. "This is a joke, isn't it? You're a grifter, and you think that tricking me into thinking you're my...my daughter will...get you something, but it won't. I'm not rich, and I don't have a Renoir in my dining room, and—"

"The only thing I knew about you was that you were a demanding, buttoned-up bitch, and you threw Martin and me out because you wanted the lifestyle but not the strings." Sam took a breath. She used to believe that, and she knew who to thank for it. Martin couldn't even leave her with a fond memory.

"I never—" Anne turned around. "He was charming, and elusive. Reformed, he said. For five years I went along with it, and then half the collection I was curating went missing, and—" She snapped her mouth shut. "None of that matters. You...Are you? Really? Because if this *is* some weird revenge thing from Bradley, I swear I will—"

"I'm engaged to a really rich guy," Sam pointed out, not sure why she hadn't realized Anne might not even believe any of this. But then she'd had time to go through most of the stages of grief or being lied to already, even if she'd kind of stopped at acceptance and being really pissed off at the same time. "I don't need whatever it is you might have. And I don't need the publicity that would follow me if I helped Martin rob your exhibit."

Anne kept staring at her like she had antenna on the top of her head, but Sam put up with it for the moment. She'd been staring at the other woman's profile all morning, and fair was fair. She resisted the urge to fold her arms, and just looked back.

"You have the same freckle," Anne finally said, reaching out one shaking finger and touching Sam's forehead. "I mean, you have several freckles, but I remember that one. Straight over your left eyebrow, halfway between your eyebrow and your hairline. And your right eye has just a tiny bit of brown in it." She drew a long breath. "You're her," she whispered. "You're Sarah Jane."

"'Jane'?" Sam repeated. "Sarah Jane. I think so. And I wasn't holding out on you. I mean, I was, because I knew Bradley Martin was Martin Jellicoe, but I didn't know about the daughter thing until last night. Rick—well, his lawyer, Tom Donner—looked into you to try to figure out why Martin would be targeting you. It all kind of weirds me out, so if you don't—"

Anne threw her arms around Sam's shoulders and back, pulling her in tight. The older woman's whole body was shaking, and Sam abruptly worried that she was going to have a heart attack or something. Crap, Sam didn't like being smothered, but she did get it. That was why she stood still and let Anne hug her, and even patted the other woman's back a little.

"It's a lot, I know."

"He…he changed your name. I should have realized. Bradley Martin, Martin Jellicoe… Dammit. Why Jellicoe? Is it because of *Cats*? He took you to see it, and you bugged us about getting a pet cat for weeks."

Cats. "Fuck," Sam muttered. "Jellicle cats. Cat burglars. God, I'm an idiot."

"You were barely more than a baby. I looked…everywhere. I tried finding some of his friends, tracking him down, and that was when I realized I knew literally no one from his life."

"Did you know he was a thief?" Sam asked, straightening the second Anne relaxed her hold a little.

With a humorless laugh, Anne put her palm against Sam's cheek. "I fell for a bad boy. He said he'd meant to rob the exhibit I was putting together, and instead he fell for me. And I bought it."

"He might have meant it," Sam offered. "Five years without doing a burglary is a looooong time for Martin."

"Yes, he apparently resisted until the Smithsonian jewel exhibition came to town, with me in charge of staging. That was before I went to work for Sotheby's, and the last event I was employed by Smithfield for."

"He got you fired."

"He got me arrested. But then I really didn't care, because that night he only came home long enough to grab you and his stupid backpack, lock me in a closet, and leave. If the police hadn't come, I would have been stuck there for God knows how long."

"Jeez. I don't remember any of that, except for him cutting my hair and dying it black. I don't..."

"You don't remember me," Anne finished for her, cupping Sam's face with both hands now. "That's okay. But...He told you I was a bitch? Did you—"

"He told me some lies," Sam interrupted. No need to dwell on the details. "Enough to make me stop asking questions and never go looking for you. Eventually I'll learn that *nothing* he ever says is the truth."

"At least he kept you on the legitimate side of his business. You've made good use of that."

Okay, this was the really tricky part. Just knowing that Anne hadn't kicked them to the curb, that she had looked for her daughter, didn't mean she could be trusted with all those secrets and jobs that hadn't yet run out their statutes of limitations. "Not so much," she settled for saying. "But I met Rick, and I retired. For good. And for real."

"He made you rob people? That son of a bitch."

"You can blame him for the stuff when I was a kid, but I'm a grown-ass woman, Anne. The last couple of years, since I turned fifteen, really, are all me. And I'd tell you more, but I've only had a mom for like twelve hours."

For a long couple of seconds Anne looked at her again. Really looked at her, in the way that made her wonder if she had lettuce between her teeth or something. She was probably running it all through her head, Martin and Sarah/Sam burgling through the years, hanging off wires and robbing shit, Tom Cruise *Mission Impossible* style. And that wasn't a bad comparison. "My God. Sarah," she finally whispered.

"Samantha," Sam said, shaking her head. "Sam. And I'm wondering now if he set things up to get me here, so he could spring this little surprise on you and mess us both up enough to rob the exhibit of everything but the light bulbs." She took a breath. "So, my point is, when we leave Starbuck's you will have a coffee in your hands, we will be amused at each other's wit, and we'll have no idea that we're related."

"If you're telling me the truth. I certainly haven't had time to logic myself through every possible scenario. You have a point about your association with Rick, but I suppose you could be scamming him, too."

Well, she hadn't expected *that* response. "How does that scenario go, then? Martin put me up to this so we can rob you together? And he offered me enough that I couldn't pass it up, even with Rick Addison putting an engagement ring on my finger? Does that make me related to you, or am I an actress he hired to play the part of Samantha Sarah Jane Jellicoe Martin?"

"I...don't know. It's just that you said you found all this out last night, and you're cool as a cucumber, while I'm a blubbering mess. We haven't seen each other in twenty-one years."

Sam leaned back against the door. Okay, she was going to have to trust Anne a little more than she'd anticipated. "I grew up thinking of people as marks. Targets, idiots to be robbed."

"Oh, Sam."

"After Martin and I split up, and before Rick, I traveled everywhere alone. I have safe houses scattered between here and Florida, with a couple in Europe. I'm used to relying on myself. I can count the number of people I trust in the world on two, maybe three, fingers. And until yesterday I did think you were a bitch who kicked your guy and your four-year-old daughter out of your house and never looked back, so neither did I. So sorry if I'm not all weepy, but I can guarantee you that I'm pretty freaked out. And I'm pretty fucking angry at Martin for lying to me about...everything."

Slowly, Anne nodded. "I can see that. I'm so, so sorry that I couldn't find you. There hasn't been a day when I didn't think of you and wonder where you were, if you were safe, or happy, or if you were married and had babies of your own." She gulped an unsteady breath. "I had no idea he'd turned me into Maleficent."

"And here *I* am, bad Robin Hood." Sam forced a short smile. "Do you trust that I'm not working with him? If you don't, I'll take the next flight back to Florida. That might even mess up Martin's plans, and he'll leave you alone."

She didn't entirely believe that, but if Martin had put in a word here and sent a note there, enough to send Anne after help and to ask it of Sam, then her leaving might at least throw him off his game a little.

"No. I just...You're not going anywhere, Sam." Anne clutched her arm again. Hard.

Not good, not good. Sam clenched her free hand into a fist to keep from yanking away. Normal people hugged and shit. She could put up with it from her mom, for cripe's sake.

Anne took a deep breath. "I...This was not how I thought today would go," she muttered, shaking her head. "But I've wanted every day for the past twenty-one years to go exactly like this."

"With maybe less thievery involved," Sam countered, slipping into what was probably a smile.

"That doesn't even matter today. I...I think it all boils down to the fact that you told me all this, when you didn't have to. I'm going to remember to breathe, and then we'll go out and I'll buy a caramel macchiato, and maybe you could invite me over to dinner tonight so we can actually talk somewhere that doesn't smell like pee and lemon soap."

That opened up a whole other mess of questions about how far Sam even wanted Anne in her life, but for crying out loud, the woman had found her daughter. "Deal. Let's say seven o'clock tonight. I'll text you the address. In the meantime, you hired me, you're still nervous about Bradley Martin, and the exhibition items start showing up tomorrow at nine in the morning."

"Yes. Yes." Tugging on her blouse to straighten it, Anne took a couple more deep breaths, nodded, and reached past Sam to unlock the door.

Samantha didn't pay much attention to the rest of their brief conversation because it was just the weather and being ready for tomorrow, and a "see you later" for effect. As she walked a half block away in the opposite direction of Anne to hail a cab, she almost felt like she was two people, one of them calmly— well, pretty calmly—watching a woman reunite with her mother after twenty-one years apart, and the other one just kind of weirdly confused by the whole experience.

Anne would have been happier with mutual weeping and more hugs and more…joy, but Samantha just wasn't built that way. A lot of years of experience made her approach everything with a cynical, practical eye, and while she had no problem with risking herself physically, she kept all the other stuff walled up like Fort Knox. Hell, even admitting to herself that she loved Rick had taken way longer than it should have.

"Where to?" a familiar male voice said from car level next to her.

For a quarter of a second she froze before she turned to look at the late model Mercedes stopped at the curb. "The gray color isn't bad," she commented coolly, "but isn't the model a little flashy for you?"

Martin Jellicoe, his eyes unreadable behind a pair of Maui

Jim sunglasses, curved his mouth in a smile. "It was convenient. So you're finished with the security installation, eh? The good stuff comes in tomorrow, I hear."

"Is this what you do, now? Drive around Manhattan waiting for me to come out of shops so you can try to rattle me with stuff that half the employees at Sotheby's know? I hope you didn't pay your snitch more than fifty bucks for that one."

Her father clicked his tongue. "So cynical, you are. You didn't have to take this job at all, you know, and I'd be driving around Manhattan while you were in Palm Beach."

"Yeah, sorry, not going to let you bully some poor woman because you think it makes you look cool, Martin. Or is it Bradley, for this one? I don't think it's a coincidence that this alias of yours shares initials with bowel movement."

His jaw jumped, almost imperceptibly, but she caught it. He didn't like being made fun of. "Are we doing the juvenile stuff now?" he retorted, flipping off a delivery truck behind him when the guy honked. "Do I point out that Rick rhymes with prick or something?"

"You could do that," Sam agreed, not even close to taking that bait, "or you could just drive away. I'm not keeping you here. Didn't ask you to stop by, either."

"Fine. Last warning, then. Go home. Drop this one. You won't like what happens at the end of it."

"You've told me that twice. Are you Babe Ruth now, calling your shots? 'Hey, I'm going to rob this place, so make sure you look the other way'?" Yeah, she was deliberately misreading his comments, because the more he talked about the end of this gig, the more she realized that he did mean to spring her relationship with Anne Hughes on her, shock the fuck out of her, and steal all the Adgerton collection while she lay on the floor, flopping around like an electrocuted fish. What a douche.

"Something like that. No more warnings, Sam."

"Then for God's sake, stop warning me. I get it. You want me here because you want to beat me, which you'll find even more satisfying because you've told me not to try it. Go for it, Martin. Just stop talking about it. In fact," and she pulled her phone out of her back pocket as she spoke, "I'm giving you five seconds, and then I'm calling 911. I'm done with you. Really."

"You don't know everything, kid. You should have listened to me."

"Nine," she said, and tapped the corresponding number. "One. O—"

"Be seeing you," he snapped, and pulled back into traffic, nearly clipping another Mercedes. He wouldn't care, though, because the SL wasn't his, and because he'd be ditching it as soon as he turned the corner.

Sam hit the back key and finally mashed her finger on Rick's face. "Samantha," his voice said, before the phone even rang.

"Guess who has two parents and just had a face-to-face with each of 'em?"

"Christ."

"No, me." Faintly in the background of his call a woman called out a mocha frap, and Sam frowned. "Where are you?"

"Clearly not close enough, if Martin got to you. Dammit, Samantha. I'm heading to the Victorian. I'll be there in two minutes."

Glancing over her shoulder, she turned around and started an easy trot back toward the exhibit space. "Roger that. Bye."

Earlier, she might have been ticked off that he'd once again followed her to her job site, but at the moment she was just glad he was close. He reached the corner just as she slowed down at the door. Rick didn't stop until he was close enough to reach out and take her hand in his.

"Where is he?" he muttered, his gaze shifting from her face to the view over her shoulder.

"Probably in New Jersey by now. He was in a stolen Mercedes SL. Left when I started dialing the cops."

With his free hand he dug into his coat pocket for his phone. He had a thin stack of folders beneath his other arm, she noticed. Apparently, he'd been working in some café or something, just so he could be close by her. Man, did he get extra points for that, today. "Did you get the license number?"

It wouldn't do any good; Martin would be half a mile or more away from wherever it was he'd abandoned the SL. On the other hand, she'd told him she would call the cops. There was a slight chance that he might at least stick around to see if she was bluffing. And if she wasn't, it might possibly have him thinking twice about the Sotheby's job. "It said BIGDEAL," she answered. "One word. Tinted windows. Gunmetal gray."

He lifted an eyebrow. "That's rather on the nose, isn't it?" Then someone picked up the other end of his call, and he reported that a man had just broken into a Mercedes, then passed on the information she'd given him.

It was a useless exercise, but a couple of months ago it would have bothered her a lot. Just the idea of ratting out anyone from her so-called profession, let alone her own father, would have given her the shakes. Now, though, she gave in to the briefest of daydreams where cops did catch Martin red-handed, and he went back to prison for a really long time for grand theft auto, of all things.

If she went along with that daydream, though, she would have to also consider that as soon as the cuffs went on, Martin would start negotiating. And even though he couldn't prove much of it, he could definitely point his finger in her direction enough to make the FBI and Interpol really, really interested.

"What are the odds that he's watching us right now?" Rick asked as he pocketed his phone again.

"Nil. He thinks he's a couple of steps ahead of me. Which means he'd be well away in case I did call the cops."

"Definitely long gone, then?"

She nodded.

Rick stepped forward and wrapped his arms around her. For a second Sam felt like an overfilled balloon that had just let all its air out. He was a strong guy, physically and mentally, and for a couple of minutes, at least, she could be as weak and wimpy as she wanted to be, because he would hold her up.

Sighing against his shoulder, she held onto him as tightly as he held her. "This has not been a good morning," she grumbled, then reluctantly straightened again.

As soon as she pushed at him, he let her go—mostly, shifting to grip one of her hands again. "Where to?" he asked.

She pointed forward with her free fingers. "That way."

For two blocks they walked in silence. Rick had to be going crazy wanting to know about both her conversations, but he didn't ask her. Instead, he just held her hand and walked beside her while she puzzled out her personal shit. And boy, she had a lot of that, all of a sudden.

"Anne kept grabbing and hugging me," Sam finally mumbled. "Maybe I should have just hugged her back, but you know, I kept thinking about that 'three versions of a story' thing."

"His version, her version, and the truth?" Rick supplied.

"Yeah. That was probably just an excuse, though, because I have no reason to think she was anything but exactly the opposite of what Martin described. It was too much. I'm not a huggy person."

"She believed you, though?"

"Not at first. She thought I might be working with Martin to mess with her. Then she was all, 'thank goodness you used the horrible things he taught you for good, and not evil,' which I kind of corrected her about. No details, though."

"Good."

"So, anyway, she's coming to the apartment for dinner tonight."

"I'm glad you're willing to talk to her about all this."

"What, you thought I'd just bolt?"

He shrugged. "I've heard your opinion of emotional entanglements. This is a big one."

"It's kind of spooky, sometimes, how well you know me, Mr. Addison." And even spookier to realize that not only had she let that happen, but she appreciated that he knew when to give her space and knew when to push—whether she liked that or not.

Leaning sideways, he kissed her on the temple. "You're something of an obsession of mine. What did Martin want?"

"He wanted to make sure I knew he was watching. Warned me again that I wouldn't like what happened if I stuck with this gig. I think he's planning to spring the 'Anne is your mother' thing on me," she said, doing her best Darth Vader impression, "and then lift whatever it is he's after from the exhibit while I die from shock and amazement at his big, devious brain."

Rick took a hard breath and let it out again. "I admit that I've never been fond of Martin Jellicoe," he murmured. "At this moment, though, I would welcome the opportunity to have a face-to-face chat with him."

Well, she knew what *that* meant. "I doubt anybody's ever set him on his ass. It might be interesting."

"Interesting, my love, doesn't begin to cover it."

She leaned her head against his shoulder, hugging his arm with her free hand. "Are you sure you wouldn't rather marry a nice girl from the country? Someone with a loving, supportive set of parents you could invite over for the holidays without first having to check to see if one of them has outstanding warrants, or if the other one remembers what her daughter looks like?"

"That sounds rather dull. And since with those parents you wouldn't have become you, Samantha, I have to decline."

"Yeah, but I have *so* much baggage. More than I even knew about."

That earned her a snort. "Have you met me?" he returned. "I carry about a bit of baggage, myself. Do you want a list?"

"What I really want," she said, "is to go home to the apartment and wrap myself around some Rick Addison. And to not think about anything but Rick sex for a good couple of hours."

He stopped, pulled out his cellphone, and texted something. "Roger that," he said. "Do give me a moment to tell Andre that we'll need him for tonight. Meal suggestions?"

"Spaghetti. I'm not a fancy girl. And we're not trying to impress Anne as anything but my boss. My temporary boss." That other stuff, the sticky, complicated stuff, was going to have to wait until she'd burned off some damn adrenaline.

His car pulled up to the curb, Benny behind the wheel. "Where to, Mr. A?" he asked as Rick handed her into the back seat and followed her, pulling the door shut door behind him.

"The apartment. And there's a bonus for you if we make it there in under fifteen minutes."

"Good as done," Vinny said, and revved the engine.

Rick put up the glass barrier between the front and back seats, took her chin in one hand to kiss her deep and slow, and slid his other hand between her thighs. Oh, that definitely started her engine revving, too.

9

Thursday, 3:33 p.m.

Richard flopped onto his back, reaching over to drag Samantha across his chest. "I don't know about you," he murmured, "but I feel better now."

Panting, Samantha tipped her head to give him a kiss on his jaw. "I'm beginning to think things would have been awkward if you hadn't come to New York." She chuckled. "Martin probably thinks I'm shaking in my boots right now, wondering when he's going to strike. And here I am, spread-eagled under Rick Addison while we try to break the bedsprings."

He didn't generally think of himself as a boytoy to be used for sex or any other purpose, but neither was he about to complain about being of service today. Of course, neither did he need to hit the treadmill today, either. Not after that. "This doesn't change anything, you know," he commented, still trying to catch his breath. "You're still who you are. The only difference is that you've added a few more chapters to your book."

"*The Book of Sam*, I suppose? It would have a lot of blank pages for things I can't talk about. And lots of profanity." She put her chin on her fist to look down at his face. "Can you imagine being Anne? Losing a kid, looking for her until you just…give up, I guess, and then years and years later having this random person you hired announce that she's your daughter?"

"Not to sound like a psychologist, but Anne's business is her own. All you have to figure out is you, my dear. And all that's shifted for you is that you potentially have one parent who doesn't belong in federal prison."

"Yeah, but *I* belong in federal prison. Some gift for mom, huh?"

That talk was *not* acceptable. Richard took her shoulders, lifting her so they were eye to eye. "No, you don't belong in prison," he stated. "Your father was a self-centered, egomaniacal fool who saw you as clay he could mold into the perfect cat burglar, and then he couldn't handle it when you surpassed him. You have a conscience; that's why you've chosen a career that helps you make amends. In my opinion, you using your expertise to stop other people like Martin is a better use of your time than wasting it in prison."

She shifted out of his grip and slid off him to sit up. "Wow. You've been thinking about this a lot."

"Every damn day." He caught hold of her hand as she shifted to the edge of the bed. "Get to know Anne, let her into your life and you into her life, or don't. The only thing you're obligated about right now is keeping Martin Jellicoe out of the Adgerton exhibition."

Richard didn't let out his breath until Samantha squeezed his hand back. He couldn't force her to do anything, as much as he wanted to from time to time, but at least she was listening. While he knew about all of his relatives back three or four hundred years, Samantha had been a singularity in more ways than one. Even knowing what he did about Martin only gave him a small sampling of what her life must have been like. He doubted she would ever learn anything about her father's family; even if Martin told her about them, even if Martin was his actual last name—which he doubted—she wouldn't believe a word he said.

Now, though, she had a chance to learn about the other half of her ancestry. Perhaps he put more importance to it than she did *because* his own was so detailed, but she must have had some interest in knowing where she came from. Where that strong, stubborn sense of decency came from, because that damned well wasn't anything she'd gotten from Martin.

"What are you thinking about?" he asked, when she didn't move.

Samantha sighed. "Mostly about whether in a year or so I'm going to regret taking this job as much as I do right now."

"So you don't want to know wh—"

"I found you," she interrupted, "when I was me, no tangles, no ties, and a dad I thought was dead. I'm not sure I like the idea of being Dolores Lee Jones from Nebraska."

"Sarah Jane Martin, from Connecticut," he corrected. "Though Dolores is a bloody sexy name."

With a snort she pulled her hand free of his and stood. "Don't forget that I'm fake-named after a T.S. Eliot poem. Or more likely, the Broadway musical." Naked, she twirled, making a pawing motion with her hands. "I'm a Jellicle cat."

Humor. Humor was good. That was how Samantha coped with things that troubled her. As she trotted into the bathroom, Richard lay back again. He'd been through moments where he'd worried she would flee, vanish into the night. This hadn't been one of those moments, but it troubled him at least as much. She felt guilty for detesting a mother about whom she'd only been told lies. She felt guilty that Anne Hughes had spent…years worrying about a young girl who'd barely given her a second thought. And she felt guilty that she hadn't been the picture-perfect girl she figured Anne had imagined for all those years.

And when Samantha felt guilty, she wanted to make amends.

Her comment that she deserved to be in prison had nearly stopped his heart. Prison wasn't going to happen. The possibility alone was why he kept a few select phone numbers and coordinates in his wallet. People who for a price could arrange travel across certain borders even if his own plane was stopped. Places where the U.S.—and most of the rest of the civilized world—couldn't arrange for arrests or extraditions. And he'd discreetly arranged several offshore accounts for the same reason.

The shower went on, and a moment later Samantha leaned around the edge of the bathroom door. "Wanna soap me up?"

His cock jumped. Yes, this was about burning off adrenaline and not wanting to consider next steps, but he happened to be an enlightened, supportive partner. If she required more sex, he was certainly willing to oblige. "I feel in need of a shower, myself," he drawled, sliding off the bed and padding into the bathroom.

She slid her arms up over his shoulders and leaned against him to plant a solid, open-mouthed kiss. "Let's just keep doing this and forget everything else," she suggested.

Taking her by the waist, he lifted her up onto the counter and stepped in between her knees. "They'd find our entwined, half-melted skeletons in about a week, but it would be worth it," he murmured, slowly drawing her forward and burying himself inside her.

Gasping, Samantha leaned her forehead against his. "Shower," she muttered.

With a grin he lifted her again. Her legs wrapped around his hips, and he carried her into the shower through the thankfully wide door. Hot water cascaded over them as he kept her pinned against the Carrara tile and shoved into her again and again. Samantha dug her fingers into his shoulders, giving a high-pitched, drawn-out moan as she came around him. *Damn.* That was the moment, that handful of heartbeats when he could look her in the eye and know that whichever heart-stopping stunt she pulled, however much danger and excitement she craved, she belonged to him. They fit, literally and figuratively. Eyes rolling back in his head he joined her, grunting as he climaxed.

"God, I love shower sex," she panted, planting a kiss on his mouth. He felt her lips curve in a smile. "And I love you."

"Thanks," he muttered, lowering her feet to the tiled floor and reaching for her bottle of shampoo. "Likewise."

A frown touching her face, she shoved at his shoulder. "Seriously. This wasn't just a workout. You make me feel…safe."

With a scowl of his own, Richard squeezed shampoo onto his palm. "That's…flattering."

"Come on, Brit. That's not what I mean. You know how to do all the sex stuff like a certified pro. But I spent a lot of years being able to count on me. That's it. Backpack under the bed, one ear listening for car doors closing too quietly, one eye watching for anybody who might look at me funny. Even with Stoney—he wouldn't give me up, but he would vanish if things got too sticky. You wouldn't, though." She tilted her head to look at him and reached up one hand to cup his face. "You're the only person who's ever put me first. And yes, that makes me feel safe. *You* make me feel safe. So you can suck it if you don't like that."

Wow. Richard leaned back against the shower wall. "I forget sometimes," he said quietly, "how much effort, and how much faith, it's taken you to be in my life."

"So 'safe' isn't a bad word," she prompted.

"So 'safe' isn't a bad word," he repeated. "Now I believe I promised you some soaping up."

She snorted, turning her back and tilting up her head. "Kinky."

SAMANTHA DIPPED a cracker into the jar of peanut butter and dumped it into her mouth. It was too late for lunch, but a little protein before Anne arrived for dinner would hopefully at least keep her from fainting or doing something else equally unimpressive.

As she licked off her finger, her phone rang to the theme from *Wonder Woman*. Using her peanut butter-free pinkie, she accepted the call. "Hi, Katie."

Katie Donner, wife, mom, PTA member, protector of local wildlife and avid recycler, had only done one questionable thing in her life, as far as Sam could tell. She'd married Tom Donner. But then, the guy was as upright as a human could get, so there was that.

"Sam," Katie's warm voice returned through the phone's speaker. "You've had quite a day, I've heard. Wanna talk about it?"

Rick strolled into the kitchen and stole one of her crackers. "Katie?" he mouthed.

Sam nodded. "My mouth's full of peanut butter. Give me a sec." With her clean hand she scooped up the phone and made her way to the huge living room window. After she swallowed and ran her tongue around her teeth a few times, she took a breath. "Tom told you all the stuff, I guess?"

"He said you found your mom. As I recall, you never thought of her very fondly. Was it rough?"

"Really rough. Turns out my dad made up all the sh—stuff about her kicking us out. He kidnapped me. She reported me missing, but couldn't get far enough into Martin's network to locate me."

Silence. "Wow. That's…awful. A lot of things for you to rethink. A lot of emotions. It must be so crazy. How're you doing?"

Looking at Katie's name on her phone display, Samantha frowned. Rick had said the same thing, pretty much, but he was always worried she would freak out and skedaddle. Slowly she sat in one of the ultra-comfortable chairs facing the window. Katie was…normal. If she thought all this might be crazy and weird, then feeling confused about it was…okay. "Weirdly," she said, "hearing you say that actually helps. My head's kind of whirlwindy."

"I can only imagine. Does she seem like an okay person, at least? Because I don't think you're obligated to connect with her unless you want to do that. It doesn't matter if what you've been told about her is false. You still have the right to decide whether you want to know her or not."

"I feel bad for her. I mean, for a lot of years I barely spared her a thought, because Martin said she wasn't worth thinking about."

"Made it easier for him, I bet," Katie muttered, then cleared her throat. "You didn't punch her or anything, did you?"

"No! No, of course not. I'm just…I'm not the ideal daughter, you know?"

"Oh, please. You're awesome. Do you want to get to know her? Because she's not perfect, either. She married your dad, right?"

"Yeah, she did." And she had known he was a bad boy, though probably not just how bad. Still, they both had some baggage. Some Martin-shaped baggage. "Martin's an ass," she said aloud. "Excuse my language."

"Oh, I agree. And moms can be tricky, too. Believe me, you're always twelve years old to your mother. And they *always* know better than you do and aren't shy about telling you that. So you take things at your pace. And call me if you want to vent or ask questions, or whatever. I'm here, Sam, okay?"

"I may have avoided that twelve-years-old thing, since she didn't know me then. But thanks, Katie. I'm not good with the family stuff. I appreciate it. Really."

"Anytime, my dear. You're frequently the only excitement in my life. And don't you dare apologize for that."

"Okay. Bye."

She tapped off the call and looked up to see Rick resting both elbows on the counter, chin in his hands as he gazed at her. "Is this where I say that I already told you all that, or should I just nod sagely at her wisdom?" he asked.

"Just nod, dude. She's a normal. You and I are…Well, we're not normal."

He grinned. "We're exceptional."

Well, *he* was exceptional. Today she was just happy to hear that not knowing quite how to feel was okay. Having a female friend was good. Having Katie Donner in her life was good. Even if it meant having Tom Donner there, too.

○

GENERALLY, when invited to someone's home for dinner, Anne Hughes brought wine. Red wine, usually, because in her mind it felt more festive. Tonight wasn't about being festive, though. Nor was it just any dinner.

Hefting the cloth sack she'd brought with her, she thanked the Uber driver and climbed out of his Subaru. She'd passed this apartment building on Park Avenue perhaps a thousand times in her decade of working at Sotheby's. During at least one taxi ride she remembered thinking that Richard Addison lived in the building, but that had been in conjunction with a showing she'd been arranging, when she'd hoped he or his surrogate would make an appearance. Everyone knew Addison was a collector with exquisite taste and deep pockets.

But tonight wasn't about that, either. Squaring her shoulders, she pulled open the glass door and stepped into the lobby. Marble floors, mahogany desk, and a gold- and dark-blue striped wallpaper that practically screamed "you can't afford me" greeted her, along with a tall, broad-shouldered man who stood up from behind the mahogany desk as she entered.

"I'm here to see Richard Addison," she said, even though he wasn't who she was there to see, at all.

"Name?" he said, bending his head to type something onto his computer.

"Anne Hughes."

He nodded, leaving the desk and walking over to the pair of elevators against the back wall. "When you step out of the elevator," he said, reaching in with a card and hitting a button before he shifted to hold the door open, "there'll be a door and a phone in front of you. They're expecting you, so the door won't be locked. You can head straight in."

"Thank you." She stepped into the mirrored elevator, and the door closed with a quiet chime.

She dealt with wealthy people all the time in her position at Sotheby's. They'd long ceased being intimidating, though she knew to look out for serious quirks and oddball requests that if ignored or neglected, could cost a client a very lucrative sale. But this wasn't about assessing a potential buyer, either, even though Rick Addison might well be one.

How in the world had she ended up calling one security expert, of which there were a small handful on the east coast, having that one person she called accept the job, and then discovering that this same one person was her long-missing daughter? There were coincidences, and then there was this.

It all stank to high heaven of Bradley Martin. The question that kept hammering at her was *why*. And the possibilities that she'd been running through her head all afternoon didn't lead anywhere good. At the beginning of the equation were two facts: she knew Bradley Martin, knew how he thought and how far he would go to make a point; and she knew—she *knew*—that Bradley always put himself first. This wasn't about helping her reconnect with Sarah—Sam. This was about him in some way. And they all needed to figure out how he meant to use all this.

Because for her it was all about Sarah. The little girl with the gold and copper hair who loved Disney movies and had once spent a month straight wearing Tinker Bell wings day and night, didn't much resemble the young woman who conversed in thief lingo and had clearly—because she'd admitted to it— joined her father on at least some of his burglaries.

There were other things, though. She'd liked Sam from the moment they'd met. There had been an ease to their conversation that she'd enjoyed, but now she had to review to see if she'd sensed a connection or something, or if she'd just been pleased to see a competent woman being successful in a male-dominated profession.

The elevator door opened, and she stepped into the small foyer. As the man downstairs had said, the alcove was empty except for a phone on one wall and a plain, unmarked door. Oh, and a camera set above the door that could see any visitors.

Resisting the urge to wave at it, or to straighten her coat or her hair or something, Anne took a deep breath and reached for the doorknob—only to have it pull away from her before she could grasp it.

"Hello," Rick Addison said in his smooth British accent. "Thank you for coming. Somewhere more…neutral might have been easier, but it also would have been less private." Standing aside, he motioned for her to enter.

"I expected a butler," she commented, hefting the sack in her hand before she held it out to him. "I brought wine. I'm not sure why, but it's what people do, right?"

"We have a butler," he said, shutting the door and falling in beside her, as charming and confident in a suit and tie as he had been in jeans and a T-shirt just…what had it been? Yesterday? "I haven't called him in yet; we thought we'd only be in New York for a few days."

"When did you decide you would be here longer?" she asked, watching as he set the sack down in the large kitchen. In the far corner sat a full, refrigerated wine rack, which of course they would have. God, she was an idiot.

"When Samantha learned that Martin—Bradley—was involved."

Anne cocked her head. "You know all about her, then? And Bradley Martin or Martin Jellicoe or whatever he's calling himself these days?"

"I do." He lifted the bottle out of the sack. "This a good cabernet."

"I like it. What made you decide to dig through *my* past?"

Anyone else might have been offended by the blunt question, but he continued on his way to a cabinet for a pair of wine glasses. "When *I* learned Martin Jellicoe was involved."

"You don't trust him, then? Or you don't trust Sam around him?"

"Ah." Lifting a cork puller out of a drawer, he opened the bottle. "If you think for a second this is a jest, or that either of us is working with Martin to put something over on you, we're about to have a very different conversation than the one Samantha's been fretting over for the past few hours." He set the bottle down. "Are we having that conversation, then?"

"She makes a good point, Rick," Sam's voice came from a doorway at the far end of the kitchen. "If I were Martin's loyal padawan, or if I still believed all the shit he said about Anne over the years, yeah, I might be working with him to hit her exhibit. I'd be suspicious of me, too."

Padawan. That was *Star Wars.* It was odd that at the same time she was trying to decide if she could trust this woman at all, she wanted to decipher everything about her, know her likes and dislikes, and make certain she ended up being one of the likes. Sam would like Michael, at least, and his substantial *Star Wars* collection. Anne took a breath. No. No talk about Michael or things that personal while Bradley Martin was anywhere in the state. "He took my child from me," she said aloud. "I'd be a fool to think he wouldn't stoop to using my connection with Sam—the connection I want—against me. Do I think she has anything to do with that? No. But it could still be used."

"I think he'll use it against us, too. But I don't think he knows that we know about that connection," Sam commented, shifting around Addison and going into the refrigerator for a bottle of diet Coke.

"What makes you say that?"

"He's dangling a big 'you won't like the ending' over my head if I keep going with this job. After he probably arranged for me to get it."

Abruptly Anne couldn't catch her breath. "You talked to him? You're going to have to explain that, right now."

Rick handed her one of the glasses of wine as a broad-shoul-dered man in a chef's jacket appeared from yet another door-way. "Let's take this to the front room, shall we? I prefer not to get in the way of Andre's culinary preparations."

"Andre prefers that too," Andre Vilseau said, pulling out a pair of pots and clanking them onto the counter.

Following Samantha and Rick, Anne found a large, wide sitting room, the entire wall facing Central Park made up of ten-foot-tall windows. The idea that her little Sarah lived in a place like this still didn't quite feel…real. Should she ask for a DNA test?

Sam dropped onto the gray couch perpendicular to the windows. "He drove up to me right after you and I left Star-bucks. He's totally up to something. I just can't figure out if he's after the Adgerton collection, if he's pissed at me for quitting my previous means of employment, if he means to try to drag me back into it, or if he happened to spot you or your name somewhere and decided to hurt you some more for getting over him."

"Would you? Ever go back to it, I mean." Anne frowned. "And I'm not asking because of the Adgerton collection. I...want some things from this relationship. I want this relationship. So, would you?"

"No."

Sam said it confidently enough. "I so want to believe you, Sam. I do. But I believed Bradley when he said he'd gone straight, too. I can't...This is—"

"May I poke a few holes in your Samantha-returning-to-crime theory?" Rick seated himself beside Sam, close enough to touch but not doing so. "Firstly, there's me."

"You keep her on the straight and narrow, you mean? I happen to have some firsthand experience that loving someone doesn't turn them into the human you want them to be."

"I'm on the straight and narrow because *I* love *him*," Sam stated, taking a swallow of her diet Coke. "And because I prefer living in a place where I can open the doors and walk outside whenever I want to. But that isn't what he means."

He sent his fiancée a sideways glance. "Yes. Anyway, I'm rich. And well known. It would ruin my reputation if she stole something and got caught. And because I've made her much more high profile, her disappearing after she pulled a job like this would be very...problematic."

"And not just because he would hunt me down like a Terminator," Sam added.

"Though that would have to factor into the situation." Rick tipped his glass against her bottle of soda.

Very slowly Anne took a seat on the front edge of a blue chair. Even more slowly she drank her entire glass of wine. Sam had mentioned her life with Rick as a deterrent to her being a criminal already, but for heaven's sake, they finished each other's sentences. As if they'd had this conversation before and concluded exactly what the outcome would be if she went rogue.

"The 'crime doesn't pay' axiom actually applies for you, doesn't it?" she commented around the rim of her glass.

"I've made crime pay," Sam answered. "It's paid me a lot. But I was getting tired of it, really. I had a legit job, working in art restoration, and only did the bad things if the object or the setting really interested me."

"Was art restoration how you two met?"

"Actually, I—"

"That's close enough to the truth to suit," Rick interrupted. "Because while I understand your trying to build trust and Samantha wanting to be honest with you, you've lived a rather secretive life yourself, Anne. And I prefer to keep some padding between my fiancée and trouble."

Anne wished they hadn't left the wine in the kitchen. "This morning I had this thought, that if you were a few years older, Sam, we might be good friends. Then this afternoon you tell me that you're my daughter, and my brain hasn't slowed down since. This isn't at all what I was expecting when I called you for help."

Sam grimaced. "I bet the reunion part wasn't what you were expecting, either. I know this isn't the huggy, squishy tear fest you probably wanted, but we both know Martin's involved. And that puts shit in the middle of the party."

"I have no complaints about finding you after all this time. Never. But no, this is not how I ever imagined any of this would happen. And I imagined it a lot. Or I used to."

Wow. As Samantha absorbed that bit of information, she sipped at her Diet Coke. She couldn't remember ever imagining a reunion with her mom, except in a nebulous, giving-the-woman-the-finger-on-her-wedding-day kind of way. Seeing that woman sitting there now, she was kind of glad Anne still wasn't sure about all this, because it helped her find her own balance. Reexplaining the logic of it all, hearing it all said aloud, made it more solid. More real.

"You think he orchestrated all this? Arranged for me to hire you? Because I had the same thought. And it's pretty scary." Anne looked into the bottom of her empty glass again. "Why would he go to all this trouble for either a painting or to teach you a lesson? It's beyond extreme, even for him. I was hoping you would convince me all this was just a coincidence, after all."

"I've been thinking a lot about that, actually. And a couple of months ago," Sam said, "Martin basically forced me into a gig to rob—"

"Samantha," Rick cut in, his tone sharp. "We're keeping padding between you and trouble, if you'll recall."

"She knows who Martin is, Brit," Samantha reminded him with a brief glare. "Plus, the NYPD thanked me after." Yeah, she got his caution. But at some point, if they made it through this, she liked the idea of just…telling the truth to Anne. If Rick was jealous of that, well, he'd have to get over it. "Martin forced me into a gig robbing the Met," she started over. "I turned it on its head, brought in the cops, and Martin had to do some serious scrambling to keep from going back to prison. He'd made a deal with Interpol to turn in other thieves, so a couple of years ago they faked his death in prison and pulled him out to roam free. Idiots." Samantha took a breath. "Anyway, the Met gig pissed him off, because he didn't know what hit him, and because he thought he was pulling me back into the business—not that I was going to send him running for his life."

"Bradley always did have a healthy sense of his own superiority," Anne muttered. "And a keen desire to keep his own skin safe."

"Yeah. So anyway, I think this is him trying to one-up me. He looked you up, planted that note to spook you, maybe had a fake phone call with Joe Viscanti and brought up my name so I would be on his mind or something, and here we are. Like I said, yesterday right after I left you Martin pulled up in a stolen car and warned me off the job. Again. I played it like I figured he was just trying to prove that he was the king, but I'm really starting to think that his end game is to say, 'Hey, guess what, Anne's your mom,' and then wreck the two of us while he takes whatever it is he's after from the Adgerton collection. A double tap."

"So all of this…crap is because you dented his ego?"

Samantha tipped up her soda and took a drink. "I can't quite figure all the angles yet, but yeah, I think it's to teach me a lesson."

"To teach *you* a lesson. I'm just what, then, incidental?"

"You're integral," Rick said.

"As the damn red herring, or gun on the wall, or *deus ex machina* or whatever," Anne snapped, slapping the arm of the chair with her free hand.

"I think we can all agree that Martin's an ass." Rick stood, handed over his untouched glass of wine to Anne, and sat again. "I can't even imagine how much pain he's caused you, Anne, but no part of me thinks he presently has anything charitable in mind."

Samantha slid her hand over to grip his. That was Rick, feeling compassion for the party that had been truly injured in all this mess. For her, it had been disbelief and shock and some anger at Martin, but for Anne, who'd had her toddler stolen from her and probably figured Sarah was dead at worst and never coming back at best, this must have been a horror. And on top of that, little Sarah wasn't a senator or a ballerina or whatever it was moms wanted their daughters to become. Nope, little Sarah was a barely retired jewel thief.

"I've put out some feelers, to see if anybody knows what he's after from the collection," she said aloud. "He generally doesn't take a job unless he has a buyer for something. That doesn't mean he won't pocket a few extra things to fence, but there's got to be someone after a particular item of Adgerton's."

"You have the list," Anne commented, sipping at her second

glass of wine. "I don't know anything particular about any of the items other than what the provenance or the family has told me. There are some extremely valuable items, of course, but nothing in particular that screams 'Bradley Martin' at me."

"Did you take Martin as your married name?" Rick asked, even though he and Donner would have discovered that by now, already. Digging again, then, or looking for lies. Jeez, and she'd thought she was the paranoid one.

"Yes, I did. After he emptied out the collection I was tending and stole my daughter, I reverted to my maiden name. I would never have been able to stay in this field otherwise." She blew out her breath. "Even so, I had to work at a few...lesser-known establishments before Sotheby's agreed to hire me. This will ruin my career. Again. And I'm running out of names."

"I know that feeling," Samantha commented. "But he's not going to ruin anything, because even if we don't know what he's after, we do know he's going to hit the collection, and we know how he means to put me—us—off our game. And I happen to know that short of taking a dump truck and driving it through the front entrance, Martin's going to have a hard time breaking into that building. And while he likes to break stuff, he definitely doesn't like getting caught doing it."

Actually, maybe a cement pillar or two in front of the front and back entrances might be a good idea, now that she considered it. If they had time to get them set into place. Even a pit of wet cement might slow Martin down if he decided to go Godzilla on the Victorian.

"What do we do, then? And what do we,"—and Anne gestured between the two of them—"do next?"

Samantha had been working on both of those ideas all day. "As far as the Adgerton collection, we start bringing in the items tomorrow just like we planned," she said, trying to ignore the male wall of annoyance sitting beside her. Yeah, Rick didn't like her spilling secrets. She didn't like it, either. But at some point, somebody needed to give ground. And under these circumstances, she figured it needed to be her.

"Isn't that like parading hens in front of a fox?" Anne asked, beginning to look like she was going to need a third glass of wine.

"It is. To Martin, it'll look like I'm straight-up ignoring his threats, that all I see is him challenging my abilities." That, though, touched on the thing that had been bugging her about all this, and she sat forward. "If you want to keep working with me, that is. This is your gig, after all, and me being here is going to make all this tougher."

"Do you think Bradley would back down if you went back to Florida?"

"He might. If this really is about putting me in my place, which I think it is, he might back off."

"Oh."

"If he's got in his head that using you is how he's going to take me out, though, he's probably not going to give up poking at both of us. It might get even more personal, for you at least. I've got him pretty well walled off from Rick and me. With actual walls."

"I don't want to even think about him lurking at the edges of my life," Anne stated, clenching the stem of the wine glass. "He needs to go away."

"On that, we agree one hundred percent," Rick said. "If it can be done without endangering Samantha."

Ultimately, it might just have to endanger her. However she'd originally stepped into the burglary business, by the time she'd retired she'd become a willing, fully cognizant, participant. If her dad decided to drag her down with him, she would sink. The idea of that scared the shit out of her, but being caught had always been a possible consequence of participating.

"Agreed." Anne nodded.

"Even if it can't be," she said aloud, before everyone could agree to sacrifice their own peace of mind for her freedom, "Montenegro is nice. And Brunei hardly has any typhoons."

"Why those two countries?" Anne asked.

Rick shifted, his fingers tightening around Samantha's. "No extradition treaties with the U.S."

Anne blinked. "That's...scary that you know that."

There were a half-dozen other countries, too, including one or two where Rick had made a point to do some investing. Just in case, he'd said. Yeah, in case they needed to flee the U.S. God, what a mess that would make of his life. And it was almost worse that he'd anticipated that, had shifted some of his wealth around to avoid having all his assets frozen if it came down to it. Him, the guy born and bred into money and who'd made a shitload more of it than he'd had when he started, was willing to restructure his entire life just to keep her in it.

"I just found you," Anne said, putting her free hand over her heart. "We need to find a way to stop Bradley without forcing you to live in a hut somewhere."

"Huts are cool," Samantha quipped. "We could be Gilligan and the Skipper."

"Maryanne and the Professor," Rick corrected.

"Thurston and Eunice 'Lovey' Howell," Anne put in.

Samantha's heart did a weird thump. "You know Lovey's real name," she breathed.

Anne's cheeks reddened. "I used to win bar trivia contests," she said. "Quite a few of them."

Rick squeezed her fingers once more, then released her to stand. "You two are definitely related," he commented. "I'm going to go check on dinner."

10

"So you—*you*—don't have a source who knows what Martin's after," Samantha said into her phone, her gaze out the rear door of the Victorian as another crate left the transport truck. "You could make a guess, you know. A pretty good one. You just won't. That isn't helpful, Stoney."

Glancing up from his own phone as he leaned against the wall beside her, Richard continued typing out his question to Tom Donner. If they involved the local police or the FBI his own ability to control the situation would lessen considerably, but he refused to be caught flat-footed. The more contingency plans they had in place, the better.

When Samantha tapped off her own call and shoved the phone into her jeans pocket, Richard dumped his own into his coat. "No luck?" he asked.

She blew out her breath. "I don't know if it's a professional pride thing, like his head'll explode if he makes a wrong guess about what a thief might be after, or if he wants to stay out of it, or if he really doesn't have a clue," she whispered, glancing at the horde of Sotheby's security guards escorting the pieces in from the trucks and up the stairs to their display areas. "But he won't even frickin' tell me if I'm playing three- or ten-card monte, so I got nothin'."

"It could all just be a bluff, you know," he reminded her, even though he wasn't wasting any energy believing that. "Martin could be in Palm Beach right now, stealing Picassos off our walls at Solano Dorado."

"I wish." She scowled. "How screwed up is that?"

"I'm actually more annoyed that he's the reason you can't just focus on your familial relationships. You've found your mother, Samantha."

She frowned. "Are we supposed to be in the park with her pushing me on a swing or something?" she countered, moving around him to shove a stack of boxes out of the way. "I wouldn't be here, and I wouldn't have met up with her at all, if Martin hadn't done his voodoo. Figure that one out for me."

"I can't. I'm here against orders, as it is."

"Yeah, I noticed that. You think you have a better chance of catching sight of Martin than I do?"

After the way she'd picked his pockets the other day, his own sense of capability where thievery things were concerned had been rather bruised, but that had probably been her intention. "I'm here in a support role. You know, someone who can verbally lambast without making waves in the theft prevention community."

"I can appreciate that," she returned, her expression easing just a touch. "But what I also don't want spreading in the theft-doing *or* theft-prevention community is that I need my pretty British man with me when I'm doing important stuff."

Perhaps she made a good point, but he didn't like it. It wasn't just the being referred to as decoration, but the implication that he was, essentially, making things worse by being there. "Then think of me as a weapon," he murmured. "I have the heads of at least three law-enforcement departments on my phone, and I'm not afraid to dial."

"Hm." Samantha sidestepped, coming up behind one of the Sotheby's workers. "If you take out your phone in here again," she muttered, "I'm going to feed it to you."

The big man turned his head to look at her. "I'm not—"

"I don't care if your house is on fire and your wife is having quadruplets," she interrupted. "Your phone does not leave your pocket inside this building. Is that clear?"

He looked like he wanted to argue, but Samantha just stood there, arms at her sides, nearly a foot shorter than he was, and met his gaze. Finally, he blew out his breath. "Okay. Sorry."

"Thanks."

"You think he's working with Martin?" Richard whispered when she returned to her post against the wall.

"Nope. I think he's playing online poker. But I'm not going to risk anybody taking photos of where the displays are, or what's in each one."

It wasn't often that he would admit, even to himself, that he was in over his head. Today, though, at best he was a curiosity, and at worst he was distracting Samantha when her attention needed to be—and for the most part was—elsewhere. Leaving, though, meant agreeing that he was useless, and that just didn't sit well. At all.

"Perhaps I'll give Walter a call myself, then. From outside, of course."

"Have at it. And you can tell him I said he's pissing me off."

Leaving voluntarily was better than her literally kicking him to the curb, but not by much. Outside he tapped his authorization card against the panel, alerting the system that he'd left the building, before he removed his phone from his pocket and called up not Walter's, but Tom's, name.

"Hey," Tom's Texas drawl answered immediately. "I'm glad you're still alive. I was beginning to wonder."

"You received my text?"

"Yeah, about two minutes ago."

"It's not the first time I've asked, Tom. Have you heard anyone discussing the Adgerton collection?"

"Are you guys fighting or something? No chitchat?"

"I am feeling somewhat useless at the moment. I don't like feeling useless."

"Gotcha. You *do* have a business to inspect in Passaic if you're looking for work. You know, the one that sells the cool board shorts but has a terrible customer service reputation?"

"'Stoked.' Yes, I remember. Not today."

"I'm just saying, Rick, Jellicoe doesn't tromp into *your* business. That's the one thing I like about her. So you tr—"

"Well, fuck you and the stupid high horse you rode in on. *I* would like to be able to turn Martin Jellicoe aside before he gets arrested and rats out his daughter to save his own skin."

Silence. "Okay. I get it. And I'm trying. But other than calling everybody in my old-timey Rolodex and asking if they know about the Adgerton exhibit and if they've heard of anything interesting coming up for sale, I don't really have an in. I'm a corporate attorney with a reputation for being a straight shooter, Rick."

Drawing in a slow breath, Richard closed his eyes for a few seconds. "I value you and your reputation," he said. "I won't apologize for pushing, but I understand why you draw the line where you do."

"Rick, now you're making me feel bad. If you give me a clue where to look, I'll dig into every art collector on the east coast."

"I don't have any clues. Yet. Just keep fishing, and see if anyone nibbles."

Tom sighed. "Will do. Just be careful, okay? Of you, Jellicoe, and your reputation. You've spent a lot of time and effort on carving one out for yourself."

Ending the call, Richard paced to the Victorian's doorway

and back again. He did understand Tom's reluctance to skirt this close to the edge of nefarious activities. Samantha referred to Donner as a boy scout, and he'd actually been one. And he had a wife and three children he wanted to be able to look in the eye.

Richard, however, didn't have any such qualms where Samantha and her safety were concerned. Scrolling through his contact list, he tapped Walter Barstone's name. The phone rang three times before the line connected with a noncommittal, "What?"

"Walter," he said crisply. "I'm assuming you feel fairly confident that if Samantha is arrested as a result of Martin's meddling, she won't carry any tales about you. I wanted you to know that I don't feel any such loyalty. In fact, if you leave her hanging here when she's trying to do the right thing by her own mother, I'm going to make a point of adding some difficulties to your life."

"Hey, Rick," the fence's voice returned, dry and even. "Good morning to you, too. Martin doesn't trust me, and he's got contacts I wouldn't touch. I'm digging. All I've got so far is a guy in Amsterdam who collects Alexander Calder kinetic sculptures and who's fallen off Sotheby's guest lists because he doesn't like other bidders—to the point that he's set guys' cars on fire."

Richard didn't ask how Walter knew that the Adgerton exhibit featured two Calder sculptures; he wasn't supposed to know that, either. While he didn't collect them himself, he did know that one had sold for two-and-a-half million a year or so ago. "Would Martin take a gig like that?"

"In the old days? No. Now? Maybe. Especially if it put him into a showdown with Sam. He really seems to want one."

"Why didn't you tell her about this?"

"First, it could be a red herring, and second, I don't want to point her in the wrong direction. She's better than Martin, but that man carries a grudge. I'm already on his shit list. So are you, if you hadn't realized that."

"I figured I might be. I'm not losing any sleep over it."

"Yeah, well, you live in a fortress, but don't forget that Sam managed to break in there at least twice." He took a breath. "I guess what I'm saying is I would've stopped working with Martin a long time ago if I wasn't worried about where Sam would have ended up with only him to rely on. I thought... maybe he took her because her mom was a bitch he couldn't deal with any longer. I also knew he had no damn business raising a kid."

This was a bit of a conundrum. Thanking Walter for having a hand in raising Samantha, when together the fence and Martin had both used her as a thief, didn't sit well. But Richard could agree that with Martin's influence alone, things could have been much, much worse. "I'll pass on your information about the Calder pieces to Samantha. Don't hold out on her, Walter; we both know she can handle whatever gets thrown at her, and I'd rather she feel more comfortable talking to you than going around you."

"Yeah, well, likewise."

"What's the name of the Amsterdam guy?"

"Rick, I—"

"Name."

"Shit. Daan Van der Berg. And I hope you know that you two are ruining my future employment prospects."

"Good. Retirement would suit you."

The call clicked off, and Rick texted Tom. "Drop the prior. I need a direct phone number for Daan Van der Berg in Amsterdam, and an idea of his portfolio." That done, he dropped his phone back into his pocket.

There. That was something that was definitely in Tom's wheelhouse, and it wasn't even remotely illegal or unethical. Walter might have just been throwing out random names, trying to get both him and Samantha out of his figurative hair, but Richard didn't think so. The fence knew what was at stake, and he damned well knew the consequences of Martin Jellicoe winning this round.

His own next step should have been to go tell Samantha what he'd discovered, but at this point having a name and even a probable focus of the theft didn't change all that much. They knew Martin meant to rob the exhibit.

The man he truly needed to talk to was Martin Jellicoe, or Bradley Martin, or whatever the hell his actual name was. That, though, came with its own difficulties. Not just finding the man, who was slipperier than a hagfish, but figuring out what to do with him. Getting him arrested would be simple, but that would then allow Martin to flap his gums to any law enforcement agent willing to listen—which would endanger Samantha's freedom.

Bribery was an option, he supposed, though he had no reason to believe Martin needed money. Samantha didn't; she had a bank account or two herself overseas and more than enough money to vanish somewhere and live very comfortably with or without him for the rest of her life. He assumed Martin was flush as well, since the man had apparently stolen every vehicle he'd ever driven and had never owned any of the houses in which he'd lived.

That left the third option. That one, though, he didn't care to consider too closely. Samantha would never forgive him for it, and while he felt the reasons would be justified, it also opened up a pathway he wasn't certain he wanted to begin walking. Once he'd come up with a good-enough reason for a murder, well, it made him a murderer.

In the business world, three options were a plentitude. In Samantha's world—former world—three options simply wasn't enough. Where, though, was he supposed to come up with more?

"It would help, Miss Sam, if you could point me in the right direction," Aubrey said, shifting his phone from one ear to the other as he pulled out his credit card to pay for the deli sandwich he'd ordered.

"That's the tricky part," Samantha answered, and he could almost hear her scowl over the phone. "I don't have a direction. All I have is a pending sense of doom—like we know the Huns are coming and we know we locked all the windows, but oops, we forgot about the front door."

"Thank you, Margaret," he said, nodding as he balanced the phone against his shoulder, the sandwich in one hand and an iced tea in the other. "Well, tell me what you've installed, and I'll see if I notice anything you might have missed."

There was more to her sudden anxiety than just nerves, because over the past year he'd come to know her well enough to be aware that the confidence she had in her work was well-founded. That kind of stuff just didn't worry her.

Aubrey took a breath as he sat at one of the diner's tables. This part of his job was only supposed to be a cover for his real job. *Shit.* "Or I could fly up there and take a look at it with my own peepers. A second—or third—set of eyes to look over things might give you a couple extra minutes of, you know, sleep."

"I thought you were happy being the office guy. Charlie with all his dirty, sweaty angels."

"I like being the office guy," he said, snorting at the idea of Samantha's growing crew of misfits and uncaught felons being angels. "That doesn't mean that I wouldn't be a better office guy if I went out and took a look at what you're doing once in a while. And this one's important. A contract with Sotheby's... Man, that could change things." He paused, sending a few curse words at himself. "Barstone and Mr. Donner got to join you in Scotland."

That sounded extremely whiny, even when he'd thought it might come across as a little needy. Damn, but he preferred charming someone over pleading with them. Being there might not make any difference, anyway. But at least it would be something he could show as a receipt to the FBI and Ling Wu.

"Really, Aubrey?" Samantha sighed, making him wince. "Fine. Catch a flight tomorrow morning, and get yourself a room at the Manhattan. Mention me to get the business discount. Bring one of the infrared cameras and a kit bag, since you're coming."

"Will do, Miss Sam."

"You guys are going to have to quit it with the jealousy crap, Aubrey. I'm the boss now, not a slab of bacon."

"I didn't mean it that way. I'm just…I'd like a chance to step up, you know?" he floundered, jabbing a finger into the top slice of his toasted sourdough.

"I get it. See you tomorrow."

The call disconnected, and he lowered his phone to the table. This secret agent business was becoming even less satisfying. Samantha trusted him, when she had no real reason to do so, and now he wasn't just observing. Nope, now he'd just bought himself a ticket to spar with the champ—and he wasn't at all sure he wanted to fight. Plus, even if she hadn't had Rick Addison in her corner, he wasn't at all sure he would win.

She hadn't even told him why this job was making her so anxious. For all he knew, she might have smelled the FBI sniffing around and when he arrived in Manhattan, she would be asking him to make some calls and find out if there was an open investigation around this collection, or around her. And then he had no idea what the hell he was going to tell her. As he'd tried to explain to Dean and Ling, he had no evidence that she'd done anything wrong. This, though, was the first time he was going out of his way to look for proof to the contrary.

As he ate his sandwich, he made himself flight reservations and booked a room at Addison's hotel. He'd said he meant to be helpful, so he googled cutting-edge anti-theft devices and a couple of articles on how the Louvre protected their artwork, plus the statistics for Sotheby's thefts, attempted and successful. Most of the stuff he knew already, but the more background he had, the more competent he would sound.

Once he'd returned to his late-model blue BMW he placed another call, this one to inform Wu Ling that he would be in New York for the next few days to take a closer look at what Samantha was doing for Sotheby's. He made arrangements to check in with the Manhattan office, too, just because it was good manners.

It all made him feel like he needed to take a shower. That creeping unpleasantness wouldn't go away until he'd either proven that Samantha wasn't the thief the FBI thought she was, or that she was. Either way it needed to happen soon, because the two sides pounding on each other in his head was going to give him an aneurism.

"AND WHY IS Pendleton coming to Manhattan?" Rick asked, sitting back in his chair, his coffee cup cradled in both hands.

"I don't know," Samantha answered. "I think he got jealous when Donner and Stoney got called to Scotland and he didn't. So I'll have him look over things at the Victorian House and see if there's anything else I should be charging Sotheby's for."

"What are they all, twelve?"

"I can only answer for Stoney and Aubrey, and the answer to that is yes, I think so. I get that I'm cool and awesome and everything, but I don't want a fan club. You have one of those, and those women are evil."

"I didn't ask for a fan club," he retorted, sipping his coffee and pretending not to look at the clock in the kitchen. "They did that all on their own."

"Well, same with my two guys. You have to explain Donner, because I can't." Bending over her phone, she flipped through the cameras, internal and external, at the exhibit house. They'd gotten about a third of Adgerton's items moved in, with a couple of delays because people hadn't used their damned access cards yesterday, so today they would hopefully get the rest of the shiny stuff secured in its display cases.

And then it would be time to wait. And sweat. The shit of it all was that Martin knew that, knew that it was actually easier to be a bad guy. Good guys were supposed to win every time, but bad guys only had to win once. It wasn't fair, really.

"Would you rather live here in New York without the Donners, then?" Rick asked, shaking her out of her momentary career regrets.

"No. Of course not. But we haven't decided if we're even moving here. I don't see why you needed to shake things up with them when nothing is decided."

"Because everyone needs time to think and consider," he returned, eyeing her. "Whether it happens or not, if we go, I would like them to move with us. I can't just spring that on them."

Powerful guys just expected their friends slash employees to relocate whenever they did, she supposed. In a way it was fair, because Rick had bought Solano Dorado after the Donners had taken a house in Palm Beach. He'd followed them, then. But the Donners had three kids, one of them in college but the other two with a couple more years of junior and high school in front of them. That complicated things.

She complicated things. Firstly, because she couldn't make up her damn mind, because just when she thought she was figuring out the straight life it threw Martin Jellicoe at her, or a marriage proposal, or a couple of impressionable kids who she really didn't want thinking her old life had been cool. Even if parts of it had been.

Her phone chimed, and she opened up her texts. Person unknown had sent her a four-word text. "Some nice-looking stuff." That didn't sound good.

"What?" Rick asked, setting aside his coffee and leaning forward.

Man, she was going to have to work harder at her poker face, if he was reading her that easily. "I don't know," she said. "My dad, I think, trying to rile me up." She showed him the text.

"Ignore it," he advised, sitting back again. "You can't bait someone who isn't paying you any attention."

That was some good advice. Samantha set the phone down, returning to her morning donut and scrambled eggs. Yep, it was nice having Andre around to do his chef stuff. Otherwise, it would have been Pop Tarts for breakfasts. "Okay. I'm ignoring it. Pretty random anyway, right?"

"Could well be a spam ad. You could just block the number."

Samantha took a breath, ripping another piece of donut off with her teeth. "Hardly worth the effort."

"True. Do you want another diet Coke?"

"No, I'm good. Thanks."

Her phone chimed again. *Dammit.* Maybe Rick was right. Maybe it was a two-part spam ad for butt enhancers or something. Waiting a beat, she turned over the phone and looked down at the screen. "Crap."

"Not spam?"

"Now it says, 'You'll get the rest of it moved in today, I assume?'"

His jaw clenched. "In all fairness, it could just be someone with a wrong number, and they're helping a friend move."

They both knew that wasn't what was going on, but the pretending at least reminded her that Martin was working very hard not to say anything concrete. Nothing that could come back to bite him later. Just a couple of vaguely worded texts meant to rattle her. Well, she wasn't rattled. It was barely street-level information to know that the Adgerton stuff was nice, and that it was being moved into the Victorian house. The viewings were starting in three days, after all.

She tapped her fingers against the tablecloth.

"Don't respond," he said, pointing a strip of bacon at her.

"I know that. Jeez. I'm just…I could say something really clever and biting. I hate missing a chance to be clever."

Rick snorted. "You are cleverness personified. The goddess of cleverness."

"I'd settle for patron saint of thieves and comedians, but thanks. And let him think I did block him or something. Jerk."

"I'm still amenable to joining you again today, you know," he said, flipping over the newspaper at his elbow like he'd spent more than three seconds looking at it since it arrived. "Just for another set of eyes. I could sit in the security room and stare at the camera feeds."

She wanted him there, or at least close by, because he was sure-fire backup. Nobody watched her six like Rick did. "You know, he could be taunting me to get you out of *here* so he can rob you. I mean, you do have a Degas on the wall behind me. Among other things."

Rick looked at her for a second. "Damnation, Samantha."

"Welcome to paranoid world. Enjoy your stay."

Her phone chimed a third time. Jumping, she picked it up, then blew out her breath. "Aubrey's landed. He'll be at the Victorian house by ten, he says."

"Good. At least he can provide another pair of eyes."

"Yeah." Reaching over, she snagged his last strip of bacon and stood. "I should get going. You're working from here today now, I assume?"

"No. But I'm calling in Wilder. I feel the need for a butler."

She couldn't help laughing. "I won't even tease you about it, because having somebody here all day will make me feel a little better, too."

"Good. Especially since a Martin Jellicoe fake-out to rob *me* hadn't occurred to me until you said that." Standing, Rick reached for his suit jacket.

"I doubt that's his plan, but I'm trying to anticipate everything." She slipped her hand around his waist as they headed for the elevator. "Give me a ride to work, will you?"

"That saves me from insisting that I accompany you there, anyway," he muttered, leaning sideways to kiss her temple.

Her phone chimed again. She lifted it up—and stopped so quickly Rick nearly lost his balance. There was no text this time. Only a photo of a small marble sculpture of a hand, taken through glass and on a red velvet background. One black metal corner showed at the edge of the photo.

"This is from my damned exhibit," she growled. "I locked that display case myself, yesterday."

Rick grabbed her gesturing hand so he could look at the phone. "That doesn't mean he broke in," he stated as she yanked her arm free and sprinted toward the door and the elevator beyond.

"Oh, he didn't," she snapped, seething. The damn elevator was of course on the first floor, and she jammed the button with her thumb. "Someone else took that photo and sent it to him. Someone who was in there yesterday. Someone Sotheby's hired, and whose name I fucking know. I bought them Danishes. The good kind."

Inside information. Martin had always gone for that advantage when he could, even if—as it usually did—it involved seducing some dumbass woman who thought he was a dashing whatever it was he was pretending to be. These days it had likely taken a bribe, and that irked her even more. Losing your mind over love was something she could understand. Hell, she'd lost her mind a year ago. Greed was no damn excuse. At all.

11

Saturday, 8:42 a.m.

I t was surreal, Anne thought, the way an off-center photo of a lovely piece of art could make her stomach tie itself into knots, her pulse pound so hard she thought she could be on her way to a stroke or a heart attack, and her throat close up so she couldn't pull in enough air.

She looked at the photo again, gripping Sam's phone so hard she was surprised the cover, with its illustration of Godzilla on the back, didn't crack and fall off. "Who did this?" she forced out, her voice a wavering hiss.

"That's what I'm going to find out." Sam glanced over her shoulder as security and Sotheby's employees filed in and out of the elevator or climbed the stairs with smaller items in tow. "I'm probably going to exceed my authority in a minute, so either back me up or stop me now. And no mother-daughter shit. Martin can't know that we know."

No mother-daughter shit. With what she'd just seen, that comment should have just passed by her brain to be absorbed later with everything else, but it caught her attention and demanded to be looked at, front and center. "I'll back you up," Anne said aloud.

Sam was mad. It didn't take any great empathy or insight to get that. Somehow Bradley or Martin or whatever the hell his name was had gotten around her, and Sam didn't like it. It wasn't just that, though. Sam and her father had gone from partners to rivals, and now to enemies. That angry streak, the dislike over being shown up, the hatred of having to admit an error—Anne recognized that. "This is not about your ego, you know," she said aloud, belatedly wondering if she'd just ended any chance at reconciliation with her daughter.

Sam stopped mid step and turned around again. "It's about me doing my job," she stated, her jaw stiff. "And one of these guys is getting fired today for taking enough money to make him think sneaking some photos was worth the risk of losing his job. Or her job, but I'd bet it's one of the guys." She took a breath. "If it was my ego I was trying to satisfy, I'd be hanging that guy off the roof by his heels instead of firing him."

Anne blinked. "Sam, that's—"

"That's an exaggeration," she muttered, stalking off again. "In my mind I would be, though." She put two fingers to her mouth and whistled. "Hey! Everybody within the sound of my voice! In the lobby! Now!"

That wasn't very subtle, but aside from what she'd been told already, Anne had the feeling that her daughter had moved in the world of thugs and thieves and other dangerous people for a very long time. Certainly being surrounded by fifteen large, muscular men and a handful of very capable-looking women didn't seem to intimidate her in the least.

"What's up, Sam?" Jamie asked, on his chest an exploding Death Star and a fleeing X-Wing. For a second she reflected that if her daughter's obsession had been *Star Wars* rather than

Godzilla, even Michael would have to be brushing up on his George Lucas trivia.

"Phones out, everybody. Screen up, on your palm. Now."

"Hey, we said we wouldn't use 'em in here. You can't take our phones."

"I'm not," she stated. "I'm looking at them."

"What the hell? This ain't a dictatorship. You can't make us—"

"You heard her," Anne broke in. "Phones out, face-up, in one hand." Why that would help she didn't know, but she'd said she would back up her daughter. No mother-daughter shit, though, whatever that was.

"Come on, Miss Hughes, we aren't—"

"Now."

One by one they produced their phones. When all of them were visible, Sam walked up to the ragged half circle. "A flip phone, Carl?" she said. "You can go back to work."

"I like my phone," the big security guard complained, pocketing it again.

She likewise dismissed eight more of them with barely a glance, sending them back to finishing the placement of the Adgerton items. As she walked back up the row, a tall older man with an impressive mane of graying hair stopped outside the locked front door and waved. "Are you expecting someone?" Anne asked aloud.

"Does he look like Colonel Sanders without the moustache?"

Anne looked again. "More or less. George Hamilton, maybe. His suit is blue."

"He's with me. Let him in, will you, Anne?"

"Of course."

While Sam gave the side-eye to the remaining Sotheby's and security employees, Anne backed up to the door and opened it with her key card. "Hello," she said, as the man joined her inside.

"Ma'am," he returned in a soft drawl. "You would be Miss Anne Hughes, I assume?"

"I would be."

"Aubrey Pendleton, at your service. I work for Miss Samantha. Is she…" He trailed off as he caught sight of Sam. "Ah. It's at least a ten," he said in a louder voice.

Without looking at him Sam nodded, then excused four more workers. That left five people, all men. However she'd decided on their innocence, Anne was glad it hadn't been one of the ladies. Falling for Martin or Bradley or whoever he was had proved to be a painful, scarring experience, and she didn't wish it on anyone else. Ever.

"Ten what?" she whispered.

"The iPhone model," Mr. Pendleton murmured back.

"How do you—"

"The reflection of the flash in the corner of the photo," he went on, obviously anticipating her question. "The camera lens configuration is an iPhone, and a more recent model than 10."

"That's impressive. Well done, Mr. Pendleton."

"It wasn't me. Miss Samantha spotted it and sent the photo to me to match lenses." He held up his own phone, and she looked at the picture again.

She might have noticed the slight reflection in the top left corner, but then again, she might not have done so. Not in time to figure out who'd taken the picture, certainly. "Well."

"She doesn't miss much."

"All right," Sam said, "turn them over."

"This is stupid," Drew, another member of the security team, complained. "We have work to do. It's a damn Saturday, so you're paying us time-and-a-half for nothing right now."

"Not for nothing," Sam answered, stopping in front of him. "Turn over your phone."

"No. Why do you want to see the back of my fucking phone?"

Before he could close his fingers around it, Sam's hand darted forward, and she snatched it away from him. Taking a step backward, she flipped it over herself.

"That's not yours," he growled, clenching his empty fist.

"That's a lovely confederate flag you've got there." Sam stayed out of his reach, then slapped the phone against his chest. "You're a jerk, but you can go back to work until Anne has a chat with your supervisor."

"Which I will," Anne added, making a note and then gesturing at Mr. Pendleton to let her look at the photo again. She couldn't make out anything further in the picture than the multiple out-of-focus circles of the lenses. *Ah.* That would be the point. A confederate flag would have showed up as a blur of color, anyway.

While Drew obviously didn't know how to react to all that, Sam jabbing a finger toward the elevator sent him on his way. The amount of self-confidence she wielded simply left most people powerless to do anything but exactly what she told them to. Amazing. With Bradley she had thought it charm, but she could see it now, though less arrogantly, in Sam. She knew what she was doing, and other people responded to that.

Four men remained, all of them beginning to eye each other. Sam stepped forward again, looking at the backs of the phones. One had a photo of his kids beneath a clear plastic case, and she sent him back to work as well. The other three were plain black, two cases and one just the phone itself.

"What now?" Anne whispered.

If Mr. Pendleton found it odd that he'd immediately become her confidante, he didn't show it. "I have no idea," he whispered back. "This is the part I think might be magic."

She couldn't help her abrupt grin. At least she wasn't the only one baffled by all of this. Sam didn't seem to be, but she was also facing down three men, all of whom were taller and broader than she was. Anne supposed the Sotheby's security team would come to the rescue, but it would take a moment for them to realize what was going on and another second to decide whether they wanted to get into a brawl or not.

"What now?" One of the three, Something Stefano, kept his phone out in front of him, but he didn't look happy. None of them, though, looked happy.

Sam lifted her walkie-talkie. "Rhee, which of these three was on the third floor between noon and two o'clock yesterday?" She glanced over her shoulder at Anne. "Angle of the sun."

Of course Sam had noticed the angle of the sun. And the reflection of the camera lens, and the reflection of the phone protector. For a second Anne had a flash of thought about what Christmases would have been like, with Sam no doubt guessing the contents of every gift the moment they went under the tree.

"That would be Albert Stephano," the security specialist returned, the sound echoing a little as other walkie-talkies around them picked it up.

"So what?" Stephano retorted. "That's where I was supposed to be."

"You know we have all the footage, right?" Sam replied. "You walking up, eyeing the security camera, making sure your back was to it, your arms moving a little, and then you stretching like you're the most innocent guy in the world before you walk off into the hallway."

He glared at her, and Anne found herself measuring heights and reaches and relative strength—none of which favored her daughter. "If you knew it was me you were after all along," Stefano finally rasped, "why go through all this, bitch?"

"Well," Sam said, putting a finger on her chin, "first, I wanted to know if you had the nards to come forward and save the rest of these guys a scare. Second, somebody knocked the camera in that room off-kilter yesterday, which I imagine was your doing, and I don't have footage of anything but your feet. So, pffft, you outed yourself."

"Bitch," he growled again, his hands folding into fists. He lunged forward.

"Aubrey?"

The man standing beside Anne pulled something out of his coat pocket. A moment later Stefano lay twitching on the ground, wires leading from his chest to Mr. Pendleton's hand. Anne yelped and leaped backward with what she was sure was a very ungainly motion.

Sam lifted the walkie-talkie again. "Marv? Come on in. And bring your cuffs."

A handful of seconds later, Marv pounded up from the direction of the security room. "I could've done that," he stated, looking with plain envy at the taser Mr. Pendleton held.

"This way you won't have as much paperwork," Sam said, squatting down as the security guard cuffed the hired security agent. "How much did he pay you?"

Stefano sniffed, rolling upright. "Not enough for me to put up with this shit."

"Hm. Maybe think about that while Anne decides whether Sotheby's is going to press charges or not and we're waiting for the cops. And then think about how mad I am that you tried to fuck up my first job with Sotheby's."

"It was a photo. Just a damn picture. I didn't steal anything."

"See that sign?" Sam pointed over her shoulder at the red-lettered sign on a white background affixed to one side wall. "'Absolutely no photography is permitted inside this establishment,'" she read without looking at it. "'Violators will be prosecuted.' You broke the sign law."

It abruptly occurred to Anne that the police had been called. She looked at Sam. Sarah. No, Samantha did fit her better. Or she'd grown into the name Bradley had given her, rather. But that didn't signify, because Sam and the police didn't belong anywhere near each other. "Why don't you get back to our item installation?" she suggested, hefting her iPad. "Marv and I can take it from here." She glanced sideways. "And Mr. Pendleton, as well, since he had the taser, I suppose."

"I wouldn't have it any other way," the gentleman drawled. "I'll catch up with you when we're finished here, Miss Samantha."

Sam nodded, turning to the two guys who remained. "You're all clear. Thanks for hanging out and helping me catch this guy. Sorry for putting you in the middle of it, though."

"Are you kidding me?" one of them said. "You guys tased Albert 'Big Balls' Stefano. Somebody's gonna buy me a drink tonight when I tell that story."

Chuckling, Sam clapped both men on the back and joined them as they walked up the stairs. *Good.* However ballsy she was, at least she knew to be elsewhere when the police arrived. And now Anne had a moment to worry over why no one had mentioned the camera trouble yesterday. That seemed like something she should have been told.

If that was Sam's ego getting in the way, they were going to have to have a chat. No one's ego was allowed to trump the security here. Not while Bradley Martin Jellicoe was slinking around the neighborhood.

ONE BAD GUY, stopped. Samantha took a breath as the next load of items for auction emerged from the elevator. Mad as she was at both "Big Balls" Stefano and Martin, she'd made a mistake, too. It didn't matter that with big display cases moving in and ladders coming up and down to adjust lights, cameras had been jostled for the last three days. As soon as a misalignment was noticed, it was corrected, but she'd let it go yesterday without investigating. In fact, other than noting that it had taken four minutes for the problem to be noticed and corrected, she'd ignored it.

Martin, with Stefano's help, had gotten something past her, and she hadn't even realized it until the photo had appeared on her phone. That was bad, and stupid, and an idiot mistake she would never be making again.

If it were up to her, all these guys would be off the job until after the auction. If Martin had gotten to one of them, he might have gotten to two, or three or five, more. She'd known forever that the weakest link in any security system was the human bits, and she'd still let Sotheby's decide which of their employees and contracted security personnel would be here at the Victorian house.

Maybe if she'd been raised straight and had hired employees herself who'd only walked on the legal side, she might have felt more confident about doing deeper checks on the people Sotheby's had hired for this event. She blew out her breath. And maybe they would have accused her of paranoia and over-reaching her authority. It wasn't like she could just fly half her Florida crew out to Manhattan for three weeks, anyway.

"The camera was knocked aside?" Anne said as she topped the stairs, her fingers gripping her iPad really tightly. "Why didn't you say anything?"

"They've been getting knocked around since we installed them," Samantha answered, keeping her voice down. "Yesterday Rhee noted it and sent Marv to reset it. It took four minutes. Today I know it was done on purpose, and as of now we're installing a half-dozen more cameras with views that overlap the ones we have now."

Nodding, Anne's shoulders lowered a little. "It didn't mean anything yesterday," she muttered.

For a second Samantha looked at her. "It must be crazy to be you right now," she said. "Two Jellicoes, a crazy rich British guy, Aubrey with the Kentucky Colonel accent, and three days until people get invited to swarm all over this place."

"Considering he arrived with a taser and kept you from getting punched, I have no problem at all with Mr. Pendleton."

Well, maybe he'd kept her from getting punched. And maybe she'd been an inch from introducing Big Balls' big balls to his own esophagus. "People don't fool me very often," she said aloud. "I don't like when it happens. So yeah, I'm glad Aubrey was here, too."

"Music to my ears," Aubrey drawled, entering the room and settling a key card into his newly assigned lanyard. "Most jobs, you don't have your employer ask you to bring a charged taser into work with you. This isn't even the first time we've had that exchange, though."

Samantha grinned. "Yeah, but last time it was to check the insulation around some wiring. Today you got to make a guy dance."

"Happy to oblige. Should I go get the order for those additional cameras going?"

"Yes, please. And then take a walk and tell me if you notice anything else hinky."

"This is your battlefield, but I may have an opinion or two on the aesthetics." With a half bow he sauntered back toward the main hallway.

Anne watched him go, then turned back again. "Is he gay?" she whispered.

"I say yes, Rick says no, so maybe. I've never seen him with anybody serious." Samantha eyed her mother. "Do you *like* him?"

"What? No! I was just asking." Anne's cheeks got redder. "He has a very calming presence."

"It's the accent. Like a warm spoonful of honey on a sunny summer afternoon. That's how I like to describe it, anyway. He's good at reassuring people."

"He may be handy to have around, then." With a nod, Anne

backed off again. "I'm going down to the security room to oversee."

"Sounds good. I'll keep roaming. Any cameras move, tell me first."

"Will do." She stood there for a moment. "Just out of curiosity, what is 'mother-daughter shit,' by the way?"

Ah, that. After seeing the expression on Anne's face, she'd figured it would only be a matter of time before it got brought up again. "Stefano is going to jail. I can't control what he's going to say, or to whom he's going to say it—or if Martin's talked to anybody else around here. We're keeping us under wraps right now. I don't want Martin getting even a whiff that we already know about us."

"Okay." Anne smiled, nodding again. "Okay. I was just…It didn't sound good."

"Yeah, I know. I should have worded it better. Or we could give it a code name." She considered for a moment. Most of the code words she and Stoney used had something to do with what they represented— "how's your pillow" was code for "are you in danger" —and other shit like that. "How about 'wine?'" she suggested.

"So I say, 'do you want some wine,' if you say no, that means we shouldn't talk about…personal things? That works, I think." She smiled a little. "Is it because I brought wine, the other night?"

"Yes, it is."

"I like that."

Whew. One tangle resolved. Checking her phone again to make sure the camera feeds were still up and live, Samantha trotted back down to the rear entrance as the last load of Adgerton bling arrived. Her little reveal of Stefano had gone more smoothly than she'd expected, all things considered, but getting rid of one greedy guy didn't mean the problem itself had disappeared.

Martin hadn't just found one guy and bribed him. He'd scouted out a couple of guys, decided this one was the most likely to be bribable, and had been correct about it. But Stefano might not have been the only one. And *that* was why she'd gone all in for humiliation, tasing, and arrest. Seeing a guy lying on the ground, twitching, was hopefully a much better deterrent than just threatening job termination or other, more nebulous consequences.

She took the list of items from the driver and checked them off herself as they left the truck and entered the Victorian house. Adgerton had had some eclectic taste, but a definite preference for the classics. Samantha appreciated that. She had a soft spot for pre-nineteenth century artists, herself.

As the seventeenth piece came down the ramp, she paused, looking up. A Grinling Gibbons piece from 1683, it depicted an apple tree. Actually, it was half an apple tree, part of a wall panel carved out of lime wood. Apple blossoms, leaves, apples, curved branches, lifted away from the panel with such stunning realism that she still couldn't quite believe he'd done the carving from one single piece of wood.

The last time she'd set eyes on the "apple panel," as it had been dubbed, had been five years ago, when she'd handed it over to Stoney for delivery to a discerning client of his, a guy she now knew to be Lewis Adgerton. Before that, well, it had been in the attic of one of the descendants of the artisan hired to clean it during a restoration of Windsor Castle some one-hundred-fifty years earlier. Mr. Fife had declined to return the piece to the castle, instead carving a passable fake that to this day remained on the wall in the south portrait gallery at Windsor.

Hm. She wondered whether Windsor had made a claim to get the panel back, or if Fife's version had been there long enough to become part of history. If Sotheby's felt confident enough to add it to the auction, whatever legal mess there might have been had obviously been resolved.

It was still weird to see it again, though. Somebody had cleaned it and had done a nice job with that—scrubbing time grime off the wood and leaving the natural patina of age behind was no easy task. Samantha shook herself. There she was, waxing nostalgic when she had a job to do.

"A wooden apple tree?" Aubrey noted, walking up beside her.

"Mmhmm. It's about 350 years old. Not the most valuable thing here, but man, it's pretty."

"That, it is. You've got this place wired up to its eyebrows, Miss Samantha. I know I asked to come out and help, but there isn't anything I can suggest that you haven't already installed, together with a separate backup."

"Thanks, Aubrey. You say the nicest things."

"I do try." He looked down for a moment, shifting his feet. "I don't want to step where I'm not wanted," he said, lowering his voice and nodding his chin toward the back door, "but I have a question."

She led the way out to the alley out back. *Great.* If she'd been transparent enough to broadcast her newfound relationship with Anne to a guy who'd been in New York all of an hour, she needed to retire and go live in an old rundown house somewhere in the woods. Fleetingly she wondered if Rick would go along with that, then shook herself. "Ask away."

"I get that the bad guy took a photo he shouldn't have, and that that made you more worried about security. I got to tase him, which was fun. But in order for you to know about the photo he would have had to send it to...you? Or to someone who then sent it to you. That seems more likely, and it's where I don't want to barge into anything I shouldn't, but if there's anything more...necessary I can do to help, you *can* trust me, Miss Samantha."

Back a little over a year ago, she could have named the

people she trusted on one finger, and he went by the name of Stoney. Now, a couple of people knew about her and her dad—the Donner parents, Rick, and now Anne. That was still only one hand's worth of people to whom she'd spilled her guts.

She'd never offered Aubrey Pendleton a job, but he'd just started showing up at her new office and managing it and her team way more efficiently than she could have on her own. So he'd gone onto the payroll and knew everything about her day-to-day at Jellicoe Security. But that was her legit shit.

Okay. Maybe she could edge him in sideways, see how that went, and make the big decision from there. Samantha nodded. "My dad, Martin Jellicoe, was a big-time cat burglar. He got nabbed a couple of years ago and died in prison."

"So I've heard. My condolences, of course."

"Thanks. Except that he didn't. Die in prison, that is. He cut a deal with Interpol, with the idea that he would consult on thefts past and present and help them track down bad guys and recover valuable items, like the Monet that mysteriously turned up year before last after going missing for fifteen years."

"Oh, my. So he... Oh, my." Aubrey put a hand over his mouth. "I'm glad he's alive, then, for your sake. And that he's working to do good."

"He's not." She scowled at the delivery truck as it pulled away, heading back to wherever Sotheby's stored their delivery trucks. Hm. That would be a good thing to know. She made a mental note. "I mean, he might still be helping Interpol out, but he's pretty much gone rogue. He's been lurking around Manhattan, the past few days. I'm pretty sure he's going to try to hit the exhibit, here."

"Doesn't he know you're in charge of security?"

"Yeah. I think that's his point—that I shouldn't try to go up against the old man. And he and Anne had a thing once, which I'm not supposed to know about, and I think he's being nostalgic or something."

Aubrey looked at her for a long moment. "He's the one who sent you the photo, which means Mr. Stefano was working for him."

"'Working for' is kind of overstating, I think, but yeah. He doesn't like that I'm legit, and so he keeps needling me. It's really annoying."

"To say the least. What can I do to help?"

Well, that hadn't gone too badly. Maybe her good instincts as a thief were transferring over to the light side. "If you have any contacts in the world of anti-theft installation or West Palm Beach hoity-toities, it would help to know if anybody is interested in something Adgerton collected. I can't see Martin doing this randomly. He'll have picked a specific piece to go after."

"It's not the marble hand?"

Samantha had already considered that. "I don't think so. I could just pull it from the exhibit if I wanted to. My guess is that he wanted me to know that my security isn't all I think it is. People are always the weakest link, though, so I probably shouldn't have been surprised. But I was, which makes me feel stupid and want to punch things."

He smiled. "I'm not exactly a delver into the criminal under-belly of West Palm Beach, but in some places it's not much of an underbelly, anymore. It's just right out there, in front of every-body. Ponzi schemes, Russian money laundering, all the higher end blue-collar crime. Now that I think about it, I might know who I could have a chat with." Aubrey put a hand on her shoul-der. "I don't know much about your dad, but I have a great deal of faith in you, Miss Samantha."

"Thank you, Aubrey. Hang out here if you want, or Rick found a nice coffee shop just up the street."

"The coffee shop does sound slightly more discreet. And as you are aware, I am the soul of discretion."

"That, you are. Thanks."

Stoney was far more likely to have sources, if he ever meant to cooperate, but it was a big "if" right now, and on occasion Aubrey had come through in some surprisingly helpful ways. Even if he didn't, it was kind of nice to have allies showing up. It was still her versus Martin, but she had some solid backup.

That abruptly reminded her that her star backup hadn't called her yet to see how her morning had gone. That was really unlike him. And if Rick had finally gotten tired of all her crap, well, everybody else could just go to hell.

She dialed Rick's mobile number, but her call went straight to his ultra-professional voicemail. Okay, maybe she was being an idiot. He was at his office. The one he owned. In the middle of Manhattan. He was a famously busy guy. And just because she was having a rough morning, she didn't get to expect that he would be instantly available.

Shaking her head, she returned to the interior of the Victorian house and went back to hovering over all the cases as the exhibit items were wiped clean again and placed in their safe little nests. Whenever she'd become so…dependent on him having her back, on his being available the second she decided she wanted to vent or ask an opinion or something, the realization that it had already happened bothered her.

Just as she shoved her phone back into her pocket it rang, and she retrieved it again. "Hey," she said, not disappointed at all to hear "Raindrops Keep Fallin' on My Head" and not Rick's 007 ringtone.

"Hey," Stoney's voice came back. "Just checking in. Anything new with Martin?"

"He bribed a security guy to take a photo of one of the exhibit items. I had to have the guy's ass arrested."

"For taking a photo?"

"Look, the sign says, very clearly, 'no photography.' Mainly that was an excuse to get him off the premises, though." She took a breath. "Anything new with you?"

"Nope. Crazily enough, nobody's returning my calls asking

about shit that's none of my business. I just wanted you to know that I am trying, and that your business is putting a serious dent in mine. This is my reputation, because you're a cat burglar ghost. I don't say, 'Sam Jellicoe wants to know something.' I say *I* want to know something."

"I get it, Stoney. I just…You're my buffer between the light and the dark sides."

"I know. I'm Switzerland. Except with all these questions, more than a few of my contacts have decided that I've chosen a side. And it ain't theirs. You get it, honey?"

"I get it. Do you want me to stop asking you for favors?" They both knew what that would mean—putting some distance in between her new life and his old one. No midnight calls for advice or information, and even if she never accepted his offers anymore, no more calls ever from him offhandedly mentioning a buyer looking for a Picasso and willing to pay a couple mill to get his hands on it.

The silence on the line abruptly made her want to cry. But he knew where she was headed, and that she'd chosen never to go backward. He was the one with both feet in the shadows, and he was the one who had to decide whether he wanted to stay there or not. She just…Today hadn't been the day she would have chosen to have this conversation.

"I don't know, Sam," he finally grunted. "I need to think about it. I'm just really annoyed this morning."

"I get it. We will need to decide this, sooner or later. Preferably after you walk me down the aisle, though. If you will. I mean, I was going to ask you, but then this Sotheby's thing came up, and—"

"Shut up, Sam," he broke in, his voice abruptly gruff. "Of course I'll walk you down the damn aisle. Jeez."

She let out her breath. "Okay. That's good. We can just leave it right there for now, then. I won't even ask if you would think about moving to New York if Rick and I relocated here."

"What the h—"

"Bye, Stoney," she interrupted. "Talk soon."

She disconnected the call. Boy, today was shaping up into a beauty. Next she'd probably turn around and Tom Donner would be standing there. Or the FBI or Interpol would be, or something. *Cripes.* That spooked her, so she deliberately waited a beat before she turned around. Nobody there but Aubrey, talking to Anne.

It was a good reminder, at least, that things could always get worse. And that they probably would.

12

Saturday, 2:35 p.m.

Clicking off the video call, Richard blew out his breath. Catching a guy flat-footed on his way to dinner in order to pretend interest in the man's banking empire or company or shares in something was fairly common for him. Getting someone to chat before he or she quite knew what was going on was an efficient way of collecting information and assessing weaknesses.

This call, though, had been different. Firstly, Daan Van der Berg didn't seem actually to own a company. Or any tangible property at all, for that matter, with the exception of a ridiculously huge yacht. Other than that, as far as Tom and his team had been able to dig up, Van der Berg had minority shares in two dozen banks, a familial history of questionable art acquisitions, and a couple of nebulous offshore accounts.

It screamed money laundering to Richard, but he didn't have the luxury of waiting around for Interpol or someone else to investigate Van der Berg and run him off to white-collar criminal prison. That could take decades, if it ever happened at all.

No, Richard wasn't interested in doing business with this guy, but he had wanted a chance to give the Dutchman a sideways warning about trying to illegally obtain Calder kinetic structures—or anything else about to be auctioned by Sotheby's.

With Van der Berg pretending he didn't speak English and Richard losing his patience at being played with, the threat had been more direct than he'd intended. But for Christ's sake, Tom had sent him videos of interviews where the twat spoke perfect English, with a perfect English accent.

So now he'd been warned off, with a couple of threats about financial ruin thrown in for good measure. Richard didn't like being toyed with, but if he wanted to justify his…direct approach, he could always claim that he might just have turned Van der Berg away from a life of crime.

Of course he might also have made things worse. If Van der Berg *was* the guy who'd hired Martin Jellicoe, he'd tipped them both off to the fact that Samantha knew that. He hadn't said her name, of course, but Martin knew they were engaged. Anyone with electricity knew they were engaged. It wasn't a great leap to figure out what was going on.

And on top of that, it had taken hours to track the man down and cause this potential disaster. "Well done, you wanker," he muttered at himself, turning over his cellphone.

Three missed calls. Two from Tom, and one from Samantha. Whereas Tom had left a pair of detailed messages, though, Samantha hadn't left one at all. Ignoring his stomach growling, he called her back.

"Hey," she answered, as she generally did.

"I'm sorry I missed your call. I had some overseas communications going on."

"Well, whoop-de-do. We got to tase somebody."

For a second Richard shut his eyes. His Samantha was not for the faint-hearted. "Is he arrested, or buried in the basement?"

"The first one. Anne and Aubrey handled it so I could keep my usual police safety perimeter intact."

"Good. Is that why you called? To inform me about the tasing?"

"I know you hate when I get to do something fun and you're stuck in the office." She snorted at her own wit. "That was it, mainly. I asked Aubrey to see if he could figure out if any of his snowbird Palm Beach buds might be after something of Adgerton's, but that was mostly to give him something to do that didn't involve following me around."

That was as good a lead-in as he was going to get, whether he wanted to use it or not. "I had a chat with Daan Van der Berg," he said as smoothly as he could. "About banking and wealth and collecting."

For twelve seconds she didn't say anything. He knew it was that long, because he counted. "Anything interesting come up?" she finally asked.

"No. I think I made a bit of an ass of myself, because it turns out I don't like smug people who are more lucky than intelligent. It may have devolved into fairly direct threats if he has anything to do with an upcoming robbery at Sotheby's—which also may get back to Martin, if Van der Berg is indeed his client."

He waited for the inevitable explosion. It didn't come. "Eh," she said, her voice its usual cool, half-amused tone. "I don't think it'll matter. You might have set Martin back on his heels a little, which I count as the good stuff."

"Really?" He stopped himself from saying anything else, because even he could hear in his voice the boy relieved to be avoiding a stern talking-to. "Well, I prefer when my threats are for a good cause."

"That definitely qualifies. In other news, Stoney and I had our first talk about getting a divorce."

That stopped *him* for a good handful of seconds. "Anything

interesting come of it?" He thought he sounded fairly suave for a guy whose mind had just run off in a hundred different directions, imagining a future where Samantha actually cut off all ties with her former criminal gang.

"He's thinking about it. I also asked if he would walk me down the aisle and then threw in a question about whether he'd ever consider relocating to New York. Altogether, I think I've earned a day off tomorrow."

"It will be Sunday. Sounds sensible to me."

"Good. I like to be sensible. So anyway, I've got another couple of hours here today. Meet at the apartment and stay in for dinner and a movie?"

"God, yes."

"Okay. Love you."

"I love you, too, Samantha."

Rick set his phone down and stared at it for a long moment, then tapped the intercom button on the office's phone. "Jeniah, have the car sent 'round. I'm in need of a bit of a lie down." And a beer. Or three.

Ö

AUBREY SCROLLED through the phone numbers on his cellphone, stopping at the one labeled "Joe—tennis racket repair." His finger hovered over the highlighted number while he glanced around him again.

He'd tried the coffee shop Samantha had recommended, but it was small and neat and quiet. That was no good for him. Another block down and he'd found a sports bar, filled on a Saturday afternoon with people who'd started drinking beers early and who were already arguing over games just about to begin. Loud, rowdy, and rude—much better for privacy, really.

Finally, he tapped the number and put the phone up to his ear. Two rings later, it picked up. "Ling."

"It's Aubrey," he said, shifting a little closer over his plate of wings.

"It's Saturday. I took this job so I would have people who would take calls on the weekend and I wouldn't have to hear about it until Monday."

"I didn't want this heading to you through Dean Frankle," Aubrey commented, resisting the urge to plug his other ear so he could hear more clearly.

"You mean you didn't want Frankle taking credit for something you dug up. I'm not your damn camp counselor, Pendleton. Go through channels. I'm hanging up."

"Did you know Martin Jellicoe is still alive?"

The call didn't disconnect. "No shit. You saw him?"

"No. He made a deal with Interpol to aid in recovering some of what he'd taken and turning in other cat burglars. They put out that he was dead to protect him and his sources."

"Lucky bastards," Ling muttered. "Where are you? In a bar?"

"Sports club. Manhattan."

"I specifically didn't authorize that yesterday."

"My other boss paid for the ticket. Not an extra dime charged to your office."

"Like I give a fuck about that. You have a deadline, Aubrey. This is—"

"She took the Sotheby's job because she found out that Martin Jellicoe intends to hit the exhibit," Aubrey interrupted, beginning to wish he'd taken a few more minutes to decide exactly what he wanted to say. When Samantha had told him about Martin Jellicoe and his recent doings, though, the opportunity had been far too good to let pass by. It gave him options, which made getting scolded for weekend calling completely worth the annoyance.

"You're going to have to back this up a little." At least Ling Wu sounded interested now.

"Okay. My source told me that Martin Jellicoe made that

deal with Interpol, and that he's been feeding them info *and* going behind their backs and hitting places, then setting up other thieves to take the fall. He's made an industry out of it, apparently." That might have been a slight exaggeration, but it was also a way out of this mess. Hopefully.

"How certain are you about all this? Because if you make me step on Interpol's toes for no good reason, I am not going to be happy, Pendleton. And then you're going to be very unhappy."

"I've been doing this long enough to know the veiled threats bit by heart, Wu."

"Then you also have an answer, I suppose, when I ask you if the Jellicoes could be in this Sotheby's heist thing together? She sets up security and he goes in through whatever hole she's left? It's kind of perfect."

"Sure, that might work once or twice, but it'd also hard to explain to prospective clients if everywhere she installed security got hit by a pro. Aside from that, none of the places where she's installed security have *been* hit. A couple of attempts, but nobody's made it in."

"Maybe it was all leading to this."

Aubrey rolled his eyes. "So she went public, started a business, got engaged to a billionaire, stopped a couple of robberies, and helped put a couple of really bad guys away just so she could get a contract to install security at one Sotheby's exhibit and help her dad rob it?"

"Maybe she needs a wedding gift for Addison. He collects art, doesn't he?"

"Why does talking to you make me want to slam my head against a table?" For God's sake. A thing either made sense, or it didn't. Samantha only pretending to go straight didn't make sense. She'd stuck her neck out too far, put too much into her life in Florida, made herself too public. The downside was huge, and he couldn't see the benefit of doing it as a ruse. There just wasn't one. "What I'm hearing," Ling Wu said, from his clipped tone pissed off that an agent had done something other than compliment him, "is that you want to trade one Jellicoe for the other. That's not how we operate, and you know it. Take down Martin Jellicoe if you want; it'll look good on your score sheet. But doing that doesn't make her innocent."

"Wu, th—"

"Run it past the Manhattan office on Monday. I'll coordinate with Tampa and make sure you get however much manpower you need. But you'd better be sure, Aubrey. If you get this wrong, it won't be reassignment to a desk at this damn CVS-view office, filing other people's reports, for you. It won't even be Immanuel Village in Nebraska. If the FBI loses one to Interpol thanks to you, you're done."

"Thanks for the vote of confidence."

"Oh, and if it messes with you nabbing the daughter, double forget it. I'll put a call in to Interpol and let them worry about their own mess after we get her in cuffs."

"I'll figure it out. No phone call from you to Interpol until I get back to you." Whatever leverage he had right now, he wasn't letting go of it until he'd figured out how best to use it.

"I'm hanging up now."

Tapping off the call, Aubrey set down his phone and leaned back in the padded booth seat, picked up his waiting beer, and took a deep, long swallow. Cowboys and Indians, cops and robbers, army and aliens—it had all been pretty black-and-white when he'd been a kid. Sure, he'd learned differently a long time ago, but that didn't mean there weren't still a few white hats and black hats out there, somewhere.

While he was willing to bet that whatever she'd been before, Samantha Jellicoe had put on her white hat and didn't intend to take it off, deciding *what* he was willing to bet on it—that was the hard part.

The exhibit would open on Tuesday. A week and a half after that, it would shut down and Sotheby's would auction off the goods. That left him a very small window to trap one Jellicoe, save another, keep his own job—jobs, rather—and not upset the balance he'd managed for the past nine months. For the past ten years, really.

Shit. Samantha should probably change the ringtone she used for his phone calls from "Somewhere Over the Rainbow" to the theme from *Mission Impossible*. Because two things were becoming quite clear; he'd already decided what he *wanted* to do, and there was no chance in hell any of this was going to go the way he hoped.

HER DAUGHTER TASED PEOPLE. Or had someone else tase them, which was pretty much the same thing. Anne Hughes reached into one of the smaller displays and changed the angle of the amber cane topper to make sure the mosquito inside could be seen through the glass. Very *Jurassic Park* of Mr. Adgerton, and not the most valuable piece by far, but she was also fairly certain this particular item would appear in at least a few newspapers next week when the press got their tour of the exhibit on Monday.

She'd never seen anyone tased except on TV, and it looked painful. Even so, she could certainly get behind doing that to Bradley, if he ever did show his face there. She almost wished he would, just so they could get the anticipation over with.

Then it would be over, she would know that they'd stopped him from doing still more damage to her life and to her career, and if she was very lucky, he would be back in prison—for good this time. She didn't imagine many people lied to Interpol and did criminal things while on their payroll. At least she hoped not.

How many lives had he ruined? Was it just her and Sam? And if he succeeded here, what would he do next? Would he decide to target her and everyone else in her life just because she'd tried to stop him? What would her own mother do if Bradley Martin showed up? What would Michael do? Oh, that couldn't happ—

"That is very *Jurassic Park*," Sam commented, leaning over the glass while the two workers secured the lid and made sure the alarm was live.

Anne jumped. "I was just thinking that. Plus, this is the only way I like my mosquitoes. Frozen solid and turned into decorations."

Her daughter snorted. "That reminds me of when Madame Tussaud's called and wanted to make a wax statue of Rick to go in their Hall of Billionaires."

"Really? What did he say to that?"

"He said being memorialized for having money was stupid. I think he was worried I would steal it from the museum and do stuff with it."

That made Anne laugh, even as she wondered whether other mothers and daughters had conversations like that one. She couldn't imagine they did. It wasn't one of the talks she'd imagined having with young Sarah, and she'd imagined so many of those. So many.

"Do you have plans for tomorrow?" she asked, as they moved on to make final adjustments and secure the next display case. "Other than obsessively checking the camera feeds, that is."

"I think Rick wants to go look at a few houses outside the City, but I'm not sure how far away from this building I'm willing to get."

"Houses? Are you thinking of moving here?" Did that mean Sam wanted to be closer to her family? Did it mean they had a future? Did it mean anything at all? "I mean, you have the apartment already."

Samantha shrugged. "Rick has this idea that I'd be happier and busier here, and if he moves, he wants his friend—his best friend, really—Tom Donner, to be around, too. And Donner comes with a wife and three kids."

"Wow."

"Well, they're practically attached at the hip."

"Oh, that's not what I mean," Anne said. "It's more about the wine, I think. And the vintage I used to prefer, and how it never gave up anything for me." Hell, Bradley not only hadn't given up his way of life, he'd stolen their daughter on his way out.

"Ah." Sam put a hand on her arm. "Gotcha. Yeah, Rick's pretty cool."

"But the house would be for the Donners?"

"I don't know. I think he's just getting a feel for the area. Or something like that."

For a minute she wanted to recommend her own Connecticut neighborhood, but that might come across as stalkery and creepy, especially if they were only talking about Rick's friends and where they would live. She didn't imagine any of them would want to live next door to Sam's mother, though. And she certainly didn't want to be that type of mother —or mother-in-law—either.

And now she wanted to ask if Sam had begun plans for her wedding, or if she needed any assistance with that. That conversation was another one to be saved for later, though, with fewer people to overhear. Because no one was supposed to know they were mother and daughter. Because stupid Bradley had managed to mess up even this reunion just by virtue of his existence.

The good thing about Samantha's performance this morning was that absolutely no one reached for their phone inside the premises. It almost became a problem, with so many calls going unanswered, but every weird ringtone reminded her that her remaining employees were following both Sam's rules and the sign's rules. No calls, no photography, no electronic devises but her iPad and Sam's own phone.

The press coming in on Monday would alter that, and afterward, while they could discourage flash photography, she didn't want to be tackling every prospective buyer who pulled out their phone to take a call or a discreet photo. Hm. She and Sam would have to talk about that. And about whether Bradley had been known to wear a disguise and if she thought he might try to sneak in as a tourist or future auction participant.

Would she recognize him? Anne shuddered. Not so much his looks, probably, as that…feeling of dread that had come over her once she'd realized just who he was, and just before he'd grabbed Sarah—Samantha—and taken off into the darkness, not to be heard from for twenty years. His features wouldn't even matter. It would be that sensation that gave him away. So if he knew what was good for him, he would stick with the threats and bullying, and get out of Manhattan.

"Okay," Sam said, straightening. "Let's do one more walkthrough of this floor to make sure everything's wired, secured, and ready, then we'll go down to the second floor and do it again."

"Are we going to have people here as security, now? Or just the alarm system?"

"Just the system at night. At this point security guards are the weak link, but they'll be a help with traffic control at least during the day."

"That seems very cynical, but I can't argue with what's already happened. Just tell me Rhee will be monitoring, too."

"Technically," Sam commented, heading for the next room, "nobody needs to be monitoring. The system will alert everybody, including the police, if anything at all trips. But yeah, I asked him to keep checking in, the same as you and I will be doing all fricking day and night until this is over."

This was the largest exhibit and auction Anne had put together in years, and she was very aware how closely her bosses at Sotheby's were watching. The fact that they'd allowed it all to proceed according to her direction, even after learning about her connection with Bradley Martin, both gave her warm, fuzzy feelings and terrified the living daylights out of her. "I don't suppose I could arrange for armed guards outside twenty-four-seven, anyway?"

"Don't tempt me. I'd definitely like it better if I could be on every floor and in front of every monitor all at the same time, but at some point I have to trust that we've done enough." Samantha blew out her breath, letting Anne take the lead as they descended the wide staircase to the middle floor.

"I know exactly how you feel, Sam. But yes, short of hiring a crack team of mercenaries I can't even imagine what more we could have done—except for placing a giant boulder on the roof, poised to crush anyone who touches anything they shouldn't, of course."

Sam shot her a grin. "If only."

"Unfortunately, giant boulders and mercenaries are both out of my budget. But go with Rick tomorrow. Have fun. I'll be watching the video feeds all day, I promise you. And I will call or text you if I see even a speck of lint."

"I appreciate it. I could log Aubrey in, too, if you want another set of eyes." Sam shrugged. "Or I could let you decide that. I'm just security. It's your gig."

"Which I couldn't have done without you. No matter what happens."

It occurred to her again that whether they'd figured it all out or not, whether they could talk about it in front of other people or not, she was the mom in this relationship. And moms wanted their daughters to be happy. If enabling that entailed her being even more watchful than she'd already anticipated having to be, so be it.

SQUINTING a little in the sunlight even with her sunglasses on, Samantha put her feet up on the dash so she could prop the *Best Places to Live on the East Coast* real estate buyer's book on her bent knees. "You really bought this?"

Rick glanced at her. "I had it purchased for me. Why? Are you secretly a real estate mogul in disguise?"

Man, he was testy this morning. Evidently she wasn't the only one who needed a day off. "It definitely shows all the best places to rob," she quipped, turning the page to look at more photos. It had clearly been put together by real estate people, made for possible buyers with money to burn. "Like a 'Guide to the Best Shit' catalog."

His jaw clenched. "Why do you insist on doing that to my blood pressure?"

"Maybe it's not me affecting you," she suggested. "We did just cross the bridge into New Jersey."

"There are some very nice places to live in New Jersey."

"Yeah, I know." She turned another page. "So are you just choosing the Donners' house, or are you buying it for them, too? Don't forget to scout the local school districts before you tell them where they're moving. Katie is very particular."

"That's it." Rick punched the accelerator and wrenched the Mercedes to the right, taking them off the toll road past a load of cars with people now honking and giving them the finger, down the ramp, and skidding them into a shopping center parking lot.

Bracing her feet, Samantha shut the book and faced him. "Thank God."

"Thank God what? You're maddening!"

"*I'm* maddening? You're like a giant clenched fist, Rick. What the hell is going on?"

He glared at her, blue eyes narrowed. "You need to make a damned decision," he finally snapped.

Oh, so he was putting this, whatever it was, back on her.

"Hold on. You're mad because I haven't decided if I want to uproot a dozen people's lives or not? Tough shit."

"It's not—Stop worrying about what the Donners or Stoney or Aubrey or anybody else might or might not wish to do. I bought Solano Dorado as a place to entertain, and to show off. The apartment here was an investment, a place I could go to be alone, or again to entertain. I'm not alone any longer. I don't want to live in a showplace. I want a home. With you. And one with extra bedrooms in case we ever get around to discussing whether or not we want children. Not because some CEO wants to jet in for the day and stay somewhere he can brag about when he gets home. A place with a yard, not a formal garden."

Now she was staring, and she didn't quite know how to stop doing it. She'd spent the last couple of weeks interpreting some things really, really badly. "This moving thing isn't about growing my business, then. It's not about me trying to weigh my shit against yours and me feeling guilty over making the Donners turn their own lives upside down just to suit my whims."

"Well...No." He frowned. "I didn't want to scare you."

"You really need to stop the thing where you don't tell me stuff because you think I'll run away. I said yes. I'm wearing a big-ass ring. If you want my input on a decision, fucking tell me about it."

For a minute there was silence in the Mercedes, with the exception of the score from *The Lord of the Rings* playing softly in the background. This was the part where the Fellowship left Rivendell, not knowing they'd all make it back except for poor old Boromir. Samantha hoped she wasn't about to be the Boromir of this situation.

Then Rick's shoulders lowered, and he blew out his breath. "Okay. I suppose I can't expect you to want the thing that I want when I don't tell you what the thing is or why I want it."

"Damn straight." She opened the book again. "Now get us to Glen Rock, New Jersey. There's a house I want to look at."

He put the car back in gear.

"Do we still get to have household staff, though?" she asked, flipping pages until she found the one she wanted. "Because I am *not* learning to cook."

"Neither am I. So, yes."

"Awesome."

It made a difference to know that he didn't want to move because he was looking out for her business. Or at least that that wasn't the only reason. She'd been in all but two of his houses, and while all of them had a tasteful and expensive design and a scattering of art and antiquities that would make some museums weep, she understood what he meant. They were all showpieces. Places that would be open, ready, and appropriate for a weekend visit or for a rich dude's party. They weren't what she would call "homey."

Neither, though, could she exactly picture Rick out mowing the lawn. So maybe "stately" and "comfortable" together. A place that required three or four staff members to maintain rather than twelve. "You're okay with no giant wall surrounding you?" she asked.

"Perhaps a nice sheltering line of trees, or something. And a pond or a small grove between us and the neighbors. Among other neighbors who also value their privacy."

She looked at him, studying his strong-jawed profile all over again. "You really have been thinking about this. Why the hell didn't you say you wanted to move, too?"

"I should have. You have to admit, though, you have fled my company before, and for less reason."

"Different reason," she pointed out. "Not less reason. You tried to manage me. This time you did, like, the opposite, giving me nothing to hang a decision on. Somewhere in the middle would be good."

He also needed to do some more work on the way he argued, but pointing that out now wouldn't be fair. After spending most of his life being the guy in charge, Rick didn't really argue as much as he just forcefully pointed out the way he thought things should be. While he'd made some big changes already, she got why he occasionally forgot he was part of Team Rimantha or Jellison or Addicoe or whatever they were. The point being, they were a pair. And if he wanted stuff done that concerned the two of them, he was going to have to ask questions and answer them.

Samantha smiled. She'd been a solo act for a long time, too. The main difference had been that most of the decisions she'd made had been about safety and staying clear of the law. Self-preservation. Now it was about lawns. And the other thing that people used extra bedrooms for that wasn't houseguests.

"What's so amusing?" Rick asked.

"I was just picturing you on one of those tractor mowers," she said. "I'm totally getting you one."

"Just remember that I can arrange to make the Donners our next-door neighbors."

Ugh. Katie would be okay, and the kids, but Donner? Where he could be walking his dog beneath an open window and over-hear...stuff? She made a face. "Okay. No ride-on mowers. Sheesh."

"That's right. Don't forget, I negotiate for a living." With a half-smile, Rick reached over and took her fingers. "On a different note, after this is over with, are you going to continue to go by Samantha Jellicoe? Or Samantha Addison? Or Sarah Addison? Or Sarah Jellicoe Addison? Or Sarah Hughes? Or S—"

"I'm Sam Jellicoe," she broke in, before he could start in on the Martin and Bradley last names. "I could probably be persuaded to be Sam Jellicoe-Addison because marrying you makes me a marchioness and a Lady with a capital *L*, but I am *not* going back to Sarah. Whoever I was, I'm not a Sarah anymore."

"Good. I happen to love Samantha Jellicoe."

"Even if I'm named after a Broadway musical about cats?"

Rick shrugged, squeezing her hand. "Like you said, you've grown into this name. You made it yours. I, on the other hand, am not even the first Richard Addison."

"Dude, your name didn't shape you. Your life did. Just like me. We are our parents' children, whether we like it or not." Samantha snorted. "And man, do I feel sorry for those hypothetical kids you were talking about. They have no chance of being normal at all."

Laughing, Rick released her hand again. "That's the reason people have children, isn't it? To laugh at them later?"

"And to make them carry heavy stuff when they're old enough."

"In that case, I deem us perfectly fit to be parents."

She flipped another page of the book, a little surprised that she hadn't tried to jump out of the car, despite what she'd said to him about good reasons for fleeing. "Yeah, we'll see about that." Before parenthood, she needed to stop her dad from ruining her life for the second or third or fifth time. For the last time.

13

Sunday, 7:52 p.m.

"Is this how we're going to be spending our evenings for the next two weeks?" Rick glanced at Sam in the passenger seat beside him, one leg curled beneath her bottom and her lowered gaze on her cellphone, the black-and-white glow making her delicate features pale and turning her auburn hair purplish.

"This is only the third time I've checked today," she responded. "And I only picked it up because Anne texted me to say she hadn't spotted anything."

"Which is good. It means everything is going as it should."

"Maybe I'm still not quite used to the whole 'nothing happening is the way we want it' thing. It just seems so...dull."

He could sympathize; no deal ever made him more suspicious than the one where everything went perfectly. Who would have thought that flaws and bumps would be comforting? And yet they were. They signaled that problems had been found and dealt with—which suggested that there were always problems, which therefore led to the conclusion that problems weren't always found. "It's natural to look for imperfections," he said aloud. "That doesn't mean they exist."

"Then I'm doing what comes naturally," she said, most of her attention clearly still on the camera feeds as she tapped from one to the next. "He knows I'll have cameras. He knows I'll have pressure sensors. He knows the windows and doors are all wired. How does he think he's going to get in? And more importantly, out?"

"I still maintain it could all be harmless—relatively harmless —bellowing. He's upset that you've successfully moved on with your life, and that Anne has regained her status within the antiquities' community, so he's doing his best to stir things up. To diminish what should be your pride at a job well done."

Blowing out her breath, Samantha closed the app, turned over her phone, and tapped it against one knee. "Could be, should be, might be, wanna be," she muttered. "Honeybee."

Even an idiot could see that she was trying to be rational about all this, and he wasn't an idiot. Even though Walter Barstone maintained that she was better at thievery than her father, that she could think circles around Martin and most other people, the fact remained that Martin had more or less raised her and taught her what she knew. This was her test, to prove to herself, at least, that she had surpassed the old crook.

"How about we drive around the building a couple of times before we head back to the apartment?" It was probably wrong to encourage her paranoia, but from what he knew of Martin, her worry might actually be warranted. He'd never had reason before to doubt her instincts about such things, anyway.

"I would be very okay with that. Thanks, Rick."

"I am nothing if not supportive."

In another ten minutes they'd reached the old Victorian. He drove as slowly as he could with the traffic that always surrounded the building, turned at the second corner, went back through the alley, and circled around again. "One more time, please," Samantha said, leaning her forehead against the passenger window.

Her phone rang, to the tune of "Mean Green Mother from Outer Space" from *Little Shop of Horrors*, one of those quirky movies she favored. "Anne?" he mouthed, and she nodded as she accepted the call.

"Hi," she said, putting the call on speaker. "Rick's here, too. What's up?"

Interesting, that. She disliked when he butted into her actual business, but apparently he was necessary backup where her mother was concerned. Very well. Duly noted.

"I don't know if it means anything," Anne's voice came, "but you said Bradley—Martin—confronted you from a stolen Mercedes. I've been watching, and the same Mercedes has circled our building twice now. Oh, there it is again!"

"Hold on. Rick, flash the lights."

He did so.

"Did you see its lights flash?" Samantha asked, sitting back again.

"Yes. Is that…Oh, it's you. I'm sorry. I'm just—"

"No, that's good. I'm glad you noticed. But I think we're both suffering from Martin-induced anxiety. So Rick and I are going back to the apartment now, and you're going to put down the phone and iPad and turn on the TV and watch a movie. Okay?"

Anne's sigh sounded extremely familiar. "Okay. You do the same, though."

"Yep. I'm making Rick sit through the *John Wick* movies with me. Purely for research."

Her mother snorted. "Is it too weird if I say I like to research Keanu Reeves, too?"

"Oh, good God," Rick muttered, while the two women laughed. "Goodbye, Anne. She'll see you in the morning before the press tour begins."

"Bye, Anne. See you tomorrow."

"Goodnight, Sam. Rick."

Rick made one last turn around the building then headed north toward the apartment. "You know Keanu Reeves is twice your age."

"Not in some of his movies, he's not. He's my age in the first *Matrix* movie. Ooh, we could watch those."

"No, thank you. Old Keanu is quite enough."

Samantha leaned over to kiss his shoulder. "If you grew your hair that long, I wouldn't need to watch Keanu movies."

That revved him up. "You are not making me jealous," he stated as they stopped for a light, "but I am going to give you the sex all over that couch. Then we'll see how much time you spend watching Keanu and his flowing mane."

Laughing, she grabbed his chin and pulled his head around for a deep, tongue-tangling kiss. "We should probably send Andre and Wilder home and turn off the lights before we start watching, then. Because I want all the sex with you, Rick. All night long."

Christ. He'd be lucky if they made it home first, now. He called Wilder and told him to give himself and Andre the rest of the night off, pushed his luck with two yellow lights on the way back, and practically skidded the car into the parking garage. "Come on," he muttered, exiting the car and striding around to take her by the arm as she straightened.

The garage had cameras, as did the elevator and the little alcove outside their apartment. His jaw clenched, Richard kept hold of her hand, kept his eyes looking straight ahead, and ran numbers through his mind. Lots of numbers, with lots of decimals in them.

"You okay?" she muttered, as they ascended past the lobby and the first two floors.

"Shut up," he managed.

He was fairly certain she was amused, but his goal was not to embarrass himself on camera. Damn tight jeans. She liked when he wore them, so this was her fault. Technically, it was all her fault, because she was so bloody attractive, and the way she moved was so self-assured and so sexy, that he wanted her all the time. Things like her teasing him or touching him or—fuck it all—smiling, made it worse. And now she was doing all three.

The elevator opened into their small foyer. He already had the keycard in his free hand, and luckily for the door it unlocked with his first swipe. Stepping inside with her, he shut the door and locked it. When Samantha lifted her arms around his neck, he held her off. "Andre? Wilder? Are you still here?"

Silence.

"I will take that as a no," Samantha said. "And if either of them *is* here, in a minute somebody's going to be too embarrassed to move a muscle. You hear that, Wilder? This is your last chance."

Nothing.

"Andre?" he yelled, just to be sure.

Samantha shrugged. "I guess they listened to y—"

Richard took her face in his hands and kissed her, his tongue dancing with hers. Her backside bumped against the door, and using the fine mahogany for leverage, he shifted his hands to her T-shirt and pulled it up so he could slide his hands beneath her bra and brush his fingers across her nipples.

Lowering his mouth to the curve of her neck, his kissed the place where her pulse hammered. He loved that he excited her, that she wanted him as much as he wanted her. "Arms up," he muttered, returning to her T-shirt.

"Arms up," she repeated, complying as he pulled the shirt off over her head. "Tits out."

Rick snorted. Technically they weren't out yet, but he meant to see to that immediately, pulling the front of her bra down and lowering his head to take her breast in his mouth, flicking her nipple with his tongue.

Samantha gasped. "We aren't going to get to *John Wick*

tonight, are we?" she asked, shoving his shirt up and going for the button fastening his jeans.

"Nope."

The curtains of the wall-sized window overlooking Hyde Park stood open, as they generally did, but the lights in the front room and the kitchen were out, and the nearer couch faced the interior of the house, anyway. Swinging her up in his arms, he carried her over to it and set her down on the deep cushions.

He finished pulling off his clothes and kicking his shoes out of the way, watching her as she did the same. Neither of them knew her birthday, but now, at least, he could ask Anne about it. When they'd first met she'd given her age as twenty-four, which would make her twenty-five now. He'd just turned thirty-four, which generally didn't signify except for the fact that it made him aware that he needed to stay in shape if he meant to keep up with her, which he did.

Samantha ran, lifted weights, and went through assorted other exercises he knew were meant to aid her in climbing buildings and going through ducts and other Spider-Man activities—completely legitimate ones now, of course—which left her strong, flexible, and supremely sexy in anything she wore, or nothing at all.

"Whatcha doin'?" she panted, looking up at him with a grin on her oval face.

"I'm looking at you," he said. "You take my breath away, Samantha. I adore you, you know."

"Well, that's a nice thing to say. Come here and I can promise you're going to get lucky."

"You don't have to ask me twice, ma'am."

"That's 'my lady,' if you don't mind." Sitting up, Samantha wrapped her arms around his shoulders and pulled him onto the couch and on top of her.

"Not yet," he pointed out, then forgot how to speak as one of her hands wrapped around his cock.

She pushed all his buttons, all the time, and he adored her for it. He felt revved up, like an engine, and she'd had her foot on the accelerator all evening. Slow and leisurely could wait for the second inning. And there he went, mixing his metaphors, but he didn't much care.

Kissing her again, he settled between her knees and pushed forward, sliding into her, relishing in the tight, damp heat of her. With another throaty chuckle she wrapped arms and legs around him, moaning while he rocked into her again and again.

Samantha came first, and he followed, riding on the same wave of heat and desire and need. *Jesus.* His watch applauded him for his elevated heart rate and exercise regime, and he snorted, lowering his head against her shoulder.

"Your watch is going to explode," she laughed breathily, taking his arm and unfastening the pesky thing to toss it on the coffee table. She'd already removed hers, of course. No sense letting some technician somewhere realize that Jellicoe and Addison were synched up and at it again.

"Dammit. I think I'm kneeling on a pen, too. I vote we adjourn to the bedroom."

"No kidding. I'm imagining some paparazzo with an infrared camera recording us through the window right now." She lifted her arms over her head and stretched, catlike, beneath him.

That did all sorts of very nice things to his nethers. *Good on you, big fellow,* he praised himself, and straightened to sink onto his haunches. "Well, now I'm imagining it, too." Trying to pretend he wasn't still out of breath, he stood and tugged her to her feet. "Come along, Jellicoe. That was barely the first inning. I'm going for a whole game tonight."

Turning around, she planted her palms on his chest and sank against him, tilting her face up for a long, slow kiss that he felt all the way to his toes. "Just so you know, I adore you, too, Addison."

"Hmm. Now I'm thinking double-header."

"Have I mentioned how glad I am that you finally learned baseball terms, Brit?" She took his hand, twining her fingers with his, and pulled him into the master bedroom. "Batter up."

○

WALTER BARSTONE SAT at his small kitchen table, set down his bowl of kit-made chicken Caesar salad and a fork, and reached over for the television remote. The doc had said more greenery and less meat, but this compromise was as close as he cared to get to vegetarian.

As always, he started with the world news, then went to the local eastern Florida channel. "No shit, it's hot," he muttered. "Bring on another hurricane, why don't you? Come on, my azaleas need another foot-and-a-half of rain this week."

Apparently, his azaleas would survive at least for the next ten days, as long as he kept the beach umbrella over them. Whatever the hell was going on with the weather, and whoever the hell had done it, he'd had just about enough of it.

Halfway through his salad the first local news story repeated, and he changed the channel again. This time of year was generally slow in Florida; the snow hadn't started to chase the northern snowbirds south yet, and the only criminal stuff going on was shoplifting and the occasional money-laundering or B and E or bank robbery. A couple of years ago Sam would have been sitting there with him, and they would have been talking about spending the month in Europe because the film awards season was heating up. Yachts, jewelry, idiots who rented out entire hotel floors and then forgot to create the security that would keep a self-assured young lady who looked like she belonged on the red carpet from strolling in and nabbing all the sparkly things.

But Sam was in New York right now, protecting sparkly

things, and he remained in hot-ass Florida. It was just wrong. Especially when on top of the weather he'd been asked to go to his sources—again—and use them to help Sam catch bad guys. Except he and Sam *were* bad guys. Or at least they had been. What the hell he was now, he had no idea, but it was giving him a migraine.

Even without Sam taking the contracts he offered her, requests from various people who wanted to own various things currently in someone else's possession, he'd still managed to make a couple hundred thousand dollars this past year. Together with the cash he'd been carefully putting away for the past twenty-five years, it was more than enough to buy him a vineyard or a villa somewhere in the south of Europe where he could retire, sample wine, and eat baguettes in the sunset for the rest of his life.

In the original plan, he and Sam were going to be neighbors, toasting each other across some quaint donkey trail and hiring people to do all the housework and driving and shit while they enjoyed the fruits of their questionable labors. Maybe she'd kind of decided on an early retirement, or semi-retirement, about two years ago, but unique contracts had still interested her. The one she'd taken to rob Solano Dorado of an old stone tablet had proven that. And he would have been good with her going slower and being more cautious.

All that had changed, though, when Rick Addison had entered the picture. Walter couldn't accuse him of ruining things, because Sam had never been happier, even with the huge damn risks she was taking now. Not just going straight, but going public. Getting her photo put in newspapers and magazines, and even worse, online.

Where did that all leave him, her Yoda, her daddy de facto, as she called him? Losing contacts, losing contracts, losing the trust of paranoid, scary people after he'd spent years building his secret little spider's web for gathering information—that's where it left him.

And sitting alone at his table eating a salad that had three tiny little chunks of chicken in it. Maybe he should just retire. He had some hobbies lined up, just waiting for him to have the time to try them out. He could even, if he was careful, get himself a nice place in New York, close to the city, even if he'd grown up there and didn't feel any particular affection for it.

Sam, though, had finally made it clear where she stood, and that the two of them as things were now would not mesh. He got it, but that also meant that if he wanted to stay in her life, he needed to give up the life just like she had. And he didn't have a rich, powerful British aristocrat to run interference for him.

Maybe, though, it was all shit, and she would stay on in Florida. Then he could keep playing both sides for at least a little longer and give himself time to figure out a revised rest-of-his-life scenario.

He glanced up at his sliding eyes cat clock. Time for *Jeopardy*, which meant his overseas phone calls would be starting in about half an hour. Nobody called him during *Jeopardy*. Not more than once, anyway. Picking up the remote, he turned the channel again and went to get the beer he'd forgotten.

His phone rang.

Swearing, he picked up the call, number unknown. He had a lot of calls from unknown numbers, though. "Do not, and I repeat, do *not*, call me during *Jeopardy*," he snapped, and tapped off the call. This was one of those times he missed the old-timey phones where you could slam the receiver down on the base with that satisfying thunk.

Walter took a swallow of beer and went back to his salad. Watching *Jeopardy* used to be another tradition with Sam, except that with her memory she knew most of the damn answers—despite her having a very minimal formal education. Sometimes he wondered what she would have done with her life if she hadn't had a dad who dragged her around the world and never stayed in one place for more than a month. Thank God Martin had taken to dropping her off in Florida when he had a solo job.

His phone rang again. The same unknown number. That was just asking for it. "Lose my number," he growled, picking up the cellphone and scowling. "Never call it again. If you do, I will hunt you down."

"Stoney," a voice said, low and mild. "Needed to catch you at home. And you're always home for *Jeopardy*."

Picking up the remote with his free hand, Walter broke his cardinal rule and hit the pause button. "Martin," he said, inwardly swearing. "It's been a long time."

"It has," Martin Jellicoe agreed. "I thought maybe you'd retired, what with your top two earners gone."

"Oh, you know how it is. There're always more guys out there who think they're Cary Grant. So, what can I do for you?"

"Well, to start with, Stoney, you can stop ratting out contacts to the British guy. And don't lie to me about it, either. There's nobody else in the damn world who could narrow the globe down to one guy in Amsterdam as fast as you managed it."

That would be Daan Van der Berg. Of course Addison would have called the guy and threatened him, even after their chat about confidentiality and rumors. *Shit.* "I'm not apologizing," he said aloud. "You're going up against Sam, when she's just trying to live her life. I don't know how to tell you, Martin, but you ain't Cary Grant any more, either."

"If I'm no match for her, why help her out? Why stack the deck against your oldest friend?"

"You're missing the point, Martin. Sam's making a go of the straight life. Leave her alone. Dads aren't supposed to make things harder on their own kids."

"Maybe *you're* missing the point," Martin retorted. "Firstly that letting her give up the life was a mistake, and secondly that she only went into the security business because of me. Everything she's doing is to try to beat me. I'm just making sure she knows she can't."

Walter shook his head. Always self-centered and with an elephant-sized ego, Martin wasn't going to be one of those guys who got smarter and wiser with age. Just more desperate to prove he wasn't losing a step. And trying to demonstrate that to the one person who definitely was going to notice differences between in-his-prime Martin and today Martin.

"I'm assuming Van der Berg canceled his order," he said aloud. "You don't have any reason to try to get into that exhibit now. Just leave it, Martin."

"You probably tell her she's better than I am, don't you?"

"She was. She's not doing that shit anymore."

"If she's leaving the business, she needs to leave it. Not just work parallel to it and call it good deeds. No, this isn't about filling an order, Stoney. This is about teaching Sam a lesson. She's never going to beat me, so if she wants out of this life she can go teach piano lessons or be a librarian. Every time she tries to wall me off from *my* profession, I'm going to jump her fence. You get me?"

"And if you're wrong and Addison uses his weight to get you put back in the slam?"

Martin snorted. "Then the first thing I'll do is give Sam all the credit she deserves for all the hard work she's done. Hell, I'm a generous soul. I'll even give her credit for some of my work. That's what dads do, right?"

"No. No, it isn't. At all. You—"

"Tell her what I said. You tell her everything anyway, don't you? See you around, Stoney. The where and how and when is up to you."

The line went silent. Walter waited for a beat, then set the phone back on the table. No mention of Anne or the mother-daughter reunion stunt Sam had figured Martin would be pulling, and that made it more likely. Back in the day he and

Martin Jellicoe *had* been friends. They'd shared a lifestyle and a penchant for enjoying getting hold of some really valuable things, if only as the middlemen.

When Sam had appeared in Martin's company the dynamic had changed, and he'd ultimately been relieved when the news had gotten out that Martin had died in prison. It had made things easier. Things like Sam taking a legit job as an art restorer, for one. And it had changed *him*, probably more than he'd realized. Martin might be her biological father, but having her in his life had made Walter feel like a dad.

Today she'd asked him to walk her down the aisle, for Christ's sake. And he was supposed to sit there and let Martin mess up her life again? Fuck that.

He lifted the phone again and opened one of the apps. Being careful, thinking ten steps ahead of where he was, had helped make him wealthy and had kept him out of prison. Sometimes, though, the steps had to change without any warning. And sometimes, taking a risk was worth it. Or at least he damn well hoped so.

In five minutes he had a flight booked to New York. Then he shut off his television and went to retrieve his emergency travel bag. Both Jellicoes were unstoppable forces and immovable objects, and if he was going to get in between them, he was going to do it with his eyes wide open, an escape plan in place, and all his fingers crossed. *Jeopardy* would have to wait. He was about to get in some for real.

14

Monday, 10:12 a.m.

Samantha wished that on occasion journalists, photographers, bloggers, and media people in general would leave her alone long enough that she could forget how much she disliked all of them. She jabbed a finger toward the opposite side of the first jewelry room in the Victorian house. "The exhibit is over there."

The photographer lowered her camera from her face. "Sorry, but you're news, too." Her finger moved, and the shutter clicked again.

Keeping her expression as easy as she could considering that she wanted to toss the camera down the elevator shaft, Samantha nodded. "Okay. If you keep it up, though, I'm going to make sure you're not invited to the wedding. And considering how few photographers and journalists I actually know, your odds a minute ago were pretty good."

The camera lowered further. "Really? I kind of need more than you just insinuating things."

"Give me two of your cards." Samantha held out one hand.

The woman complied, pulling a pair of cards from her all-purpose photography vest and handing them over. Samantha pocketed one and wrote down her cell number on the back of the other before she handed it back. "That's me," she said, patting the pocket of her nice pants where she'd put her phone. "Don't bug me, but give me a call after the first of the year and hopefully I'll have a date and location for you."

"I don't quite believe you," Stephanie Freven said, putting the card in a different vest pocket, "but it's worth the risk. No more photos of you today, except for any official ones."

"There won't be any official ones with me," Samantha returned. "I'm background."

"You could have given her my number," Aubrey said from beside her as the woman strolled away. "I'm happy to be a buffer."

"Are you my wedding coordinator, now?"

He shrugged. "I could be. I've been to a great many weddings. Very fancy ones."

"I'm tempted, but first you have to tell me who's holding down the office while you're here."

"I asked Bobbi Camden and George Narvaez. I figured they could keep an eye on each other."

She nodded. "I like that they're from two different teams. Good job."

"Well, we'll see when we get back, won't we? If my filing is unalphabetized, heads will roll." He nudged her shoulder when she didn't react. "I chatted with a few hoity-toities," he commented, thankfully lowering his voice. "One was aware of the Adgerton auction, but nobody seemed either overly inter-ested or evasive. In my opinion, anyway."

"Thanks for checking. It was a long shot, but we do, on occa-sion, come up lucky." Maybe that was the real problem, she reflected; she'd been too lucky in her career for too long, and now all the bad thief karma was about to unload on her like a ton of granite.

As she'd stood aside to watch Anne deliver her presentation to the press and other Sotheby's honchos and then answer every question like the pro she was, it had occurred to Samantha that this probably wouldn't be the end of it. Every time she got a job protecting something that Martin wanted or at a location he had a grudge against, he could show up again. She could spend the rest of her new career fighting off her own damned dad.

The solutions to this problem, though, mostly entailed things that she didn't even want to think about. She'd made a point throughout her criminal career of not getting other people hurt. To turn around now and wish Martin would be crushed beneath a metal door was both icky and wrong. Seeing him back in prison would be more than enough, thank you very much.

When another of the journalists started giving her sideways looks, she patted Aubrey on the shoulder. "Keep up the charm offensive as needed. I'm going down to the security room to hover like a vulture."

"Anne will appreciate you not letting yourself get put into the spotlight on her big day," he muttered, smiling at the man as he neared them.

"This is her show. She's welcome to all the spotlight she can get." Before Mr. Nosey could aim his cellphone in her direction, Samantha ducked backward, turning left to trot down the stairs to the main floor and then to the back of the house and down the utility stairs to the shut and locked door of the security room.

It opened before she could knock. "Saw you coming," Rhee said, resuming his seat in front of the monitors and keyboard.

Samantha took the chair next to him. "Everybody behaving?"

"Yep. One of the guys tapped on the glass of one of the

displays and the pressure alert went off to alert me to it, but other than that we're good. I mean, the alert was good, too; that's what it's supposed to do."

"You've got Cassie up to speed on everything so you'll have some backup?" Cassie Veldez was apparently a newbie to Sotheby's security division, but she had a good eye, and Samantha hadn't gotten any weird vibes from her. She didn't read like a Martin plant, anyway.

"I do. And even though they think we're a bunch of paranoid idiots, I did like you asked and got Sotheby's to do random checks of the system and display from their office every couple of minutes. If something looks hinky, they can notify the cops from there."

"Good. The more eyes, the better."

He sent her a sideways glance. "You know, us getting hit and the black hat getting caught is the only way Sotheby's will ever spring for this much security again."

"Yeah, I know. One of the perils of a job where the ideal summary is 'nothing happened.'"

A yellow light blinked in the bottom left corner of monitor three, and at the same time a two-tone alert sounded. Rhee sat forward, zooming in to the indicated panel of glass to see some random guy's hand making a stupid handprint all over it. "Same damn guy as before," he grunted.

Before he could acknowledge the alert and reset it, Samantha shifted. "Wait."

"In five more seconds, the alert's going to sound."

"Let it."

In five seconds, a loud buzz echoed through the rooms of the Victorian house. "Please refrain from leaning on the glass displays," an automated male voice said.

The guy jumped, stepping back from the display. In the middle of the room, Anne smiled then explained about the top-of-the-line security system Sotheby's had installed to insure the protection of all the Adgerton pieces.

"Heh," Rhee snorted, resetting the alert even though the system was ninety-five percent automated. People-proof, or so Samantha hoped.

"I still think we should have gone with a Darth Vader voice, but that one definitely does the trick," Samantha observed.

Marv unlocked the door and walked in, a clipboard in his hands. "I ran all the credentials, Sam," he reported. "Everybody checks out."

"See? And you didn't have to frisk anyone."

The security guard grimaced. "Thanks for letting me test out the wand, anyway."

"It was a good show. You'll make the news, and everybody will see that Sotheby's isn't fucking around where security is concerned."

"That Bradley Martin guy, especially. I almost wish he would show up. We'd get this kind of funding for every exhibit if we actually nabbed a cat burglar in the act."

"That's what I said." Rhee seconded him. "Hey, the guy in the blue hoodie's been leaning in the plaster and ceramics doorway for five minutes, and he's giving me a partially blocked view of the lefthand corner. See if you can get him to move, will you?"

"You got it." Marv set down the clipboard and headed out again.

This was all going really well; everything was working the way it should, problems with the angles of the sun and the glass reflections had been minimized, every sensor was green, and Samantha still kept most of her attention on the outside cameras. She knew what Martin looked like. He wasn't inside the Victorian. That meant he was outside. The only thing was, she didn't know where, exactly, he was lurking.

So this was how it was going to go; her sitting, waiting,

monitoring, and nothing happening—until it did. Or it didn't. And now, from what Rhee and Marv had said, if Martin and everyone else left the place alone, Sotheby's would think Anne had overspent on security, and one Sam Jellicoe had overdelivered at an exorbitant price. So neither outcome looked particularly good for her.

That was Martin, though, wrecking everything within arms' length to make one of his stupid "I'm better than you" points. And he had the remarkable ability to do it remotely. Nope, he didn't even need to show up at all for her future Sotheby's job prospects to go down the drain. Jerk.

He could ruin Jellicoe Security the same way. Call in a vague threat every time she got a new contract, and Samantha would overdo it on the security. She knew she would, because Martin pushed all her damn buttons, and extreme security was the only way to keep him out—wherever he actually happened to be. Her good reputation would slowly change to mention her paranoia, her excessive reliance on expensive, cutting-edge technology, and in that final stab of irony, the way nothing ever happened, despite her dire warnings.

Maybe she needed to focus on stolen-item recovery, after all. At least that way other people knew something had happened, and she just needed to show up with the missing whatever-it-was. No fuss, no muss, and she could bust windows and bad people's alarm systems to her heart's content.

Sure, security installation was a better long-term career option, but if she was going to have to factor in Martin Jellicoe every time she went to work, she wasn't so sure it was what she wanted, after all. There had to be an easier way to stop him than dropping an anvil on his head, Wiley Coyote style.

"Okay," Anne said, reviewing her to-do list one last time, "catalogs printed. Maps printed. Auction date set, notifications posted and placed in catalogs. Tickets printed. Staffing arranged for. Employees screened." She glanced up. "What am I forgetting?"

"Parking validations?" Sam suggested, squatting to pick up a stray piece of paper from the floor of one of the exhibit rooms. She examined it, crumpled it, and dumped it into her pocket.

Neither of them seemed willing to leave anything to chance. Not even suspicious pieces of paper. "We have those, too. And the restroom's been checked, and we have fresh toilet paper and hand soap."

"It all sounds good," her daughter commented, leading the way down the stairs. "I'm still tempted to sit here on the landing all night, just in case."

"You and me, both. He didn't used to be a tease, you know. If he said he was going to do something, he did it. But that was back when he was Bradley. Maybe he's learned patience."

"It's not patience. He's already set the date and the time he's going to try to break in. The rest is about running us as ragged as possible until then so we make mistakes. All it takes is one, if you're any good. One mistake somebody else makes, and bam, you've got a Picasso under your arm."

Anne paused in the foyer. "But you can't plan on mistakes. He must have a plan to get in regardless, yes?"

"Oh, I'm sure he does. But I think I blocked every way he could get in unless he's a human mole now and can dig underneath the building. But I put sensors in the floor, too, so we'd know as soon as his mole head popped into view."

"In that case," Anne commented, still reluctant to leave the house to its electronic protection alone, "would you be interested in joining me for dinner? I'd like some non-work time for the two of us to just…chat."

"I'd like that, too, but as far as we want Martin to know right now, we're just coworkers. After the auction, maybe."

That hurt a little bit—okay it hurt a lot—but she did understand Sam's reasoning. Some obvious reluctance at turning down the invitation would have been nice, though, instead of what she was coming to recognize as her daughter's standard direct approach.

"Definitely then," Anne said aloud. "May I ask what you have planned for the rest of the day?"

"Aubrey bought me a guide to getting married, so I may look through that. Or burn it. I haven't decided which, yet. And I need to check back in with a couple of people to see if they've figured out anything new about Martin's plans, or his target." Sam gave a small grimace. "You?"

"I thought I'd give my mother a call," Anne answered. "I haven't told her about you yet. Still trying to figure out how to do that without giving her a heart attack."

"I have a grandma? Wow. It never occurred to me to ask. What about a grandpa?"

"Your grandfather died about twelve years ago. Lung cancer. He could not give up the cigarettes."

"I'm sorry. You know, I kind of remember chasing some big guy with a beard around a yard and yelling at him to drop the cigarette. Maybe I dreamed it, though."

Good heavens. "No, that was real. He'd go outside to light up, and you'd chase him until he gave it up, though I actually think it was because you liked the piggyback rides."

Sam smiled. "That's cool, then. I do remember something." A horn honked outside, and she turned to look through the nearest window. "And that's my ride. I'll see you about half an hour before opening tomorrow, right?"

"Yes. Definitely. You and Rick have a good evening."

"Thanks. You, too."

They headed outside together, and Sam looked over her

shoulder as she locked the door and made sure the alarm was set. This was it. No more fiddling, no more alarm tests, no more practices. Everyone interested in anything Adgerton had ever collected would be coming by starting tomorrow at nine o'clock. "Should we post a photo of Bradley by the ticket booth and in the security room? It just struck me that you may be the only one who might recognize him." She might, as well, but it had been twenty years—and for some reason she kept imagining him making his appearance in a trench coat with a fake moustache.

Sam shrugged. "He talks a big game, but I doubt he has the guts to just stroll in. I've warned him that the next time I set eyes on him, I'm calling the cops. He might think I'm bluffing, but he probably also wonders if I'm not."

Anne looked at her daughter for a moment. "Are you?"

"Nope."

Abruptly that struck her as being very...sad. What a life this woman had known. A life nothing like the one her mother had intended for her. "I'm sorry to have you in the middle of this."

"I'm not. It was bound to come down to a him or me situation, and I've got backup now. Plus, there's you. It's all his loss, as far as I'm concerned. He didn't have to do the things he did; he chose to do them. People *can* change. I know that, because I've done it."

"I really want to hug you right now."

"That's some good wine, isn't it?" Sam said, grinning as she headed to the edge of the sidewalk.

"Yes. A very fine vintage." Now they were at code words and turning in people's fathers, and the exhibit hadn't even opened yet. The next few weeks were going to be a hoot.

She lifted a hand to hail a cab. As one pulled to the curb, she opened the back door and slid in, giving her address. At this moment, the thing that kept her from tearing out her hair and running away, screaming, was the idea of after. After this was finished, Martin would somehow or other be gone, and she would still have a daughter back again. The holidays were coming up. Thanksgiving. Christmas. She had no idea what someone gave to a young woman who could acquire anything she wanted practically by thinking it, but she looked forward to the challenge.

The after had family gatherings, at least one wedding, laughter, and a hundred other things she'd just begun to imagine. The idea that Bradley Martin had both caused the separation and the reunion didn't make her look on him with any sort of kindness or forgiveness, especially when he could theoretically continue to create problems for Sam, but she couldn't help wondering if some small part of him felt bad for what he'd done and this was his twisted, horrible way of making amends.

Her phone jangled in her pocket, and she jumped. "Mr. Pendleton?" she said, pulling it free and tapping on the little green phone image. "Are you trying to reach Sam?"

"No," his soft, cultured drawl came. "I was hoping I could have a word or two with you, Miss Anne, if you have the time. Is there somewhere we could meet?"

"Um, sure. There's a deli around the corner from my apartment. Will that work?"

"That would be lovely."

She gave him the address. "Say twenty minutes?"

"I will be there with a hot cup of coffee for you."

Hm. Aubrey Pendleton was a fine-looking man, if a bit... overgroomed. Not that she was after another relationship. She'd been avoiding those for the past two decades. But a cup of coffee? That, she could manage.

○

"IF I PROMISE to bid on something, can I be there on opening day?" Richard asked, wondering when he'd last asked permission to do something. Mutual consent was one thing, but even if he felt like an idiot asking her, he did not want Samantha resenting his presence.

She unbuckled her seat belt as Benny pulled up outside the hotel's main entrance. "You will attract attention."

He got out of his side of the Mercedes before Benny could come around and open the door for him. "I'm not the only one. This is a well-known collection. Other big names in buying things—or their minions—are going to show up. Are you going to stop them at the door, too, so they don't distract the staff?"

She blew out her breath, nodding as Vince opened the lobby door for her. "Thanks, Vince. Hey, do you know who Lewis Adgerton is?"

The beefy concierge narrowed his eyes. "He's the dead rich guy, isn't he?"

Ha. "See?" Richard put in. "Everyone knows."

Samantha kept walking toward the elevators. "Fine. But you can't just bid. You have to buy something."

"Like we're at a PTA bake sale?"

Snorting, she grabbed his hand as the doors slid open. "That's right. Mom has to sell her stuff, or she'll think people don't like her baking."

"Very well," he conceded. "I will buy something."

"Then you can come."

"Thank you." The elevator doors opened on their small, private foyer, and he stepped in front of Samantha, shoving her backward even as he caught sight of the dark, hooded figure standing by the apartment door. With his free hand he reached into his coat pocket for the butt of his .45. *Jesus.*

"Wait!"

"It's me, it's me," Walter Barstone said on the tail of Samantha's protest, reaching up to push the hoodie off his head. "Hey, there."

Taking a deep breath, Richard let go of the pistol. "That's it.

Vince is supposed to inform us when we have people lurking for us."

"Vince? The lobby guy? Don't blame him. I came in the back way. Spent an hour sitting in your living room until I decided that would be creepy and I came out here to wait."

Richard brushed by him and pulled open the door. "It's still creepy," he stated, walking into the apartment.

"Yeah, but less creepy."

"Okay, Stoney," Samantha took up. "What are you doing here?"

"We need to have a chat. A face-to-face one."

That was *never* a good thing. Walter Barstone never meant anything good for Samantha, however much credit he deserved for at least keeping her from turning into her father. Richard took a breath. Perhaps the fence wasn't so bad, then, all things considered. "Then you should come in," he said. "Wine, beer, or diet Coke?"

From Samantha's expression his acceptance of this newest bit of chaos surprised her, but hell, he'd known her for a little over a year. Chaos followed her like a crazy, rabid dog. He was becoming accustomed to it.

"Beer," Walter said, making his way to the living room.

They'd intended to go out for dinner tonight, so Andre hadn't come by to cook for them. Another best-laid plan now gone astray. "Should I order a pizza?" Richard asked aloud, pulling out his phone. "Mexican? Chinese? Indian?"

"Can I get a salad with some chicken or something in it?" Walter asked. "I'm trying to eat healthier but not starve myself."

Beer in one hand, Samantha stopped in her tracks, turned around, returned to the kitchen, and reemerged a moment later with a bottle of water and her ever-present diet Coke and no beer. "Why are you eating healthier?" she asked, handing the bottle of water over to the fence.

"Really, Sam?"

"Your DNA is eighty percent tacos, Stoney," she returned, dropping onto the couch and curling her legs beneath her, catlike. "And twenty percent beer. Explain the salad."

They were family, Richard reminded himself. To him, Walter was an annoyance. To her, he was closer to her than her own father, and she certainly trusted him more than she did Martin —and with good reason. When something changed, she noticed it. And she worried.

"I just had my annual checkup, is all," the big man commented, opening the water and eyeing it like he worried it would bite him. "My cholesterol's creeping up. Therefore, three salads a week, a walk every morning, and fewer beers."

"And you're sure that's it? You don't secretly have consumption or something?"

Snorting, the fence downed a swallow of water. "Nope. Or the Black Death plague."

"Good. What the hell are you doing here, then? Yesterday we were talking about…vacations from each other."

"Amicable separation," Richard amended, placing an order for pizza and a chicken Caesar salad and then texting Vince to let him know it would be arriving in thirty minutes or less.

"I remember," Walter answered, sending a glare over his shoulder at Richard. Their mistrust was mutual. "Started daydreaming about that villa in France I always talked about. You know, the one where you lived on the next hill over?"

"With the little donkey path in between? I remember."

Richard folded his arms over his chest. She wanted a villa in France? Well, he could do that. And he could buy her some donkeys. That would take a lot more maneuvering than a move to New York, but the effort was beside the point. Why hadn't she ever mentioned a villa to him?

"Yeah. I was daydreaming myself out there on the veranda, sipping some wine in the sunset, and then my damn phone rang. Martin."

"Shit." Samantha straightened. "What did he want?"

"He wants you to be a librarian." Still looking like he expected a crocodile to be swimming in his bottle of water, Walter took another swig.

"Come again?"

Richard walked into the kitchen, pulled two beers out of the refrigerator, and returned to hand one to Walter. "This seems like an alcohol sort of story."

"Amen to that."

"Stoney."

"Sorry, Honey. I need a drink first." Unscrewing the cap, Walter tilted the bottle back and took a long drink. "There we go. Much better. So yeah. He wants you to stop dipping your toes into his world. To stop throwing fences up in front of him, because he swears he will jump them each and every time to keep proving that you're not better than he is. Which you are, but which he would never admit."

"Did he actually say librarian?"

It seemed like a frivolous detail to him, but Richard was well aware of how her little crime family operated, with their code words and seemingly throwaway phrases that actually meant things that were likely to give him a heart attack later. "Does that mean something?" he asked aloud.

"He said librarian or piano teacher."

Samantha sat back. "He probably got that out of *The Music Man* movie. He thinks that's what 'normal,' quote unquote, women do. Unmarried women, that is. Jackass."

"Well, sure they did, a hundred fifty years ago. In movies." Richard sat beside her and unscrewed his own beer. "Not that I would ever say anything to credit Martin, but perhaps that's his way of saying he wants you to have a normal life."

"Nah," Walter countered. "It's his way of saying that Sam's ticking him off and he wants her to get away from his business." Clearing his throat, he took another drink of beer. "And the reason I booked a flight here as soon as I hung up with him is because I had the feeling that he's planning on lowering the hammer on you, honey. A 'lesson you won't forget' type of thing."

"You're choosing sides, then." Samantha sat forward. "And you know what that'll mean."

The fence looked at her for a long couple of seconds. "You asked me to walk you down the damn aisle. I can't do that if one of us is in the slam. And Martin said if you turn him in, he's going to start talking about you. Give you all the credit you deserve, plus the blame for some of the shit he pulled, probably under Interpol's nose."

"Maybe you should have started with that, Walter." *Fuck.* That had been the sticking point all along—that if they did stop Martin and managed to get him arrested, he would turn around and provide all that pesky missing information about Samantha that had kept her well under the radar for the past ten years. "Would he, really?"

"To get himself back in good with Interpol or shave a couple of years off a sentence? In a heartbeat." Slumping back again, Samantha took a drink of her soda like she wished it was gin.

Richard brushed his fingers across her cheek. "Then you leave this to me," he murmured.

She slapped his hand down. "Why? So you can kill him? You've got a temper, Rick. I'll give you that. But you are not going to murder anybody and wreck your own life. There are like, hundreds of people who rely on you for their livelihood."

"I am not—" Richard stopped, swallowing hard. Jesus, he couldn't even say the words aloud. "You are not going to prison. I am therefore giving you three choices."

"Oh, you're giving *me* choices? When did—"

"Stop." He glared at her until she closed her mouth. "One, you can shut off the alarms and let Martin take whatever the hell he wants. Two, you can stop him however you planned to and take the consequences, at which point we will move permanently to Brunei or Austria or France, because they—"

"No extradition treaty with the U.S.," Stoney cut in. "We've got all those countries memorized."

"Yes. No extradition. Or, three, you let me deal with Martin, and we proceed as planned."

"All I need to do is keep him from getting in there," Samantha stated, her jaw clenched. "I'm doing that. I've done it. Short of slamming a trash truck through the building, he's not getting in."

"And what about your next job?" he asked. "Do you really want to go through this every time you contract with somebody to provide security?"

"No, I really don't," she snapped. "That doesn't mean I want to jump over the Grand Canyon of idiot ideas to murder, though."

"Neither do I. It's my worst-case scenario. No, my second-worst. The worst is you going to prison."

"Wow," Walter commented from his seat in the chair. "Not even I was thinking about offing Martin, and I'm the bad guy in this trio."

"I will protect Samantha," Richard insisted. "No matter the consequences. But I am ready to hear other plans that leave Martin permanently out of our lives and unable to implicate her in any crimes."

Yes, it sounded violent, and yes, he did have a mean streak that had last showed itself when he'd found his ex-wife in bed with his ex-friend and he'd hung her out to dry with the lawyers —after filling her apartment with dirty mattresses up to the ceiling. This wasn't anger over betrayal, though; it was fear, about what prison would do to his Samantha, and about what not having her in his life would do to him.

Samantha's phone rang, and she glanced down at it. "Vince," she said, accepting the call. "The pizza's here already?" She listened for a second, then uncurled from the couch and stood. "Send 'em on up."

"Who?" Rick asked. "We're in the middle of something here."

"I know that." She walked to the door, her attention on Walter. "Sorry about this, Stoney. In my head we did this over dinner somewhere nice, and you would be wearing a tie."

The fence scowled. "Wha—"

She pulled open the door and stepped backward. Anne, Aubrey Pendleton on her heels, walked into the apartment. No one had wine this time, Richard noted as he rose. Old-fashioned or not, an English gentleman always stood when a woman entered a room. Especially one that would shortly be his mother-in-law. "Anne," he said, nodding. "Aubrey."

"Rick. Hi, Sam." Anne started forward, her arms lifting, until she caught sight of Walter. Immediately she stopped. "I forgot the wine," she said, in a tone that would have alerted anyone within a ten-block radius that something was suspicious was afoot.

"That's okay. Anne, this is Walter Barstone. Stoney, my mom, Anne Hughes."

Walter shot to his feet, nearly dropped his beer, set it on a side table, and shook droplets off his fingers as he came forward. "Very pleased to meet you, Ms. Hughes," he said, wiping his hand on his pants before he stuck it out to her.

Anne shook it. "Mr. Barstone."

"Stoney, please. I mean, we're kind of family."

They both glanced at Samantha. "I suppose we are," she said with a quick smile. "But we've got some trouble."

"Yeah, we do." Samantha returned to her seat and curled up again. "It occurs to me that I should've become an adventurer cryptozoologist who free dives after man-eating squid. That would've been more sensible."

"You don't like seafood," Stoney observed, resuming his seat across from Samantha.

"As if disliking calamari would be the main reason not to dive into a man-eating squid's tentacles." Samantha watched as everyone took seats and Rick wordlessly upped the pizza and salad order to account for additional people, being civilized even if he had just suggested offing Martin Jellicoe.

Samantha had on occasion seen Rick's temper, like when he'd ripped apart her emergency go-bag and tossed the contents into the pool at Solano Dorado. But it had always been a controlled, pointed anger, with enough thought behind it to figure out how and where to do the most damage. Not the smack-you shit, ever, because she wouldn't have tolerated that, but more the I'll-ruin-you-and-your-entire-company-for-lying-to-me-about-your-actual-net-worth shit.

Kill Martin? Sure, she'd thought about how much easier her life would be now without him in it, but Rick only knew the bad stuff. There had been the odd spaghetti dinner and a beer before she was old enough to drink it, the way he'd taught her things she'd been able to use later on her own that had saved both her and the heist from going sideways.

"Okay," Anne said, accepting a glass of wine from Rick and handing a second one over to Aubrey. "I'm not quite sure how to start, here."

"Maybe Stoney should go first," Samantha suggested, gesturing. "He flew in with news."

She sat back as her surrogate dad, a Ving Rhames stunt double in slacks and a neat pink-and-blue dress shirt with short sleeves now that he'd shed the black hoodie, recounted what he'd already told her and Rick. As she watched, a couple of things occurred to her: first, while she'd talked around enough things to give Aubrey an idea of her past, he didn't look the least bit surprised at hearing details; and second, what he *did* look was seriously worried. And he *never* looked worried. Smooth and amiable were his superpowers.

Him together with Anne didn't make much sense, either,

because while he was a distinguished-looking older man, she'd always had the feeling that he was gay. Rick disagreed, but she'd been around her office manager far more than he had. Aside from all that, none of this had date vibes.

When Stoney finished, everybody needed a drink refill. Rick obliged, again being the perfect host even while he was probably still thinking of the best way to off Martin and get away with it. If this was the Upside Down, Manhattan version, Samantha didn't much like it.

"Aubrey," she said, accepting a second can of soda from Rick, "we're trusting you with some stuff here. I know you probably knew, but now it's official. I hope you're okay with getting the whole story."

"What she isn't saying," Rick took up, sitting beside her again, "is that you now know some things that could have consequences for Samantha. Unpleasant ones. We should have asked where you stand first, but you're in it now. And we're trusting you."

The sometime social-events-escort gulped down the rest of his wine like it was water. "I can't sugarcoat this," he stated, looking over at Anne.

"Let me start," she countered, "and we'll take it from there."

"No. It's too late." Aubrey faced Samantha, his ruddy face pretty pale for a guy who tanned professionally. "I know who you are, Miss Samantha. I've known for nearly ten months, now."

That would have been about the time they first met. "Did I say something that tipped you off?" she asked. What was so horrible about that, she didn't know. If he'd been keeping her secret for more than nine months already, she owed him a steak dinner. A couple of them.

"Yeah. 'Jellicoe.' Miss Samantha, I'm with the FBI."

A couple of things happened at once. Rick, one hand diving into his pocket, stood and put himself between her and Aubrey;

Stoney stood up so fast he knocked his chair over backward; she started choking on the mouthful of diet Coke she'd just tried swallowing; and Anne put both hands over her face and sank deeper into the couch cushions as if she was trying to hide.

Samantha noted all of it in a second, at the same time pounding herself on the chest and fighting the weirdest thought that she wished she could be an old-fashioned fainty woman and just black out and wake up after somebody else had taken care of everything.

Aubrey moved his hands away from his sides. "Hey, we're all friends here. Nobody get any crazy ideas," he said, his drawl deepening and his gaze on Rick's pocket.

"Careful," Stoney warned, still ducked behind the tipped-over chair. "Nobody say anything but 'lawyer.' Don't answer anything, don't admit to anything."

"Everybody take a breath," Aubrey advised.

"Lawyer! I want my damn lawyer!"

It all began to sink in. FBI. *The FBI*. In her house, in her office, in her life. How the fuck had she not known that? She liked Aubrey Pendleton. She trusted him. "Is Aubrey Pendleton even your real name?" Samantha asked when she'd coughed the rest of the soda out of her lungs.

"Yes, it is. And before you arrived on everybody's radar, I was ratting out old ladies who stole jewelry and old men who stole from their own banks. I was good at it, too."

"Stop talking," Rick growled. "Walter, there's some climbing gear in the left bedroom closet. Get the rope."

"Yep. I saw it earlier." Looking very happy to be leaving the room, Walter rolled to his feet and took off running across the living room.

Samantha stood up, moving slowly and deliberately until she stood beside Rick. "Take your hand out of your pocket."

"No."

"I get it," Aubrey said, despite Rick's warning. "You put a

samurai sword through a guy's shoulder because he threatened Miss Sam. You protect her. Think about it, though. There's a reason it's me sitting here, and not a bunch of guys with bullet-proof vests."

Rick stared at him. "You'd best have a very good story," he finally said in his crispest British accent, blowing out his breath. He pulled his empty hand from his pocket. Samantha knew he had a gun in there, though. Nobody was getting shot on her watch. Not if she had anything to say about it.

"Don't try to be charming, Aubrey," she suggested. "Just tell me what the hell is going on."

"Okay. But that guy you put a sword through, Rick? I burned down his house. So give me a minute to say a few things, if you don't mind."

Samantha blinked. "Y—That was you?"

"He was creepy," Aubrey supplied, as if that was sufficient. It did make her think about a few things, though, so maybe it was.

"Okay," she said, keeping a hand on Rick's arm. "Talk."

The story he told, about going from small-time white-collar criminal-finder to being assigned to stalk her, made Samantha's hair stand up on end. For nine months the FBI had been actively investigating her, and she hadn't had a clue. She'd always prided herself on being alert, being one step ahead of whoever might be after her, but this time the lack of handcuffs had nothing to do with her or her actions.

"I don't get why you haven't given them enough to put me in the slam, yet." Samantha picked up Rick's discarded beer and took a swallow. A good buzz would have been nice, but the wiser part of her didn't like giving up that much control, so she set it back on the table.

"That's the part that's been bugging me, too. And them." Aubrey took a deep breath. "You've mentioned bits of things, enough that I could look up unsolved heists and figure out to which one you were referring. But...you came out of the shadows, Miss Sam, when you didn't have to. You were literally a blank page with a whole bunch of question marks on it. And since you stepped out, you haven't done anything wrong. Hell, you've even caught a couple of bad guys and turned them in."

"You admire my style of vigilante justice?" she suggested, ignoring Rick's unamused growl.

"In a sense, yes. This...I mean, I watched you in real time. You gave up the life. A very lucrative life. I don't know if you feel like it's your penance, or you just changed your point of view, but you stepped away and you haven't slipped. Not once. Sure, you've done a couple of shady things, but those were to help people."

"Just get to the point, will you?" Rick finally snapped. "What is it you want? Because you're not taking her out of this room."

"He's been stalling the FBI," Anne finally said. "Looking for a way to keep everyone happy *without* putting you in prison, Sam. When you told him about Martin, he thought your father's presence could be...useful."

"It won't be." Stoney had picked up his chair, but he continued to stand, the bulk of the furniture between him and the door and the rappelling rope in his land like a lasso. For him to even stay in the room with an FBI agent surprised Samantha; he reacted to the law the way some people reacted to walking into a spiderweb. "Martin'll rat Sam out if he ends up in jail over this. He told me so. Which is why *I* flew up here."

"The way I see it," Anne countered, her voice taking on a matter-of-fact mom tone that Samantha remembered hearing from Katie Donner when she'd had it with her kids, "we have a trap set. We have a rat. And we have a rat catcher. Don't tell me there isn't something we can figure out to get Martin far away from here and not endanger Sam. Think, people."

Stoney glanced from her to Samantha. "Jesus," he muttered. "You *are* related."

"So you won't turn me in?" Samantha asked, sitting down

243

again to lean her elbows on her knees and putting all of her attention on Aubrey Pendleton. "Or you won't turn me in if you can get hold of Martin, instead?"

"Neither one," Rick stated, his jaw still clenched. "Both end with you in jeopardy."

"Stoney, is there anything that would keep Martin's trap shut?" Samantha continued. Rick's white knight thing was cool, but right now he was a roadblock to any thinking, in or out of the box.

"You mean like did he ever kill someone and only tell me about it? No."

"Is there a job, then, that if anybody knew he did it, would get him in bigger trouble than what Interpol or the FBI could threaten?"

"No," Stoney answered. A second later, though, he set his second bottle of beer on the side table. "Hold that. Let me think for a minute."

Rick faced her and grabbed her hand. "It doesn't matter what we might speculate about," he muttered, catching and holding her gaze, "because it is too much to risk."

"Look," she returned, keeping her voice low, too. "I'm freaked out. I nearly jumped out the front window when Aubrey said those three letters I won't even repeat because they give me hives. But if he's looking for a way to keep me out of trouble when I'm already on the white hats' radar, I'm going to try to help him find it. So go call Donner or something, because right now you are not being helpful."

He blinked, then took a step backward. Good as he was at hiding what he was thinking, she saw this one plain and clear. He was pissed off. And hurt. She tried reaching for his hand, but he moved out of the way and stalked to the main bedroom door, walked through, and slammed it shut behind him.

"Sam," Anne whispered, shifting over to take his place.

"Yeah, I'm going to pay for that one later," she muttered.

It occurred to her that he might have just decided she wasn't worth the trouble that seemed to boil up around her, and that he *was* on the phone with Donner, arranging to have her excised from his life. That she'd pushed him too far. That he'd realized what a fucking mistake he'd made in falling for her in the first place.

Vince rang the buzzer with the pizza, and Anne got up to take it from him. That was good, because Samantha wasn't sure she could move. Everything felt cold and frozen as a block of ice, and however much she needed to be thinking of a way to get herself out of this mess, every bit of her stayed focused on that door at the far end of the room.

What had she done? *Crap.* Taking the private plane tonight to France or Austria with Rick wouldn't be so bad. In fact, it could be pretty awesome. Of course he'd get all of the assets he hadn't already moved in case of this emergency frozen, the aunt and uncle and cousin he'd just reconnected with after ten years would start pretending neither of them existed, he'd be booted off all the executive and charity boards he currently sat on, and he'd lose the bulk of the art he'd spent his life collecting, and never be able to do legit business anywhere outside the country where they landed ever again. But hey, they'd be together, right?

Stoney went into the kitchen and pulled down some plates, and she shook herself. "Did you open *every* cabinet and drawer?"

He shrugged his broad shoulders. "Pretty much. I got bored waiting for you."

Making herself stand, she put two slices on one plate and a single on the other, picked them up, and headed for the bedroom. "Keep thinking," she said over her shoulder.

The door wasn't locked, at least, and balancing both plates on one arm, she turned the knob and stepped inside, shutting the door again before Rick could bellow at her to get out or something.

"'I'm not helping'?" he repeated, turning from the far

window. *"I'm* not helping. After everything I've done to keep you safe and to allow us to stay together if something ever—"

"You went right to DEFCON one," she interrupted, beginning to think she should have taken another beat or two to figure out exactly what she was going to say. "The thing is, I want to stay. Here. With you. With Stoney and Anne and even all the Donners but Tom. With your plan, yeah, we'd be safe, but we'd also be fugitives and everything would be ruined for you."

"I don't c—"

"I know you don't care," she cut in again. "Or you say you don't, which is nice. But I happen to like this life, now. The one I have with you. Therefore, if we can scrounge together a fifty-one percent chance to salvage the situation without murder or me getting arrested or us fleeing to parts unknown, and if it maybe involves just a little mayhem and subterfuge, I am going to take that risk. So stop jumping straight to planetary destruction mode before we check out all the other levels of peril. Okay?"

He stared at her, his Caribbean-blue eyes shadowed in the half dark of the bedroom. "My plan stays on the list," he finally said. "It can be at the bottom of the list, but it remains our DEFCON one option. Is that clear?"

Samantha exhaled, not remembering when during the conversation she'd begun holding her breath. They were still a thing. She hadn't wrecked it. "I would definitely choose you and France over FMC Carswell. That's the women's prison in Texas where they keep the highest escape-risk inmates. Which would be me."

"I know what it is. Federal prisoners aren't allowed conjugal visits. That's unacceptable." He tilted his head a little. "The pizza's here?"

"Yeah." She held out the plate with the two slices. "You get it, right? I don't want to have to run for it."

He took the plate, and her hand. "I get it. I don't like being told that I'm not helping, but I get it." Slowly he tugged her closer. "You want to stay in this life. With me."

Setting her pizza on the bed, she lifted up on her toes and kissed him, tangling her free hand into his black hair. "Yes, I do," she breathed, leaning her forehead against his.

"Then let's find a damn way to do that."

15

Monday, 8:17 p.m.

Martin Jellicoe lowered his binoculars and pulled another slice of pizza out of the box sitting beside him. Rooftop dinners. He didn't much like them, because he preferred to enjoy a meal and have it accompanied by a drink with an umbrella in it, but he'd definitely become accustomed to them over the years.

Not so much these days, because it turned out that it was a much easier gig to get in with a heist crew and then get paid by Interpol to rat them out before they could actually rob anything. Of course there were the jobs that were too tempting to pass on, where he went in and liberated an item himself and then left a fake fingerprint or a strand of hair from one of the young guns who thought they'd cornered the market on high-end burglaries.

He lifted the binoculars again. Sam and Stoney and Addison and Anne and some older guy who looked like George Hamilton. With that tan he had to be from Florida, probably Sam's office manager. At least the voice he'd heard matched with the guy that he saw now. Her crew, though, was a joke. The only thing missing was that lawyer Addison usually hauled around with him.

Tonight it looked like they were going over strategy to stop him again. Stupid waste of time, but supremely predictable. He'd put in the call to Stoney, and of course Stoney had gone to warn his best source of income, who had in turn called in the Sotheby's lady and the tan man. And so the crew had gathered, with the timing of a clock.

Yeah, Sam had an ego on her. Just because she'd gotten lucky turning on him—*him*—in the middle of the Met job, now she figured she was just better than he was. Fuck that. Anybody who knew anything in his line of work learned right at the beginning that while a lucky turn might get you a prize, being lucky didn't make you a good thief.

But then she'd gotten lucky, and suddenly she thought she was the best. She probably hadn't even batted an eye when Sotheby's had decided to call her in for a prime opportunity. No, she probably thought she deserved it. Sam would never dream that her dad had called into the Met to pretend to do an article about the theft and Ms. Jellicoe's heroics right before he'd sent an anonymous email to Sotheby's asking some sharp questions about their security—and right before he left that note for Anne.

Everybody was so damned predictable in this world. Even Sam, and before she'd gotten too good to work with him she'd actually shown some real promise. Unless her engagement with the rich guy was just to get close to his shit so she could rob him, Martin didn't see the point of it. Four years of trying to be a normal had nearly killed him. Signing up for a lifetime of sitting in front of the TV and folding towels? No, thank you.

Sam knew, too, that without the thrill of the grab, life was a damn, dull pot of shit, and as her dad, it was his duty to both point out her flaws and short-sightedness to her, and to remind her that nobody was allowed to go against him without facing consequences. Maybe he'd thought about that last bit more than the first one, but that was her fault.

Leaning back against the A/C unit behind him, he finished off the slice of pizza. Not for the first time he wished he could hear the conversation behind those big-view windows, because Anne would have told Sam about Bradley Martin robbing her before, and Sam *wouldn't have* said that Bradley Martin was Martin Jellicoe, because she'd gone around announcing her own name and Sotheby's wouldn't have kept on the daughter of the guy threatening the exhibition—and Sam would have been drooling at the idea of working with Sotheby's.

Well, his call to Stoney had gotten the gang together for their meeting, and so he needed to get to work. Idiots. Working so hard to figure out a way to stop him *and* protect Sam, and thereby giving him the opening he'd been waiting for to get inside the old house.

He packed up his shit and headed down the back staircase of the office building again. If this didn't convince Sam to either give up the life or jump back into it with both feet—and to apologize for trying to show him up—well, he would be doing it again. But with the surprise he had ready for her and Anne, he doubted she'd be in any shape to keep working in security after this. A shiver ran down his arms. Man, he'd been saving this one for just the right moment, and it was finally here. He hoped one of the Sam gang was recording their meeting, because he wanted to watch this later, if he could.

Stealing a Tesla parked down on the street, he made his way uptown to Sotheby's and the old Victorian house a few blocks past that. Dumping the car again was easy, and he picked up the tools he'd stashed behind a dumpster close by, then zipped up his jacket, pulled the hood over his head, and strolled the last half block to where his latest treasure lay, just waiting for him to retrieve it.

In various disguises he'd walked this block maybe twenty times since Sam had arrived in Manhattan. He'd seen the security she brought in, watched parts of various tests, checked the details of cabinet-makers and the sensitivity levels the window alarms were capable of, and the same with the display panels and pads. She'd wired the place against everything from him to Houdini.

Hell, she'd even had some concrete pilings put in to keep a trash truck or something from crashing into the building—a route he'd favored early on. Her point had been that nobody could sneak into that place and get out again without being seen and identified. In doing that, though, she'd neglected a couple of things.

Martin pulled a paint gun from his duffle. Staying at the edge of the shadows, he splattered green paint over one camera, then the other that overlooked the street in front of the exhibit house. Easy. And a method Sam had been known to use, herself.

Then he pulled the phone he'd stolen out of his pocket and dialed Anne's mobile number. "Hello?" she said, her voice the reedy, annoying one he remembered.

"Anne. Good to talk to you again," he said, putting a smile into his voice. "It's been a while."

He could almost hear her frantically gesturing at the apartment's other occupants. "Bradley." Her voice wobbled even more, now.

"Thought it was time I give you a call," he said expansively, squatting down beside his duffel. "You and Sam Jellicoe have been working pretty hard to keep me out of your exhibit, haven't you?"

"Of course we have. You threatened to steal from me. Again."

"I did steal from you before, didn't I? So maybe I owe you one. Take a look at Sam standing there staring at you, why don't you?" His voice had a slight echo in his ear now, so he knew she'd put him on speaker. Good. Fewer misunderstandings and misinterpretations, that way. "Sam Jellicoe. She's what, about twenty-five, do you think? And that last name of hers—what is that, something she started using after she went to see *Cats*?"

"Shut up, Bradley," Sam's voice came, tense and hard.

"Sam! Hi." And she was calling him Bradley, so his hunch about her not telling Anne Hughes everything was spot on, as he'd figured it would be. "I thought you might be listening in. That's good. You see, Anne, Sam Jellicoe there knows some things that you don't. For instance, I don't go by Bradley Martin these days. I use the name Martin. Martin...Jellicoe. Sam didn't want you to know she was my daughter, so she didn't tell you that. And Sam, Anne didn't tell you some things, either. Namely that she and I were married once, and that we had a kid together. Anne wanted to name her Sarah, but I preferred Samantha."

"What the fuck are you talking about?" Sam yelled, her voice shrill.

He grinned into the phone. So predictable, people were. Even the ones who had a little talent. "That's a lot of information, isn't it? I'll put it all together for you. Anne took her mom's maiden name, I guess, after I left, but her married name was Anne Martin. Sam, you were born Sarah Martin. Mom, meet kid. Kid, meet your mom. And don't ever accuse me of not putting family first. I arranged this reunion, after all. Now you two talk amongst yourselves, and I'll give you a call later to catch back up. Good night."

He hung up, pulled a grenade from his bag, primed it, and tossed it at the front door of the exhibit house before he dove around the corner. *Let the fireworks begin.*

"DID HE HANG UP?" Sam mouthed, stalking forward to lean over the phone.

"Yes. He's choosing *now* to drop his bomb?" Anne asked, scowling at the screen. "Who does that?"

Shit. Samantha dove for the bedroom. "He's going in. Right now."

At the same second her phone, Anne's phone, and her mom's ever-present iPad began clanging with alerts. Tossing her phone to Rick, she kicked off her pretty blue flats and yanked on her way-more-practical athletic shoes. No time for her black thief outfit; slimming and practical or not, the clock was ticking. Fast.

"The cameras out front aren't working," Anne called, her voice shaking. "And half the sensors downstairs are registering pressure alarms. What do—"

"I'm going in," Samantha stated, pulling on her black hoodie. "You guys do the things we talked about, and do them fast. Because I aim to have him in jail by morning."

"I'm going with you," Rick stated, handing her phone back to her. "Just in case he has a different idea. Walter, call Tom and let him know it's happening right now."

"I'm the phone guy now?" Stoney complained, even as he pulled his phone from his pocket.

Aubrey already had his phone out, his complexion way paler than his tan should have allowed. She still wasn't a hundred percent about him, but over the past year she'd become a fan of the everybody-gets-a-second-chance mantra. Pendleton was key, though; if he backed out, or couldn't pull off his charm thing, she was going to be in a shitload of trouble, and on several fronts.

"Oh, I'm getting a fire alarm, now." Anne looked up as Samantha trotted past her. "Please be careful. My job isn't worth losing you again."

Samantha squatted in front of the table standing against the wall beside the door. She thudded her fist against one of the faux side panels and popped it open to pull out the small backpack she'd shoved in there months ago. When she straightened, Rick stood between her and the door, his gaze on the backpack and his arms folded over his chest.

"You still have a go-bag?" he snapped. "After all this? How can I—"

"It's not a go-bag," she interrupted, grabbing his arm and turning him back toward the door. "It's an emergency equipment bag. No toothbrush or fake passports or anything."

"I was wondering where you had it stashed," Stoney commented, then turned away. "Donner? No, don't hang up. This is official shit."

"Oh, my," Anne breathed behind them, and then they were out in the foyer and calling the elevator up.

"What *is* in there, then?" Rick asked as they stepped into the mirrored elevator. "And why did you hide it from me?"

"Rope, pliers, tape, hammer, screwdriver, knife, a can of spray paint, and a couple other things I might need if I have to get into or out of somewhere fast. And I didn't tell you because you would worry that I was going back to the dark side or something. Which I'm not."

He took a breath. "I should tell you, then, that I visited Sam Gorstein a couple of days ago, just to ask a few general questions."

Now she wanted to argue about who didn't trust whom and why he was allowed to go behind her back when she couldn't keep a single secret, but with the backpack over her shoulders she knew exactly how that conversation would go. "My name twin? Let's give him a heads-up, then. The cops and fire'll already be on their way. They may even get there first."

"Will Martin still be there?" he asked, pulling a key fob from his pocket. The car that beeped surprised her—the metallic blue Mercedes GLE. He was going for SUV muscle, which meant they might be breaking some traffic laws. Cool.

"Depends on how fast we get there. From the alarms it

sounds like he rammed something through the front door, which wouldn't be easy because of the concrete barriers. But he's not being quiet or careful, and he knows the cops will be automatically dispatched, no matter how shocked Anne and I might be by his stupid 'Leia, she is your mother' shit."

"So he's actually just making this a smash and grab? For actual loot?" Rick slid behind the wheel and turned on the engine as she buckled herself in on the passenger side.

"You're getting good at the lingo," she noted, her adrenaline pumping despite the fact that this was probably the hinkiest plan she'd ever come up with. "And I don't know. Maybe he just wants to toilet paper the place. I can't figure him out anymore. He doesn't have Van der Berg as his buyer, thanks to you, but most of that stuff would have black market bidders drooling like rabid dogs. He could unload any of it pretty easily."

They roared up the street, taking corners faster than physics liked, and dodging taxis and Ubers like they were standing still. Rick wanted to get her there before Martin left, then, however he felt about the plan. He told his phone to dial Sam Gorstein's mobile number, not his work phone, and that surprised her.

"You guys exchanging Christmas cards, too?" she asked. "Just how chummy are you with the white hats?"

"Sometimes it's handy to know someone on the inside," he commented. "You have some unconventional acquaintances, too, I believe."

The call went to voicemail. Frowning, Rick glanced at her. "Martin Jellicoe is currently breaking into the Sotheby's exhibit I mentioned," he said, his voice a low growl. "Samantha will be there trying to head him off. Do not let anyone fucking shoot her. And call me the hell back."

"That was...direct." She pulled her black leather gloves out of the hoodie's pocket. Habit, yeah, but also handy protection from broken glass.

"I'm angry." They squealed around another corner. "And you're excited, which scares the shit out of me."

"I'm not excited. I'm pissed off." Okay, maybe she was a little excited, but there were a handful of unknowns up ahead, a very small window of time to figure them out, and the possibility of confronting Martin on equal ground. It was more about being mentally ready than being excited.

One more left-hand turn on a red light, and the Victorian came into view. "Christ," Rick grunted, stomping on the brake half a block from the building.

The front doors were missing, along with a portion of the wall surrounding them. No, they were actually there, but with the glass broken in and the frames bent like a couple of pretzels, they were more abstract art than door, now. *Shit.* "What the hell did he use, a grenade?" she snapped.

"You are not equipped to repel explosives." Rick faced her. "Leave it to the police."

"We can't do that, because they'll never get him. And then he'll do this again. What if he decides to grenade our wedding or something?" She released her seat belt and shoved open the SUV's door. "Do not follow me in. You watch from out here, and let me know if he gets by me. And tell the cops not to Dirty Harry their way in there. You or Gorstein slow them down a little, if you can. Anything that gives me a minute."

"They will listen, even if I have to occupy them with arresting me to get the message across."

"Okay." She took a breath. "Go time."

Rick caught her arm before she could hop out of the car. "Be careful," he ordered, his scowl giving away just how worried he really was.

He didn't like it, but he wasn't trying to stop her. God, she loved that about him. Samantha leaned back in, gave him a swift kiss on the mouth, then slipped out of the car. Keeping low, she crossed the street, dodged the chunks of concrete and metal, and ducked into what was left of the lobby.

The sprinklers worked; water covered everything, a shinier sheen on the shiny floor, dripping off displays, and generally making navigating the mess even more difficult. She'd seen her dad do some crazy things to get whatever they'd been hired to steal, but *never* had he resorted to explosives before. This would have been ridiculous, except that he'd just raised the danger bar so high she wasn't certain what he might be willing to do next.

Maybe that had been the point, though: to scare the shit out of her, make her hesitate if the "hey, we're family" thing didn't work, so he could get away with whatever loot and point he was trying to make. Rolling her shoulders, Samantha bypassed the elevators and headed for the security room. Toward the rear of the main floor the house looked okay, but water had definitely made a mess of everything, had wrecked the walls, and had played havoc with the electronics.

The plain, unmarked security door was open, and she leaned around the corner of the doorframe before she stepped inside. Well, Martin had been there, too. The screens were okay, but the computers were all trashed. At least that part made sense to her, because if Martin had taught her anything, it was to avoid being caught on camera.

In a way, though, the mess of circuits and wires was a good thing. It meant he'd spent time in here before he'd moved on to whatever he was after. She was catching up. The sound of sirens began echoing up and down the canyon of buildings around them. She couldn't tell distance or direction, but there were definitely a lot of them and they were getting close.

Staying against the back wall, she climbed the stairs to the second floor and stopped on the landing, crouched and motionless. Hearing anything on top of the patter of water and alarms and the outside chaos was nearly impossible, but she listened anyway. A few taps, a click, what might have been cloth shifting, and she turned to continue to the top floor.

Up there, at least, the mess was minimal. Except for the sprinklers, some items tipped over, and a couple of display cases shifted by the blast, she couldn't see any damage at all. If Martin knew what he wanted was on the top floor, he might have decided a blast was worth the risk to his stupid commission, as he called the items he burgled. It was still a bad decision—but it did reinforce that robbery hadn't really been the point of all this.

Keeping low and silent on her toes, she edged into the middle of the floor. Another tap that could have been a tool against a display case, or just the house trying to settle after getting its foundation rocked, but she moved toward the north-ernmost room. The jewelry room.

Two of the display cabinets were missing their glass tops, and a third had a circular hole cut through the front. She noted that in passing, though, keeping her attention on the shadow that shifted in the far corner, putting something sparkly into a backpack.

"Hi, Martin," she said.

16

Monday, 9:52 p.m.

"You really are stupid enough to show up here, huh?" Martin said, zipping the pack closed and sliding his arms through the straps. "And after the gift I just gave you? Hell, I figured that made us even."

"You mean you telling Anne that she's my mom so I'd roll around on the floor, weeping? We figured that out a week ago. Put the stuff down. Never thought I would have to say this, but it isn't yours."

Finally, he glanced over at her. "Cops are here. Fire department is here. The chances of *you* getting out without being seen are close to zero, Sam. That whole 'daughter of renowned jewel thief Martin Jellicoe' problem of yours is really going to start circulating on all those sites where you've been smiling for photos for months. Sucks to be you. I did warn you, though."

"Yeah, you've got it all figured out, don't you?" she retorted, keeping her arms loose at her sides. "Except the part where you aren't supposed to steal some lady's kid and then use the two of them against each other to try to score some loot you don't even need. What a shit father you are."

Martin straightened, stalking up to her. "A shit father, am I? Who taught you everything you need to know to survive out there? Not just survive, either, Sam. Excel. If not for me, you'd be some librarian somewhere in the Midwest, and you for damn sure would not be engaged to Mr. Fancy Pants." He had the nerve to smile at her. "Consider that while you're explaining what happened here to the cops. I'm dead, remember?"

"Because of you, Martin," she retorted, warming to the argument and a little surprised at the venom she could hear in her own voice, "I hated Anne for years. I thought she abandoned me. Us. But it was all you. You wrecked at least two lives for your damn ego and your itchy fingers."

"And you went and took a reunion with your dad and turned it into a police fest just because you didn't like your cut."

Samantha frowned. "'My cut?' I didn't like you trying to force me back into the life after I found a way to be happy out of it, you turd."

Sniffing, Martin turned his back. "All that says to me is you needed this lesson, because you didn't learn a damn thing the first time." He headed for the window that would be the farthest from the explosion below, on the opposite side of the building. He already had a rope slung over his shoulder, so he meant to rappel down, count on surprise and timing to avoid being spotted, and then just vanish into the night—to do it all over again the next time she managed to find a really cool security gig.

"I learned way more than you think," she countered, following him. "And you're sticking around this time. You owe a few people some explanations. The not being dead, Interpol's deal that you've obviously shit all over, the stolen stuff on your back. All that."

"Mm-hmm. I know you've talked to Stoney, because I saw him eating pizza in your apartment. I wasn't joking. You turn on me, I turn on you. With interest, because I am that generous. So step back, and if you make it out of here, maybe go retire and have babies or something. Who knows, maybe I'll stop by and visit one day."

Well, that was the worst thing he could possibly have said. When he turned to anchor the rope around a heating pipe, Samantha stepped forward, pulled the knife from her pocket, and sliced through the rope he carried before he could turn around. "No deal."

Martin whipped around and stiff-armed her backward. "Are you fucking kidding me? What kind of amateur shit is that?"

"I don't want you out there in the world anymore," Samantha said, the words harder to utter aloud than she'd expected. For her entire life he'd been the epitome of footloose and fancy free, after all, and she'd just declared that she meant to box him up. "You're too dangerous, and too careless. I might have had security guys in here, walking the floor, and you what, threw a grenade at the front door?"

He was already glancing around the room, no doubt trying to figure out an alternative exit. "You had it wired up pretty well, I'll admit," he said, focusing on her again. "And…you have a backpack. If I know my girl, and I do, that means you have a rope, too."

Without warning he lunged at her. Samantha dodged him, folding the knife against her thigh and shoving it back into her pocket as she sidestepped. She was *not* going to stab him by accident or something. "I don't have a rope," she lied, "because I'm not trying to escape. I work here. Remember?"

"If you make me get sloppy, somebody's going to get hurt." He grabbed at her arm again, but she saw it coming and shifted behind one of the displays.

Yeah, she had him kind of trapped, or temporarily stumped, at least, but now the problem was how she meant to keep him there for the cops. Panicked and mad seemed to be her best choices. "Come on, Martin," she taunted, "you've been arrested before. Just relax and let it happen."

"No, thanks. I try not to repeat my mistakes. Hand it over and I'll go. Say whatever you want to the cops. I don't care; I'll be out of the city in an hour."

She moved again, keeping some big, heavy things between her and him. "Is this the part where you bargain? Wow. You're bad at it."

"That's enough, Sam. I'm your dad. You don't want the headlines of me being tossed in the slam, and you know it. Addison for damn sure won't like it. Give me the fucking rope, or I'm going to throw you down the stairs and slip out while they try to find all your parts."

"Bargaining, threats, you're doing it all in the wrong order. You're supposed to be pleading, now." She slipped her hand between her backside and the backpack.

Martin came over the top of a display and smacked her in the head as he landed on her shoulders. They both went down, the back of her head hitting the floor hard when his weight kept her from curling up. "I'm not playing," he growled, and jerked the backpack off one of her arms.

It took her a second to focus her eyes. "Neither am I," she snapped, yanking her other hand free, pointing the taser she held squarely at his chest, and pulling the trigger.

His eyes went big, he made a crazy gurgling sound, went stiff, and fell onto his side. Samantha squirmed out from under him, not sure if the water would make the electrical current travel from him to her, but definitely not wanting to get shocked.

"Sam," he wheezed, trying to sit up. She pulled the trigger again, blinking hard and staggering at an abrupt and nauseating tsunami of dizziness. Damn, that knock on the head wasn't going to go away.

"Nope. You had your chance," she countered, retrieving her

backpack and with her free hand digging into it for a pair of plastic cuffs. With no lock to pick, they were way trickier to get out of than normal cop cuffs.

"I'll rat you out. I swear it. You and Stoney."

"No, you won't." Shoving him onto his stomach and shaking her head, dizziness slamming into her every time she shifted her stance, she used her knee for leverage and yanked his hands back one at a time until she had him restrained. That still wasn't enough, though, so she grabbed the remains of his rope and knotted them around his knees.

"Code four," a low voice stated behind her. "Suspect in custody."

She whipped around then fell sideways onto the floor, noting to herself that she must look like a deranged cat woman, trying to crouch and fumbling with the air, her hair bloody and the part not mashed down by the water sticking out from her ponytail. "Gorstein," she said, squeezing one eye shut. "Good timing."

"Yeah, well, tell that to the girl I left sitting in a very swanky restaurant while I hauled ass over here." He shoved his pistol into its shoulder holster, the rest of him managing to look blond and handsome and put-together despite the water and the smoke and crackling electricity.

"Do you like her?" Samantha panted, rolling onto her back-side and putting her fingers against the back of her head. Great. Broken glass made for a great hair decoration, until it cut her scalp open. That felt like it needed stitches. She hoped Stoney was still around to do it. And Rick was not going to be happy.

"Yeah, I do."

"Then stop referring to her as a girl." She picked up Martin's backpack, very aware of her dazed and really angry father glaring at her from a few feet away. "Do you want to take the loot down to log in as evidence? The stuff I saw him stash is worth about three-and-a-half million, I would estimate."

Samantha glanced down at her dad. That didn't track. It was peanuts. "What else were you going to take?"

"Three million isn't enough?" Gorstein asked, taking the backpack and opening it to look inside. "Jeez."

"Not for him." She looked around the room again, still blinking to focus both her eyes and her thoughts. He'd been stuffing the jewelry into the pack when she arrived, and then he'd announced that he was leaving. That didn't mean he hadn't had something else in mind before she'd caught him.

Hm. He had the rope ready, so the window there *had* been his intended exit. The rest of the loot was probably close by, then.

As she pivoted toward the door, she saw it. Half hidden by one of the displays and wrapped in plastic, a plaster bust of a woman's head, a penis over one eyebrow and forming into a nose, looked back at her. "The fucking Picasso. I knew it." Moving over to it, she carefully lifted the heavy thing off the floor. "It's made of plaster, Martin! What the hell? You set it down in water?"

"It's wrapped up," he grumbled, groaning as Detective Gorstein yanked him to his feet. "I can't walk, you idiot. She tied my legs up."

"So she did. Stand here, then." Gorstein looked over at her. "How much is *that* worth?"

"At the auction, probably a hundred million. On the black market, half that, I'd guess." Samantha checked the plastic wrapping, making sure no water could get anywhere near it. This bust was a first effort by Picasso; a year later he'd recreated it and refined it in bronze, but this was the first one. Utterly irreplaceable and absurdly delicate. "You can't have it," she added.

"I don't want it. Put it somewhere safe, and I'll have one of my guys take some photos of it. We don't need any of this, really; Jellicoe here has enough heists to his name that he practically has his own wing at the FBI."

"I don't know who you think I am," Martin snapped, "but *her* name is Jellicoe. Her father is dead."

"So I've heard."

More cops, followed by the fire department and then almost immediately by Sotheby's security bigwigs, started flooding the building. Once she had some credentials she could verify, she handed off the Picasso and, holding onto the safety railing, made her way back down the stairs, keeping an eye on Martin as three officers escorted him outside. Three wasn't enough, but the taser seemed to have knocked the wind out of his sails. For the moment, anyway.

"Sam," he barked, as they made him do the hands on his head, feet apart thing and searched his pockets before they put the metal cuffs on him—the ones that were easier to get out of.

"Hey, Gorstein," she called, approaching. "He'll get out of those, you know."

"Get out of—oh, right. Leg shackles and somebody sitting next to him in the car, Greer. Multiples everywhere. The FBI is on the way, but we are not losing him before they sign for him."

The biggest cop in the group nodded. "You told us."

"No, you don't understand," a hard British voice came from off to her left. "I'm with her. And I *will* walk over there."

She wanted to see Rick, wanted him to bundle her up, scold her for taking chances, and drive her to the emergency room—which is where way too many of her jobs these days seemed to end up—but this wasn't quite finished yet.

"What?" she asked, approaching Martin.

"You're cutting your own throat," he stated, letting the cops shove him into the back of a police car, "you ungrateful bi—"

"Goodbye, Martin," she said, gazing at him. Hopefully it would be the last time she set eyes on him, but that depended on a lot of other people doing what they were supposed to do, not one of them screwing up, and a bucketload of luck.

"This isn't over!" he yelled, the last part muffled as the door shut.

"You're bleeding," Rick said from directly behind her.

She turned around, then took a half step back when his arms lifted. "Do not hug me. As long as he can see me, I do not need anything from you. Got it?"

"That wasn't part of the plan," he muttered. "He hurt you."

"He body-slammed me and I fell on my head and got cut by a piece of glass. Then I tased him." She shrugged. "Twice. Where's Aubrey?"

"Still at the FBI Manhattan office. He left right after you did. I'm still not sure we should be trusting him with this, Samantha. A few days in Paris won't hurt anything. Please."

It wasn't just the word, but the sound of his voice that made her really look at him. He wasn't just worried. He was scared. Scared that he would lose her. And still he was following her playbook. "I really love you, you know," she murmured. "A lot."

"Likewise, my heart. May I drive you to the hospital?"

"Stoney can sew me up."

"Can and will are two different things, my dear." He gestured her toward the street.

"Did you see what he did? It was a grenade. An actual grenade. We are not going to be able to open tomorrow."

"Mm-hmm." He stepped away, saying something she couldn't make out to Gorstein, then came back again. "We're good to go. This way, before you tip over. Because if you do, I will grab you, you know. Audience or not."

Rick led her to the SUV and opened the passenger door for her. "I'll get the seat all wet and yucky."

"Benny will clean it up. He likes to be busy."

Now he was just humoring her, but her head was really starting to hurt, and a couple other things were beginning to hit her, too. "I just sent Martin away for life."

"You gave him every chance to walk away," he countered,

sitting behind the wheel and guiding them around the herd of police cars and fire trucks. "Far more chances than I would have given him."

"Can he still see us?"

Rick glanced in the rearview mirror. "No. We're around the corner."

"Okay. Pull over, will you?"

"We are going to the hospit—"

She opened the door, he slammed on the brakes, and she leaned out to barf on the street. Yeah. She was living the dream.

Richard looked down as the phone in his hand vibrated. The text message, the fifteenth in the last half hour, didn't make him any happier than the other fourteen. He'd had no idea that Team Sam would be so chatty. "I'll be right back," he said, standing.

"What?" Samantha demanded from the bed next to him. "Did he slip the cuffs?"

"You have a grade two concussion, Sam," the nurse checking her vitals said. "Do not sit up."

"It's Anne," he said, turning back and putting one palm against her shoulder to keep her prone. "They won't let her into the E.R. I'll go break her in."

"Oh, it's immediate family only, right?"

"And fiancés. Don't move."

"Not going anywhere. I have a grade two concussion."

"So I heard." Glancing over his shoulder at her, he slipped around the edge of the privacy curtain and down past the row of curtained beds. Two heart attacks, a man who'd fallen off a bridge and landed in a shopping cart, a case of hypothermia, and a few others he hadn't been able to figure out yet, but he imagined none of the other E.R. patients had been body-slammed by their own dad and had then tased him into submission. At least he hoped not.

He pushed open the emergency room door. Anne Hughes stood at the main desk, her color high and her purse clutched against her side like she wanted to use it to bat the clerks out of her way. "Anne," he called.

"Mr. Addison," one of the staff said, heading in his direction, "we have security protocols here for a reason. You can't—"

"She's family," he interrupted, lifting an eyebrow. It was his haughty look, according to Samantha, but since the man only frowned and returned to his station, he decided it worked well enough.

"Thank you," Anne said, stepping past him into the hallway. "I answered all the questions to prove I knew her, but evidently her birthday isn't January 19th any longer, and her mother's maiden name is Connor."

He offered his arm, and she wrapped her hand around his sleeve. "That's after Sarah Connor, the heroine of *The Terminator*. She's been here before, and we had to fill in the blanks. Of course we had no idea that *her* name was Sarah, or she'd probably have gone with Ellen Ripley from *Aliens*."

"Well, I'm no Sarah Connor. Or Ripley. That's for sure." Anne frowned. "Is she disappointed, do you think? I mean, I'm glad she knows I'm not some heartless witch, but I never found her. She found me, and I didn't even recognize her standing there, right in front of me."

Taking a breath, he edged them over against one wall, out of the way of the gurneys and staff careening up and down the hallways. "Samantha is prickly," he said. "She uses sarcasm and humor to shield herself, and that leaves people charmed, but not knowing her very well. Just let her be prickly."

"But that doesn't answer my question. I'm not larger than life. Bradley—Martin—is."

"She wants a relationship with you, Anne, or she would have

turned down the job the minute she figured out who you were. In my experience, patience is invaluable. Give her time, give her space, let her come to you."

"Like she's a scared baby deer?"

"More like a cautious Tasmanian devil. She's nearly bitten my fingers off a few times, but she's still here. She wants to be here. And she wants to know you."

Anne nodded, grabbing his hand and squeezing it. "Thank you. I know how much you protect her, and I appreciate you trusting me to be around her. I will be patient. And not try to hug her so much."

He grinned. "Yes, hugging is definitely something to work up to. And just be aware, she looks a bit of a wreck. Seven stitches and a concussion."

"Bradley Martin needs to go to hell and stay there."

"He doesn't know it yet, but that's where he'll be sometime in the next forty-eight hours or so."

"Good. Will you be there? I want someone to be able to tell me he's not getting out of this. That he isn't coming back."

That same worry nagged at him, and he knew from the way Samantha interpreted every text that came to his phone as an alert that Martin had escaped, she didn't have much faith in the justice system, either. "I'll be there. As long as you'll be here, with her."

Anne nodded, blinking away obvious tears. "I'm not going anywhere."

Approximately eighteen hours later, Richard could count the number of hours he'd slept over the past two days on two fingers. Samantha had done much better than that, but if the doctor didn't release her soon, she was going to go out the window. He knew that, because she'd told him so right before he'd left the hospital. Well, he'd warned Anne about Samantha's prickly side, but keeping her in that bed for another twelve hours or so would definitely be a test of the thickness of her hide.

"I think I'm breaking the law just letting you be in here," Detective Sam Gorstein grunted, pushing open a door and motioning for Richard to precede him inside the room. "You and Jellicoe make things so hinky whenever you show up that I never know if I'm getting fired or promoted by the time you're finished."

"You were promoted last time," Richard said, taking a seat in front of the two-way mirror and declining to look at the neighboring room's occupant just yet. "And this is only our second call to you. That's hardly a 'whenever we show up' pattern."

"Two for two. That's a pattern." The detective sat opposite him. "That's really her dad, huh? I thought he'd be taller. And have lockpicks for fingers. Edward Lockpickhands or something."

"He doesn't look it now, but he can be charming." Finally Richard turned to look at his future father-in-law. They'd put him in jail orange, but his brown hair just going to gray remained disheveled, hopefully from the electrical shock Samantha had given him as much as from the fire sprinklers and their tussle. The fact that he'd struck—or jumped on, or otherwise put hands on—his own daughter, on Samantha, made him want to find out how much it would cost to bribe the NYPD for a few minutes alone with him.

"No punching the glass," Gorstein cautioned, and Richard realized he'd coiled his right hand into a fist. "You're observing. And only because the FBI said you could."

As if on cue, Aubrey stepped into the small room beyond the mirror. For Christ's sake, Richard had underestimated him, as had Samantha. It was ridiculous how close they'd been to disaster for the past nine months, and without even realizing it. Aubrey Pendleton could have destroyed...everything.

And yet, he hadn't. Richard had warned the detective about Martin Jellicoe's charm, but both men had already succumbed to Samantha's. It hadn't even been conscious on her part. Being in her presence was simply enjoyable. Fun. Unique. Inexplicably satisfying.

He knew that, because he'd fallen for her the moment he'd set eyes on her. No, that wasn't quite true, because he'd barely registered her presence before she'd shoved into him and the ensuing explosion had knocked him barmy. That second time, though; he remembered that. Dropping through his office skylight like Cat Woman and offering a partnership—a little over a year ago, a lifetime ago, and yesterday all at once, his life had flipped in the air and landed on its arse, and he'd never been happier.

"Are you just going to stand there?" Martin said, his gaze on Pendleton. "I have a deal with Interpol. I'll talk to them. Not you, Beach Glow Ken."

"That's charming?" Gorstein muttered.

"No, that's still royally pissed off that his daughter got him arrested," Richard noted. He shifted a little, glancing at the cop. "You know he's likely to say some things that aren't true about her, yes?"

"I've seen moms lie on a Bible about their own sons, and vice versa, to get themselves out of trouble. But I'm not an idiot, either, Rick. And yeah, I know, we've had this conversation. And no, I don't want you to make my life a living hell. And yeah, she's made some really interesting and kind of admirable choices given who had the biggest influence on her growing up. So just relax a little. Unless he has photos and fingerprints, I'm intending to believe very little of what he yaps about."

It didn't hurt that Martin was a bigger fish than Samantha. Not because he'd broken more laws, but because he'd left traces of a trail from time to time. Samantha had said she thought he did it out of pride, wanting his victims to know they'd been had by the best of the best, but it had come back to bite Martin once. This time, Richard wasn't certain what use Pendleton would make of it. The man had been declared dead once already and recruited by Interpol.

"You haven't called Interpol yet," Martin said, sliding his hands along the surface of the metal table in front of him. They'd shackled him to it, but after Samantha's warnings, Richard was half-convinced her father was already loose and just pretending to be caught because it suited him to do so. "I'm not talking until you do."

The ladies' companion-slash-FBI agent finally took a breath, not moving from his place by the door. "A facility with a private room, a garden, a gym, a library, a movie theater, a putting green, and a climbing wall," he said in his smooth Southern drawl.

"What's that? What you'll offer me if I confess all? Don't make me laugh. I know you're a friend of Sam's. You run her idiotic office."

"I do. I'm also Special Agent Aubrey Pendleton, FBI. I like to keep busy."

Martin cocked his head. "Sam hired an FBI agent? Jesus. I told her going soft would kill her."

"Let's stay on topic, shall we? Private room, garden, putting green, climbing wall, and the other stuff I mentioned. Can you picture it?"

"I'm not going to your damn Club Fed. Call fucking Interpol."

With a nod Pendleton moved forward, set a folder on the table, and sat opposite Martin. "I have. I—and my bosses—have spoken to them at length. You nearly made off with a hundred-million-dollar Picasso, you destroyed half a Sotheby's auction site, and you blew out windows for a block around the place."

"Small change. And I didn't leave with anything. I stole nothing. B and E, maybe, but that's it. I'm just keeping in practice. I have to have a reputation or none of the heist crews'll trust me enough to feed me information that I can pass on to Interpol."

Richard kept his attention on Aubrey, watching to see if he would fall for any of it, hesitate in going through with the plan they'd concocted...thirty hours ago? And every moment after that infinite one while he'd been stuck outside the Victorian house, waiting in his SUV, had been so full of chaos and ten-every-minute deals that it would take him weeks to catch up.

"In exchange for the putting green, etcetera," Pendleton went on, opening the folder and ignoring most of what Martin had said, "you will keep your damn mouth shut and confess to any and all robberies, break-ins, et cetera, I ask you to."

"You mean Sam's." Martin sat forward. "No."

"I have a list of crimes to which you haven't confessed yet, even though you were supposed to come clean to Interpol. You will admit to all of them. Further, if anyone comes to you looking to pin a crime on your daughter, you will take credit for it. We will make it known that you did your best to keep Samantha away from your illegal activities when you were raising her, and while we understand that she might have learned something about how to go about identifying security weaknesses and how to pick a lock, she has never, to your knowledge, committed a crime."

Martin snorted. "That's rich. How do you think Adgerton ended up with that Picasso cast in the first place?"

Rick frowned. She hadn't mentioned that to him. Then again, for all he knew, every time they visited someone's home she could claim a momentary ownership of their works of art. That was...unsettling.

"If you'd care to try to make amends with Interpol, you're welcome to rat out anyone else you choose, but blaming your own daughter for your shit because you're too much of a coward to accept responsibility for your own actions? That's pitiful."

Pendleton spoke with every ounce of Southern indignity he could gather, and silently Richard applauded him for it. *Take that, you bastard.* His phone beeped, and he pulled it from his pocket to look at the text.

"Hey, no phones."

"Samantha's still in the hospital," Richard stated. "Her mother says if she passes the next couple of tests, they'll release her in a few hours." And if nothing else came of Anne's return to Samantha's life, he was grateful for her now. He wouldn't have left Samantha at the hospital with anyone else.

"Okay. No *more* phone stuff."

"That is the lamest deal I've ever heard of," Martin was saying, all venom now that his substantial ego had been besmirched. "Interpol. Now."

"If you don't agree, then I do have something else we can arrange for you."

"Let me guess. Four walls, bars, and concrete. Send me. I'll be out in a week."

"Huh. Yes, there will be concrete—a pad for exercising, which you'll be able to access for one hour each day. The other twenty-three hours will be spent in a cell with no bars, a door with a very small window and an opening for fitting handcuffs and delivering food, and no window. A library cart will come around bi-weekly, and there's a small television behind plexi-glass in one corner. I kind of like this one, myself, because you can just blab away about whatever you want, and nobody will be listening."

"Inter—"

Pendleton slammed his fist on the table. "You made Interpol look like chumps, after they've spent a lot of money on your ass just to have you fling shit in their faces over and over again. They're happy to be rid of you."

Martin stirred a little. Uneasiness? God, Richard hoped so. "You can't keep me locked up somewhere with no access to attorneys. What I say will get heard. And I can say a lot."

"Well, the thing is, Martin, you're dead. I have your death certificate right here, signed and notarized. You have no rights, because you're a corpse. You're inconvenient, too. The only reason I have that first offer for you is because the government is willing to provide you with a comfortable stay in exchange for the assurance that you won't go breaking out of things and causing a stir. Kind of a gentlemen's agreement, held together by the threat of what'll happen if you do make trouble. Get it?"

"So I just get forgotten? No deal. Lock me up tight. I'll give it a week. Maybe two."

Finally Pendleton pulled out the opposite chair and sat. "Look at it this way. You're going away. You're not getting out. And after all those statutes of limitations expire and your daughter decides that she's famous and wants to write herself a memoir about all her thefts and adventures and cash in on being Mrs. Addison, every reporter in the world will call her a liar and say she's trying to make bank on *your* reputation. So would you rather be comfortable and watch those interviews on a giant TV about you being the greatest cat burglar in the world while you drink iced tea, or on a tiny one in a steel room behind plexiglass with toilet water to drink?"

Oh, he was good. Those FBI psychologists and their "how to make a deal with a narcissist" tactics had come through in a damned impressive manner. And for the first time Richard was glad of Martin's notoriety; if he hadn't been such a big fish, and if they hadn't been anxious to close the books on all those unsolved thefts, the DOJ wouldn't have cared about making deals, and none of them would be sitting where they were right now. Instead, Martin would probably be gleefully ratting out Samantha to anyone who would listen.

"That would twist her up, wouldn't it?" Martin snorted. "I

like your style, Pendleton. She won't be able to take credit for her shit. Ever. Because you're giving it all to me. The art, the Viking treasure hoard, the jewels, all of it."

Beside Richard, Gorstein shifted a little. "'Viking treasure hoard?'" he muttered.

"Something he invented, no doubt," Richard said, though he would be asking Samantha about that later.

"No parole, I suppose?"

"No parole."

"I will get out, you know, sooner or later. It's just going to happen."

"It won't, but you're welcome to try. If the nice room with the windows and the movie theater isn't enough to keep you around, the concrete and plexiglass place will always be available."

"So you're authorized to pitch me this offer, without anybody else in the Bureau or whatever signing off on it? Or are you just trying to get me to sign away my life before anybody figures out what you're up to?" Martin leaned forward. "Because you know I could make you a lot of money. Your own trained cat burglar on a leash. And by a lot of money, I mean millions. Millions. The first thing I confiscate and sell, you're a million-aire. Just like that. And I'm not bragging, because that's how I make a living. You could tell whoever your bosses are to go screw themselves. Just retire and be rich."

He slid his hands out of the cuffs.

Richard lurched to his feet, but before he made it to the door, a scrambling Gorstein on his heels, Pendleton was shoving Martin against the wall, a pair of cops pushing into the interrogation room behind him.

"I was just demonstrating that you can trust me," Martin said, his voice, like his face, somewhat smushed.

"I only want two words from you, Mr. Jellicoe. Or Mr. Martin. Or Mr. Bradley—whoever you want to claim to be. You either say 'putting green,' or 'concrete pad.' Those are your choices."

"I wanna talk to Sam. And ease up, there. I don't swing that way."

"Sam never wants to see you or hear from you again. Wasn't the taser enough to convince you of that? So which is it going to be, Martin? Because honestly, I had to pull some strings to get you the Club Fed deal. Everyone from Interpol to the DOJ would be *much* happier with you in a tiny cell."

It hadn't just been Pendleton pulling strings and making deals. Tom Donner had hit the ground running yesterday morning, and in exchange for all of this, Richard would be making some generous investments in some countries where the U.S. wanted to make some diplomatic headway. The number of favors he owed now…It was worth it. If Martin went away, it would all be worth it.

Samantha's father shook his head as best he could with three men wrestling him back into handcuffs. "No. I want to hear it from him." He jabbed his chin toward the mirror. "Come on, Addison. You really going to let these guys take care of everything for you? You just put down some cash and tell somebody else sweep away your problems?"

"Yes, that's exactly what you're going to do," Sam Gorstein cautioned, motioning Richard back to his seat. "That's why you called us in the first place. To do this legally. Or mostly legally, anyway."

The idea of having a last, definitive conversation with Martin Jellicoe practically made Richard salivate. This was the second time in a year the man had made his own daughter's life miserable, and both times he'd seemed perfectly fine with leaving her to take the blame for his misdeeds. They were working in was a very slender gray area as it was, and it wouldn't take much for someone to raise a complaint that would put everything in front of the press and the courts, draw it out for years, and end with both Jellicoes in prison.

He looked through the glass at Martin, his hands locked behind him, as they shoved him back into his chair. The older man's ego had done this to him, made him unable to resist pulling a job that would prove he was a better thief than his daughter. It might have worked, if not for the oddball crew of misfits Samantha had gathered around her. And as much as he hated to admit it, he was one of the oddballs.

"You deal with me, Mr. Jellicoe," Pendleton said. "There is no other deal coming."

Martin glared at the agent for a long moment. "Fuck it. I wouldn't mind taking credit for another Rembrandt or two. And make sure you include the Faberge egg from Milan and the Viking shit."

Okay, now Richard had several questions for Samantha, but they'd done it. Finally. "I'm finished here," he said aloud. "Care to walk me out?"

"I would be extremely happy to walk you out of here," Gorstein said, climbing to his feet. "I suggest you go collect Jellicoe and walk all the way back to Florida."

Richard paused in the doorway, glancing over his shoulder at the detective. "We're thinking of moving here, actually."

"For the holidays?"

The hopeful lilt in Gorstein's voice made Richard grin briefly. Another oddball. "Permanently."

"Oh, for fuck's sake."

17

"What the hell is this?" Ling Wu, head of the CVS-adjacent office of the FBI, strode into the small office the Sam gang, as Aubrey had always thought of them, had taken over in Manhattan's police precinct. "This is not what we agreed to, Pendleton." He waved a folder in the air for emphasis.

Aubrey stood up, because that was the polite thing to do, and gestured at Mr. Gorstein behind his desk. "Wu, Sam Gorstein of the NYPD. Detective Gorstein, Ling Wu, FBI."

"Explain yourself. Because to my eyes it looks like in exchange for having the most infamous cat burglar in the world stay at one of our finest confinement facilities, we get—" He looked down at the folder he held, though he didn't even bother to open it—"nothing."

That "we" was the key word here, Aubrey knew. "I get that it's frustrating we can't blast this all over the front page of the *Post* and the *Times*," he said, sitting again and crossing his ankles, "but this is definitely a feather in our caps. Martin Jellicoe, alive and caught red-handed doing evil *and* in a comfy cell for life. Because of the Palm Beach FBI. You know it had to be comfy, or he would be picking locks and escaping every ten minutes."

"You don't—"

"And we got the DOJ to agree to this, without any publicity for them, either. How many times do they get to handle a dead man wanted in eighteen countries?"

"You know why th—"

"Oh, excuse my manners. Have you met Tom Donner?" He gestured at the tall former Texan seated next to him and not looking much happier than Ling Wu. "With the short time frame we had, Tom did some impressive hoop-jumping to get this all put together. He's an attorney based in Palm—"

"I know who Donner is. I know who all these people are. I told you what I wanted from you, Pendleton. This is not it. Let's discuss it outside, shall we?"

"Yeah, we all know you wanted the other Jellicoe, too," Donner drawled.

At that, Ling's eye twitched, which was satisfying. The Sam gang knew what was up, and even with only himself, Donner, and Detective Gorstein present, it was the first time in a while he'd felt like he had someone watching his back, rather than trying to stab him in it. "There is no there, there, as they say," Aubrey took up. "I got you Martin Jellicoe. Who's conveniently been declared dead and has no rights. He's off the street, after he wound Interpol around his pinkie and stole pricey shit around the world on their dime. We have him. The CVS branch of the FBI."

"No, *you* have him." Ling slapped the folder against his thigh and well-pressed trousers. "Your name is all over this. Where's the 'authorized by' and 'plan put together by' shit? This is *not* the way the game works."

And there it was. "Ah," Aubrey said, sighing. "After all these years I know better, but damn if I'm not still disappointed when somebody proves me right. We took a bad guy off the streets, Wu. That's what we do."

If Ling clenched his jaw any harder, he was going to have to go see a dentist. "Hallway, Pendleton. Now."

Standing again, Aubrey motioned him toward the door. "The hallway's good with me," he said. They left the office, and he pulled the door shut behind him. "I'm not going to apologize for not giving you more credit. You kept sending me after Samantha, no matter how many times I told you she's gone legit. I offered you Martin Jellicoe, and you practically spat at me. I figured I mentioned you enough in the report, though, that you'll get space in the Lake Worth office. Maybe not a prime window office, but I can't do everything for you."

Ling leaned closer. "One, you made the FBI look like it's willing to ignore criminal activity just because it's convenient to do so. Sam Jellicoe might be legit now, but she still has crimes attached to her resumé."

"Not really. Her dad confessed to just about everything we thought might have been hers."

"Two, you falsified your report to make Sam Jellicoe sound like she's up for a halo award. I don't care if she helped bring him down. She's a criminal."

"Innocent until proven guilty."

"And third, yeah, you crapped all over your boss. I don't like it. At all."

"This is where you tell me I can stay on in Palm Beach if I want, or I can transfer to one of several promising assignments that've opened up, right? That I made the department look good to the rest of the legal community?"

Ling waited while a uniformed cop walked up the hallway. "You'll be able to avoid Immanuel Village and Nebraska, for now. But I'm going to file a complaint about this, and I am going to make your remaining years in the FBI hell. Every minute of them."

Well, that was what he'd expected. Aubrey nodded, pretending that his heart rate hadn't accelerated a bit and that little, pesky worries hadn't begun tapping at his brain. He was good with all this; that, at least, he knew. Samantha deserved a chance, and he'd helped get an active investigation off her back, at least for the moment.

He shrugged. "I filed my retirement papers this morning with Bob Harris in Tampa," he said. "And I'm thinking of relocating to New York. Maybe I'll work in an office, maybe I'll be a dog walker. Haven't decided yet. But I'm done with pricks like you who call any of this a game. Martin Jellicoe used a damn grenade to break into that building. And we made sure he won't ever be doing that again. So, go fuck yourself, Wu."

For a minute Ling looked like one of those drunk guys who knew he was about to get clocked but still couldn't resist throwing a punch. Then he took a breath. "That's how it is, then. This isn't over, Pendleton."

"It is definitely over. Go sign your shit and collect your prisoner. And for God's sake, don't turn your back on him, and don't go anywhere alone with him. He'll have you wrapped up and stuffed in the trunk before you can say, 'I'm an idiot who should've listened to Aubrey when I had the chance.'"

Then, without waiting for his soon-to-be former boss to conjure up another vague threat or insult, Aubrey turned around, went back inside NYC's office, and shut the door on Ling Wu.

"Nicely done, Aubrey," Donner commented. "You know, I haven't really gotten acquainted with you, but you pulled one over on Sam Jellicoe for better than nine months. I'd like to buy you a beer."

Gorstein cleared his throat and stood. "Well, I haven't slept in two days, I only got through appetizers for dinner night before last, and I've been existing on M&Ms and Doritos since then. I say we go grab some lunch. And make Addison pay for it."

The attorney grinned. "I am in complete agreement. I flew out here so fast yesterday I didn't even pack a suitcase. I had to buy toothpaste. Sam Jellicoe wins again."

Detective Gorstein paused, one hand on the doorknob. "So is she out of the burglary business, or is she pretending? Because I've been checking up on her, too. If you take even twenty percent of the unsolved high-end thefts over the last ten years, that's…billions. Her dad couldn't physically have been everywhere. Some of them happened at the same time."

Donner sent a glance at Aubrey, who shrugged. "She says she's legit," Pendleton offered, "and I've never seen her do anything crooked while I've worked for her. I wouldn't have done all this if I thought she was faking."

The attorney nodded. "Rick might put up with a lot where she's concerned, but if she is up to something, she's fooling him, too. I think she's legit. Just don't tell her I said that."

The fact of it was, and Aubrey thought they'd all realized it at about the same time, that they'd simply all chosen her side, and they were all going on blind faith that a young lady who'd had her hands on everything from Monets to the bust of Nefertiti meant it when she'd said she was retired. If this was a long con or some elaborate ruse, God help the world, because he wasn't going anywhere, regardless. And he didn't think the rest of her new gang were, either.

○

"I DON'T NEED to be hand fed," Samantha complained, trying to peer around Rick's shoulder to see the television. "And stop telling Andre to make the rice mushy. My head got damaged; not my teeth. And you're making me miss the movie."

Rick glanced behind him and went back to scooping up

spoonfuls of the mushy rice Andre had left for them this morning. It was pretty good, actually, but she was complaining more about the principle of the thing. If she was getting hand fed, she wanted it to be grapes and shit.

"You've seen it already," he said. "Godzilla wins."

"But Godzilla and Kong are about to fight Mechagodzilla. That's the best part."

"Take another bite."

With a sigh she paused the movie, leaned forward to set the remote down on the coffee table, and took both of his hands in hers. "I am okay," she said, meeting his gaze and wondering if there were any other bazillionaires in the world who hovered. There for damned sure weren't any others who looked as sexy as Rick while they did it.

"Nine stitches," he said, settling on the edge of the couch as she scooted toward the back to make room for him. "Class two concussion. That's a football player-level concussion. No standing or walking without assistance for two more days. That is not okay."

"Yeah, but you should see the other guy," she quipped, then frowned. No, Martin was not a happy guy, and he wouldn't be unless or until he realized that he wasn't going anywhere. If he didn't figure out a way to escape, that was—which was an entirely possible scenario.

"You did the right thing." He leaned down and kissed her on the mouth. "No one's dead, you're the only one who got hurt, and he's not going to be able to make any more trouble for you, or for Walter, or for Anne."

It wasn't just that, though. While she'd been barfing, the team—her team—had managed to pretty much close an open investigation on her and solve two dozen unsolved thefts; she had a mom again, and well, the Victorian house was all over the local news today, along with the information that one Samantha Jellicoe, fiancée of Rick Addison, had prevented an original

Picasso from disappearing into the world of black-market collectors. *The Today Show* was looking for her to do an interview, Anne had reported, but that wasn't going to happen.

Rick's phone beeped, and he lifted it off the coffee table. "Tom's on his way up. Be nice; he wrote up a lot of the paperwork, woke up some judges, and leveraged the DOJ—and he's not happy about it."

Great. Now she owed Donner one. Probably two, because he'd flown to New York with like ten minutes' notice and had hit the ground running. "I'll be nice if he's nice," she conceded.

Two solid raps on the door, and then it opened, Donner strolling inside their apartment. "I haven't been here in five years, at least," he said, heading for the view out the front windows. "It is a nice place."

"It's good for the two of us," Rick agreed, making his way over to shake hands. "Thank you."

"About that; I'm going to take some criminal law classes, and you're paying for them. This is ridiculous, Rick. I help you buy companies. I don't work with the U.S. government to find companies *they* want you to buy and oversee to help spread democracy worldwide, and I don't write up legal ways for people to be thrown in prison for life without a trial."

"Martin already had a trial," Samantha pointed out, sitting up a little as Rick stuffed another pillow behind her. "He was found guilty. Then they declared him dead. We didn't do any of that. And that's cool."

"Yes, I suppose it is. It made things easier, anyway."

"Easier," Donner grumbled, eyeing her.

"But you're buying companies to help spread democracy? You didn't say anything about that."

Rick shrugged. "It couldn't wait for you brains to stop spinning."

"Thank you." Good cause or not, it sounded extremely expensive. They were going to have to have a chat about just how much he owed to which people, now. Sheesh. One concussion and everybody went crazy.

"And so the suckage into the Dark Side begins." The attorney sat in one of the chairs by the window. "Pendleton had it out with his boss and announced his retirement. I think Detective Gorstein's gonna get a bigger office and get promoted to lieutenant. How's your—how's Ms. Hughes doing?"

"Sotheby's isn't too happy right now," Samantha answered, "but at least they showed what it does take to break into one of their exhibit houses. She's still overseeing it, and they still want to open the auction preview at the old house because of the publicity. They've already started digging out wrecked concrete and putting in new windows and doors." And to her specifications, which was good. She hadn't been all that certain Sotheby's wouldn't come at her with a lawsuit for attracting trouble.

She could thank Rick for that not happening, though; whether he said or did anything or not, Sotheby's didn't want to risk pissing him off. So she owed him another one, too. Again.

Their door opened again, this time without the lobby informing Rick they had a visitor. "Hey," Stoney said, strolling in. "How's your pillow?"

"Nice and fluffy," she said, grinning.

He headed into the kitchen. "Good."

"You don't even knock now?" Rick asked, glancing down at his phone as if it had betrayed him.

"I don't like being announced," the fence said, as if that explained how he'd managed both to avoid Vince and not trigger the elevator camera. "I'll knock next time, though."

"Thank you, Walter."

"Grab me a water, will you, Walter?" Donner asked. "And by the way, Pendleton's on his way here, too. I hope you really wanted to hire him full-time, Jellicoe. He may get tossed without a pension."

"That won't happen." Still hovering, Rick shoved aside her

pillow mountain and sat in its place so she could lean back against him. Her eyes had stopped crossing on their own, and she'd stopped feeling like she was riding backward on a roller coaster, so no permanent damage. On the outside, anyway. Inside was going to take a little time to figure out.

"We are not challenging the FBI to a fight, Rick," Donner stated. "Not over the pension of a guy who's been spying on you."

"Spying on us but not telling tales." Pointing that out, Samantha held a hand up. "Diet Coke, Stoney."

"What am I, the waiter?"

She snorted. "By now you probably know where everything is in here better than Rick and I do. And yes, please knock next time. We might have been nudie or something."

Rick stirred behind her. "Maybe we should stay in Florida, after all," he murmured. "More walls and more doors between us and them." He kissed the top of her head beside her stitches and bandage. His phone beeped again. "Pendleton," he commented, checking.

"I don't think it matters," she answered, considering. "These guys are going to follow us no matter where we go. There's no escape."

After a triple knock, the door opened, and Aubrey, carrying a box of doughnuts, walked in. "I didn't know if we were going to have another strategy session or not, but I could not pass the bakery without going in. Have you seen these things?"

Rick's phone beeped again. "Oh, for God's sake," he muttered, picking it up again to look. "Anne."

"Oh, good. I wanted to know if I still have a job with Sotheby's. I mean, all the downstairs displays are going to have to be replaced, and a guy with my name did the dirty deed. If I were them, I'd kick me to the curb and then drop garbage on me." And that would suck, because she'd played an inning in the big game, and the idea of doing security installations for Sotheby's and other auction houses, larger venues, even museums had nearly made her giddy. Martin had poofed that away with his stupid grenade stunt. At least it would be his last. She really, really hoped so, anyway.

"They won't."

Rick's matter-of-fact statement made her crane her face up to look at him. "Do not bribe Sotheby's," she ordered. "Do not offer to buy Adgerton's entire collection so I can get a gold star. If I messed up, I messed up. I can try again."

"I'm not bribing anyone, despite the apparent lack of faith on the part of all my friends and family," he said. "What happened will be good for their bottom line. Having your name continue to be associated with them will be good for their bottom line. You stopped a theft in a rather spectacular manner, and you did it when it would have been easier not to."

"That's me, hero-woman."

A quiet quartet of knocks sounded at the door. With some grumbling Stoney, one arm laden with waters and a soda, detoured over and pulled it open. "Hi, Anne," he said, and continued on his way.

"I'm not interrupting, am I?" Anne asked, taking a step inside the apartment.

"No, you're not. We have doughnuts," Samantha said, motioning her to come in. "Am I excommunicated from Sotheby's?"

"You are not. And neither am I, surprisingly enough. Evidently some rather big collectors emailed the management this morning and stated that if and when they ever parted with any of their own items, they wanted to work with me."

Samantha elbowed Rick's ribs. "That's bribery, man," she whispered, though what she really wanted to do was turn around and hug him and give him a big old wet kiss. Her hero-man.

"Nonsense."

"And you foiled a robbery, even if it wasn't quite the way any of us had envisioned. So we're both looking good at the moment. I suppose the final decision will come after the auction, when they see how much money we've made."

"You're going to make a great deal of money." Rick accepted the soda from Stoney. He unscrewed the lid and lowered it down to her.

"And you're certain you're all right?" her mom pursued, coming closer to squint down at the top of Samantha's head. "You were more than a little loopy yesterday. I can't believe they let you leave the hospital."

"I passed all the 'I'm not a zombie' tests, so they had to. And it's all part of the job. I've had worse. I'm fine."

"I am very, very glad to hear that." Anne clenched her hands together in front of her. "And Bradley? Martin? Whatever we're calling him now?"

Aubrey cleared his throat. "On his way to a comfy prison for life. With the threat of a very uncomfy prison if he makes trouble."

"Thank goodness. Thank…everything. He's…the trouble he's made for you, and for me, for everybody, is unforgivable. Good riddance."

Life with him had made her what she was, but Samantha certainly understood the sentiment. And shared it. "Double good riddance," she commented.

Anne grimaced, twisting her hands. "I know it's kind of short notice, but I wondered if you and Rick would care to join me for Thanksgiving at my house in Danbury? You could meet your grandmother, Sam. Or meet her again, rather."

They'd planned to do Thanksgiving with the Donners. "I don't know if—"

"It was just a thought, of course," Anne broke in, her cheeks getting red blotches on them. "I know how busy you two are."

"Can we let you know by the end of the week?" Rick asked,

always more ready with polite stuff than Samantha was. He'd had a lot more practice.

"Certainly. It's just…" Grimacing, Anne squatted down in front of Samantha and leaned close enough that she could smell her mom's coffee breath. "I would really like for you to meet Michael," she whispered.

"Ooh," Samantha breathed back, smiling. "Is he your guy? Don't tell Aubrey. I think he's sweet on you."

"You keep telling me that Aubrey is gay," Rick put in, his own voice low and conspiratorial. "What's the real story, then?"

"Actually," Anne replied, taking one of Samantha's hands and squeezing it, "I didn't dare mention him while Bradley was anywhere around, but Michael is your younger brother."

Samantha and Rick sat up straight at the same time. *"What?"*

THE END

DISCOVER MORE BY SUZANNE ENOCH

Contemporary Romantic Suspense
Flirting with Danger
Don't Look Down
Billionaires Prefer Blondes
Twice the Temptation (half historical, half contemporary)
A Touch of Minx
Barefoot in the Dark
A Kiss in the Dark

Wild Wicked Highlanders
It's Getting Scot in Here
Scot under the Covers
Hit Me With Your Best Scot

Standalone Historicals
Something in the Heir
Every Duke Has His Day
A Duke Never Tells

Regency Historicals
Lady Rogue
Stolen Kisses

The Bancroft Brothers
By Love Undone
Taming Rafe

With This Ring
Reforming a Rake
Meet Me at Midnight
A Matter of Scandal

Lessons in Love
The Rake
London's Perfect Scoundrel
England's Perfect Hero

Anthologies
One True Love (from The Further Observations of Lady
Whistledown)
A Touch of Scandal (from Lady Whistledown Strikes Back)
Take Two (from I Loved You First)

The Griffin Family
Sin and Sensibility
An Invitation to Sin
Something Sinful
Sins of a Duke

The Notorious Gentlemen
After the Kiss
Before the Scandal
Always a Scoundrel

The Adventurers' Club
The Care and Taming of a Rogue
A Lady's Guide to Improper Behavior
Rules of an Engagement

The Scandalous Brides
A Beginner's Guide to Rakes
Taming an Impossible Rogue
Rules to Catch a Devilish Duke
The Handbook to Handling His Lordship

Standalone Short Stories
Good Earl Hunting

The Scandalous Highlanders
One Hot Scot (a short story)
The Devil Wears Kilts
Rogue with a Brogue
Mad, Bad and Dangerous in Plaid
Some Like it Scot

No Ordinary Hero
Hero in the Highlands
My One True Highlander
A Devil in Scotland

Traditional Regencies
The Black Duke's Prize
Angel's Devil

ABOUT THE AUTHOR

A lifelong lover of books, Suzanne Enoch has been writing them since she learned to read. She is the author of two well-received traditional Regencies, 24 and counting England-set Historical Romances, four contemporary Romantic Suspense novels, and a growing number of Scottish Highlands Historical Romances.

A native and current resident of Southern California, Suzanne lives with a green parakeet named Kermit, some very chirpy finches, and a small army of Star Wars figures (including a life-size Yoda). Her books regularly appear on the *New York Times* and *USA Today* bestseller lists, and when she's not busily working on her next book or staging fights with action figures, she likes to read, play video games, and go to the movies with her large and supportive village.

Website: http://www.suzanneenoch.com

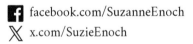

facebook.com/SuzanneEnoch
x.com/SuzieEnoch